She lifted her head to meet him, and the sweetness of it filled him with joy.

When their lips touched, they both jolted at the shock of it. There was fire between them. And magic, like her shirt said. And a tenderness the like of which he'd never experienced.

He brought her against his body and cupped her nape, giving her lips another pass. Her breath shuddered out, and her hands gripped his shoulders as she kissed him back.

Closing his eyes, he brushed her lips again, changing the angle of his head to enjoy the right side of her mouth and then the left. Her lips were warm and soft, and while his heartbeat had settled some, its pace increased for a whole new reason.

Her.

He'd dreamed of kissing Megan Bennet, and those dreams were finally a reality.

As he lifted a hand to caress the exposed line of her neck, she moaned against his lips—the softest of cries, but it reverberated through his bones.

OTHER AVA TITLES TO BINGE

The Unexpected Prince Charming Series

Love with a kiss of the Irish...

Beside Golden Irish Fields

Beneath Pearly Irish Skies

Through Crimson Irish Light

The Merriams Series

Chock full of family and happily ever afters...

Wild Irish Rose

Love Among Lavender

Valley of Stars

Sunflower Alley

A Forever of Orange Blossoms

A Breath of Jasmine

The Love Letter Series

The Merriams grandparents' epic love affair...

Letters Across An Open Sea

Along Waters of Sunshine and Shadow

The Friends & Neighbors Novels

A feast for all the senses...

The House of Hope & Chocolate

The Dreamer's Flower Shoppe

The Dare River Series

Filled with down-home charm...

Country Heaven

The Chocolate Garden

Fireflies and Magnolias

The Promise of Rainbows

The Fountain Of Infinite Wishes

The Patchwork Quilt Of Happiness

Country Heaven Cookbook

The Chocolate Garden: A Magical Tale (Children's Book)

The Dare Valley Series

Awash in small town fabulousness...

Nora Roberts Land

French Roast

The Grand Opening

The Holiday Serenade

The Town Square

The Park of Sunset Dreams

The Perfect Ingredient

The Bridge to a Better Life

The Calendar of New Beginnings

Home Sweet Love

The Moonlight Serenade

The Sky of Endless Blue

Daring Brides

Daring Declarations

Dare Valley Meets Paris Billionaire Mini-Series

Small town charm meets big city romance...

The Billionaire's Gamble

The Billionaire's Secret

The Billionaire's Courtship

The Billionaire's Return

Dare Valley Meets Paris Compilation

The Once Upon a Dare Series

Falling in love is a contact sport...

The Gate to Everything

Non-Fiction

The Happiness Corner: Reflections So Far

The Post-Covid Wellness Playbook

Cookbooks

Home Baked Happiness Cookbook

Country Heaven Cookbook

The Lost Guides to Living Your Best Life Series

Reclaim Your Superpowers

Courage Is Your Superpower

Expression Is Your Superpower

Children's Books

The Chocolate Garden: A Magical Tale

BENEATH PEARLY IRISH SKIES

THE UNEXPECTED PRINCE CHARMING BOOK 2

AVA MILES

To Shane, Emer, Ita, Donnachd, Tish, Ciara, and the rest of the bunch for being the dearest of friends—and to their animal gang, namely Poppy and Jen as well as Yankee, Frisky, Miracle, and Raj, who have given me more joy than I could ever have imagined.

Prince Charming...

Some women say he's too elusive.
Others long for him with all their hearts.

But what is the truth?

Is he a real person
or only a myth?

Even if he is waiting in the most obvious of places—Ireland—
the land where dreams,
like rainbows, materialize when you least expect it,
he might be the most unexpected of men.

The real question is: will you let him love you?

CHAPTER ONE

The greens and blues of the curved ceramic pitcher reminded her of the rolling Irish hills outside her pottery studio.

If Megan Bennet weren't so sick to her stomach, she might have laughed at herself. She could still talk like a potter, even after a ten-year hiatus from teaching and practicing her craft. And she could certainly appreciate others' work, as evidenced by the pitcher sitting a few yards from her. She'd bought the piece at a secondhand shop, savoring the longing it had stirred for her last art. Before, the only thing she'd longed for was her lost husband. But all the talking and appreciating in the world wasn't going to get her anywhere because she wasn't able to *work* like a potter.

Her first ceramics classes started a week from today, so that was a problem. Students from surrounding villages in County Mayo were going to show up at the new Sorcha Fitzgerald Arts Center in Caisleán, expecting to be taught, and the view from the ceramics studio, however breathtaking, wasn't going to distract them for long. Her students would be more focused on what was between their hands: clay primed for molding.

She looked at the deflated blob on the pottery wheel in front of her. This was her twentieth attempt at throwing a bowl. *A simple bowl.* Before her now-deceased husband had told her to stop working, she'd formed a million of them. Back then, she could have done it in her sleep.

Now it was as hard as pulling herself out of the depression she'd been mired in since her husband had been killed in the line of duty in Afghanistan.

How was she going to show people how to throw clay if she couldn't do it herself?

She had a lot riding on teaching again. She needed to make it work because ceramics was the only thing she'd ever been good at. It was also the only way she could give back to her cousin, Betsy O'Hanlon, for allowing her and her eight-year-old son, Ollie, to live rent free in a cottage on her property. Sure, Bets seemed happy enough to host them, but Megan hadn't forgotten that it was her sister, Angie, who'd been issued the original invitation to teach at the arts center, not her. Megan had tagged along.

Coming to Ireland had jarred her out of the misery she'd felt after losing Tyson and their life ten months ago, but while Angie had found herself—and an incredible Irishman to marry—in Caisleán, Megan had a long way to go. Financially, there was no rush since she had Tyson's death annuity, but she wanted to make something of *herself.* She needed it, for her and for Ollie.

Pottery had given her a sense of purpose once. She hoped it would again.

No pressure, right?

Her ceramics mentor, Barry Travers, used to say the clay was a reflection of what was going on inside a person.

As she glared at the misshapen lump she'd just been trying to center, she had to be honest. The buff white mangled mess looked pathetic. Unrecognizable. Just like her.

She'd lost her center. These days, she wondered how much of one she'd ever had.

When Tyson had told her she didn't need to teach ceramics anymore because he would take care of her when they got married, she'd agreed. She'd never wanted to displease him, and deep down, she'd loved hearing him talk about "taking care of her." She hadn't known what it would actually mean: giving up parts of herself. Now she knew what folly that was, and she refused to fall into that trap ever again.

"There you are," she heard a familiar voice say from behind her, the lilting accent as soothing as a gentle Irish breeze. "I was on my way to the farm and thought I'd see how you were getting on with the clay."

Turning on her stool, she tried to smile at Kade Donovan. Since the day she'd met him at his pony therapy farm, she'd thought him the kindest man she'd ever met. He'd given her son pony rides, shared his beloved Jack Russell terrier, Duke, with them, and taken them both under his wing. In doing so, he'd become one of her best friends.

She'd started helping him at his farm occasionally now that Ollie was back in school. Being with Kade had become her favorite new pastime, whether it was mucking out the stalls, feeding the animals, or leading his gentle ponies that healed children as well as adults.

She could tell him anything, she knew, and because she could, she let her shoulders slump in defeat. "Not good. The clay and I are more adversaries than friends right now. I'm trying not to freak out."

He shrugged out of his fall navy jacket and set it on one

of the nearby stools. The tempestuous wind making the verdant green grass dance outside the studio windows had played with his dark mop of hair in an appealing way. His brown eyes were as warm as the full smile on his face. "Talk me through the problem. Step by step. We'll figure it out, Megan."

There it was again. His solid, reliable support. From the first moment he'd shown up at her cottage to give her son a pony ride, he'd been there with a willing ear to listen and a shoulder to lean on. No one she'd ever met could calm her nerves the way he did. "Kade, I can't center the clay, and that's the building block to throwing pottery. When you and the six other students show up for the evening pottery class next Tuesday, how am I supposed to teach you anything?"

"Have you ever had this problem before?"

She sputtered. "Ah... I don't think—"

A sharp pain shot through her head as a memory flashed into her mind, one of gripping a messy blob of clay on the wheel. She'd just met Tyson while waiting for a friend at a crab shack. He'd asked her out, and she'd been so nervous leading up to their first date, she hadn't been able to center the clay. The same thing had happened after he asked for a second date.

Her chest grew tight as the past washed over her. She'd been an emotional wreck, not knowing why someone like him would want to go out with her. He was a hot, cocky, handsome soldier on the rise. Later he'd told her the reason was because she was a lady, the kind of woman a man wanted to come home to and make a family with—a very different woman from the troubled single mother who'd never been there for him.

The pressure to be what he'd wanted, something she'd chased with her own father, had been excruciating. There could be no slipups. Pretending to be an elegant vase when all she considered herself to be was a serviceable mug had made her spine rigid and her heart cold.

Only recently had she finally admitted to herself that their marriage hadn't been perfect like she'd pretended, and it had hurt. Bad.

She fisted her hands, trying to hold it together.

"You're remembering something." Kade's voice was quiet, yet compelling.

Her throat was suddenly sore, and it demanded she rub its length. She didn't talk about Tyson much—not even to Ollie. Until Ireland, the memories had been too painful. Here, she'd finally broken out of her depression and started working through her grief. Although she'd admitted her grief wasn't just for Tyson but for the woman she'd become. "It happened when Tyson and I first started dating."

He walked over until he stood before her. "Can you tell me why, Megan?"

More memories surfaced. She'd found herself in this same position, hunched over an uncentered lump of clay, the day he'd told her he was going on a mission, the first of many. Sleeping had become problematic. She'd still been teaching then, her class filled with intermediate students. Everyone knew how to center their clay. Everyone but her. So she'd turned to hand building ceramics to sell at arts and crafts fairs.

She hadn't centered her clay after that, she recalled at last. *Oh God!*

"My whole life changed when I met Tyson," she said, her voice breaking. "I was worried about him fighting overseas."

It had rocked her center.

But so had knowing he wasn't really happy being

married to her or having Ollie. Otherwise, he wouldn't have volunteered for those extra missions and stayed away from home so much. That, she feared, was on her.

She hadn't been enough for him. In her heart, she felt she'd never been enough for anyone.

"It's only natural you were worried about him." Kade paused a moment. "But that's not the reason you can't center the clay now, is it?"

Her breath was stuck in her chest. "No, it's not."

"What do you really fear, Megan?"

Her laughter came out unbidden. "Do you have all day? Some days I think I'm more frightened than one of those hurt and scared horses you heal."

The right corner of his mouth tipped up. "Don't you remember what I told you about them? All that's needed is consistent care, kindness, and time. The rest takes care of itself."

"But I don't *have* time!" Her outburst echoed in the room. "I have a week. I don't think I'll be able to do it, Kade, and that scares me. Every time I get close, my disc starts to wobble." She'd be a failure. Again.

"Wobbling discs, eh?" he said, rolling up his sleeves, showing his tanned forearms. "I imagine there's a rhythm to it, right? Rather like riding a horse. You've learned to do that fine."

He'd hoisted her onto a horse on a sunny summer morning only a few weeks ago, the same day he'd asked her to help him on his farm. That day had changed her world. She'd felt empowered and larger than life as they'd ridden through the fields with the wind at her back.

Her chest tightened again. Meeting Tyson had changed her world too, only it hadn't made her feel empowered or larger than life. She'd felt afraid. Small. And wanting. Like

8

she'd never catch up to his vision of what he wanted from her. She'd never told him that or anything else that wasn't supportive, and sometimes she wondered what would have happened if she had.

Defeat was starting to cloak her, and she shook it off like a dog shaking off the rain. She didn't want to go back to feeling that way. "So if clay is like horses, an encouraging yet unwavering hand is all I need, right?"

God, if only...

"Indeed, and people are no different," he said in a tone resounding with certainty. "Now, let's see if clay feels the same way."

She blinked in surprise. "You want to help me?"

"Why not? We have over an hour before our next client comes for a pony ride."

Our client. She still wasn't used to Kade saying things like that, like she had a share in his business because she was volunteering her time, but it made her heart swell inside her chest. Those two words made her feel special. "Okay, but don't laugh."

He put a gentle hand on her arm. "Why would I laugh? Megan, I would never do that to you or anyone. Come now. Grab what you need and let's try this."

"You might get dirty."

His rich laughter filled the ceramics studio, and a lock of brown hair fell over his wide forehead. "I work and live on a farm. I'm always dirty."

"Good point."

Yet he never seemed to *look* dirty, whether he was wearing jeans or cargo pants with a T-shirt or windbreaker.

Her clothes were another matter. The ones she'd brought to Ireland weren't faring well. She hadn't envisioned she'd be working with clay again, let alone animals.

Looking down at her lilac sweater and black pants, she saw they were covered in clay despite the tan apron she'd bought in town. At the farm, she usually wore a knee-length windbreaker or rain jacket to cover them as best she could, along with her new black wellies and a pair of jeans she'd succumbed to buying.

Her clothes were all wrong for what she was doing, as glaring as a red flashing light on a highway. The clothes she'd always worn—good girl clothes—didn't feel right anymore. And her old pottery outfits of loose cotton pants with a plain or striped T-shirt from Talbots weren't appealing either.

She heard Barry's voice again. *No center. No pot.*

He'd shake his head if he could see her now.

Firming her shoulders, she walked over to the wedging table and tore off a hunk of clay from her twenty-five-pound bag. God, she'd made a mess to clean up. Every misfire on the wheel led to more clay that needed to dry out before being useable again. She wedged the mass, pushing it with the heels of her palms to shape it into a perfect ball. Wedging the clay wasn't lost to her, thank God. Barry had always said it was rather like kneading bread, and she agreed. Finished, she brought it back to her station.

"What was that step?" Kade asked as she sat down in front of her wheel and turned the switch on.

"Wedging makes sure there are no air pockets in the clay and it's uniform in composition."

"It looks like you're working something out of the clay and yourself when you do that," he remarked as he pulled a stool over and sat down beside her.

Maybe it was the proximity, but he seemed so large all of a sudden. Sitting on the stool clearly wasn't comfortable for him, given his height of six foot four, so he angled his legs open with his hands on his knees.

They often stood together by the ponies, but this was a little unnerving. With every breath she inhaled his scent—a little soap, a little land, and a lot of male.

She became aware of him.

As a man.

It wasn't the first time this had happened, of course—Kade was handsome, after all, and nice and compelling. Anyone would admire him. In her journal, she'd rationalized these moments away as a sign that she was coming out of a long depression. Parts of her that had been shut down for a long time were finally waking up.

What she couldn't bring herself to write down was that she was attracted to him. It felt wrong. Tyson had only been gone for ten months. Besides, Kade was her friend, and she didn't want to mess that up.

"Are you all right, Megan?" he asked, gazing at her calmly with those steady brown eyes of his.

She took a breath. "Just nervous about trying this again."

"No need to be nervous. You've done this millions of times in the past. Show me how it's done."

She really wanted to, but she was so afraid of letting him down—of being judged or found wanting. Gritting her teeth, she faced down her biggest personal nemesis: herself. She couldn't keep giving up or letting life put her down. It was time to make a stand. "All right, I'm starting."

She took another breath before slapping the clay in the center of the wheel and adding a splash of water over it from her bucket. Cupping it between her hands, she slowly pressed the foot pedal and started the wheel turning. Putting downward pressure on the disc, she increased the speed, working with the centrifugal force. She held the clay in the middle, but she could feel it start to bolt under her hands. So she increased the speed, hoping maybe she could catch up to it. But the disc of clay shot to the right and spread across the wheel into an uncentered lump.

Again.

Taking her foot off the pedal, she bit her lip as frustration cloaked her. "That's how it goes. I can't even get it centered to start forming a cylinder. Kade, that's like beginner ceramics."

"You're being hard on yourself." He put a gentle hand on her arm again, his scent filling her nostrils. "What do I always say?"

"You're doing better than you think," she repeated. Usually she got teary-eyed when she heard him tell this to his clients. Like when one child cried because his misshapen hands made it hard for him to hold the pony's reins.

"Come," Kade said softly, his chest seeming so broad and comforting. "Try again. This time I'm going to get behind you and steady you a little. Your shoulders were shaking, as were your arms. How many times did you try this today?"

She gestured to where she'd dumped all the wet, uncentered clay on the drying slab. "Probably twenty."

"Twenty is a lot of work on the body as well as the mind, I imagine, especially with the speed of that wheel. Grab some more clay, Megan. Let's try it again."

After securing another ball of clay, she sat back down. Kade moved his stool until he was directly behind her. When she inhaled his scent this time, her belly fluttered. She hadn't felt desire in nearly a year, but it was undeniable. She shifted on her stool, her shoulders locking with tension. Maybe if she breathed through her mouth and ignored him, the feeling would fade.

"I'm going to put my hands over yours and follow your lead," he said, his voice a low rumble that seemed to hum through her.

Oh God!

When his arms came around her, she bolted like the clay. "Sorry."

"Easy, now," he said, drawing the words out softly.

Like she was one of his horses. His body felt so masculine and strong behind her. Then his hands covered hers, and she jolted in place. His touch was arousing and soothing all at once, making it impossible to deny her attraction to him. She studied his large callused hands. She noted a small scar next to his thumb and wondered about it. But she couldn't form the question. Her mouth had gone dry.

"Focus on the clay, Megan," Kade said in a low voice. "You know where it needs to go."

She took one deep breath and then another. But all she could see and feel were his hands. So she closed her eyes as she increased the wheel's speed.

Barry's words echoed in her mind. *Centering is all about feel. You don't need your eyes. You need your heart.*

The clay settled in the cradle of her palms, and she let herself *feel.* The smooth earth against her skin. The speed of the motor. The wheel holding everything in place. Kade's arms banded around her to anchor her as her arms started to shake.

Another shiver rolled through her body as his chest pressed lightly against her back. The clay started to wobble under her hands, but she forced it back to the center.

A wave of intuition washed over her.

The clay didn't like to be forced any more than she did.

It simply wanted things to be easy between them, the way they used to be.

Before things had gotten hard with Tyson. Her mind spit out memories of him waving goodbye from his black Ford Jeep. He'd always been leaving. When she was pregnant. When she was a scared and unsure new mother and their newborn son wouldn't sleep. When Ollie first started kindergarten and couldn't stop crying.

He'd left for the last time around the holidays last year and hadn't come home. He never would. Old pain and hurt radiated through her as she cradled the clay, crying.

Her heart was like a messy piece of clay, and she couldn't take it anymore. She needed a new one, free of all the sadness of the past.

She would make herself a new one.

Hadn't that been the reason she'd been drawn to pottery? She'd watched a potter at an arts center work when she'd gone on a field trip in tenth grade. The woman had told them the great thing about pottery was that you could make anything you wanted. "The sky's the limit," she'd said and shown it was true by making one magical piece after another. Until that moment, Megan had never imagined such possibilities were available to her, and she'd found herself wanting to do pottery. She too wanted to be able to make anything.

Now, sitting in front of the wheel with Kade behind her, she opened up to the limitless potential she'd once believed in.

Her hands seemed to merge with the clay, a feeling she'd thought lost to her. But no, it was a feeling she could recapture. She formed the clay into a centered mound and pressed her thumbs into the disc to open it up.

"There you go, love," Kade whispered in her ear.

He embraced her then, and she welcomed the comfort. His warmth and gentleness had more of the shards around her heart falling away. When he pulled away, her hands seemed to fly with the clay. She opened her eyes and watched as she pulled the wet clay into what Barry called a jello mold with a bottom. Then she cradled the walls and started to pull up. Gently. Because that's what it needed.

The clay moved with her, and she shaped it until it was six inches tall. Before she knew it, she was angling her hands and pulling the walls out on the diagonal to form the sides.

As the bowl formed, joy shot through her heart, thick and heady, like the rain that was now tapping against the windows.

She grabbed her plastic scraper and lightly pressed it to the clay bottom of her bowl, smoothing the curve. She firmed the rim and slowed the wheel's speed until it stopped completely. That ugly misshapen clay had transformed into a thing of beauty.

Her breathing was harsh in the silence as she stared at it, her chest full of raw emotion.

"I did it!" she whispered, feeling more tears swell in her eyes.

"You sure did," Kade said behind her, putting his hands on her shoulders. "It's beautiful, Megan. It might be the most beautiful bowl ever made."

She turned on her stool, bumping his well-muscled leg. He moved to give her room, and they faced each other. His brown eyes looked as warm and inviting as usual, but it was the smile on his face that had all the tension leaving her. She gripped her apron, fighting the urge to hug him.

"I don't know if it's the most beautiful bowl in the

world, but I'll take it. In fact, I'm going to give it to you when it's finished, Kade. To thank you."

He shook his head. "No, love."

"But I want to."

"You keep it, Megan. It has your all your passion and sorrow and joy in it. When you look at it, let it help you remember how you got a piece of your soul back today."

Her throat grew tight. Oh, these Irish. They had a way of talking about life and people with a poetry she hadn't known existed outside of books. "A piece of my soul?"

"The very same." He pushed a lock of her hair behind her ear, the clay dry on his fingers. "Didn't you feel it?"

She met his eyes, the gold in them shining brightly. The color reminded her of the browns and golds in the temmoku glaze she loved. She would use that glaze for this soul bowl. To remind herself that he'd been there the day she got her center back. After ten long years without it.

"Thank you, Kade." She took his hand and squeezed it. "But I still want to do something for you."

"You're doing it," he said, his mouth tipping up on the right as their hands continued to touch. "Every time you take a step forward for yourself. It's like watching a newborn foal take its first steps and then race across the fields with wild abandon."

She was rather like a newborn colt, she supposed. A little unsure of herself but eager to explore her new freedom. She squeezed his hand again. Noted the clay staining his skin and rose to grab a rag. "Let me get that for you."

She started rubbing the clay off his hand the same way she would Ollie's face after ice cream—until she became aware of Kade's stillness. He was always a contemplative man, but this kind of stillness was different somehow. Her gaze flew to his, and the banked heat she saw had her inhaling sharply, the sound audible in the studio.

Could *he* be attracted to *her*? No, it wasn't possible. He was too wonderful. Too handsome. She was Megan, plain and dull.

"Maybe you should finish up," she said, clearing her throat and laying the cloth on his hand. "I acted without thinking."

"I liked it," he said softly.

Her gaze flew to his again, and this time there was no room for doubt. She *knew* that look. Sure, she hadn't seen it in a very long time, but she knew it all the same.

Kade smiled ruefully. "It had to come out sometime, Megan. I'd like to trust this was the right moment, but there's no reason for you to feel worried or rushed. I feel as I do about you. You know that now. It doesn't change our friendship. Think on how *you* feel. We'll talk when you're ready."

Warmth and a little giddiness washed over her as he stood and walked around until he was in front of her wheel. He *did* like her!

"It really is the most beautiful bowl in the world, Megan," he said, studying it. "Do you still want to work at the farm today, or do you need some time to yourself?"

"No," she said softly, her heart beating hard in her chest. "There's a child coming, and I promised you I'd help."

He nodded. "Then I'll see you soon."

When he left, she sank onto her stool. Kade liked her. That made her feel special and priceless but also small because *how* could he like her? She was...

The bowl caught her eye, and she put a hand to her chest. She didn't want to act like this anymore—to feel lucky for being admired, to feel worthwhile only because she'd caught a man's attention. No, she wanted to be like her new creation. Beautiful because she was herself.

Tension squeezed her ribs. This was too much, too soon. Wasn't it? Tyson hadn't even been dead a year. Even if their marriage hadn't been great before he'd died, didn't she need to wait a little longer to go out with another man?

Except this wasn't just *another man*. This was Kade.

He was the kind of man scientists should clone. The world would be a whole lot better if they had a bunch of Kade Donovans walking around.

Kade had helped her center her clay—and herself.

What had Tyson done? Rocked her center and left her alone, again and again.

Anger reared up, the hot, searing variety that made her head spin. She'd made Tyson the center of her life—*the center*—but he hadn't taken care of her or Ollie the way he'd promised.

He'd left her like an uncentered lump of clay. She fisted her hands together again, feeling the urge to hurl something across the room so she could hear it shatter. Because that was how she still felt inside sometimes. *Shattered.*

She took deep breaths until she'd calmed, pausing to wipe the sweat at her temples, and reminded herself that all she needed to focus on was centering her clay and teaching her class.

That was true, and yet she couldn't forget that look in his eyes and her response to it.

She needed to orient herself to this new possibility between them. Deep down she knew it had the potential of being even more beautiful than the bowl she'd formed today.

If only she was brave enough to explore it.

CHAPTER TWO

S unlight was streaming into the stables for a change.

Kade paused from mucking out the stall and leaned against his pitchfork. He took a moment to enjoy the quiet and the light as it wrapped around him. He'd awoken happy like usual—his mum had said he'd been happy from his first moment of breath—but there was a new excitement in him.

Megan was finding her way and setting roots in Ireland, something he believed would make her happy—hopefully with him. After yesterday, she knew how he was feeling, and he'd seen in her eyes that she felt the same. She was going to need time to sort things out, of course, as evidenced by her quiet yet searching demeanor at the farm yesterday afternoon. Good thing he was a patient man.

His longest standing pony nudged him in the back.

He laughed, turning to rub Winston's black and white neck. "She's a lot like you were when we met. Hurt and scared but with the biggest heart. You didn't know what you had in you, but I did. Took you some time to figure things out."

Winston neighed and nodded vigorously.

"Glad you decided to let me help you," he said, starting to work again and whistling the pub classic "Wild Rover."

"It's lovely to see you're whistling this morning, Kade," he heard a female voice say.

Winston startled next to him, and he put a calming hand on the horse's side as he turned his head.

Sorcha Fitzgerald stood in the sunlight in the white dress she always wore when she visited him. Some ghosts seemed to have an unlimited wardrobe, and others continued to wear their last earthly outfit. Kade had never figured out the particulars. It didn't change the reason for their presence.

"You have a right to be upbeat, certainly," she continued. "Things are going well with Megan."

He couldn't help but smile, both from the pleasure of seeing his old friend and from her recounting of things. "I thought you were around, although you haven't shown yourself. I smelled your orange scent on my way to the arts studio yesterday."

"It's a fine place to have named after me, don't you think? I'm glad Carrick finally saw sense and donated it to the village. No point in building a house for someone who's dead and can't enjoy it. I'd much rather be venerated this way."

Kade snorted. In life, Sorcha Fitzgerald had possessed a sharp humor about the way of things. Dying didn't seem to have changed it. She'd returned months ago to help her husband, Carrick, find new love with Megan's sister, Angie. And since Sorcha was nothing if not stubborn, she'd announced she was going to help Carrick's friends too. Or at least Kade. He looked forward to seeing what she had in mind.

"The arts center is going to enliven the souls of a lot of people, Sorcha. Much like your poetry did for you and those who read it. Maybe one day a poet like you will come and teach there."

"A grand thought." She cocked a brow. "Are you saying you read my poetry, Kade Donovan?"

Winston nudged him in the back, and he continued to soothe and pat the pony as a few others neighed in their stalls. Not all of his animals saw spirits. Kade couldn't say why some did and some didn't, but the same was true of people. He'd always seen them. Like his granny had. Carrick saw spirits too, yet he had only seen Sorcha for a time—and so Kade had discovered another mystery. Ghosts could choose not to be seen, even by those who naturally possessed the sight. Living in Ireland, he knew anything was possible, but still, life held plenty of secrets. He recalled a piece of Sorcha's poetry along those lines.

"'The sunshine strikes a patch of land, and the secrets held in the soil retreat into holy springs for cleansing.' That might be my favorite passage."

Her mouth curved. "You have a romantic Irish soul as well as the biggest heart in the county. It's one of the reasons I always liked you."

He watched as her brown hair billowed in the sunlight as if touched by wind in another place. "Is that why you're helping me? I understand why you helped Carrick. He was your man, and you wanted him to be happy again."

She fussed with her sleeves. "Maybe I'm helping you because of how you took care of Carrick after I died, but we're getting off track. I'm here to talk about Megan."

He hadn't expected a straight answer. Spirits were still people, after all, and they had minds of their own. He'd stopped trying to figure out why some stayed around and others didn't. "Then talk."

This time she snorted. "Megan is unsettled after realizing you have feelings for her, which she shares, by the by."

Hadn't he seen as much in her eyes? He knew better than to think it meant their seas would be calm, but he'd call it progress. "I'm glad for it, but she's still fighting to sort out the past. I hadn't planned on sharing my heart with her yesterday, but it's like I told her. I trusted it was the right moment."

"You helped her find her center, and that's a tremendous gift, Kade. Something her deceased husband never gave her."

He crossed his arms. "Oh? Do you spirits all know each other?"

She scoffed. "No, he's passed along to wherever his next place is, but I looked into him. I don't like him. And you know I've always been inclined to admire a brave man fighting for a cause."

While he didn't have the slightest idea how she could "look into" such a thing from the beyond, her words confirmed what he'd suspected. Hadn't Angie bit her lip to keep from talking poorly about Tyson the other night at the pub? "It's hard to be angry with a dead person."

"And yet Carrick managed to be mad at me for three years," she said, tracing the Celtic symbol of the Trinity knot on the wall of the stall, one he knew bespoke of eternal love. "But that's Carrick. Megan is the softer kind. She's the sort to get stampeded by life, whereas you know how to calm the stampede. Both inside and in the fields."

"Why not bring calm to chaos?" he asked. "I've never liked fighting myself."

"Neither does Megan, although both her father and her

dead husband made it their profession as soldiers. You're a complete contrast to what she's known, but she's opening her heart to you, a great measure of trust. Now that she knows about your feelings for her, you must walk a fine line, my friend."

"Don't I know it." He'd seen Megan's bones go lax when he'd called her *love* yesterday, and again later, when he'd shared his passion for her. "She's only recently come out of the cocoon she's been in."

"You're both going to have to walk other fine lines shortly. I'll be here to help with that too." She stilled, frowning. "Yours is coming now."

The sunlight vanished with Sorcha, and the quiet ended in the familiar clomp of heavy boots.

Dad.

Since he rarely came to Kade's shed, the reason must be important—something Kade would have gathered without Sorcha's warning. He'd also sensed something was brewing in the yard earlier. The wind in his dad's part of the yard had seemed angry, stirring up dirt and dust as he walked through. He deposited Winston back in his stall and shut the door as Duke gave a loud *ruff* to warn him of the company.

"Morning," his father called, striding across the cement floor, stamping his powerful energy into the ground with every step. "Fine morning so far after the rain these last days."

He leaned back against the stall's door, eyeing his father. They didn't start conversations about the weather as a rule, although weather was often discussed. It was Ireland, after all, and they were farmers of a sort. "'Tis. Something on your mind, Dad?"

Killian Donovan rarely showed anything but strength,

but today he ran a hand through his thick silver hair before nodding. "It gives me no joy to say it, but say it I must. This farm breeds prize horses, and with it comes clients who are looking for a certain buying experience. Not everyone who comes here is easy with some of the people you help."

Kade locked his jaw and gave a flick of his hand, ordering Duke to leave the stables so he wouldn't bark at his father. "Keep going."

"The land you stand on and the house you live in is paid for by the horses I breed and sell." His dad blew out an aggrieved breath. "I know we've had row after row about you not wanting to take your part in our business, but the current way of things isn't working."

"I know you don't understand why I want to run a pony farm and heal horses—"

"I *do* know," his dad shot back, dark eyes blazing. "I was there the day my friend carried his boy to our farm, tears streaming down his face, with you running at his side, crying as well. It was one of the worst days we've ever seen and not one I ever want to repeat."

The emotion of that terrible sun-drenched summer day had never fully left Kade. He and one of his best childhood friends, Ryan Hughes, were driving with his father in the tractor. The fields had been a vivid green, and the rut they'd hit had jarred his bones. Ryan had fallen out the back of the tractor and cracked his head open. The ten-year-old boy had never been the same. In some ways, neither had Kade.

Since they'd always ridden ponies together, Kade had continued the tradition after Ryan's injury, not knowing how else to help his friend. His ponies had always calmed his friend and lightened his burdens.

Later, when Kade was older, he'd discovered there was a profession called pony therapy, and he'd felt as if he'd discovered his life's purpose. His skill at calming and healing horses even when he was young had been well known. Why couldn't he do the same with people? Only that had never suited his father, who'd always intended for him to breed horses with him and run the farm. Continue everything he'd built—the common custom.

"Then, knowing that, what is the problem?" Kade asked, comforted when Winston rested his head on his shoulder.

"I need you to contribute to the farm. It seems only fair, given that I've allowed you to work on the land for nothing."

His patience was fraying like a dry rope, and he took a few deep breaths to calm himself. "We've discussed this, Dad. I'm happy to pay you for the land I use and any taxes."

"It's not enough," Killian said. "I need your help with a mare. She's a prize, son. As graceful as the curves of the hills around us and as fast as a wind coming in from the sea. She has champion bloodlines. But she hasn't gotten pregnant in the two years I've tried, and I want a foal from her."

He knew the horse, and in truth, her name was ironic given their discussion. "Legend."

"I've had her scanned by four different vets. Nothing is wrong with her."

Kade shook his head ruefully. "She hasn't liked your choice of studs."

His father threw up his hands. "I've never had a problem like this. I promised Joris Christiansen a foal from her. You know what he pays."

Joris was a Dutch financier who had a keen interest in horses and racing. He'd won a Triple Crown with a horse from their farm. "Joris trusts you. Tell him you'll give him another foal."

His dad stalked over to the stall beside him. "He has a

sense about Legend. He thinks she could produce a Triple Crown winner with the right stallion. As do I."

Kade didn't often grimace, but he could feel his mouth bunching in response. "I understand your situation, Dad, but if I agree, this opens a door I keep telling you I don't want to go through."

"You don't want your birthright, you mean!" He gestured to the stables. "Who's going to keep everything I've built here going if not you? The Donovans are their own legend in horse breeding. Son, you love horses and this land. It's in your blood just like it is mine."

"Not like that, Dad." He strove for patience. "I've tried to tell you, but we never seem to reach an understanding. We're going to change that now. I will help you get a foal from Legend on the following conditions."

His dad's mouth twisted. "You'd negotiate with me? Your own father?"

"Yes, and that's the way of it." He pressed away from Winston, knowing he needed to stand tall as he laid out his terms. "Are you hearing them?"

"I'll hear them, although I might keel over dead because my only son, the man I want to give all I've built, wants to lay out terms like he's a client coming to our very own farm."

Kade waited for him to settle down before saying, "In exchange for helping with Legend, I want the thirty acres that go along the beach and cut across to Kenmore Abbey."

"But that's prize land—"

"You'll still have one hundred and seventy acres left, Dad," Kade said, well aware he could have asked for more. "You don't need the views to breed horses, whereas those views would be quite lovely on a pony ride as well as the house I plan to build for myself and the family I hope to have."

Killian made a shocked sound. "When did you think about having a family after breaking poor Mary Kathleen's heart? Is there something I don't know? Clearly your mother doesn't, or she'd have told me."

He decided not to argue about the status of Mary Kathleen's heart. He knew she was glad he'd called a halt to them settling into something that wouldn't have fulfilled them. Now she had four children with a mechanic in a nearby town and seemed happy, although not everyone remembered that.

"I'm only thinking ahead," he answered, although he was thinking about Megan and Ollie. She loved the beach, and he thought she'd like having a view of it from their house, should things go as he hoped.

"Thinking ahead and then some, I'd say." Killian tromped around the entry of the stables. "Asking for thirty acres from your very own father."

"Take it or leave it, Dad." He hated the harshness of his own voice, but his dad only respected strength. He and Megan both had fathers who liked to fight.

"I'll take it, seeing as how you haven't given me another option." Killian's jaw ticked. "You have from now until January to do whatever you need to do with Legend to prepare her. I'll arrange for her to come down to your very own stables today. If something isn't wrong with her body, it has to be in her head, and supposedly you heal both things."

He did and was proud of it. "I want our agreement in writing."

Killian pursed his lips as if the whole discussion tasted like sour milk. "Fine, but you'll hear my terms if Legend isn't expecting by the end of January."

He wasn't a nervous man, but a ripple of fear trembled in his belly. "State them."

"You will either join me in helping with the farm, or you will find another place for your pony therapy with all its brightly colored bridges, wind chimes, and playground equipment."

His father hated those things, complaining they marred Donovan land. This, he knew, was the source of his dad's complaint about his wealthy patrons expecting a certain kind of buying experience. No denying it—he saw the distasteful looks they gave him when he rode by with his special needs clients. Kade tried to understand people, but when someone scoffed at or snubbed another human being, especially the children he helped, he was at a loss. Bottom line—he didn't want to work with people who felt that way about others, something his father couldn't fathom.

Kade rubbed the back of his head. Maybe his father had maneuvered him to exactly where he wanted him. Ah well. Maybe it was always going to come to this. "Just so we're clear. I won't be giving up my business. I believe in what I'm doing."

His dad met his gaze without flinching and said, "So do I."

"Then I agree on one more condition," he said, sadness creeping into his voice. "I choose the horse for Legend, and we do it the natural way. No insemination."

"You don't know breeding like I do since you've eschewed all I wanted to teach you," Killian said, crossing his arms over his massive chest. "I'll choose the stallion—"

"You haven't gotten it right so far," Kade responded. "You're going to need to trust me on this, Dad."

"I can't, and I won't."

Wasn't it ironic that Megan trusted him, despite having

only met him a few months ago, and his own father couldn't? That hurt.

"This is my business and my deal with Joris," his father stated in a hard tone. "I won't allow for a horse with the wrong bloodlines to be joined with Legend."

Kade knew when his dad became as immovable as an oak. "Fine, then we'll do it together. What about covering the mare naturally, like I asked?"

"I've done that successfully in the past, so I'll agree this time and show you how it's done." His father laughed dryly. "Maybe you might take to my way of things if we work as partners."

Another maneuver? "Or we'll drive each other mad," he quipped, as that was more likely.

His dad extended his hand. "It's a deal, then."

Kade shook on it, holding his gaze. The way his father squeezed his hand spoke of a power struggle he had no interest in entering.

He smelled Sorcha's orange scent then. My, was he glad she was going to be around to help him with this as well.

He feared he was going to need it.

CHAPTER THREE

If anyone had told Betsy O'Hanlon that she would be having coffee with a sexy sheep farmer every day of the week, and at sixty years of age, no less, she would have laughed herself off the closest chair.

When her Bruce had died after thirty years of marriage, she'd resigned herself to that part of her life being over. Mostly. She had three grown sons, one of whom still lived with her. Despite Liam being twenty-five, she was happy for the company in the large O'Hanlon manor house. She had great friends. Business concerns. What did she need a man for, really?

As Donal O'Dwyer kicked out his long legs, reeking of earthy masculinity, she had to admit there were plenty of reasons to want a man around. Particularly a clever and handsome one like him, whom a woman could depend on as much for weeding in the garden as for a hearty laugh.

Donal's thick silver hair reminded her of the puffy clouds in pewter and white in the sky outside her windows, and she was always tempted to run her hands through it. Of course, she wanted to run her hands over other parts too.

His broad shoulders and chest were tantalizingly displayed by the simple navy work shirt he had on. He might be sixty-three, but he was somehow more vital and masculine than a younger man. Downright yummy. Could a woman her age say *yummy*?

Or hell, maybe her eyesight was going along with her marbles. He had her so hot she couldn't see straight. She kept losing the keys to her red Mini Cooper after seeing him —one set last week and the other this week. For the past three infernal days, she'd looked everywhere, as had her friends. Of course, they all thought it a good laugh that she was so horny she was losing things. Talk about embarrassing.

When her son had suggested purchasing ginkgo biloba capsules to improve her memory, she'd had to admit to her boy that she wasn't losing it. She was distracted by Donal O'Dwyer.

The infernal man.

He fixed his deep-set green eyes on her, the strong planes of his face knotting as he worked up to a question— one she'd been waiting for.

"When are you planning on agreeing to go away with me?" he finally asked as she took her first sip of coffee.

Hot coffee that scalded her mouth. "Ouch!"

"Let me see your burn," he said, cupping her chin. "I might have some salve for that in my car."

"I'm not a sheep," she said, wishing he'd said something about massage oil instead because that was what she'd prefer he use on her.

She opened up her fridge for some ice. But the ice in her ice trays was melted, and the other frozen items were dripping.

"Dammit! The fridge is on the fritz again."

"I'll look at it after my coffee," Donal said as she strode back to the table. "Do you want me to kiss it and make it better?"

Yeah, she kind of did. She leaned forward, and he kissed her—light as a snowflake. He could make her swoon with a kiss like that. Man alive, she *was* horny and no amount of alone time together was helping. Being together offered a wonderful sort of companionship, but their relationship wasn't only about holding hands, drinking coffee, and going out to dinner. No, they were too hot for each other for that. They needed to have sex, *the hot, sweaty, until dawn* kind.

She fingered the petals of the Love's Magic roses in the white vase in the center of the table, doing her best to remember she was an adult, not some young woman ruled by her urges. She'd had fun before meeting Bruce and more fun *with* him. Then they'd married, and things had changed between them. Having the boys had taken a further toll on their sex life. Same with growing older.

She wondered how Donal's relationship with his Margaret had gone. Should they talk about it? Damn, but it was weird to be in such uncharted territory. All of her friends still had their husbands. There was no one she could talk to about dating later in life. Deep down, she knew there was only one person to talk to about it. And he was patiently waiting for her response.

"I know what you're really asking me. About going away." Good Lord, she sounded like a young schoolgirl. Felt like one too, when she remembered what he'd said about going away to Paris. Oh, to go there with Donal and stroll along the Seine...

He took her hand away from the rose and simply held it. "Do you now?"

"You're asking when I want to go to bed with you."

There, she'd said it out loud and in a stronger voice. "Truth is, I haven't decided. Once we start, you'll be over here all the time."

"Damn right I will be, since I expect you'll prefer we use your bed," he volleyed back, clearly amused. "But take your time. Once that horse bolts, there will be no getting it back. I want you to be ready for me."

Inside, she agreed with him. She *did* need to be ready for this next step. Even so, she appreciated his patience. He'd been courting her for months and had never once rushed her.

The thing was, she hadn't been with anyone other than Bruce in thirty-two years. Her body had changed, but so had her heart. She liked to think it was wiser now. Truthfully, it wanted more fun and freedom. She wasn't sure both were possible with a man. Marriage, while wonderful, had a way of tying a person down, even when you loved someone.

And she and Donal did love each other.

"Are you still wanting to get married?" she asked boldly.

He laughed heartily, a sound as warming as the smell of baking bread. "Maybe we should have sex first and hang around together more. I need to see if you hog the covers or snore. You need to let go of your fear that all I want you for is to cook and clean."

"I didn't say it *exactly* like that," she said, trying her coffee again.

"You said and I quote, 'You know how you Irishmen are.' Like we wear furs and carry around clubs in our jeeps."

"I could have sworn I saw a sizeable club in your Mercedes when we went to dinner the other night. The night I lost my keys."

"You know what kind of club that is." He shot her a look, and she had to hold back a chuckle. Leave it to him to

33

joke about his manhood. No doubt he'd known it would make her laugh *and* make her belly tight with desire.

He liked to joke with her, but he also gave her what she needed, everything from passionate kisses to pleasant hours reading in her parlor or his greenhouse, where he'd bought her her very own chair in hot red.

She hadn't expected Donal O'Dwyer. She'd known him and liked him for decades, but never like *this*. Why, the fool man had planted an entire rose garden for her.

"You like sex, don't you, Bets?" he asked straight out, his green eyes suddenly narrowing.

"Oh, Jesus, I thought you were only having *coffee*," Liam said, stopping a few steps into the kitchen. Then he turned right back around and walked out.

"Liam O'Hanlon, come back here!"

That was another reason why she was dragging her feet. Her son lived with her. Sure, he was an adult, but he lived down the hall. *Down the hall*. He approved of Donal, but she was a little weirded out by the setup. Because she expected she was going to be really loud with Donal.

Maybe she could buy Liam earplugs. Yeah, she could see that. *Here, son. Please shove these into your ears at night so you won't hear your mom shouting Donal O'Dwyer's name at the top of her lungs.*

Liam had never brought a girl home, knowing it was a house rule. Until now, they hadn't talked about changing that rule now that he was a grown man. Should she bring it up? Jesus, she didn't need questions like this at her age. It had to be bad for her blood pressure.

Her son appeared again, peeking into the kitchen with a knowing grin on his face. "You sure, Mum? I can grab my coffee and a roll and head to the parlor for breakfast."

"Don't be ridiculous," she said, fighting the urge to rise

and serve him like she'd done most of her life. Maybe it was how she'd been raised—a woman took care of things—as much as her days as a bartender. Whatever the reason, she had to stop herself from falling back into old patterns with her sons. And she imagined the same would also be true with Donal, should they become a real couple, married or not.

Pulling on the gold hoop in his left ear, her son made a face. "I don't want to be in the way. It's no bother, Mum."

Her heart hitched a little at that. This was his home as much as hers, and that was something she'd never see change. "Come. Sit. We're finished talking."

"Are we now?" Donal asked softly. "We'll pick this topic up another time."

She nodded. "Yes, we'll talk."

He kissed her cheek and stood. "I'll see to the fridge and do my best to cool down."

If that didn't melt her on the spot...

He headed over and pulled the fridge out and looked behind it. She frowned as Donal pounded the back of it, muttering swear words in Gaelic like she didn't know their meaning.

"Is it on the fritz again?" Liam asked, sighing audibly. "Mum, you need to call it and get a new one. I know you love it, but this has been going on since Angie and Megan arrived."

"Do you know how hard it was to find a red refrigerator?"

"If it doesn't work, what does it matter?" Liam asked. "I can paint a white one for you if you'd like. Good morning, Donal, by the way."

"Morning, Liam," he replied, his head buried behind the fridge.

The back door opened, and she glanced over to see Brady McGrath holding a letter as well as a stack of envelopes. "Good morning, all. Bets, I brought your regular mail along with this letter addressed to you at the arts center."

"Thanks, Brady," she said, smiling at her dear friend Siobhan's son, so much like another son to her. But now the moment with Donal was *definitely* over. She wasn't sure if she was frustrated or relieved. Probably both.

"Grand day, isn't it?" Brady said, dropping the mail beside her and then opening the cupboard for a mug and pouring himself a cup of coffee, something everyone did on a chat.

When she'd first come to Ireland, she'd been shocked to discover that the postman—and pretty much everyone else —simply walked into one's house unbidden and expected coffee or tea and sometimes a biscuit. She didn't mind people popping by, but it had presented a glaring problem to her, a newly married woman.

She'd suggested locking the doors. Bruce had laughed at her naiveté, saying people would make a big deal of it since it wasn't the custom. They'd ask you why you'd locked them —cringe—or peer into the windows to see if you were dead or had fallen since your car was visible—double cringe.

Or they'd call the Garda, the Irish police, to look for you.

Flummoxed, she'd asked how anyone had sex outside their bedroom during the day if people just popped by all the time. One didn't, he'd said and brushed it off, hurting her feelings.

Their sex life had changed because of it, sadly, some of the spontaneity seeping away. As she looked at Donal fiddling with her fridge, she realized she didn't want to be limited to that kind of sex again, the kind that only happened at night in a bedroom, when no one could pay a call. She was sixty years old, and most of her life was behind her. She didn't want to settle for the status quo.

She liked being alone with Donal. She *craved* being alone with Donal. Hell, she wanted daylight sex and in-the-parlor sex and on-top-of-the-kitchen-counter sex. At-any-time-of-day-and-location sex.

How was she going to do that in Ireland? And would Donal go for it? She simply couldn't let it go now. She and Donal had another chance at something hot and special and fun.

This she wanted to talk about.

"Knowing you, it's been grand for other reasons than the weather being dry," Liam said, pouring his own coffee and sitting down beside Brady at the table.

"I've had some lovely biscuits from Mrs. Cashe this morning. She gave me a whole bag to bring home with me."

Bets leaned back in her chair as she settled into the visit. She loved this kid. He did more than deliver the post. He delivered hope and connection, which was why he scored so many treats. "I heard Mrs. Kelly gave you some blackberry jam the other day."

He patted his flat belly. "It's been a good summer with fall looking promising."

"How many jars of preserves did you garner so far?" Liam asked, tossing him a bread roll, which he swathed in butter from the butter dish.

"About a baker's dozen, I think," Brady responded with his mouth full.

"A very good run then," Donal called, poking his head out and grinning.

Brady only grunted and took a sip of coffee.

Bets sorted through the mail. When she came to the letter addressed to her at the arts center, she noticed the return address was from the town council. She slit it open and pulled out the typed letter and started to read.

And quickly saw red.

Especially since it was signed by Tom MacKenna, her recent nemesis, the official party in the trio of village busybodies who seemed determined to make her life difficult. Tom's wife was a pill and her best friend was Bets' sister-in-law, who hadn't liked her from the get-go.

"Oh, those bastards!" She felt her heart rate kick up. "I could hit something."

"What is it?" the three men in her kitchen asked all at once.

Bets waved the letter in the air. "Those village eejits are going to screw up our new arts center before it's really taken off. It wasn't enough for them to close it down when it was on my land. Now, they want me to cover the operational costs for the center, saying there's a budget shortage. Advertising, taxes, utilities, and salaries. The whole shebang."

"What?" Donal shoved the fridge aside and was beside her in a moment, reading the letter. "Oh, Jesus. I had a bad feeling something like this might happen."

Liam grabbed the letter and Brady leaned over to read it alongside him. Both started cursing.

"You did?" she called out in an outraged tone. "Well, I didn't! They paved the road and the parking lot and paid to finalize the building without complaint."

She'd been happy to cover everything when the arts center was on her land, but when they'd closed her down out of her sister-in-law's spite and Tom MacKenna's collusion, that had ended her financial involvement. Managing the center was all she'd agreed to.

"Mum, this is outrageous!" Liam said.

"Total rubbish," Brady added.

Donal uttered a sigh as heavy as morning fog. "If I'd known what Carrick was planning, I would have told him to make sure they agreed to cover *all* the operational costs. I've seen this kind of thing before. They got the building ready for use so the village could *say* it has an arts center. How it goes after that isn't their problem. Especially if they think they can bleed those involved for more money."

His eyes blazed as he said so, making her proud. Donal was easygoing until he wasn't.

"They said they were fully behind the arts center," Liam said. "Now they're going to withhold funds? They might as well board up the windows and let the mice have their way with the inside. Angie and Megan are going to be crushed."

Yes, she'd thought of that. Her American cousins were teaching there, and it promised a new path forward for both of them.

Was this their way of trying to force her to resign from managing the center? Tom and company hadn't liked her stepping into that role, she didn't imagine, after they'd gone to so much work to close her arts center down.

"Let's not tell them anything yet," Bets said. "I'll look into this and see what our options are."

Her shoulders felt heavier all of a sudden. If she was all tied up with finding a solution to this problem, she wasn't going to have the mental or emotional energy for intimacy— not to mention the problem of finding physical space for it. People would be popping by to talk about the arts center if she didn't head this off quickly.

Donal ducked his head out from behind the refrigerator

again, his green eyes steady and understanding. "We'll be helping you too, *mo ghrá*. You're not alone in this."

She loved hearing that as much as she loved hearing him calling her *my love*.

Her shoulders lightened a fraction, and she rose and walked over to him. Dammit, she was not going to let Tom MacKenna and company mess with her personal life. They had to find a way to clear the path—of everything. They needed to get the arts center independent and functioning, and they needed to find a way to have the kind of sex she wanted. Assuming he'd want it too, of course. Piece of cake, right?

He opened the refrigerator door when she reached him, fiddling with something in the back. "Your cooling fan is out, Bets. And I believe I found your keys."

When he held them up, unbidden laughter surfaced. "Of course they're in the fridge. I brought home those fresh eggs you'd given me." And promptly opened the freezer for ice to press against her hot neck.

His mouth twitched as she grabbed them from his hand. Putting her hand on his strong back, she lowered her voice to say, "Donal, to answer your original question before we were interrupted... Yes, I happen to really like sex."

His green eyes gleamed down at her. "Good to know. We'll talk more, then."

Damn right they would.

CHAPTER FOUR

M egan slowed her car to a halt on the country lane. "What in the world?"

The cows had words spray-painted on them.

Date.

Ask.

Cute.

But these weren't poetic words like the ones her future brother-in-law, Carrick Fitzgerald, used to spray on his sheep to honor his late wife's poetry.

Ollie pressed his face against the window. "Someone stole Uncle Carrick's idea! On cows. Ugh! Uncle Carrick should never have stopped doing his sheep. Mom, does that cow say *Steak?* That's so wrong. I can't wait to tell the guys at school."

Megan wished she could wash her eyes out. *Steak?* Was that supposed to be a bad joke? She looked at a few more. *Savage. Biscuit. Teatime. BBQ.*

What was this farmer thinking? She racked her brain to see if she could remember whose fields these were, but she only had a vague recollection of it being a young farmer.

She grimaced as she scanned the thirty or so black cows clustered together in the center of the field. They weren't cute or cuddly like the sheep. In fact, they were a little scary as they stared back at her. Were their eyes red? Or was the red spray paint on them somehow making it seem that way? "I like the sheep better."

"Me too."

She saw a motorcycle coming on the road behind her and recognized it as Liam's Triumph. No one but Liam had one in the whole of Caisleán. The village said it was because he had an unearned optimism about the weather. Megan thought he had a positive view about everything.

He pulled up behind her, took off his helmet, and dismounted as she and Ollie exited the car.

"*Oh, Jesus!*" Liam lamented, slapping his hand to his forehead. "He's done it! He's done it but good."

"Who did?" Ollie asked, racing over to stand beside their cousin. "It's awful, isn't it, Liam?"

"It's a disaster! But why anyone would expect anything else from Keegan O'Malley, I wouldn't know."

Megan stilled completely. There was a Keegan O'Malley signed up for her pottery class!

"*Wetser? Beor? Diger?*" Liam stalked the road, gesturing to the cows.

"What do they mean, Liam?" Ollie asked, extending his little arm out in a mirror image of his hero.

"They're—" He pursed his lips and shook his head.

Megan knew what that meant. "Irish words you probably don't want to learn, Ollie."

Liam patted the brown mess of hair Ollie hated to use a brush on. "At least not until you're older. Oh, he's ruined it! I can hear every heart in Caisleán and the surrounding towns breaking once they hear about this. Everyone loved

Carrick's spray-painted sheep. That was Sorcha's poetry. This is pure rubbish."

Megan grimaced. She was still trying to recover from learning the owner of the cows was going to be in her Tuesday evening class.

"Rubbish means garbage, Mom," Ollie said, taking her hand as the entire herd started to stalk toward them. Sure, there was a barbwire fence between them and the cows, but still. Full-grown cows in Ireland were huge. Eight hundred to a thousand pounds huge.

"Thanks for telling me, Ollie," she said although she'd known the meaning. "Maybe we should get back into the car. They look menacing."

"Ah, they're only having a look at us," Liam said, putting his hands to his waist. "Nothing to be worried about. My dad had cows. He'll be turning in his grave at this monstrosity just like the other farmers we've lost. I know Keegan wants to make a mark on the village, but this wasn't the way of it."

"Just how old is he?" Megan asked, wondering if he'd joined her class hoping to meet girls.

Her pottery mentor, Barry, had confessed at the studio one night, when they were all loose from drinking wine and throwing some big pots, that he'd taken his first class for the girls. *Who knew my center would be the clay and not the chicks?*

She suddenly remembered Barry's final words to her. Since she'd been journaling and opening up her mind, more and more memories had been resurfacing. *Isn't it interesting that me and the clay are losing you to a guy?* Barry hadn't said anything else about her decision or her relationship with Tyson—he was a "live and let live" kind of guy—but his final hug had been heavy with goodbye. They'd never

seen each other again, and she'd missed him. They'd been...
friends. All her fellow potters had shared that connection.
She hoped her students could become a community like
she'd had back then, but people had to be there for the right
reasons.

If Keegan had signed up to meet women, he'd likely be
disappointed. There were only three of them in the
Tuesday night class. The other students were men: Eoghan,
Liam, and Kade. She had no idea why Eoghan wanted to
learn a new craft at his advanced age, but she admired him
for it. Liam had told her he'd had a taste of it before on a trip
overseas. Kade had said he thought it would be uplifting.
Truthfully, though, she wondered if he wasn't attending for
a girl. *Her.* Who knew what kind of atmosphere they'd have
with that group?

"Keegan's twenty-seven," Liam said, plucking a tall
blade of grass and worrying it between his fingers. "To hear
him tell it, he's in the middle of a midlife crisis, what with
not being married yet. You have only to look at the words he
sprayed on his cows to see why the girls in Caisleán don't go
out with him."

"He's weird," Ollie said.

"He's a gas," Liam said. "Funny. Or trying to be. I'm not
feeling it."

Megan wondered if Keegan was weird or simply misun-
derstood. She'd also felt the pressure to get married and
have children. In fact, she would have had more of them,
but the timing of Tyson's short home leaves had never been
right after Ollie. She hadn't gotten pregnant again.

"Can I call Uncle Carrick and tell him, Mom?"

Megan looked at her watch. "No, we need to get you to
school. It starts in ten minutes."

"At least I can tell Mr. Fitzgerald," Ollie said, because

his teacher was none other than Carrick's brother, Jamie. "But we don't have to be in such a hurry. I'm always early."

Even though she'd been on a lightening-up program with Ollie, she still made sure they arrived on time every day. Some lines she didn't want to cross. Still, she she'd stopped being a smother mother. Ollie loved to play outside and soak up male attention from their friends and relatives, so she'd gotten out of his way. For the first time in a long time, she and her son were getting along.

Liam laughed. "My mom always had us there fifteen minutes early too. It's the American side. Come on, Ollie. Let's leave this sorry spray-painted lot and get you back in the car."

"Where are you going today?" Ollie asked, racing over to him.

Liam scooped him up, making her son giggle. "I'm off to the corner store for some milk. Mum forgot to buy some when she went shopping yesterday. She's out of sorts."

He laughed. "Because she likes Mr. O'Dwyer, right?"

"Ollie!" Megan gasped.

"What?" Her son made a funny face. "She does. Boys make girls crazy. Aunt Angie says it all the time."

Liam tilted his head to the side and grinned. "Girls make boys a little crazy too. Unless you do yoga and meditation."

"Ugh!" Ollie called out. "I hate yoga and meditation. Uncle Carrick says you're going to get stuck in one of those poses. What's it again? Something with your dog?"

"It's downward facing dog." Liam tapped him on the nose when he caught him. "Not Carrick's style, but I still love him. Megan, how's the meditation going for you?"

She'd tried to quiet her mind last night after Ollie had gone to sleep, but her thoughts had strayed to Kade. He hadn't brought up their conversation in the pottery room three days ago, acting as easygoing as always. She'd written in her journal instead. The pages could be summed up into one phrase: she didn't know what to do.

Liam stopped his gentle roughhousing with Ollie. "You all right, Megan?"

"Mom burned our dinner last night," Ollie responded. "It was so gross. Burnt spaghetti is the worst."

"Not as bad as the monkey brains I had in Kenya," Liam quipped, making her son gag.

"Liam, please tell me you did not eat that," Megan said, turning away from the cows.

"I did, and it was disgusting." Liam put his hands to his own throat like a little boy, gagging along with her son. "My older brother dared me. Ollie, hear this wisdom. Never let anyone dare you into doing something. It's a mistake. Every time."

"I won't, Liam," Ollie said, sniffing the air. "Someone is putting poop on the fields."

Megan caught a whiff of bovine in the air herself, her face bunching from it. The Irish countryside was picture perfect for the eyes, but sometimes it was downright putrid for the nose.

"We call that slurry," Liam said with a laugh. "Now, you have another Irish word. Off to school with you. Megan, do you need anything at the store?"

"We need milk too!" Ollie answered, opening the car door. "Ugh! I have to shut the door fast so the poop smell doesn't get in the car. Bye, Liam."

Liam's shoulders were shaking as the door slammed. "He's a trip, as Mum would say. I'll drop the milk off on my way back. Anything else?"

Another journal? she almost asked. She'd written pages

last night, much like she used to do in letters to Tyson, some of which she hadn't had the courage to send. Her chest tightened.

Liam put a hand on her arm. "Is the clay still bothering you?"

"No, actually. I finally centered the clay and made my first piece."

With Kade's help.

"I told you Ireland would be balm to the senses." He pointed to the overcast sky. "Is there anything more beautiful?"

"Liam, it's been cloudy for two weeks. I'm missing the sunshine."

"You'll get used to it," he said with a wink. "Part of the charm. It's like the old saying. *No rain, no rainbows.*"

She loved Liam but she almost rolled her eyes at that piece of "wisdom."

"Now, take Ollie off to school," her cousin said, walking back to his bike. "We'll talk when I bring your milk."

Talk? She wasn't sure that was a good idea. She wasn't sure she was ready to talk.

When she got into the car, Ollie bounced in his seat. "Mom, I think we stayed too long. I'm actually going to be late."

She sighed as she turned the car on. "We're fine."

Liam raced past them on his motorcycle, making Ollie cheer. "He's totally the best. Like Kade. And Uncle Carrick. And Brady and Declan and Mr. O'Dwyer. Mom, I'm so glad we live in Ireland now. I love it here!"

She met his eyes in the rearview window. "Me too, honey."

When they arrived at school, Jamie crossed the schoolyard immediately. "Everything all right? You're never late."

"We stopped to see these crazy cows spray-painted red," Ollie nearly shouted. "The farmer stole your brother's idea, Mr. Fitzgerald, and it's awful. Liam called it rubbish."

"Carrick's idea?" Jamie asked, his brow furrowing. "Who did?"

"Liam said it was Keegan O'Malley," Megan said.

"Not him!" Jamie moaned. "How bad is it?"

"He spray-painted *Steak* on one of the cows," Ollie said, bobbing up and down like a fishing line looking for Irish trout.

"Jesus, Mary, and Joseph," Jamie cried out. "It's awful, then."

Megan had to bite her lip to keep from laughing. The Irish had a way of making life theater. "As awful as it gets."

"Kids!" Jamie called out to the others milling in the yard. "We're taking a field trip. Up the road. Grab your coats."

Megan blinked at him. "You're going to walk there?"

"It's a nice ten-minute stroll," he said, his eyes narrowed. "I'm not waiting until school's out to see this monstrosity."

"I told Mom we should call Uncle Carrick." Ollie raced off to join a group of boys who'd emerged from the school with their raincoats.

"Oh, I'll be calling him," Jamie said, his brown curls in a riot on his head. "Jesus, Sorcha will be mad as a hornet over this."

Megan jolted. "Why would you say that? She's passed."

"Don't mind me," he said, rubbing his skull. "I'm mad meself sometimes. All right, kids, let's go see what Keegan O'Malley has done to his poor cows. Have a good day, Megan."

Megan watched as all twenty children followed Jamie

down the country road. She shook her head. The small village school wasn't anything like the one Ollie had attended in Maryland, where everyone was in a grade according to age. The kids in his class here ranged from eight to twelve years old, with Jamie using multiple lesson plans for the various ages. Ollie loved it so far, saying it was like going to summer camp. He had new friends, which delighted her.

But it still threw her that they were going on a cow field trip.

As she passed the animals again on the way back to her cottage on O'Hanlon land, she caught sight of more words.

Pretty. Girl. Smile.

Her arms rippled with goose bumps, and she found herself thinking of the first day they'd arrived in Ireland. Carrick's poetic sheep had greeted them. She'd seen a message then too. *Here. Be. Good.* It had given her chills, much like the cows' message today.

Maybe there was something to those scary-looking cows, after all.

She was cleaning up their breakfast dishes when she heard Liam's motorcycle roar out front. Moments later, he was knocking on the door and calling her name as he let himself in, something she was mostly getting used to.

"I'm in the kitchen," she called out.

He appeared with a wry grin and a bottle of milk and a gift bag in his hand. "You know... Maybe Keegan's words aren't complete rubbish. When I passed by coming here, I saw some grand words. *Lovely. Date.* That's what I'm having tonight with a girl in Crossmolina on this fine Friday. Met her at a barbeque last weekend."

"You seem to like dating," Megan commented as she wiped her hands off with a towel.

"What's not to like? I get to spend time with a beautiful woman. Learn about her. Romance her. Enjoy her."

"Do you want some tea?" she asked, and he nodded. "You don't mind it not being permanent?"

"What's permanent, really?" Liam grabbed two mugs from the cupboard. "You would know that better than most people. I don't mean to sound crass. I figure we have people in our lives as long as we're meant to. Sometimes it's of our choosing. Sometimes it's not. You know me. I try to live in the moment, especially after I lost my dad so young. The other stuff—the planning and the hoping for and the worrying over—is only wasting energy until it's right in front of you."

She filled the kettle, her mind struggling to process it all.

"You want to tell me what's bothering you?" He pulled out some Lyons teabags and plunked them in the mugs. "If you've centered your clay, I would think your problems are over."

She wouldn't call Kade a problem. Her chest tightened as if there were a vise around it and part of her was struggling to break free. "I don't know that I should say."

Except whom else could she confide in? She and Angie were doing better in their relationship, but she couldn't imagine talking to her about this. They'd decided to let each other live their own lives without any sisterly interference or comment, and Angie was too involved in her past with Tyson not to have a strong opinion.

"Why not?" He came over and put his hands on her shoulders. "I know we're long-lost cousins, but I think we're also good friends."

"Me too," she said, the bonds around her chest easing a moment. "But you're also good friends with the person I need to talk about."

He smiled, a rich and enchanting smile. "At last! You and Kade."

She pressed her hands to her face. "How did you—"

"I have eyes, don't I?" He tapped his temples as if to punctuate the point. "I know Kade well, and I'm starting to know you. You're a good fit for each other."

"But—" The kettle's whistle blew, startling her.

"Let's have our tea and sit," he said, taking over the preparations.

When they were situated in the front parlor, she rose to turn on a light. The skies were gray, making the cottage feel small and gloomy. "I don't know where to start."

"Start at the beginning," Liam said, "and then see where it takes you."

She told him about centering her clay with Kade at her side. Her voice broke when she reached the part about the memories it had unleashed, including her revelation that meeting Tyson had knocked her off her center. "I hadn't remembered that until the other day, and it broke my heart. It also made me angry, like *I want to throw something* angry."

"Maybe you *should* throw something," he said, blowing the steam coming off his mug. "There's an infinite amount of rocks on the beach. I've always found it therapeutic to hurl them into the sea and listen to them crash against the other rocks in the shallows."

Megan touched the edge of the small table and studied her cousin. "You don't strike me as an angry person."

"I wouldn't say I am as a rule," he said, sipping his tea. "But I have been. When a girl I was dating went out with another guy in Inniscrone. When my dad died. When Wyatt and Rhys left for South Africa because they couldn't handle living here without him being around. We all get angry, Megan. The trick is to let it out before it hurts us. From the look of it, you have a lot to be angry about. Maybe it's time to let it out."

"And what about Kade?" she asked, gripping the table's edge.

"Isn't he your friend? Liking him doesn't change that. Just talk to him. He's one of the best listeners, and he's known for his patience. The question is: do you want to start getting to know him in a different way?"

She thought of how it felt to have his arms around her. As comforting as a warm fire and yet as exhilarating as riding a horse through a golden Irish field. "A part of me does want that, but Tyson hasn't even been gone a year. Aren't there rules about that? Wouldn't that make me a bad person?"

Liam set his mug aside. "Following your heart is never a bad thing—quite the contrary. I hesitate to ask this, but maybe you just think on what I'm about to say."

Her stomach tensed. "Okay..."

"You've told me your marriage was far from perfect, and neither of you had been happy for a long time. Do you think Tyson would have waited a year if you were the one who'd passed?"

A bubble burst in her belly, something hot and painful. "Wait? No, he wouldn't have waited." Her anger was back, and it was starting to pulse under her right rib. "Liam, I don't know this for sure—"

He met her gaze unflinchingly. "You think he cheated on you."

She gripped her knees when the table no longer felt like enough to anchor her down. "He was gone so much, and it wasn't always fighting. There were lots of weeks of what they call R&R. In Dubai. In Cyprus. In Mykonos. He told me soldiers need downtime from fighting—which I understood. He also said the government wouldn't pay to send him home the whole way. Even if that was true, he was never upset about it. I thought he should be upset that he couldn't come home to me and Ollie. Especially when it was Ollie's birthday or mine. Or the holidays. But I don't think he wanted to come home. He looked happy in the pictures he sent or when we talked on FaceTime. So, no, he wouldn't wait."

She stood, needing to move suddenly.

"Maybe it's not fair to talk about Tyson like this."

"That's your choice," he said quietly.

"I feel so conflicted."

"Is that how you feel with Kade?" Liam asked, resting his arms on the table.

She shook her head. "No. I always feel happy around him. And calm and appreciated. Other than you, he's the best man I know."

His mouth tipped to the right. "Thank you. Well, I believe you have your answer."

Her hand pressed to her chest. No, her heart. It was glowing. "Yes, I believe I do."

"Here's the thing about the past, Megan. You can try and put the pieces together like it's a giant jigsaw puzzle, but you'll only waste months and drive yourself mad. I say burn the fucking pieces and be happy." He rose and kissed her cheek. "I have a feeling it will look good on you."

She gave in to the urge to hug him. "Thank you, Liam. You can't know how glad I am that we're friends. Not just cousins."

"I feel the same. Now go and open your gift. I thought you might like it. See you, cuz."

She went into the kitchen after the front door closed

quietly. The roar of the motorcycle sounded outside as she peered into the bag. A bright patch of soft yellow fabric greeted her, and she pulled out a cotton T-shirt. Holding it up, she laughed. *Visualize Sunshine.*

Only in Ireland... Now that was something Keegan O'Malley should spray paint onto his cows. She detoured into her bedroom and closed the curtains—you never knew who might pop by—and pulled off her sweater. Before changing into the T-shirt, she surveyed herself in the small wall mirror. She'd lost weight after Tyson had died, too steeped in depression to have much of an inclination to eat. She was rail thin. Would Kade find her attractive?

He did, she remembered, as she pulled the shirt over her head. His brown eyes had been filled with it. She was the one who needed to see that in herself.

A T-shirt had never been her style, but when she looked at herself wearing it, a ribbon of shock twined through her. She looked...pretty.

Pretty. Girl. Smile.

She did smile, and her face seemed more radiant in the gloamy light of her bedroom. Apparently those words had been a message she needed to heed.

Now it was time to find Kade.

CHAPTER FIVE

L egend wasn't quite sure what to make of him.

Kade eyed the mare in her new stall in the stable between Winston and Majestic. He'd wanted her to be flanked by two of his softest ponies, and from the neighing he'd heard, he could tell they were giving the mare a huge welcome.

Lifting his hand gently to let her smell him, he waited. Smell wasn't the only thing that assured a horse, although it helped.

"We're going to become good friends," he told the russet-colored mare.

Fear and longing warred in her brown eyes. Kade had always marveled how two such polar emotions could exist in one being, whether animal or human. The mare had scars, but he didn't need their origin to heal them. He did that with love, gentleness, and attention.

He'd been doing the same with Red Zephyr, whom he was healing for a client after the stallion had broken his leg in the Dubai World Cup. No, he wouldn't race professionally again, but his leg was healing nicely. Kade thought he might run again. The horse would wither without it. Roaming the pasture Kade had him in behind the shed wouldn't be enough for him long term.

"You make yourself comfortable," he told Legend, stroking the side of her neck gently at last. "You're among friends."

Another tremble overtook the mare, and at eighteen hands, it came off as a rumble of thunder.

"She's a beauty," Sorcha said, appearing beside him.

The horse stomped her foot in her stall. "You can see her, eh, Legend? Hello, Sorcha."

"Hello, Kade."

She seemed to float to the stall door and reached out a hand to Legend. The horse studied her for a moment and then edged back.

"Seems she's not ready for you either," Kade said, chuckling as Duke trotted over with a *ruff* and tried to press up against Sorcha's leg only to shake his head when he met nothing but air. "She's not real, my friend."

"I'm more real than some," Sorcha said with a laugh. "I would caution anyone who can see spirits not to hang around that bog down near the abbey. There are some frightening ghosts down there."

He snorted. Usually he ignored those who roamed the ruins of Kenmore Abbey. "Why are you here?"

"Good news." She lifted a finger to her ear as Duke gave a bark and raced out of the shed. "Megan is on her way. There's progress in the air. I only popped by to tell you not to mess things up. It took a lot of doing to arrange a compelling message for her today with Keegan O'Malley's cows. They aren't anything like Carrick's sheep."

"I heard about that," Kade said. "The pictures Jamie sent around were mad."

"Keegan's only looking for love like most," Sorcha said. "Wait until you see what miracle Liam worked with Megan. I inspired him to buy a gift for her. He might not see or hear spirits like his dad or brother—yet—but he senses the energy of things. Enjoy this moment, Kade, but since you are still a man, I thought it best to tell you to mind yourself."

She disappeared before he could decide if he wanted to shoot off a clever reply. Mind himself? Because he was a man? Oh, death hadn't changed her.

Then Megan walked into the stable, Duke trotting proudly next to her.

She was wearing a yellow T-shirt. So unlike her. The phrase *Visualize Sunshine* had him smiling. "You look beautiful, Megan. Let me guess. Liam bought that for you."

Her mouth parted. "Yes, he did. How did you know?"

Telling her about Sorcha might be strange this early, so he went with another explanation. "They're selling those shirts at the yoga studio he sometimes attends. I saw it in the window. It looks lovely on you."

She ducked her head, looking young and unsure. Both looked good on her.

"I thought we might have that talk," she said, her voice as soft as her footsteps as she took those first hesitant steps toward him.

"I'd love that," Kade said, smiling already, waiting until she met his eyes.

Those large brown eyes of hers latched on to his, and her mouth formed a small smile in response. The twin emotions of fear and longing radiated in her gaze, reminding him of Legend. He could all but feel her heart pressing against its old confines, wanting to expand. He'd seen the gentleness and love inside her as well as her exhilaration riding across the fields, something they shared. She had such a huge heart—for him and Ollie and Liam and the people they served, as much as the animals around her. He loved that heart of hers, one she wasn't sure of yet. He reminded himself to be patient.

"How does a walk on the beach sound?"

"Great." She was clenching her hands at her sides. "Is that a new horse?"

He patted the mare. "This is Legend, and she's going to be around for a while. She's still a little skittish, but she's learning the way of things."

Megan edged closer. "She seems a little big for pony rides."

"Indeed," he said, laughing when Legend stomped her foot again. "Putting your foot down already? Megan, she's here because of a deal with my father. He needs help breeding her."

Her hand lifted to give Legend her scent like he'd taught her. "I didn't know you did that kind of thing for him. Is this something new?"

"It's a one-time deal between us." His diaphragm started locking up as he said it, which told him he needed to process some deep emotion. "We have old business—like many parents and children. I'm hoping this will go a long way toward addressing it."

"Good," she said, uttering a delighted laugh when Legend nibbled on her fingers. "Oh, she likes me."

"Kindred spirit." Kade leaned against the stall, wanting to push a piece of her hair over her shoulder as an excuse to touch her. "Come on. Let's take that walk. Actually, I thought we might ride there. The tide will be out, and it's a special place I'd like to show you. Sound good?"

Legend gave a soft neigh as Megan removed her hand.

"It sounds wonderful," she said, a touch of awe in her voice. "I've always thought riding a horse on a beach would be..."

"What?" he asked as he opened Blaze's and Majestic's stalls.

She made a face. "Romantic."

He started to saddle the ponies. "Why do you think I suggested it?"

This time he spotted a flush on her cheeks. The yard was quiet as they left the shed, leading Blaze and Majestic out with them.

"Another day of nothing but gray skies," Megan said in a mournful voice. "I'm going to have to wear my T-shirt every day to turn this weather around."

Kade tipped his head back and studied the clouds. "I think they're beautiful. Pearly, even. Hard to imagine more beautiful skies than these. Great for cloud watching and dreaming."

She turned up her face too but stared at him instead of the clouds. "*Pearly skies.* Kade Donovan, do you ever have a negative thought? A bad day?"

He thought about his recent upset with his father. "I had to walk off some anger and sadness only a few days ago, and I expect I have more that will need addressing."

She swallowed thickly. "Was it because of me?" she asked in a low voice. "Because I didn't comment on what you said the other day?"

Pausing, he dipped his head to meet her eyes. "No, love. When you come to my mind—as you do often—you light up my heart. The other issue is with my father, and it's been a longstanding problem."

She had trouble maintaining eye contact, but she tried valiantly, he could tell. "I don't know what to say when you tell me things like that."

"You don't need to say anything," he told her as he formed a step with his hands for her to use to alight Blaze's saddle. It took trust to accept such help, or at least it did for her, and he felt how far they'd come. "Unless you'd like me to stop saying them."

Their hands reached for the reins at the same time, but she didn't pull away when they touched. In fact, she settled her palm over his and met his eyes unflinchingly. "I don't want that. I appreciate everything you say. No one else has ever said those kinds of things to me before."

He smiled as he checked her stirrups and saddle one last time. "Good."

With practiced ease, he swung onto Majestic and nudged her into a walk down the path that would take them to the stretch of beach he had in mind. Megan wiggled in her saddle for a few steps until she settled.

"Did you know that riding a horse is rather like centering the clay?" He matched Megan's pace to keep even with her. "You need to be in a good place with yourself to ride. The horse knows if you aren't. I've seen grown men get pushed around in such moments. Fly off, even. You seem to be faring well on both accounts."

She laughed with a richness he only heard from her when she was around his horses, and it scattered a few black rooks in the surrounding trees. He cherished the sound. There was a rare freedom to it.

"I love riding," she said, patting Blaze's coat. "I feel tall and powerful. And I've only started centering the clay again. I've made a few more pieces on the small side the last couple of days, but I have a long way to go."

Did she expect another hiccup? "But you have it back. You're ready for your classes. Don't forget it."

Her smile was more of a grin, the kind devoid of life's weight. "I won't."

"If you do," he said, leaning over in his saddle to touch her arm, "I'll help you remember. Let's canter."

They picked up their speed. Again, she needed a few beats to find her rhythm, but she was posting nicely. She'd been a good and eager student. He still wondered what had happened to convince her she wasn't good at anything. He hadn't seen any evidence.

When they reached the beach, he carefully led her through the low tide to the small island at the edge of the shore. The horses splashed in the clear water, seaweed dancing in the shallow current. Majestic pulled a little on the reins, wanting a drink, and he patted to let her know she would have it in a minute.

"I've never been out here before," Megan said, looking at him with a grin, "but I've seen horses grazing on the island and wondered how they came to be there."

"They're from our farm," he said, "and there's a path leading to the top of the hill with sweetgrass for them. I thought you'd like to come. This place has been a favorite of mine since I was a boy."

They cleared the right corner of the island. A heron took off, its massive wings flapping audibly. Large boulders dotted the shore, ones he used to play leapfrog with.

"There's a grey seal by the rocks straight ahead," he pointed out. "A group of them comes here in autumn for breeding or to give birth."

She gasped. "Liam said they were around, but I've never seen one."

"Good. Then my surprise is what I'd hoped. Let's have a better look."

Megan rode tall in the saddle, and they shared a smile.

The seal started its funny movements across the sand, which he'd always thought looked like the breaststroke on land by a giant dirigible. Yet it moved fast and with purpose to the shallows and soon disappeared from sight. As they neared, a trio of seals made quick work of doing the same. At the tide's edge, Kade gave Majestic the cue to halt, and Megan and Blaze came to a stop beside them.

"There's more of them!" Megan exclaimed as a few others maneuvered off the large rocks and made their way across the sand and into the sea.

"I used to love watching them when I was younger," he said, his heart full as he spotted a seal bobbing his head out of the water as if equally intrigued with them. "I might have wanted to adopt one. My mum usually let me keep whatever animal I wanted, but this time she put her foot down. Although she did give me an entire salmon to feed my friend."

"What a wonderful memory. I don't know your mom well, but she seems like a nice woman."

He swung out of the saddle and crossed to help her down. Gazing down at her flushed face, he couldn't help but trace her cheek. "You need to ride on the beach more. You're glowing."

She touched the place he'd caressed, almost as if testing for an imprint. "I'd love to."

He patted the ponies to send them off a few yards. Their training ensured they wouldn't wander.

He and Megan faced the water, a few seals visible in the bluish gray sea. "But I still don't know what to do about this."

"By 'this' you mean what's between us?" He turned his head and smiled. "How does riding more on the beach sound? Going out to dinner?"

She blew out a breath. "That isn't all we're talking about. We've been spending time together for months, and I love that, but this new thing between us would mean more... Kade, I'm still working through some issues."

"I know you are, love, and I'm glad you are." He held out his hand to her. "As for us... How about we start here?"

Her brown eyes gleamed and then darkened. She took another breath. A light caramel color punched through in her irises before she grabbed his hand. He could feel the change in the way she touched him. There was an electric receptivity to it that called to the man inside him, like how he expected the tide felt about the moon.

"I can do that," she said softly as she gave him a new smile, one alight with rare treasures like the sea glass under their feet.

"Then everything else will fall into place," he responded, raising her hand to press a gentle kiss to it.

They held hands for the entire stretch of the beach with the horses trailing behind, the smell of oranges hanging around them.

CHAPTER SIX

Megan had never been to a budget meeting before, and given that her pottery classes began tomorrow, this wasn't the day she would have chosen for her first one.

It had all started with a text from Bets last night. *Hi Megan! Don't panic but the council has decided it won't cover the arts center's operational costs. I'm hosting a meeting to talk about solutions tomorrow at eleven after Donal and Carrick do some last-minute pushing back of their own. We're going to figure this out. Trust me.*

The message had instantly sent her into a tailspin. When the shock receded, Megan had felt the urge to pull the covers over her head and ignore the issue. She'd written in her journal instead, talking about her old habit of avoidance and then tore the pages up into her version of a jigsaw puzzle and burned them like Liam had suggested. She might have even danced around the fire.

But she wasn't dancing now. Her stomach was already in fits about tomorrow's class, and this added stress only made it worse.

The fact that her usually beaming sister was wringing her hands next to her on Bets' settee in the front parlor as her cousin and Siobhan McGrath, the arts center knitting teacher and Bets' dear friend, made tea made her feel slightly better. The clacking sounds of china from the kitchen grated on her frayed nerves, though.

Not even the memory of another walk on the beach holding Kade's hand could ease the tension in her belly. Breathing took effort. The center had money troubles already, and that was no way to start. Angie knew it well, having gone through what she called the budget roller coaster before in Baltimore.

"Carrick said he could kick himself for not making this part of the conditions for his donation," Angie muttered. "His focus was on getting them to agree that we could teach any form of artistic expression such as nudes. Not the day-to-day expenses."

Angie's painting classes had gotten into trouble for teaching nudes, stirred up by Mary Kincaid and Orla MacKenna, Tom's wife. Ultimately that complaint had prompted the county council to close Bets' fledging arts center. Carrick had donated the house he'd built to serve as a city-run arts center, which should have solved the problem. But if they couldn't afford to pay the operational expenses of the center, it would close.

They would be out of jobs.

Or at least Megan would be.

Angie taught five art classes, sure, but her painting career was taking off again, and her Irish roots would be oak-tree strong once she married Carrick after the new year. Megan had only started to think of Ireland as her new home, but Ollie loved it and so did she. Now there was this beautiful and tender thing between her and Kade, as fragile as a newborn. She needed to teach and make ceramics to stay.

They had to find a solution.

The two women appeared, a complete contrast to each other. Siobhan was five ten with silver hair and a round face, while Bets was a whirl of energy at five four with orange-brown hair and an angular face that suited her thin frame. Siobhan carried a plate of biscuits and tea cakes with a warm smile. Bets carried a tea service and had a tight mouth.

Megan couldn't imagine forcing anything down, but she thanked the women as they settled in, Siobhan into a tapestry-covered armchair and Bets onto another settee.

"I think Donal and Carrick are back," Bets said, cocking her ear. "I'm hoping for good news but I don't know that they'll be bringing it."

"Donal and Carrick thought it was worth a try," Angie said, tapping her fingernail against her teacup. "They couldn't wait to confront the council about the notice."

Megan set her tea on the coffee table and crossed her legs to stop her foot from bouncing nervously, listening for the sound of boots clapping in the front hallway.

When she finally heard them, Megan turned to watch Donal and Carrick stride into the room. The older man was already shaking his head. Carrick's jaw was clenched.

"So it's as I thought—a complete waste of time," Bets said, dumping a sugar cube into her tea with such force the hot water spilled over the rim.

"Did you punch anyone?" Angie asked Carrick as he kissed her cheek and sat on her other side.

"I thought about it, and I'm not a violent man. When

we told them you weren't planning to pony up the cash, they had the cheek to propose that *I* should pay for the expenses since *I'd* donated the building. As I'd saddled them with a burden."

"That center isn't a burden," Siobhan said enthusiastically, her round face tense. "It was good of you to donate it as you did."

"Thank you." He nodded in her direction. "I said they were mad. Hadn't they paid to finish the center in the first place? Something has clearly changed, and I demanded to know what."

"That's when I stepped in," Donal said, dropping onto the settee beside Bets and putting his arm around her shoulders. "I served on the council until recently, and I know the way of things. Tom wasn't going to let anyone be upfront with us—even though I wanted to confront the lot of them."

Donal had resigned from the council over the snafu with Bets' art center. Megan rather admired that, even though the thought made her belly tighten further. They had a real fight on their hands, and she'd never been a fighter.

"Breathe, Megan," her sister whispered next to her.

When she tried, she could barely squeeze air through her windpipe. Her sister took her hand, the touch sweet and yet firm, and she finally managed a short and painful breath.

"I wish they had the guts to say why," Bets said, giving the floor a stomp. "They make me so mad!"

"They weren't going to say why, *mo ghrá*," Donal said, rubbing her leg.

"It's a new low," Siobhan said, pouring the men tea, "given how much the community is behind this."

"No doubt." Carrick swore under his breath. "But

Donal took a hard line with them. Tom burned rubber out of the parking lot."

"You did pretty well yourself, Fitzgerald," Donal said, thanking Siobhan when she brought him and Carrick tea. "We got them to agree to a paltry monthly sum for the center. Unfortunately, as the director, you're going to have to find a way to make up the rest, Bets."

"I was prepared for that," Bets said, making her orange-reddish bob dance. "It's not going to be fun though. I'm going to have to become a grant writer. Gads!"

"And we're going to have to resort to *fundraisers*," Angie said with a moan. "I still have nightmares about the ones I held in Baltimore. In the end, none of it was enough. I lost my job, and they closed the arts center I was managing. Budget cuts suck. I can't believe I'm facing the same situation here. Where is that luck of the Irish everyone talks about?"

"I've never seen it," Bets said with a sad shrug.

"If I have to sell some of my sheep to keep it open, I will," Donal said, chucking Bets under the chin.

"Me as well," Carrick said, rubbing Angie's arm in comfort. "Don't worry. The arts center will stay open. You have my word on that."

Megan trembled at the conviction in his voice. She believed him.

"Oh, Carrick, I love you," Angie said, hugging him briefly. "But we agreed you would not put up your personal finances for the center."

"*Our* finances," he said, fingering her engagement ring.

"I like the sound of that," she said with her first easy smile, touching the top button of his blue work shirt. "However, no one should be spending their own money on what is being publicly touted as a community resource. Trust me on this."

"I agree," Bets said, "and while I love you guys for considering it—I could fund it too—we shouldn't. It sets a bad precedent in the community. Plus, according to my research, it might hurt our chances for a grant."

"It will." Angie made a face. "When private money comes in, public funding always goes down."

"You would know best," Carrick said, glowering. "But I'm retaining the right to help if needed."

She laid her head against his chest for a moment. "If you don't stop, I'm going to get all emotional. That's why I love you."

"And I you, Yank."

Megan felt tears rise in her eyes. Angie, who'd been married previously—and to a real jerk— had admitted this was the first time she'd experienced this kind of support in a relationship, and that's why she knew it was going to last.

That wasn't something Megan had ever experienced with Tyson.

The image of Kade taking her hand yesterday came to mind. When he told her something, she believed him too. Would they be able to have this kind of a relationship? A flash of longing rocked her heart. She wanted to find out, which meant they really needed to keep the center open.

"I think we should hold a craft fair," Siobhan said, munching on a biscuit. "The holidays would be a grand time for it."

"How much money do we need to make up?" Angie asked, her brow wrinkling. "I love the idea, but from what I know, you won't make nearly as much as you think and it's a lot of work. Unless people donate goods for free, which is rare. Tell me the figure you got the council to agree to, and

I'll run the numbers right now. Carrick, can I use your phone to calculate?"

Megan watched as her sister inputted the number Carrick mentioned, which made Bets groan in despair.

"Megan, how often do you plan to run the kilns?" Angie asked. "Those are going to be our biggest electrical expense."

Her stomach dropped to the floor. Would they consider cutting her classes? "My students are beginners so right now, so probably only once a month, with the first firing being next month." She bit her lip. "I know ceramics is the most expensive art in an arts center."

"Megan, I know what that wooden face means," Angie said, giving her a pointed look. "We aren't going to stop teaching ceramics."

"Of course we won't!" Bets exclaimed so enthusiastically that her silver earrings moved like playground swings. "We're running an arts center, and we will hold all manner of classes. Even though this budget issue is going to constrict us from bringing in resident artists. Room and board might not be enough to tempt them."

"To come to Ireland and live without rent?" Angie asked wryly. "You'd be surprised, cousin."

"Maybe you're right," Bets said, biting into a tea cake. "Time will tell."

Megan wondered how much time they had given the figures they were discussing. "Don't we need to make money fast to keep things running?"

Angie's nose scrunched. "If you're not running the kiln until next month, we have a little more time. We only have two classes at night—yours and mine—and it's fairly light out, which will cut down on electricity costs."

"Jesus, maybe we should light candles," Donal said,

rubbing the back of his head. "No! That's ridiculous. You run the power you need. I can talk to the utilities people and ask for extra time and maybe even some luck."

"I thought you said there was no such thing," Megan said.

"Luck in Irish means the thing yer man throws in that's a little extra," Carrick said. "Like a set of tires when you buy a car."

Megan shook her head. "Who's your man?"

Angie gave a weak chuckle. "It's Irish for 'some dude.' I'm still trying to figure out when to use it in conversation. Anyway, I think we have enough until the end of the year. Classes stop mid-December."

Megan gulped. "Four months."

That didn't seem like a lot of time to figure out their funding situation. Angie must be thinking the same thing because her sister was wringing her hands again.

"I'm going to apply to the Arts Council of Ireland for a grant," Bets said with a grimace, "but my concerns are twofold. It might be a lengthy process, and any money that comes in will be managed by local authorities. Which is why we're in this jam to begin with."

"That doesn't sound very encouraging," Megan said tightly.

"From my experience," Angie said, "arts councils usually want to see a place established for a while before they fork out cash. We shouldn't count on it immediately."

"Still, I say we try early," Bets said. "I'll need some help with the grant."

"You have it," Angie responded.

"What about a gallery showing?" Siobhan asked, resting her blue teacup on her leg. "Angie held a very successful one in August."

"Except gallery showings should be money in an artist's pocket. They're meant to grow his or her name," Carrick said, kicking out his feet. "Angie is just getting that back. Giving her proceeds away would undercut her success."

Personally, Megan thought Angie was a better artist now than when she'd had some fame in her twenties. She agreed with Carrick—Angie's art was too valuable to be auctioned off for the arts center. But maybe *she* could help. "What about me?" she asked. "I'm not interested in growing my name."

Angie swung her head in her direction. "Maybe you should be, Meg."

Staying here in Ireland was more important right now. She needed this job. Besides, if she didn't have access to the wheel and kiln, she wouldn't have a way to practice her art. The equipment was too expensive and cumbersome for her to buy for herself. Painters had it better in that regard. "Maybe. But I don't have a reputation in the ceramics world like you did in the art world. I need to build everything from scratch. Literally."

She thought of Kade's words. *Things will take care of themselves.* If she wanted to make a name for herself, it would have to happen gradually, piece by piece. And it would need to start somewhere outside of the classroom, even if it was at a fundraiser.

"What are you thinking, Meg?" Angie asked.

Her tongue grew thick in her mouth as everyone looked at her. She panicked. No one ever liked her ideas. No, that wasn't true. Kade did. And Liam did as well. She was no longer scared little Megan who didn't have a thought in her head. Or at least she didn't want to be.

"Maybe we're thinking too small," she said, swallowing audibly. "I mean, it's a community arts center. People here value that. They like to be together. Pop by for a chat. Be social at the pub. Why not create a fun event for the community? I can make items to sell, but it sounds like we need some serious cash, the kind a simple sale won't bring in. What do the Irish like to do most?"

Bets leaned forward on the edge of her seat, and she wasn't alone. Megan's insides did a flip in response, and she found herself bursting with a new feeling. Pride.

Donal made a humming sound. "An event the community would pay serious money to attend? A horse race."

"A horse race?" Megan squeaked. In a million years, she hadn't expected that answer.

"It's perfect," Carrick said, slapping his knee. "It's an old tradition in Ireland. People would pay to come to a kind of country fair where they could watch the race and be entertained."

"What about kids?" Megan asked, clearing her throat. "I used to take Ollie to all sorts of festivals. Halloween was a big one. We'd go to a farm and have a hayride. Pick pumpkins. Maybe watch a carving contest. Have food. There might be drinks and a band for the adults. I mean, we're surrounded by farms."

"Oh, don't worry, Megan," Carrick said with a wink. "People would bring their kids along to see a horse race."

"Believe me, they would." Bets started tapping her feet on her faded Aubusson rug. "This could work!"

"How much did you pay for this kind of thing in the States?" Donal asked.

While they weren't talking about the kind of event she'd ever been to, she based it on what she knew. "Anywhere from thirty to fifty dollars for adults while children are somewhat cheaper. All inclusive. I could ask Kade about giving pony rides. People would like that, I'd think." She knew he would help her in anything.

"They would." Bets tapped her mouth. "The horse race will be harder to control since it requires us to secure a wider area of land."

"I agree," Donal repeated. "But we could try and cordon it off."

"We would need a prize for the winner of the race," Carrick said.

"People will donate," Siobhan said. "The shoreline has been a preferred track."

"I'll talk to Killian about that," Donal said. "He's the best one around for such things."

"So we're having a country fair of sorts around a horse race," Bets said, drawing the words out. "Food, drink, and music, with crafts for buying along with other items donated by the community. The horse race would be in the early afternoon, let's say."

"I can knit a bunch of items to sell along with Megan's ceramics," Siobhan said. "I'm sure a few other people in the village would donate things as well."

"Agreed," Bets said, holding up a fresh tea cake. "Now we only need to decide on when. Let me pull up the community calendar on my phone and see what's already scheduled. The calendar is rather full up to mid-December."

"So we do it on St. Stephen's Day," Siobhan said enthusiastically.

"When is that?" Megan asked as she and Angie shared a look.

"It's the day after Christmas and has a grand tradition in Ireland," Donal answered, "although not as strong perhaps as a few generations ago. You'll hear it referred to as the Day of the Wren by some. While no one throws rocks at wrens anymore for causing bad luck—"

"Good God!" Megan said, shuddering.

"It's a grand holiday for socializing, horse racing, and partying," Donal continued. "In England, it's called Boxing Day. No boxing though."

"That always confused me," Carrick said with a shake of his head.

"People will still have relatives visiting, and they will be longing for something to do with them," Siobhan said.

Angie nudged her. "We will too. Mom and Dad will be here for the holidays and my wedding. God help us!"

Megan's stomach burned. She loved their parents, but she didn't want her mother to treat her like a baby—or her dad to call her one. "I'll buy them tickets the moment they're available," she said, making Angie chuckle.

"A local St. Stephen's fair would fit the bill nicely, I'd be thinking," Donal said.

"It would also give us plenty of time to organize the event," Angie said, her mouth tight. "Which is good. Especially since Carrick and I are getting married on New Year's Day."

Days after this fair...

"It's going to be a grand wedding, Yank," Carrick said, taking her hand. "You'll have plenty on your plate."

Everyone was assuming Angie would head things up like usual. Her sister was experienced, sure, but she had a lot going on. Maybe too much. This was the perfect time for Megan to show she was on a new path and that Angie didn't have to do everything.

"I can organize the fair," she said brightly.

The whole room stared at her. Angie might have blinked.

Bets waved her finger in the air as if getting used to the idea. "It *would* be a great way for you to get to know the community better, and they you. I'll be buried with this grant application."

Donal shot her a look Megan didn't understand. Bets, in turn, rose from the settee and came over to stand beside her.

"Are you sure you want to lead this, Meg?" Angie asked. "I only ask since I know you have a lot going on too."

Keeping busy would keep her focused, and that meant moving forward. With her life. With her son. And hopefully with Kade. "It will be good for me."

Angie nodded. "You'll do great, and we'll be here to help when you need anything. I have templates from past community events you can use as guides. Although I've never raised money with a horse race."

"You'll need a local helper for that, Megan," Donal said after a moment. "Someone who knows how to encourage people to donate money for a good cause and how to wrangle them if it comes to it."

Bets crossed her arms. "Who are you thinking?"

"My dad, Eoghan O'Dwyer," Donal said with a slap of a hand to his knee. "He's in your ceramics class, so you'll be getting to know him. He was good on a horse in his day, and he's well respected around town."

"I'd be happy to have his help, Donal," Megan said, hoping it would help the pit in her stomach. All of this was so new to her. But new was good, right? And she would meet more people in the community. She wanted that for her and for Ollie.

Siobhan clapped her hands. "Eoghan is perfect! And he's an ace at dealing with Cormac O'Sullivan, so we might get a cut of the local gambling."

Even Megan knew about the town's elderly bookie. The

whole village bet on pretty much anything, which he kept track of in his black book.

"My thought exactly," Donal said, leaning forward. "I'm hoping he can encourage Cormac to whip the village and the surrounding towns up into a fever over the horse racing. I'd prefer to raise the money we need ourselves than to be beholden to the government."

"Me too, although I'll apply for the grant all the same," Bets said with a frown. "Well, it sounds like we have a plan."

"It's going to be grand," Siobhan said. "I say we nail down the horse stuff straightaway and then start selling tickets. People tend to buy a little closer to an event here in Ireland."

"I'll get on the horse stuff right away." Megan clasped her hands together to keep them from shaking. What did that entail? She was glad Eoghan would know.

"You wait until after your first class, Meg," Angie said. "I remember mine well."

So did everyone in town, given a few of the local men had shown up nude on a dare.

"Might be nice to have a little spectacle," Megan said with a harried laugh.

"Maybe better to wait until after this first week of classes," Bets said, watching her with knitted brows. "I imagine you're a little nervous after all this time."

Understatement of the century. "I was trying to make a joke. Clearly not well. I didn't mean anything crazy. It's just...it would be nice to have some kind of icebreaker in case things don't go as planned."

Because her hands were shaking, and shaking hands didn't center clay well.

Mold the clay, mold yourself, her old teacher had said.

With her new challenge of organizing the St. Stephen's Day fair, she was about to find out how good she was at molding herself. But first, she had to center the clay and teach her classes.

Her entire future rested on it.

CHAPTER SEVEN

Donal stayed on in Bets' parlor after everyone else left. His expression was ruminative as he ate a fairy cake. What was he thinking?

Oh, who was she kidding? He was probably here to talk about sex.

"Something on your mind, Donal?" she asked, grabbing a fairy cake herself and taking the settee across from him.

He wiped his mouth. "We're going to need a permit for the St. Stephen's Day fair."

"*Shit.*"

"Yes." He rubbed the back of his neck. "Tom MacKenna has taken over that job now that I've resigned."

"Double shit."

"I think we should expect more trouble from your sister-in law," Donal said with an ominous frown. "Mary sabotaged your victory at the rose competition over a month ago. Whatever feud she has with you clearly isn't over in her mind. Orla is along for the ride, as is Tom, being her husband and all."

"Why can't people simply live their own lives?" She had

no interest in poking at Mary Kincaid. Hadn't since she'd first arrived in town to meet Bruce's family. Mary had told her she would never fit in—not in the O'Hanlon family, not in the village, and not in Ireland. Bets had been shocked by her rudeness and hoped the years would quiet it. Instead, Mary was still buzzing about like a mad hornet.

"Some people are mean to the core, and she's one of them," Donal said. "She was a jealous little girl in braids, I remember, and her jealousy over you having the O'Hanlon land and being so well liked in the village has never been more on display. Plus, she came by with her baked goods after my Margaret died, hoping my eyes would rest on her. Now they rest on you, as you know. More salt, I expect, in addition to your roses being more beautiful than hers. I expect your petals are too."

She waggled her eyebrows at his cheek. Petals, indeed. She wanted him to see them too—at some point. Yet another reason they needed to figure out a way to check Tom and company for good. The profits from a fair, even a successful one, would only take them so far. Her grant would take them further. It had to. But he was right about the permit, and she groaned. Another thing for her to sort out. He wasn't seeing her petals anytime soon at the rate they were going.

"Every time I hear about you not going for Mary's baked goods, so to speak, it puts a smile on my face. I bet that put her girdle in a knot all right."

"Like I'd want that shrew." He crooked his finger to her.

She got up and crossed to him. Because she needed some assurance he was going to see her "petals" sometime in the future. Only they hadn't had *her* talk about spontaneous sex. Why have it when they didn't have the space for intimacy?

"What is it?" she asked.

"You look tense again." He pulled her onto his lap, scattering crumbs on the rug.

"Couldn't you have waited until I'd finished my fairy cake to grab me? I'm going to have to vacuum, and I only do that on Wednesdays."

"I'll do it," he said with a snort, "and not just to show you that I can clean up and don't expect you to be doing it for me—should we get married and all. Of course, I'd still be liking to have sex with you first. Assuming you can pencil me in now that you have the writing of that grant application. Did you arrange it to elude me?"

Elude him? She fantasized about him five to ten times a day. Like a guy. She was losing her keys. She'd burned out the batteries in her vibrator. Next thing she knew she'd be blowing a fuse. "Don't be ridiculous. I told you we'd have sex. But we need to have the time to have it, and right now, I have the grant to write and the permit to secure without getting blocked by Tom." How in the hell was she going to do that?

He tipped up her chin. "I'll take care of the permit."

"You will?" She wanted to hug him. "How?"

"You focus on your grant," he said, kissing her lightly on the mouth. "Bets, I suspect the lack of time and space isn't the only reason we aren't having sex."

Okay, maybe a part of her still wasn't ready yet. "Keep going."

"Since we're talking about it and not having it, I was wondering..."

Good Lord, here they went. "What?"

He paused, stroking the yellow butterfly in the right corner of her blue leggings, before saying, "Are you of a mind for oral sex?"

She met his gaze straight on, knowing her brows were in her hairline. "Are you joking with me right now?"

He looked away and cleared his throat. "No."

No? She wondered why he wasn't meeting her eyes, and then she noted his cheeks were red. Red! "Donal O'Dwyer, are you *blushing*?"

He dumped her gently onto the couch and stalked to her front window, his boots making the boards creak. "God, I hope not. This isn't an easy topic for me."

What in the world was he talking about? "You'd better start at the beginning."

His hand cruised along her windowsill as if brushing away dust. "Margaret went to convent schools."

Suddenly Bets understood. "*Oh.*"

His back muscles were tense through his green work shirt. "It isn't easy to say, but she wasn't for it. Early on, I tried to talk to her about it, saying it was all right when a man and woman were married."

Had they waited until they were married to have sex? From the sound of it, they had, which was likely common enough back then. She believed in respecting other people's beliefs, except if they intentionally hurt other people. This was a little different. "But she wasn't comfortable."

"No, neither with the giving or receiving." He grabbed ahold of her windowsill again. "In fact, we stopped talking about anything related to sex, and that's not something I want to happen with us. So that's why I'm asking you this and why I want you to tell me what's really bothering you."

They would get to that, she thought, her heart warming in her chest. "It can't be easy to talk about Margaret like this. Or yourself."

"It's not, but it needed saying." He turned, putting his hands to his hips. "I am embarrassed, Bets, not only to be having the conversation but because I haven't had the experience."

"Do you want to?" She rose from the settee, knowing she needed to cross to him.

His cheeks deepened in color, but his proud bearing offset the vulnerability in his eyes. "Very much. Both the giving and receiving, *mo ghrá*."

"Then we'll do that," she said, finally reaching him and putting her hand to his chest.

He rolled his eyes. "I feel like an idiot. I'd like to assure you that I'm a good lover, but I've only been with Margaret, and there were rules, ones I found...confining at times. I loved her—you know that—but our views about sex weren't the same. I fear our marriage bed suffered for it. The only thing I can promise you is that I'll give you everything I am and everything you ask for—if you want me."

Her heart ached, hearing that admission. "I do want everything—but most of all, I want you."

He leaned down and kissed her gently. "Think me an old fool?"

"No," she whispered, cupping the back of his head. "Never."

She knew men and their pride. She understood how hard it had been for him to share this with her, and it emboldened her to do the same. "Your instincts were right. There is something I wanted to discuss. How do you feel about having sex in daytime hours and anywhere in the house besides the bedroom?"

His mouth tipped up on the right, and his green eyes sparkled like the fields in the morning light. "I'm in favor of it, not having had the experience."

With that admission, she went a step further and said,

"When I first came to Ireland, I didn't like the way my sex life with Bruce changed because people kept popping by."

Donal nodded. "I see the way of it now. It does have a way of curtailing things, doesn't it? It's like I told you. Once that horse bolts, there's no getting it back. I'm going to want to do everything, Bets. Anywhere. Anytime."

"Good!" Her belly tightened at the very thought. "Interested in starting a little right now?"

She would talk to Liam later about changing the house rules. Right now, all she wanted was Donal. She sank to her knees in front of him.

"My God, girl. You're not thinking—"

"I am." Her hands undid the top button on his pants and then unzipped them slowly, his desire evident, making her mouth water. God, she'd been waiting a long time for this.

He grabbed her hands, groaning as he halted her progress. "Bets, I want this more than anything, and if I'd known you would even think to do this, I wouldn't have called—"

"Hello!" a male voice called out. "Donal, Bets, where are ye now?"

Bets scrambled off her knees. *"You called your father?"*

He quickly secured his pants, wincing. "I thought to tell him about St. Stephen's after Megan left. Oh, Jesus, this is a disaster. The first moment everything is going my way…"

She smoothed her hair back, hoping she didn't look like some sex kitten who'd just been on her knees. "In here, Eoghan."

The older man appeared, singing a tune softly in Gaelic. "I can come back if ye need," he said with a knowing grin.

Bets pasted a smile on her face while Donal tensed

beside her. "Don't be ridiculous. Come in. We have fairy cakes and biscuits. Would you like some tea?"

"That would be grand, yes," Eoghan replied, taking his sweet time lowering onto a chair in her parlor.

Before she could dash to the kitchen to grab some ice and press it to the back of her hot neck, Donal leaned in to whisper, "I'll be thinking up a solution for this popping by problem, Bets, I promise, and we won't be doing anything else until then. I can't stand the torture."

She chuckled all the way to the kitchen despite herself, having her answer.

CHAPTER EIGHT

C entering the clay and oneself is an ongoing process, Barry used to say. *When life throws you a curveball, the clay shows you how far afield you are from your center.*

She had another curveball now—the arts center's financial difficulties—and the lump of uncentered clay trailing across her wheel was certainly a sign. She tried to look on the positive side. She'd centered it for a few beats, but when she'd tried to pull up the walls of the clay into a cylinder, the clay had buckled. Summation: she could center the clay but not hold it.

Even with a plan—forget that she was leading the organizing of the fair—she worried about the outcome. What if they didn't make enough money? She'd be out of her job.

Who was she kidding? If she couldn't center her clay and teach her first class *in thirty minutes*, it wasn't going to matter. They'd fire her. Maybe not today. But a teacher who couldn't center her clay or teach others how to do so was useless.

She didn't want to be useless anymore.

Grabbing her plastic scraper, she cleaned the wet clay off her wheel, determined to start again.

"Hi, Mom!"

She looked up to see Ollie holding Angie's hand. Her son had on the "farm clothes" Carrick had bought him—a green hoodie for Mayo's Gaelic football team and brown cargo pants with navy wellies—while her sister wore jeans and a burgundy jacket dotted with iron-on flowers and paint splashes. Megan looked down at her plain russet apron covering tan pants and a navy blue sweater set and felt a little stab of something.

"Hey, Megan," Angie said with a smile.

"Hey, you two," she responded, smiling back.

Their clothes reflected their personalities as much as their art did. Angie's roots were earthy and bohemian while Megan's were the boring, lackluster kind. Angie drew landscapes and nudes in hot oranges and reds in her new series. Back when she could center her clay, Megan had crafted serviceable mugs and the like in cool blue tones.

God, she was tired of being so serviceable and cool. When she looked at Angie's paintings these days, she wished she had the courage to be a little more daring. Like she felt when she rode a horse or wore the yellow T-shirt Liam had given her.

Maybe it was time to do more than hold Kade's hand.

She inhaled sharply. Where had that thought come from? He hadn't asked her out on a date yet. He knew she had a lot on her mind, what with the arts center and her upcoming classes, and she figured he was giving her space and time.

She realized she didn't want it. *Well, well, Megan Bennet. Maybe you're more of a firebird than you thought?*

"I thought you were going to help Carrick with the sheep," she said, setting aside her plastic scraper.

Ollie made a dramatic showing of rolling his eyes. "We were, but he had to go help Mr. O'Dwyer with some crazy ram that got loose, so Aunt Angie thought we'd come here and tell you to break an arm."

"It's a leg, Ollie, but your mom knows you say it to wish someone luck." Her sister glanced at the clay disaster and gave a valiant smile. "You're going to do great, Meg."

Her throat thickened. "Thanks, Angie. I'm a little off after our budget meeting."

"Me too," Angie said with a wry glance. "I had so much trouble painting this morning that I finally stopped fighting it and fingerpainted. It helped."

Angie was struggling too? That made her feel less alone in her uncentered state. Tears filled her eyes, but she forced them back. This was no time for tears.

"It's going to be okay, Mom," Ollie said, racing over to kiss her cheek with a loud smack. "Uncle Carrick told me to tell you and Aunt Angie that every chance I get."

That dear man.

Ollie put his finger to his small rosebud of a mouth. "He said you were having growing pains. Like when I grew an inch last year and my legs hurt. Are you getting taller? I thought adults stopped growing in high school. Wow, your hands are really dirty, Mom, and you made a huge mess. You *never* do that."

Kids were great for dispensing wisdom in one moment and sidetracking to something completely different the next. "Clay is a messy art," she said, wiping her hands on her apron.

"Why haven't you ever let me do this?" he asked, poking

at her lump of clay and giggling when it stuck to his finger. "It looks fun."

"It is fun when you and the clay are friends," she said, wiping off his fingers with the old towel she kept near.

"Why aren't you friends?" Ollie asked.

How was she supposed to explain this to an eight-year-old? "We haven't seen each other in a long time."

"Oh," he said, turning around in circles like the sheep did, something he loved copying these days. "Like when Dad came home from one of his tours and you didn't know what to say to him. Man, that was so weird."

Her mouth parted in shock, as did Angie's.

"Okay, Ollie," Angie said, coming closer. "We're going to get out of your mom's way since her class will be starting soon."

"You're so lucky Kade and Liam are in your class, Mom. I wish I could be."

"Maybe she can teach a children's class next term," Angie said with another encouraging smile.

She heard her sister's message. The center would stay open. And she, Megan Bennet, would find her center again. She wanted to believe that.

"Thanks for stopping by," she said, hugging her sister without touching her with clay hands and then plunking a kiss on her son's head. "Ollie, you go to sleep on time for Aunt Angie. It's not summer hours anymore."

"Yes, Mom! Come on, Aunt Angie."

"Good luck, Megan. See you later."

She eyed the clock as they left. Twenty minutes. She had twenty minutes to find her center again. She cleaned her mess off the pottery wheel and grabbed another ball of wedged clay. She'd lined them up like baseballs waiting to be thrown. She plopped it in the center and hand formed it into a disc.

Wetting her hands in her water bucket, she cupped the clay and pressed the foot pedal to increase the wheel's speed. "Come on," she told it, feeling it buckle in her hands.

She pressed harder.

The disc shifted to the left, the lump resembling the state of Massachusetts. Terrific.

"Oh, this is impossible!" she said, hunching over the wheel on her stool.

"Nothing's impossible," she heard a familiar voice say.

"That's right," another dear friend's voice said. "You're saying it wrong, Megan. It's *I'm possible*."

She looked up at two of her favorite people.

Liam shot her a cheeky wink. Kade's brown eyes were steady as he met her gaze, a warm smile transforming his strong jawline. He still had on his farm clothes of a thick cotton navy shirt, jeans, and boots, all a little dirt smudged. Man, did he look good. She felt her cheeks warm before she shook herself.

She had class. In twenty minutes.

She was lucky they were here—only she wasn't sure their moral support was going to change what she had going on inside. No one could give her back her center.

"I'm possible," she repeated and winced. "Even I don't believe in myself. Oh, what am I going to do? The other students are going to be here any moment, and I can't keep my clay centered. I'm going to have to teach pinch pots."

"That wouldn't be a bad way to go," Liam said, shrugging out of his worn jean jacket and hanging it on the coatrack beside the door. "I like hand building myself."

When he turned around, she read his black T-shirt. *Eat, Clay, Love.*

"Liam, where in the world did you get that shirt?"

Kade turned and eyed their friend.

Grinning, Liam said, "Bali. There was this gorgeous potter there who taught classes. It was hot. What can I say? We hooked up while I was there. We made some love and some pots, like in that movie *Ghost* with Patrick Swayze and Demi Moore. And both were grand, let me tell you. She gave me this shirt to remember her by, and it seemed only right to make it my class shirt."

Laughter bubbled up inside her and spilled out. "Bali! Oh, Liam. That story is so you."

"It really is," Kade said, pulling a stool over to her wheel where she sat. "Now, let's talk about you, Megan. You'll have a lot to cover for the first class, won't you? Tools and process and the like? Start there and see where you are a bit later. You have it back, Megan. Trust in that."

She wanted to touch him, she realized with a shock, so she awkwardly touched his leg. "Thank you for the reassurance."

"The problems with the arts center aren't helping," Liam said. He knew everything, of course.

"No, they aren't."

"The community will rally around you and the center, and the St. Stephen's Day fair will be successful, don't worry," Kade said. "You settle into that knowledge, and it will help."

She reached for his hand, and happiness radiated through her as he curled his fingers around hers. Initiating contact had never been easy for her, and she never would have imagined doing something like that with Tyson. He'd...

She cut that thought off. She didn't want to think about Tyson. She wanted to hold on to this feeling. With him.

"Okay, we have a plan," she said. Nodding to the

pitcher on the wedging table, she added, "And my favorite pitcher to use as inspiration."

"The greens and blues are like the Irish hills," Liam said, crossing to examine the pitcher. "I've never seen a glaze like this."

"Neither have I," Megan said, touching the run lines of the glaze. "The store had no information on the piece, and I couldn't find the potter online from the signature on the bottom."

Every potter had a signature, even if it was a symbol. The mark of the individual was sealed in fire for all time. Megan had always loved that. Her signature had been a simple MN carved into the clay. At that time, she'd been Megan Newcastle—her maiden name. She needed to think about a new signature.

"Soon you'll be making pieces as beautiful as this again and again," Liam said, touching the exquisitely curved handle.

"God, I hope so." As she heard voices in the hallway, her stomach flipped. "They're here."

Kade put a gentle hand on her lower back, something he often did when she got flustered. He could calm anyone with a mere touch. She'd seen him do it with upset or aggravated kids and also with animals. She took a deep breath and felt herself settle, as if all the tension was draining out of her.

When she looked up at Kade again, he was smiling at her like always. She'd never met anyone who smiled as much as he did.

"You're going to do great," he said, squeezing her hand before releasing it. "Be easy with yourself. It's been ten years since you've had a class. Anyone would be nervous. But you'll remember the way of it."

She gave a brave smile as she tried to believe it.

"And we'll be here for you," Liam said, putting his arm around her sweetly and kissing her cheek. "Megan, this is going to be a grand adventure."

"An adventure," she repeated, liking the sound of that.

"Where will you be sitting?" Kade asked. "Liam and I thought we'd flank you for support if that's okay with you."

"I'll be sitting in the center of the back aisle."

"Perfect," Kade said. "We're happy to help you lift anything that's heavy as well."

"Thank you."

She heard laughter in the hallway as well as the clip-clop of heels. Turning toward the door, she had to bite her lip to hold back a smile. Two young women dressed like they were headed out for a night on the town had walked in. She knew her only other female student by sight, so she surmised they were Sarah Roycrof and Hollie Meyler.

"Hiya, Liam," called out one of them, a curly-haired brunette.

The other, a dyed blonde, called out his name as well, fluttering her fingers in a coy wave. She watched as Liam strolled over to speak with them, his pirate grin firmly in place.

She thought about Barry's comment about guys showing up for pottery to meet women. It seemed it went both ways. She leaned close to Kade and whispered her suspicions.

He laughed softly. "Everyone loves Liam. Look," he added, nodding to the door, "Eoghan is here, and he's not wearing his streaking outfit."

The older man had on faded brown pants and a thread-bare jacket, which mostly came as a relief, although some rogue part of her wished he'd distract her students like he had with Angie's first painting class months ago. "Hello, Eoghan."

He lit up when she walked over to him. "Hello, Meg. I was planning on popping by your cottage to talk about the St. Stephen's Day fair, but Bets and Donal told me to wait until after our first classes. Tragic turn, this mess, but don't you worry. I've been doing some scheming already. We'll put things to rights and then some."

She almost hugged him. "I'll be happy for your help."

He patted her hand. "As will I with the pottery. Ah, it's a grand night out for our first class. Not a breath of wind or rain despite how cloudy it's been."

"I almost wished you'd worn your boxing robe tonight, but you appear to be a serious student."

He waggled his overgrown white brows, his brownish green eyes dancing. "I thought you'd throw me out on my ear, so I'm minding myself. Despite the bets people in the village placed with Cormac O'Sullivan."

They'd bet on it? Oh, of course they had. Months ago, that would have horrified her, but she found herself laughing.

He put his hand on her arm. "I wanted to learn this craft too much to be on the books with you."

He meant *in trouble*, she realized. "I think it's wonderful you want to learn."

"My brother, Callum, God rest him, was a potter before and after WWII," Eoghan said. "I thought it might help me become closer to him before we meet in heaven. Something to talk about over a pint, if that's allowed up there."

Her heart swelled in her chest. She still wondered about the afterlife and where Tyson had ended up. It bothered her that she wasn't completely sure. "That sounds like a wonderful idea."

He dragged his wispy hair off his forehead. "You have a few more arrivals, love. I won't be keeping you any longer."

He walked off as her last two students arrived. Keegan O'Malley had his head down as he spoke with chic Lisa Ann Walsh, who owned the hair salon. Megan hadn't had a haircut since arriving, and she'd looked at the salon's blue door with trepidation. Her hair was a mess with tangles from the wind. She didn't know what to do with it, but she was too scared to do something drastic.

Scared.

And she wondered why she was off her center.

"You have quite a group on your hands," Kade said, coming up beside her.

"My other two classes don't have any men in them, so the dynamic will be different." She surveyed the group. She had four bachelors, two women interested in Liam, and Lisa Ann.

"All right, everyone," she said cheerfully, facing her class. "Let's get started. I'm Megan Bennet, from the States as you probably know. I'm also Liam O'Hanlon's cousin—"

"That's so great," the young woman with dyed blond hair said with a sigh. "I'm Sarah, by the way."

Megan wondered how long Liam's ceramics seraglio was going to last. They were going to get clay all over their nice clothes and ruin their manicures.

"How about we go around the group, and everyone can give their names?" she asked.

"Everyone in Caisleán knows everyone," said the woman she now knew was Hollie.

"Megan doesn't," Kade said softly. "Hi, I'm Kade Donovan and I own the pony farm."

Everyone else followed suit.

"Great! Let me walk you through your individual shelves and hand out your ceramics kits."

After showing everyone their personal space, she enlisted Liam and Kade to pass out the clay packs. "In your kit, you will find essential ceramics tools and an eleven-kilo bag of stoneware white clay."

The ruffling of bags sounded as people started to go through their packs.

She picked up the tools included in the kit. "Let me walk you through some basics. These are your three trimming tools, which you'll select based on the size you need. Once you throw a pot, you'll dry it to what we call leather-hard and then trim off the excess clay around the base to make a foot."

She made a motion of the process with her hands before continuing.

"This is your wire cutter to cut the thrown pot off the wheel. These are your scrapers—both the plastic and wooden ones have a purpose beyond the practical need to scrape the excess clay off your wheel, but we'll get into that later. This metal needle tool is what you'll use to check the thickness of the base of your pot, and lastly the sponge... He will become your best friend and your vehicle to both apply and remove water while throwing your pot."

She pointed to the three industrial sinks against the wall. "Water is essential to throwing a pot—and by pot I mean anything you can throw on the wheel you're sitting in front of. How much water will be an ongoing journey, as you will see. Rather like our journey in life, I guess."

Her gaze rested on Kade's then. He was watching her quietly, and he nodded as if to encourage her. She could feel herself finding her way, and the sensation was powerful.

She *did* know what she was doing.

"Ceramics is the fusion of earth, water, and fire—some would even say wind since you need wind to feed the fire. Irish folklore speaks a lot about the elements, so this kind of talk might be familiar to you."

"Like a piece in my soul," Liam said, patting his chest.

She smiled as his fan girls sighed. "Irish pottery is famous around the world for its use of Celtic symbols as well as some very special clay found in areas like Cashel. Eoghan just told me his brother was a potter."

"Was that Callum?" Lisa Ann asked, already wearing a black apron that looked like it came from her salon.

"It was indeed," Eoghan answered. "A fine man, although he wasn't long with us. But we're interrupting the Yank."

She smiled, knowing the Irish could go on with their stories. "You might have had family who worked with the clay, or you might find inspiration from another source. Wherever it comes from, I hope you will infuse your own passion and history into everything you make. Which leads me to a question. How many of you have done ceramics before? I just learned about my cousin's experience."

"Do those paint your own pottery places count?" Hollie asked. "A girlfriend had her birthday party there."

"That would make you familiar with decorating and handling fired pots, which is good, but throwing them is another step." She looked around the room, but no one else raised a hand. "So Liam is our only student with experience at the wheel. Anyone ever make shapes out of Play-Doh? Do you have that in Ireland?" Crap, she'd forgotten to check.

"We have that," Lisa Ann said helpfully.

"Good, then that's also something you can do. Hand

building. I'll do my best to run you through the various options as we go along."

She fisted her hands at her sides as a lull came over the room. She needed to start a demonstration. There was only so much information people could absorb, especially on the first night. But she was delaying. *Say something, Megan.*

"I'll just do a little demo to show you what to do," she said, her tone overly bright.

Megan walked to the clay she'd set aside. When she picked it up, she handled it gently, letting her hands feel it. Centering started with feel, and if she focused on the clay, maybe she wouldn't remember how tight her stomach was as everyone watched her.

"This is about one kilo. You can weigh your clay on the scale on the wedging table. That's about the weight you'll want to start with. It makes a nice mug or a small bowl or vase—great when you're first starting out."

Like her.

"You'll want to wedge the clay like you're kneading bread. Come close if you want to see what I'm doing. This stamps out any air pockets in your clay and makes it more uniform to throw."

She demonstrated the technique.

"I'm going to throw a simple cylinder and make a mug," Megan said, praying she could manage it.

She sat down at her station as people clustered around her. Sweat formed at her temple, even as Kade pulled his stool close. She took a deep breath, searching for his scent, and it calmed her. Plopping the clay onto the center of the wheel, she turned the wheel on and pressed the foot pedal to give it speed.

"You're going to physically place the clay in the middle as best you can, flatten it into a mound, cupping your hands around it, and then start the wheel. Convention has it that you center better with medium to high speed rather than a slower setting, but as you will discover, you need to find the best way for you."

Boy, did she ever. Right now.

She bent over at the waist, applying pressure to the mound.

Pressure.

She felt it in all the eyes trained on her. The clay started to bolt. She could feel her frustration growing, but she fought back, remembering how she'd centered it for the first time in ten years. With Kade by her side as he was today. She closed her eyes and gentled her hands. In less than a minute, she knew it was centered.

"Aha!" she said spontaneously to her class as she opened her eyes. "The first hurdle. It's centered."

"You're in your Zen space, cousin," Liam said with a grin.

She blew out a breath. If only. "Now I'm going to form a cylinder by opening up the clay disc with my thumbs to form a thick wall of clay that will resemble a jelly mold with a bottom."

She did exactly that, rewetting her hands to create more ease with the clay.

"As you see, I only use a little water. Now I'm going to place my fingers on either side of the clay and start to pull up."

"Megan, do you want to check the bottom for thickness?" Liam asked, looking over at her.

She wanted to kick herself for forgetting. "Yes, thank you. Now I'm going to measure the thickness of the clay floor by how much it sinks into the needle."

She cut the speed and the wheel ground to a halt so she could check.

"I have the perfect amount—you'll want about a half inch. Wait. For you that's a little over one centimeter. I'm still learning the whole metric system."

Frankly it drove her nuts sometimes, especially in cooking.

Stay focused, Megan.

"When you're new, you might have a little more, which you can trim off. Only don't go less because you won't have enough clay to take your pot off with the metal cutter. Also, a thin floor cracks easily. Not good. A leather-hard pot shrinks about ten percent when it's fired. Okay, enough of that. Let's make the walls of this mug."

She started the wheel again and pulled them up firmly but gently, pressing down on the rim.

"That move I just did keeps your rim—and your pot—centered."

She took a breath as it started to wobble. *No, please stay.*

"When you start to create your walls, the centrifugal force can throw things off center." She pressed on the rim, bringing it back in line. "You want to keep things straight and tight."

She heard a few snickers and found it eased some of her tension. As she knew—heck, everyone who ever took pottery knew—the language could be fairly salty.

"You think that's funny," she decided to say, "wait until you learn how to pull a handle for your mug."

Liam barked out a laugh. "It's pretty naughty, let me tell you."

Lisa Ann started fanning herself, much like Megan had the first time she'd seen handle pulling, which pretty much resembled making a male appendage before smoothing it flat. Even Kade's mouth was twitching.

"Pottery is an earthy art."

And it had a mind of its own. When she went to finish the mug, it wouldn't cooperate. Its mouth was too small, and her walls weren't wanting to stay wide. She decided not to fight it.

"You're about ready to see why pottery is an art," she said with a laugh. "This piece of clay—every piece—knows what it wants to be. It's telling me now that it would rather be a vase."

She stopped trying to force it and let go. The vase formed beautifully before her eyes, another lesson. Don't force something to be something it doesn't want to be.

"That's incredible," Hollie said, leaning forward on her heels to see.

"Good job, cousin," Liam said. "That will be one fine vase."

Staring at it, she felt emotion rush into her throat. Her first demo hadn't been perfect, but it had worked. She looked over to see Kade's reaction, and his smile stole her heart.

"So now we're going to use the wire to cut under the vase, and then I'll grab a bat and we'll do one of the most dangerous things in pottery. Take your piece off the wheel."

The irony was rich to her. You could have your center and make something beautiful, only to have a horrible moment and lose it all. It felt like an appropriate metaphor for her life, except she was coming to realize that what she'd had wasn't as beautiful as what she might yet have.

She walked to the shelf for a drying bat and held up the disc, forcing away her barbed thoughts.

"As you can see, this has absorptive material to help the

pot dry. You're going to put plastic over it once you have the pot on it and then let it dry until it's leather-hard. Then you'll trim it next week."

She dipped her sponge in her bucket and dribbled water around the outside of the pot on the wheel.

"Now I'm going to grab my cutting tool and run water under the pot with the tool."

She demonstrated with aplomb and wanted to shout for joy.

"All right, on to the last step."

She cupped the sides gently and lifted it off and onto the drying bat.

"And there you have it, friends."

Kade started to clap and the others joined in. She turned a little pink but found herself smiling. She'd done it!

"Okay, let's get you guys started."

She went around to all the students as they began their work. Some had taken notes from her demo, she realized. Others just waded in. Kade, for example, was efficient and fearless. While her other students struggled to center the clay, he was the only one who got it on the first go-around. Somehow she wasn't surprised.

"Well done," she said, meeting his brown eyes. "I wasn't sure you'd take to it."

"I've always liked to build things," he said with a smile. "And I had a good teacher."

She grinned and made sure to move on to help Sarah, who had discovered using too much water could be a disaster. Her clay disc had ended up in her freshly laundered lap. Megan suggested people might consider wearing an apron like Eoghan and Lisa Ann if they worried about soiling their clothes, although the clay did come out, she assured them.

By the end of the three-hour class, a few of her students —Liam, Kade, Eoghan, and Hollie—had managed to make a cup or a bowl. Liam's was gorgeous, of course, while the others were thick and a bit misshapen. But she knew they would always remember their first pot. She'd kept her first creation and used it as a candy bowl.

Not everyone left with smiles after cleaning up. The determined or competitive ones who'd struggled with the craft weren't happy with their results. She'd been like that with everything except pottery. Learning anything new had always been excruciating for her, and the new craft or subject would be unappealing until she managed to accomplish something worthwhile. If that didn't happen quickly, she'd give up, thinking she couldn't do it. That pattern had become a way of life, one she was eager to break out of.

With pottery though, once she'd graduated high school and stopped living with her parents, she'd taken to it so easily. Funny, she hadn't realized how much being out from under their roof had made a difference.

"We're headed to the pub for a late drink," Liam said, putting his arm around her and squeezing her sweetly. "To celebrate our first class. Want to come?"

She thought about Ollie, and how Angie and Carrick would be waiting up for her. They were newly in love. She didn't want to keep them from alone time. She shook her head. "Another night."

"I'm buying the first round," Eoghan said with tears in his eyes. "It's not every day a man learns something new he loves. I could feel my brother helping me from heaven."

"That gave me chills," Lisa Ann said, brushing her arms.

Oddly, it had given Megan goose bumps too. "I'm glad you enjoyed it so, Eoghan."

"Megan, it was grand," he said, clutching her hand for a moment before releasing her.

"Wasn't it?" Liam said. "I love feeling the clay in my hands again."

She hugged her cousin. "You're so good at it."

He chucked her under the chin. "You are as well, cousin. Well, we're off."

She waved at the group. She was aware of Kade remaining behind, and she was happy for it. When the studio was finally empty, she turned to him. He was sitting on a stool, resting his hands on his long, open legs.

"First class in the bag!" She blew out a breath. "I can't thank you and Liam enough for being here. I wasn't sure if you were serious students when you told me you were going to sign up."

He rose and walked over to her. "I thought I might take to it, and I wanted to learn more about what you love."

That rolled through her, making tears fill her eyes. "I don't have enough words to say thank you."

Her journal was filled with such words. After their first walk on the beach on Friday, she'd written three pages on all the things she loved about Kade under the heading *Gratitude*. Afterward, she'd drawn hearts and smiley faces in the margins, needing to express more of her emotions. She had a lot for this man.

He gazed down at her quietly, his eyes traveling over her face. "It's a joy to see you coming alive again. Every day I wake up, I know I'm going to see another facet of the amazing Megan Bennet."

The amazing Megan Bennet. Her heart raced at the compliment.

"Come on," he said, cupping her elbow. "I'll walk you out."

She locked up, aware of him following her progress.

When they reached the gravel parking lot, he shifted on his feet in the cool fall night. "Megan, you did wonderful tonight. When you go home, make sure to savor it. Come, let's get you into your car. Then I'll follow you home."

The stars were brilliant overhead and the night so dark she felt a twinge of nerves about driving home, although her cottage on her cousin's land was barely five minutes away. They drove on the other side, and she was still getting accustomed to that as much as the narrow roads.

"You don't have to do that," she said, but she liked that he'd offered. The men around here were like that, and there was a part of her that appreciated it.

"You're still new to driving in Ireland. It will make me feel better to see you home safe."

Tonight had been her first night out alone since coming to Ireland, her first night of doing something for herself. As the wind rushed around her, she felt a little giddy from that newness.

"How about another ride along the beach tomorrow?" she asked, smiling as she recalled how she'd written a long journal entry about their ride so she could read it again whenever she wanted to recapture the feelings, ones she knew were beautiful and rare. She didn't take moments like those for granted. "I'll be finished with my second class at one."

Oddly, she wasn't scared of yet another class. Wasn't that something she'd write about in her journal later as something to be grateful for? She'd gotten through tonight. She would manage tomorrow.

"I'd love that," he said, the planes of his face looking so masculine in the soft light in the parking lot.

Spontaneously, she rose up and kissed his cheek. "I'll see you tomorrow."

He pressed his hand to her back, the touch laden with the new promise between them. "That you will, love."

When he called her *love*, it unlocked something long buried in her heart. Hope. Happiness. Contentment. All those feelings made her think anything was possible.

Precious feelings Megan Bennet wanted to embrace as much as the man in front of her.

CHAPTER NINE

His dad was going to be stubborn.

Even though Kade wasn't surprised, he still had to fight the bite of frustration rising inside him as he patted one of the five horses his father had presented to him. The giant black Oldenburg nickered as if he sensed the tension in his father's stables. "Dad, none of these stallions are going to work for Legend."

"Why not?" he asked, pointing to a beautiful chestnut Dutch Warmblood. "Titan would be perfect for her. As would any of these stallions."

Kade walked over to his father so they were only a meter apart. "Dad, none of them are gentle enough."

"Gentle?" he scoffed, his mouth twisting. "This is breeding, son. Not pony riding."

Duke chose that moment to pad into the shed. He'd told the dog to stay in their part of the yard, and it was unusual for him not to listen. Sorcha's doing? "You asked me to help you find a horse Legend would accept. None of these will do."

His father put his hands on his hips and glared at him. "How do you know?"

Duke gave a *ruff* as he said, "I know."

"What about Red Zephyr?" his father pressed.

He'd thought about it and dismissed it. Sometimes two animals—or people—who were healing could help each other, and both would benefit from the connection equally. This wasn't one of those times. "Not a good match either."

His father tapped his foot a moment, looking like a vexed horse, before saying, "Then what are we going to do, eh?" He started to lead the horses back into their stalls, and Kade stepped in to help as his father's trainers had wisely left the shed.

"Show me some other horses that meet your criteria," Kade said, opening the Marwari's stall and putting a hand on the horse's flank when he stomped a foot, mirroring his father. "None of that now."

"That one's trouble," his father said. "Mind yourself, or he might take a chunk out of you."

He snorted. They both knew he'd never been bitten by a horse. His father had a few scars from them, but then again, he liked to struggle and battle with everything. Kade understood it fed something primal inside of him—he just didn't possess the same instinct.

"You're supposed to put Legend in the right mind for breeding with a horse of my choosing," his father said, pushing a black Arabian back into his stall when he showed a spurt of rebellion. "Not make my life harder."

"Dad, I'm not trying to make your life harder," he said, nudging the Marwari into his stall.

"So I need to search for a gentle horse with great breeding." Killian's voice dripped with sarcasm. "Any suggestions then? We're talking about a Morgan or an Appaloosa, right?"

"Or a Connemara pony," Kade said, expecting an explosion in response.

"We've had this discussion before." His dad secured the last stallion in his stall. "I am not using a Connemara for breeding."

"It would be a good choice for Legend, Dad."

His growl made Duke race out of the stable. "Why?"

His father knew why, but Kade said patiently, "Connemaras are known for their athleticism and heart. Legend already has plenty of speed and heart. The match would be sound."

"You give me an impossible task." His father stomped over to the Arabian. "You think Joris will accept anything other than the best in a foal?"

"He'll accept whatever breeding you do, Dad." Kade rubbed the back of his neck. "You know your business."

"But a Connemara isn't my choice," Killian said, his mouth tight.

"Be open." He checked his watch. "I have to go. You're going to find the right horse, Dad. I somehow think it will be right under our noses."

"Wait a minute!" his father called as he started to walk away.

"Yes, Dad," he said, setting his hands to his hips impatiently.

"Eoghan O'Dwyer came by this morning to ask me to host the horse race they're planning for this St. Stephen's Day fair for the arts center." His scowl told Kade what he thought of that. "He mentioned Donal's concern about securing a permit for the event. It seems he and his father remembered that my mother took care of Tom MacKenna's grandmother back in the day."

Kade felt his mouth twitch. "Never say the O'Dwyers aren't canny. They think Tom will remember that and give you the permit."

His dad nodded crisply. "Yes, that's the way of it. I know they're hoping to use one of my sheds for the rest of the events they have planned. Do you have any views on this?"

With Megan and the center involved, he definitely had one. "I'm for it. All the way. Megan Bennet even asked if I would be willing to give pony rides to the children. It would be easier to do that here than elsewhere."

"I hate having people on my land that I don't know," his father said, grabbing a pitchfork and leaning on it, "but I know your mother is going to be for this."

They both knew he didn't want to fight Nicola. "It's for a good cause, Dad, and it would mean a lot to the village, and me especially."

He studied him. "You like the Yank then? I wondered why you asked someone with no horse experience to help around here."

Kade didn't want to talk about these particulars. "I know my own mind."

"If I grant them permission to hold their fair here, will you agree to use the horse I select for Legend?"

Kade laughed, making the older man's mouth twist. "I can agree, but Legend won't. I'll see you later, Dad."

He strode out of the shed, not wanting to engage in the conversation anymore. Megan would be arriving shortly for their ride to the beach.

He checked Red Zephyr, liberally applying plantain salve to the horse's leg. The break was healed, and the tendons were knitting together nicely. He ran his hand down the leg, anchoring more energy into the bones. They would begin to exercise him soon, and by the New Year, he was hoping the horse would be running again like he'd been born to do.

When he heard Megan's car, he walked over to greet her. Duke was already racing around her legs.

He didn't have to ask how her second class had gone. The radiance on her face told him. "Another class in the bag, as you say?" he called out.

She lifted her hands over her head for a moment. "I made a mug this time. No deviations. The women are nice. A few older ones and some mothers with kids in school. We had fun. It feels so good, Kade."

"Then I'm glad I can share it with you," he said, remembering the sweet kiss she'd given his cheek last night. Beyond the progress it indicated, he'd liked feeling her touch. As a man. As *her* man.

He'd continue to let her take the lead, and he would match her pace. "Are you ready to go riding?"

"Am I ever!" Her eyes were full of a new fire coming from inside her. "And I want to go fast too."

He'd been sensing that. Blaze was a good pony for her, but he was starting to wonder if she needed something faster, all her own. Ollie would like his own pony as well. He'd keep an eye out. It was like he'd told his father. The answer would be right under their noses.

After saddling the pony, he helped her onto Blaze. Legend neighed loudly. When he looked over, she had her gaze on him, longing in her eyes.

"You want to go too?" he asked, walking over to her. "Then let's do it."

Both of his girls seemed to need a little speed today.

When they reached the beach, he realized he did as well. With a father who'd pushed him to compete in the horse shows as a kid, he'd purposefully limited his racing and jumping time to when he was alone with friends.

"Megan, I'm going to let this girl work some things out." Himself too, he realized. "See you by the seals."

Gently kicking Legend into a canter, he let her warm up slowly. Soon she was straining for more speed, so he gave the nudge. She made the sand fly as she flew across the beach. Kade let the sensation rush over him, feeling the mare's heart thunder in her chest. When he brought her back down into a canter and finally slowed, she was breathing hard but lighter. He felt the same way.

"You're going to breed a champion all right," Kade said, stroking her neck.

Sorcha appeared in front of the horse, making her step back. He tightened his hold on the reins to calm her.

"Megan looks happy," the ghost said, watching as Megan and Blaze raced more carefully across the beach. "She's soaring over obstacles. It's a heady feeling."

"It is at that," Kade said, spotting a few seals watching them from behind the rocks.

"You're right to be patient with her," Sorcha said, bending to touch the water lapping under her bare feet.

"Do you miss the tangible world?" he asked when her hands passed through it.

Her mouth tilted up, and she shook her hair out. "There's something tangible where I am, and its beauty is grand. It's only good memories of wading through the shallows that had me doing it just now. Memories have a powerful influence on us—good or bad. Megan is still battling hers. Perhaps you are as well."

His brow knit. "Me?"

"I haven't seen you look that free on a horse in some time," she said, putting out a hand to Legend. "You don't ride for fun anymore. Not the way you used to with Ryan. Or with Carrick and the other boys."

"Are you a mind reader too?" he asked. "I was just thinking about those times. We used to race our ponies across the shoreline with the sole purpose of scattering seagulls."

"Except Brady, of course." She laughed heartily. "He always rode one of his family's many donkeys."

"Hence the name of the Brazen Donkey."

She nodded. "It's a good name for a pub. I remember those days well, as I was often on the beach collecting shells. Why did you stop?"

He gave her the pat answer. "We grew up."

They both knew it wasn't completely true, but he'd never told anyone about the time his father had caught him racing—and pressed the point about him competing. He'd been thirteen. Kade had done what he usually did with his father. Chosen the path of least resistance. He'd stopped racing completely, which had equally angered his father until he'd left him alone.

He'd made peace with missing it, or so he'd thought. Until recently.

"You're right about growing up. Except you're the only one who still has horses. Yet you don't ride them except to exercise them or heal them. Something to think about. I'll leave you."

Her wink was her final riposte before she disappeared. He would think on what she said as much as this old feeling resurrected inside him. But right now, he simply wanted to be with Megan.

When she reached him, she slid off Blaze and ran over

to pick up a large white seashell curved from the circles of time in the sea. "Look what I found."

She clutched it to her chest like a treasure—like Sorcha had as a girl, he recalled—and he dismounted to join her. She took a few steps and bent over again. "Red sea glass! Oh, what a day!"

He leaned down and picked up a beautiful green piece of glass and held it out to her. "That's the beauty of life. Every day presents us with more miracles."

She raced over and hugged him. "I love it when you talk like that. Come on. I've been wanting to take my shoes off and walk in the shallows."

This was something he hadn't done much of either lately. He rarely walked along the beach in bare feet except when he took the time to visit Achilles Island. Taking his shoes off, he tossed them away from the surf. "Why haven't you before?"

Her grimace was enchanting as she set her shoes and socks carefully on a nearby rock, well away from the tide, and then walked back to him. "Oh my God! The water's cold."

"It's the Irish Sea, love. It's always cold."

"Right." She padded out of the water. "The old reason was that Tyson worried about me being by the water. I got over that after I arrived here, so here's my current predicament. I'm a recovering clean freak. I love the beach, but I've never liked sand in my shoes. Or the car. Or the house. Or the laundry basket. Pretty much anywhere."

He took her hand, the one holding her seashell. "Sand looks good on you, Megan."

Their eyes met, and he watched her chest rise as the awareness between them grew. He stroked the side of her palm and heard her breath catch.

"Ireland looks good on me," she said softly.

He pushed a lock of her hair behind her ear. "It does at that, love."

She gave a small smile and then lowered her eyes. He dropped his hand, sensing she needed time to become used to his touch.

When she busied herself with picking up more sea glass, he simply watched her. Some things couldn't be rushed, and he wasn't inclined to try. His father, though... Kade thought about their tugging and pulling over the way of things.

It hadn't always been this way. His father was the one who'd taught him to ride, and Kade's first race across this beach had been with him. Back then, his father had thrown him in the air in delight, his booming laugh making sand crabs withdraw into their shells. Their enjoyment had been pure then—no words about competing or being a man or besting one another. Time had ruined that, and his heart hurt for it.

When was the last time they'd laughed together, only the two of them? He couldn't remember.

"You look sad, Kade," Megan said, standing up.

"Thought of my father, love," he answered, picking up a rock and throwing it into the sea.

"I wish mine wasn't coming." She closed the hand holding her treasures. "I wish Angie could have found a way to invite my mom only. You must think I'm terrible to say that."

"Not at all. You've dropped a few hints here and there about your parents. I know she's a nurse and he's a senior military officer who's been hard on you. I imagine the Jack Nicholson character in *A Few Good Men* minus the cover-up."

"You have him right, except he's more handsome, I suppose," she said with a sigh. "He parented us like we were privates in basic training. He even bragged to his friends about it."

"That mustn't have felt very caring or encouraging." He worked with kids and knew what they responded to.

"It didn't." She tugged on the collar of her windbreaker. "I tried to be what he wanted. I remember us hosting a Memorial Day barbeque for his work colleagues when I was fourteen. All the women had mostly straight hair to their shoulders—no bangs or frizz like I'd seen at school—and they wore sweater sets and neutral pleated pants. I thought he'd like me if I looked like them. He laughed a lot at that party, and trust me, he didn't laugh like that at home."

Maybe it was his own thoughts about his father and racing, but he could see so clearly how she'd become the woman she was trying to leave behind. "It seems like the way you're going—not trying to win his approval anymore and be who you want—is working well."

She gave him a hesitant smile. "I still feel vulnerable at times, but I'm feeling stronger in it all."

"It shows," he said, picking up a piece of green glass and handing it to her. "In fact, it looks downright beautiful. I can't take my eyes off you when you're like that."

The words hung heavy in the air. He watched her swallow thickly.

"Good to know," she said, coughing to clear her throat. "I'm going to have to keep really busy with the St. Stephen's Day fair so I can stay that way. By the way, do you have a favorite local band? We talked about finding one for the event."

He decided the abrupt change in subject meant she needed time to process what he'd said. So he didn't press her. "I have a few favorites," he said, laughing when a seal gave a bark as a seagull buzzed it. "You'll want one to donate their time possibly?"

"Yes, although I expect that will be tough. Musicians deserve to be paid."

"You're donating all the money you make on your pots," he pointed out.

"But I work at the arts center. I need it to stay open. We both know I'm not the greatest farmhand."

He threw back his head and laughed, making a seal bark again. "That sounds like an American Western movie. Megan, love, I don't have you around for that. I have you around because you're good with horses and children, and I like being around you."

He also wanted them to share their passions, which was why he'd enlisted in her class.

"Good with kids?" She wrinkled her nose. "My son is just starting to like me."

"It probably helps that you're recovering from the clean freak thing," Kade said with a wink. "He's a boy. I remember liking to play without a thought to my clothes. To give my mother credit, she knew we loved to roam, me and Shannon. She'd have us strip off our clothes in the laundry room in the back when we came in especially muddy."

"But she let you roam, as you said." Megan dug her toe in the sand. "I wasn't letting Ollie do that before."

"You are now, love, and look how he's thriving."

Her smile started slowly. "He *is* thriving. He loves school, and he likes playing with friends after it or being with Angie and Carrick and Liam. And *you*."

"He'll remember the freedom you've given him, trust me." Kade looked at his watch. "I don't want to go back, but we have a client."

"Maybe you can come by and watch a movie with me after Ollie goes to bed," she said, ducking her head. "Angie mentioned watching *The Wind That Shakes the Barley*. She thought it gave a good historical perspective on recent Irish history."

He'd seen it and liked it very much. "I'd love to. Do you like popcorn?"

Her smile turned into a grin. "I do."

It's a date, he almost said. "Then I'll bring some."

She tried to brush off more sand before giving up and tucking her treasures into her jacket pocket. He helped her into the saddle and gave in to the urge to race a little more when Legend showed the inclination.

When they reached the yard and saw to the horses, he watched as she greeted ten-year-old Jakub Doyle and his mother. When the autistic boy had first come to him two years ago, he'd vacillated between being terribly withdrawn and wildly frustrated with his difficulty in communicating how he was feeling and thinking. Kade had been working with him on that, and although it was an ongoing process, the boy had flourished.

Jakub had been shy with Megan at first, but she'd shown him pictures of Ollie, and by the end of their first joint session, he'd started hugging her around the waist and asking about her son.

It had made Kade fall even harder for her.

After preparing Jakub to ride, Kade helped him onto Winston, who always made him laugh by his habit of bowing. Even Legend was charmed by it, Kade had noticed.

When Jakub asked Megan about Ollie's school, she told him about how much he loved Jamie, his teacher, and that his favorite subject was science, something Kade already knew. Ollie was always asking for help identifying trees and plants and why an animal would do this or that.

When Megan asked Jakub about his school, the boy grew quiet as they crossed the new bridge Jamie and Liam had helped him build last month.

"I don't like school, but I'm afraid to tell my mom," Jakub whispered, his hands tightening on the reins from his distress.

Megan looked over Winston where she was walking on the other side of the boy. He nodded for her to respond.

"Ollie used to be scared to tell me things," she said, patting his leg. "He used to tell his aunt how he felt, in fact. But you know what? One day he got angry at me, and he told me everything he'd been feeling, and boy, was it a big deal. I'd had no idea he was so unhappy. I asked him to tell me what he was feeling from then on, so neither of us would have to get so upset."

Jakub bit his lip. "It's better that no one be upset. I don't like yelling."

Loud noises bothered him, and Kade had encouraged him to hum or sing a song when he put his hands over his ears to block them out, including a jet ski by the shore. It had seemed to help.

"No one does," Kade said, loving this part of his job. "But it's okay to be upset."

"Kade and I were just talking about being upset ourselves," she said, giving him a smile.

"I have something in the shed that might help," Kade said, prompting Jakub to let out a cheer. "Now, why don't you tell Winston to turn?"

The boy extended his right rein like Kade had taught him. "I like that he understands me."

Kade knew the feeling. The unspoken communication

between him and horses had been one of his earliest joys. He could look into their eyes and know what they were feeling or what they wanted. His father had the same gift. Kade hoped he would let it lead him to the right match for Legend. Because he understood where Jakub was coming from. He didn't like that kind of tension either.

When they reached his shed, Kade went into the small room off the tack room and grabbed the item he'd prepared.

Jakub had his arms around Winston's neck. "I love you, boy!"

Megan put her hand on the boy's head gently after he leaned forward, communicating he was comfortable with her affection. Kade's heart soared. How could she not see how good she was with them? By her own account, she'd been bullied as a child. She understood what it was like to feel different. Like the people who came to him.

"Jakub, this is for you," Kade said, handing him the clear plastic jar. "There's water and glitter in it. Go on and give it a shake."

"Wow!" he breathed out as colors danced in the liquid, much like snow in a snow globe.

"When you start to get upset, I want you to shake this and watch the glitter. When it settles, you're going to feel calmer. Then you try and talk to your mom or anyone else you need to share something with. Let's give this a try. Okay?"

"Okay." He launched himself at his legs and hugged him. "I love you, Kade!"

He put his arm around him. "I love you too, Jakub."

"And I love Megan," the boy said, running over and giving her a hug as well.

She had tears in her eyes, as she often did in the face of such unconditional love and acceptance. Her arms went around the little boy, but he quickly pulled away to show off the glitter jar. At the car, Kade helped Jakub in and buckled him up. His mother was fighting tears and mouthed *Thank you* to them both before they drove off.

Megan gave an audible sniff, and when Duke appeared at her side, she picked him up and hugged him. "Do you think it would be okay for Jakub to play with Ollie? He really likes to hear about him, and I thought it might be nice for Ollie to meet a new friend of ours."

He walked over and put an arm around her. "I think that's a great idea, love. So will his mother."

"You did beautifully with him. Like you always do. How did you know to make that glitter jar?"

"I read," he responded. "When I came across the idea, I knew it was going to be helpful."

"It's like a jar of dreams, with the colors dancing around," Megan said, her voice wistful.

He tipped up her chin to look into her eyes. When he saw the longing in them, he knew his answer. He kissed the top of her head and went back into his shed, coming out with one for her.

"For you, love." He continued to hold her hand as her fingers curled around it. "May all your dreams come true."

When she wrapped her arms around him and laid her head against his chest, letting him hold her, one more of *his* dreams came true.

CHAPTER TEN

In her whole life, Bets had never talked so much about *it* without having any of *it*. Even though she knew she was imagining it, she could smell sex in the air between her and Donal when they were together. Donal had assured her that he was working on their problem. And so was she...

Not that living with Liam was a problem, of course, but they needed to have a discussion about sex. They were both adults, and...

Oh, who was she kidding?

She was going to be sick.

"Hey, Mum," Liam said, knocking on her office door. "I found your keys."

Her blush was infantile, and she darn well knew it. "Lovely. Where?"

He bit his lip. "They were on top of the fridge this time. You couldn't see them because you're such a shrimp. I bet you were getting some ice. We're going through it pretty fast for fall."

"It's been especially warm for an Irish autumn."

He cocked a sandy blond brow, the little shit. "I hadn't noticed."

Her glare put a smile on his face as he crossed their ancient Aubusson rug and put her keys on the antique desk. "I still haven't found the other set."

God knew where she'd put them. "We'll keep looking."

He sank into one of the high-backed chairs across from her. "How's the grant writing going?"

"They seem to excel in the art of detailed questions," she said, her mouth twisting. "I'm not pleased with the couple of grants we barely qualify for. We haven't been around long, and that could be a problem. They have more offerings for graduate students or the newly graduated who want to work with the arts. Still, that information could come in useful. Angie sent it out to some of her old artist friends and teachers and asked them to do the same."

Bets had jokingly suggested that Angie should send it out in the old chain letter style, which had made them both laugh.

"I feel really good about those ripples actually," Liam said, resting his ankle on his knee. "I know you and Angie are looking for a new artist to come next year. The right person will find her way here. It's a she, I think. And she loves the light but she's not a painter."

She got chills. "Your intuition is fairly flawless these days, so I'm going to tell myself not to worry. I look forward to her falling into our laps."

"It's all the meditation, Mum," he said, flashing her a smile. "If we didn't already have a potter in residence, I'd contact Aspen in Bali. We meditated pretty good back in the day."

She smirked before realizing this was her segue. Had he cued it up for her? "Speaking of girls like Aspen..."

"Mum, there are no girls like Aspen around here. But I know the right girl will come find me eventually. In the meantime, I plan on having my fun and living my life. As should you."

She blinked. Yep, he'd cued her up but good. "Liam, I—"

"Me first." He put a finger to his lips as if shushing her, looking like a little rascal. "Mum, Declan just bought Summercrest Manor, and he's asked me and Brady to move in with him in a few weeks. Jamie refused. Said it was too creepy."

Bets put her hand behind her ear as her mind went blank. "What did you just say?"

He came around the desk and sat on the edge, laying a grounding hand on her shoulder. "It's time, Mum. We're both growing up. You have your life with Donal to enjoy, and I'm still finding my purpose, although it feels closer than ever. I can't tell you what these last three years with you have meant, Mum. For it to be just us. I'll always treasure them."

Rare tears filled her eyes as he leaned over and hugged her. "Dammit, Liam. You made me cry. I was going to talk to you about having sex in the house. You don't have to move out."

He held her chin, like Bruce used to do when he really wanted her to listen. "Yes, I do."

She nodded and brushed away her tears. "I don't know what I would have done if you hadn't been here after your dad died and Rhys and Wyatt left."

"I don't know what I would have done either," he said, wiping his nose. "We binged on all those action-adventure series like *Justified* and *Black Sails* because it felt good watching people who had it worse than we did, losing Dad."

Her throat thickened because she heard what he didn't say. How she'd sometimes lain in bed all day in dirty pajamas. How he'd joined her with ice cream or popcorn to make an event of it. "You can't know how much it meant to have you here when I was feeling like that."

His beautiful green eyes gleamed. "Yes, I do."

"Shit, I'm going to start bawling if we don't stop this." She rubbed her face. "Liam O'Hanlon, you're a good man, and I'm the luckiest mother on earth to have you as my son."

He kissed her cheek. "And I'm lucky to have you for a mum. Not too many mothers would talk to their adult son about having sex in the house. Were we going to divide up the rooms?"

"Stop it." She punched him lightly. "A root canal was looking more tantalizing."

Standing, he tapped her on the nose. "The Universe always provides, Mum. I hope you have sex soon. You can't keep losing your car keys. You won't be able to go anywhere."

When Donal finally figured out a solution to their problem, she was fine with not going anywhere. They could stay home and have sex all day. Anywhere.

"I wonder what you're thinking about, Mum." He laughed when she threw Post-it notes at him. "I'll be leaving you. I need to pull some things together to go over and do an energetic clearing of Summercrest. It's a mess of lost dreams and longstanding grudges and some things I won't tell you about because I don't want you to have more trouble sleeping."

"I won't even ask how you're going to do that," she said with a shiver.

"Another beautiful gift from Bali. We're going to bring it back to what it once was—what we all want in the end: a place of promise for a wonderful life. You have a shot at another one yourself. I hope you take it, Mum."

Oh, her boy. "I love you, Liam."

"Love you too, Mum," he said, putting his hand to his heart. "Think you can find some time for us to have a few movie nights before I move out?"

Her heart throbbed in her chest. "You're the one with all the girls and nights out."

"I was giving you space," he said with a knowing look, surprising her. "Besides, you'll always be my number one girl."

My, how she liked the sound of that. "I'd love to have a few nights with you like that." Only this time there would be a different kind of sadness. Her boy was moving out.

"I'll be making the popcorn since you always singe it. How does this Friday sound?"

"Wonderful. I'll buy some ice cream."

"One last thing, Mum," he said, holding out his hands like he was testing heat from a stove. "Like I've told you before, Wyatt and Rhys and me really like Donal for you. So you should know, I'll be out of the house for at least three hours if you'd like to call him. I can also bunk somewhere else tonight. Or you can put a handkerchief on the door-knob of your room of choice."

"Oh, get out of here," she said, waving her hand at him. "We're not having sex just yet."

His brow rose. "Do you need to talk about why not?"

"I'd rather eat frog legs!" She stood. "Out! Go clear that creepy manor. Sounds like you have your hands full."

"I have a hunch that Sorcha is going to help me." He grinned. "I feel her around sometimes. I always did like that girl."

With that, he left. She sank into her chair. Sorcha. Bets

had suspected she might be around after catching a whiff of her orange scent months ago, when her cousins had first come to Ireland. She'd meant to ask someone about it, but her focus had shifted to other matters: finding more money for the arts center and having sex with Donal.

She reached for her phone and texted him.

Liam is moving out in a few weeks. How is your side of our problem coming along?

She waited for his charming reply, full of his usual misspellings, which she'd learned had less to do with an ignorance of grammar and spelling and more to do with the size of his hands. They were really big.

Like other things.

She headed to the fridge for an ice cube as her body blazed with heat. Her phone beeped with his response as she cracked the ice tray and pressed the cube to her hot neck.

I have a lead on somethang Brilliant. Are you good with Liam moving Out? He'll be happy lving with Declan and Brady, although Summercrest is haunted. I Believe the Old stories.

Another chill touched her skin. She wasn't surprised he already knew about the move. News traveled fast in Caisleán, and Summercrest Manor would be a hot topic for gossips. Locals thought it was haunted—Donal included, clearly—but it wouldn't be after Liam did his clearing ceremony. The boys had loved sneaking onto the grounds when they were kids, but Liam was right, Jamie had never enjoyed tagging along. Declan, however, had said he loved the dungeon and that one day he'd buy the place, and so he had.

Liam and I had a nice talk, and I'm good with it, although I'll miss him. Any news on our permit for St. Stephen's Day?

She tossed the dripping ice cube into the sink and waited for his reply.

Yes. Dad and I would like you to meet us for dinner at the Merry Fiddler tonight at half six. We're as giddy as a spring ram to show you our play.

That sounded encouraging. She couldn't wait to see what they had in mind.

When they arrived at half six, Bets was wearing gold heels, peacock earrings, and a deep blood-red lipstick that seemed perfect for the occasion. Donal had his hand to her back as they followed Eoghan and the server to the table in the corner, which happened to be right next to the spot where Tom MacKenna was dining with his wife, Orla, and Bets' nemesis, Mary Kincaid. Something told her that was no coincidence.

Eoghan called out a cheeky greeting, and Tom buried his head in his menu, his wife pursing her lips. Mary, though, shot Bets a look of pure menace as Donal patted her hip in front of the entire restaurant.

"You're so bad," she whispered as he helped her into her chair.

"I can't wait to show you how bad," he said into her ear, making her flush with heat.

Thank God she hadn't driven tonight. She'd have lost her keys for sure. When the server came around, she didn't need to look at the menu. The Merry Fiddler did one thing well—fish and chips—although they dabbled in stir-frys. God knew why, but Irish food was still a mystery to Bets after all these years. She ordered a Guinness while Eoghan and Donal both went for whiskey.

Then she waited...

She was halfway through her Guinness when Killian and Nicola walked in. Her dear friend and fellow Lucky Charm caught her gaze immediately and grinned like a cat who'd found the cream. Killian led her to a nearby table and helped her into a chair, but he didn't sit down. No, he walked straight over to Tom MacKenna's table.

"Hi, Tom! How are you faring?"

The weasel looked over sharply. "Fine. You?"

"Grand," Killian said, taking out an envelope and laying it on the table. "I was going to drop this off earlier, but I had a horse bolt on me. What luck to run into you and your wife. Mary, good to see you."

Killian had a killer smile he brought out to deal with assholes, be they rich, entitled jerks looking to buy horse-flesh or people trying to do wrong by others. From the way his mouth couldn't decide on an expression, Tom didn't know what to make of it.

"Shall I look at it now?" he asked with a short smile, finally committing to an expression. "Given our family's history, if you need something urgent, I'm happy to help."

Killian rocked back on his boots, hands on his hips. "I'm glad to hear it. I've decided to be a good citizen and host an event on my land. I've never asked for a permit before—you know how I feel about my property—but I did my best to fill everything in."

Tom turned gray as he realized what the permit was for.

Bets had to bite her cheek to hold back a smile as Orla's mouth puckered and Mary's hefty bosom heaved.

"I'd been hearing about a St. Stephen's Day fair to support the art center," Tom said, clearing his throat.

"My land has a good track for the racing," Killian said. "I'll have to give up one of my sheds as well for the day, but it's for a worthy cause, and the pony rides my son will be giving to all the children in the area will keep the holiday season alive in their hearts. I'm sure it will be the talk of the village for years to come."

Game. Set. Match.

Donal gripped her knee under the table, his elation palpable. Eoghan took another drink of his whiskey. They had him, and they damn well knew it. Oh, Donal and Eoghan were dear men for bringing her to witness this.

"I'm sure it will be, with you and your land involved," Tom said, coughing this time like he'd swallowed a fishbone.

"So I can count on the permit going through, then." Killian held out his hand for a shake.

Tom eyed it before shaking it. "I'll make it official tomorrow."

"I'll be by for the official confirmation," Killian said with a nod. "Thanks, Tom. Orla. Mary. Enjoy your dinner."

He didn't so much as glance at Bets and her companions, but Killian was cool when he needed to be. Nicola sent her a smile before kissing him full on the mouth when he sat down beside her at the table.

Bets moved her chair closer to Donal, away from Mary Kincaid's glare. Her sister-in-law had lost this round. If she and Orla had planned on blocking the permit, they couldn't now. Not even Tom would be bold enough to go back on his word—and handshake, mind you—after so many of the townspeople had witnessed it.

She stared in wonder at her two dinner companions. Eoghan was humming an Irish tune she didn't recognize, while Donal caressed the back of her knee under the table.

"Dessert is on me," she said with a grin. "*Slainte.*"

When Donal took her home after dropping his father off, dessert was indeed on her—again. She climbed onto his lap in the front seat of his Mercedes and kissed him until they were both breathless.

"Now who's bad," he said with a groan as he let his head fall back. "Hopefully tonight gave you faith, Bets. If my dad and I can find a way to check Tom MacKenna, I'll be able to find a way for us to have uninterrupted sex."

She kissed him one last time, making herself groan as he rubbed his hips against hers. "Make it fast, dammit."

His laughter followed her as she opened the car door to hop out. "Did you find your other set of keys yet?"

She glared at him and then slammed the door. But she did find her keys that night when she decided to do laundry because she was too worked up to go to sleep. They were at the bottom of the laundry basket, mixed in with the clothes she'd torn off in her haste for a cold shower last week.

Liam was right. They'd better have sex soon. God only knew what she'd forget next.

CHAPTER ELEVEN

They had the permit for the St. Stephen's fair.

The story of the ambush at the Merry Fiddler Thursday night had reached Megan through Kade, whose mother had texted him the good news. They'd been watching another movie on her uncomfortable settee at the time after she'd finished another successful pottery class, and she'd launched herself at him, making him laugh.

"Everything is falling into place, love," he said, holding her gently.

Almost a week later, she was starting to believe that. She and Kade had spent time together every day, either riding horses and walking on the beach or watching a movie at her house after Ollie went to bed. Her Tuesday and Wednesday night classes had gone well, and she expected the one she had tonight would be equally successful.

When she returned home from dropping Ollie off at school, Eoghan O'Dwyer was waiting for her. The ninety-three-year-old's brown and green eyes sparkled. "It's time to get serious about our fair, girl. Can you meet me on the teal bridge overlooking the river that cuts through the village at ten tomorrow?"

"I can," she replied.

"People will have money in their pockets and be in high spirits," he said, "having been paid for their week of work. It's a good day to make the rounds and ask for donations."

Given the way he and his son had handled the permit affair, she wasn't surprised at his canniness. "It sounds like I couldn't have a better partner." She knew they needed prize money for the horse race and some additional expenses like the band, although Kade was hoping to convince one of the groups he liked to waive their usual playing fee.

"You can't at that," Eoghan said, "but I have a lot of years on you. I'll be happy to share some of my secrets with you."

She loved the offer, although she didn't have a clue what he meant.

On Friday morning, she paced in front of her dresser as she tried to decide what to wear. Her farm clothes seemed too informal, but her pale blue sweater set didn't look right.

She was trying too hard.

Compromising, she tugged on her farm jeans along with the sweater set, hoping she didn't look like a polar bear in the tropics. Before she left, she shook her Dream Jar, holding the intention that her dreams were falling into place, like the glitter dancing in the water.

When she met Eoghan, he beamed and kissed her cheek. "Smile, girl. We're about to have our way with the village. Now, take my arm and let me do the talking. If I feel like our prey would be more amenable to giving money to a beautiful art teacher such as yourself, I'll pat you on the back. All right, we're off."

She clutched her navy handbag as Eoghan led her to the

center of town. Talking to people had never been easy for her. When she'd agreed to take point on this project, she'd imagined making phone calls or sending letters, not approaching people face-to-face. And his supposition that they'd give money because she was a beautiful art teacher? Her mind couldn't wrap itself around that. She'd been told she was nice-looking, but no one had ever said she was a beauty. And who could blame them? She'd looked like every other conservative female in the greater Washington, D.C. area: well dressed and styled but like one note in a song, not meant to stand out.

"Take a breath, girl," he said, stopping at the garden plot in the center of the square, bursting with roses and begonias in yellows and whites. "You're going to need a medic if you don't relax. The secret to asking for donations and the like is to go to your friends first. Afterward, you visit your enemies and talk up what the other kind folk in town have contributed. Guilt sometimes works wonders, but let's hope we don't have to dish out too much."

Guilt?

"Eoghan, I'm not sure—"

"You're going to do grand, Megan," he said, taking her elbow and leading her into their first store, The Final Chop. "We're among friends. Your sister will soon have the owner as her father-in-law if you'll recall."

Only Seamus Fitzgerald wasn't the one who greeted them—it was Declan McGrath. She told herself this wouldn't be so bad. Although the butcher's assistant had a unique sense of humor, he was a good friend of Kade's and Carrick's and had been present for her first taste of whiskey to toast the official opening of the arts center.

He looked up after severing a large piece of raw meat with a giant gleaming cleaver and grinned, a dimple showing in his right cheek. "Megan Bennet! Welcome, girl. You're in terrible peril, for sure, if Eoghan O'Dwyer is accompanying you."

Terrible peril? She'd never get used to the way these Irish talked. "Hello, Declan."

"Insulting me, already, Declan McGrath?" Eoghan gestured to the cleaver. "You're the one in terrible peril, what with buying Summercrest Manor, even if you got it for a song."

"Why do you think I asked Liam to move in with me?" Declan wiped his hands on his apron. "He'll have all that nonsense cleared out, and if he doesn't, Brady will talk the spirits into a second death."

Liam had told Megan about his new lodgings, but he hadn't mentioned any of this. Suddenly she wasn't as excited about visiting him in his new home. "Congratulations."

"I heard about the play you and your son executed on Tom MacKenna," Declan said to Eoghan after nodding her way. "Our Mayo football team might win a championship if you and Donal were coaching."

"They might at that, but I'm still skeptical given the curse. They won't win until the last two players from the 1951 championship team die. Stupid they were, celebrating while a funeral went on."

Curses and ghosts? She knew this was Ireland, but Megan still clutched her purse as a shiver stole over her.

"Hello, Eoghan!" Seamus Fitzgerald called out as he emerged from the meat locker in back, hefting a large rack of beef. "Megan. It's fine to see you. How's your boy? Carrick said he hasn't begged to be saved from my other son at school. Jamie must be actually teaching them something."

She knew he was joking. His wife had been a teacher

until her recent retirement. "I've never seen anyone so excited about going to school. It's all he can talk about. He wasn't this happy at his old one."

"Jamie is a right fine teacher," Seamus said, "even if he gave Mary Myers nightmares after taking them to see Keegan's spray-painted cattle. *BBQ* and *Steak* were especially troubling to some of the children."

"Clearly they're not future butchers," Declan said, and the two men shared a laugh.

Megan only managed a weak smile. Eoghan, however, joined in with a laugh that sounded like a thunderclap, surprisingly loud for his thin frame. "Vegetarians for sure, the end of this country."

"Well, that's enough of that talk." Seamus grabbed a whetstone and started sharpening his cleaver, the sound whisper soft and scarier for it. "I suspect that since the two of you are together, you're here about the St. Stephen's Day fair."

Eoghan patted his green wool jacket shot through with purple stripes and took out a small black book. "We are."

"It's for a great cause," Megan blurted and then almost kicked herself.

Declan knuckled a lock of black hair back from his forehead. "My mother...Siobhan," he added for Megan's benefit, "was telling me and Brady last night over dinner how much she wants to continue teaching knitting classes there."

"So, I'll be putting you down for a hefty sum," Eoghan said. "What about the horse racing?"

"Not for me," Declan said, wiping his cleaver on his apron and cutting another rack of beef. "My brother has a mind to take part in it, although I suspect he'll want to ride one of our family's donkeys."

Donkeys? She was so lost.

Eoghan sputtered. "Why can't Brady ride a horse for once?"

"He'll be worried about falling off. Doesn't think people would like seeing him deliver the post with a black eye or worse," Declan said with a laugh.

"The widows especially would fuss over him and his eye," Eoghan said. "I heard tell he's received nearly twelve jars of preserves so far. I should have been a postman meself and not a sheep farmer."

"Better to raise sheep," Seamus said. "You and your son have some of the finest lambs around—second only to my son's, of course. Put me down for the horse racing. I'm hoping Carrick might race too. We'll see who crosses the finish line first."

"From your lips to God's ear," Eoghan said. "I'd challenge my Donal, but I don't have a widow to tend my sore bones like Brady does. Shame that. Well, we'll be leaving you, except we'd like to know what you might donate."

Seamus walked over to the till and popped the drawer, drawing out some euros. "How does two hundred sound?"

"And a few steaks perhaps for conciliation prize?" Eoghan asked, nodding to the ones lying in the counter. "They're fine steaks, Seamus."

"*I'll* donate the steaks," Declan said and dug out his wallet. "Along with a hundred euros for the prize money. Buying a house has my account a little light at the moment."

"Then we're all the more grateful," Megan said, flashing him a smile.

Seamus leaned his elbow on the counter. "Megan, girl, you like steak?"

She wasn't much of a steak eater, but Ollie enjoyed it, and she imagined Kade might too, so she nodded. Maybe she could make him dinner, another sign to him that she was settling into their relationship. "I have some errands—"

"I'll drop them by your house as it's on the way," Declan said helpfully.

"I don't know when I'll be home—"

"No bother. I'll just pop them in the fridge for you."

She nearly laughed. People came by the house all the time. Ollie loved it, but Angie had admitted that she still found it a little weird too. "Thanks, Declan. Thank you both."

"Thank *you* for volunteering to organize this event," Seamus said, his thick silver brows furrowing. "It can't be easy being new to the village, but trust me, everyone will do their part to help make the day a success."

"What he's saying, Megan," Declan said, putting a companionable hand on the man's shoulder, "is that you needn't worry. People want the art center to stay open. Even if it's only to spit in Mary Kincaid's face."

"Personally, I'm hoping you ask Tom MacKenna to race and let the fates decide," Seamus said, flexing his arm muscle, a considerable size for his age. "He's up to no good, and he knows it. He doesn't come in here anymore, knowing my feelings."

"Like we'd serve him," Declan said, disgust lacing his voice. "Doing the dirty work of two women. It's rubbish."

"Well, we stopped his dirty work this time," Eoghan said with a nod. "I didn't like Donal having to resign like he did."

Megan hadn't realized how personal this was for Eoghan. Donal seemed so capable, but this man was his father.

"Well, we'd best be off," Eoghan said with another look at the butcher counter. "No steak for this old man?"

"If you have the coin, always, you old codger," Seamus said with a grin.

"I'll donate one your way as a reward for recent events," Declan said, packaging up one and handing it to him. "Have a fine day, Megan."

"Thanks, Declan," she said. "See you later, Seamus."

When they left the store, Eoghan extended his free arm to her. "You did right fine, Megan. We have three hundred euros and some free steaks, and we've only just begun. I knew the village would do their part. Let's see what else we might raise."

They went into store after store, and it followed a similar pattern. People asked about each other's families—something she loved about the Irish—and then there was a bit of teasing. Some talked about the coup that had secured the permit. Others brought up the weather. Still others mentioned Keegan's cattle. The village was up in arms about the words he'd used, although Megan had found a few messages helpful. She hadn't gotten to know Keegan well yet, but she hoped to change that in her class.

Eoghan was a clever sort. When the townspeople started reminiscing about Carrick's sheep and how much they missed the poetic words of Sorcha Fitzgerald, he'd remind people about the arts center being named after her, and sure enough, they always made a strong donation.

The biggest surprise came when they reached the bookshop, One More Chapter, owned by Kade's mother. Shannon, his sister, embraced her and then proceeded to ask Eoghan whether women could enter the horse race, something that hadn't been established.

He scratched the thin wisps of silver hair covering his head, clearly flummoxed, and Nicola covered her hand to disguise a smile. Megan couldn't imagine why a woman couldn't race, so she kept quiet.

"Usually the horse racing is for the men only." Shannon anchored her hands on her hips, glaring at the older man. "But aren't we part of the village too?"

"Is this some kind of independence stand?" Eoghan asked. "Girl, I'm all for you racing. I'd let my own granddaughters do it if they weren't in Dublin."

"So it's open to women?"

Eoghan nudged her. "What do you think, Megan?"

"I don't see why gender should matter."

"Good, then it's decided." Shannon shook back her long brown hair. "Megan, you should know that this town and Ireland herself has a long way to go when it comes to treating women fairly. Hence why I had to ask."

Eoghan uttered a squeak, making Nicola laugh outright this time.

Waving her off, he turned to Shannon. "Ah, you should talk to your old schoolmates, Riona and Ceila, when they come visit me and their father. Now, we must be going, but before we do, we'd be wondering about your interest in making a donation."

Nicola took some bills out of her purple skirt and extended them. "I saw you making the rounds and was ready for you."

"I hear we have you to thank for Killian agreeing to hold the event on your land," Megan said.

"We have a good race course and some nice sheds you'll be needing given the weather that time of year." Nicola put her hand on Megan's arm and gave her a soft smile. "We need to keep our Yanks happy."

She stared at the elegant woman with the short white-blond hair. Happy? They wanted them both to be happy? The sweetness of the comment enveloped her.

"With me helping, their path will be lined with unicorns, fairies, and rainbows," Eoghan said in that charming way she was coming to love.

"Thank you for the donation and the help," Megan said, awkwardly reaching out and touching the woman's arm in return.

This was Kade's mother, and while she didn't know her well, the same thread of kindness ran through mother and son. Looking at Nicola, she could also see where Kade's cheekbones and brown eyes had come from. When the older woman took her hand and smiled, Megan found herself smiling in return.

"Megan, come up to the house for tea after you finish a late pony ride," Nicola said. "I'm usually home around five. Please bring Ollie if you'd like, although I've heard he loves to play around the farm."

"Thank you, Nicola. I will."

Shannon shot her a knowing smile. Did she know about what was developing between her and Kade? They hadn't gone out in public yet, but she was his sister. Megan sent the young woman a smile as Eoghan took her elbow.

"We'll be off since everything is sorted," Eoghan said with a crisp bow of his head. "Good luck."

"You've put me down for the horse race, then?" Shannon called as they walked past the new release section and out the door.

He gave a crisp wave over his shoulder. "She's always had spirit, that one. I'm not sure a bookshop is where Shannon's heart lies, but she'll find her way. All right, we're off to see Gavin McGrath at the Brazen Donkey."

She glanced down at her watch. It was only eleven

thirty in the morning. Were they going to offer her a drink? Most likely. This was Ireland. What was she going to do?

She tripped over the weatherstrip of the door, causing everyone to look over. The pub was already doing brisk business. The two televisions had on a horse race and a soccer game. Five tables were full, and the ten barstools were all taken, mostly by gray-haired men. Her stomach clenched when Gavin McGrath came through the flapper door and charged toward them, all six foot six of him. He grabbed Eoghan's hand and shook it exuberantly before turning to Megan.

"You're finally darkening my door then, girl," Gavin said. "I heard from my son that you'd paid the butcher shop a visit this morning. I'm ready for you. Eoghan, you can put me down for the horse racing as well as three hundred euros for a donation. I need to keep my Siobhan happy, don't I?"

"That's very nice of you." When he sent her a quick wink and grabbed her hand, she found herself letting him lead her to the bar. She looked over her shoulder. Eoghan wouldn't save her—he'd stopped to talk with some of the men clustered at a table.

"Fergal Kennedy, move out of the way for the lady." Gavin toweled off the area as the older man exited his seat, taking his Guinness with him. "Come, Megan! I'll get these other fellows to open their wallets too." He hoisted her onto the recently vacated red leather barstool, lifted the flapper door, and then he was grabbing a glass and a bottle of whiskey and pouring her a drink.

"It's a bit early," she said, looking at the generous pour.

Gavin leaned forward, scratching his cheek. "Only have a sip, then. Make an old man happy. And I don't mean Eoghan, girl."

She lifted the glass and touched her lips to it. Liquid fire was a usually a good description for whiskey, but today she tasted warmth and caramel as well. A cheer erupted in the pub.

"To Megan Bennet!" Eoghan said, hoisting a whiskey in the air. "*Slainte.*"

No one had ever toasted her. The feeling was as warm as the whiskey. "*Slainte,*" she replied with an easier smile, taking another sip. The flavor really was nice after she got over the fire on her tongue.

"Now, who's going to help keep our beautiful new arts center open?" Gavin asked, taking a green and blue houndstooth tweed cap from the hat rack and waving it above his head. "And me own wife from crying every night over its potential closing."

Oh, the Irish and their drama. She kind of loved it.

"I can give you a handkerchief for her tears, but little else," one of the ancient men at the bar said with a wink in her direction.

Megan startled. She'd never met so many men who winked before coming here.

"But for this pretty Yank, I might part with twenty euros," said the winker with blue eyes as he dug out some bills.

Pretty? Her? Funny how Eoghan had said something similar. Maybe the effort she'd put into lightening up and being more herself was making her appear more attractive. People talked about the extra light in someone's eyes and face when they were happier. These days she mostly was. Suddenly she remembered the message on Keegan O'Malley's cattle. *Pretty. Girl. Smile.* She caught sight of herself in the mirror behind the bar and did just that.

"Ah, she is a pretty one at that," Fergal Kennedy agreed from his post against the wall covered in old Guinness paraphernalia, the best of which included a bright toucan balancing two pints of beer on his beak with the saying, "Lovely Day for a Guinness."

"What do you teach at the center, love?" the man to her right asked as Gavin handed him the hat. He slid in some bills and handed it off to someone else.

Suddenly all the men seated at the bar stopped their conversation and leaned forward, pints in hand. She took a hasty sip of whiskey to embolden herself. "I teach ceramics. Pottery."

"We have the finest clay in the world," Fergal said, throwing in some money and passing the hat to the next man. "Are you going to be selling your pottery at the St. Stephen's fair?"

"I am," she said, clutching her glass. Of course, she would need to spend more time at the studio if she was going to make enough pieces.

"Well, I'll be looking forward to seeing your treasures," Fergal said with a wink.

"Stop your flirting." Eoghan gave a squeak. "Fergal, you leave that nice lady to herself. She doesn't want to be caught up with the likes of you."

"And this from my first cousin," Fergal said with a hearty laugh, coming over to the bar and putting his elbows on the top. "I hear he's taking your pottery class. Watch out for him. He's been trouble since he was born, me own mother used to say."

Clearly trouble worked for the O'Dwyer men. They had their permit in hand for the St. Stephen's Day fair, after all.

"If you're first cousins," Megan said, reaching for her drink and taking a sip, "does that mean you're in your nineties too?"

He gave another laugh. "No, I'm only eighty-eight, and I feel as young as a spring lamb."

"I fear having that lamb served at my table," Gavin said with a laugh, pouring a Guinness slowly. "Tough meat that."

"Oh, stop, you'll break my ancient heart," Fergal said, clutching his chest. Turning back to Megan, he said, "I hear you've been helping Kade Donovan at his pony farm. A good boy, that one. You're lucky to be working with him. You must be special as well as pretty."

Again, she almost rocked back on her barstool. Oh, how she wanted to wrap that compliment up and take it with her everywhere. She caught sight of her hair in the mirror. Her long brown hair certainly didn't *look* special. It was straight and plain and unassuming. She was fairly certain her freshman yearbook picture would show the same hairstyle. She touched the ends, her fingers catching in them. The Irish wind made brushing out her hair painful and time consuming. These days she dreaded doing anything with it.

Maybe it was time for a new look. Something that made her feel more special and pretty. She didn't know Lisa Ann well, but she felt more comfortable with her now. Perhaps the time had come to visit the shop with the blue door.

"Gavin," she called. "Do you know if Lisa Ann's shop is open around lunchtime?"

The man appeared with the whiskey bottle and a sparkle in his eyes. He studied her, his silver brows furrowing. "You thinking about a change? Shorter, I think. Maybe a bob to set off that fine chin of yours."

"How did you guess that?" she asked in shock.

"Bartenders in Ireland know everything," he said with a smile. "Come on, Megan."

"Where are we going?" she asked.

Gavin lifted the flapper top of the bar and slid out, towering over her. "Lisa Ann is my cousin, and we'll see to it that she puts you in her chair straightaway. She's the best hairdresser in town."

"Maybe I should tell Eoghan—"

"Does that old rascal look like he needs help?"

She looked over her shoulder to see him gesticulating widely, making the men laugh. Honestly, she couldn't imagine Eoghan ever being caught flat-footed.

Gavin handed her purse to her and helped her off the barstool. "He'll press a few more holdouts for a donation as he tells his tales. Fergal, keep watch while I'm gone. I'll be checking the kegs and the bottles when I return."

Megan startled. "If you're worried about leaving the bar—"

"No, girl, that's just a bit of craic," he said, pausing at the bar's green front door. "Fergal, I'm grabbing your hat since there's a bit of rain and my own is full of cash."

Slapping the blue and cream hat on his head without waiting for an answer, the giant gangly man led her onto the street and then down the sidewalk. The gentle shower wet her hair quickly, and she wrinkled her nose as the rain touched her face. She'd given up using an umbrella. No one used one, and she'd looked conspicuous.

Gavin waved into the stores they passed and said hello to a few people standing in a shop's open doorway, smoking, but he didn't stop, keeping a gentle hand to her back.

"Here we are," he said, pointing across the street and waiting for a few cars to pass before crossing.

When Gavin opened the door for her, Lisa Ann paused in sweeping dark hair from the white tiled floor. The salon was empty but not quiet. Iggy Azalea's "Fancy" was playing loudly, which the woman turned down immediately. "Hi, Megan!"

"Hi, Lisa Ann," she responded, noting how Gavin pointed to himself as if he were waiting for the woman's acknowledgment.

"And what are you doing coming to my place, Gavin McGrath, with my very own ceramics teacher?"

"She's in need of a new look and something on the short side," Gavin said, "and I told her you were the best hair-dresser in town. Don't be making a liar of me. I'll be rushing back to my bar before all those rascals pour themselves a free one when I'm not around. Good luck."

He was already opening the door.

Megan started, "Tell Eoghan I'll—"

"He'll still be at the pub with all the rest of them," Gavin said, rolling his eyes dramatically. "I run a retirement center, didn't you know?"

That made Lisa Ann laugh out loud. "And you love it."

"I do! Come back and show us your new look when you're done, Megan. We'll toast it with another whiskey."

Another whiskey would have her falling on her face, she thought as he closed the door. Lisa Ann walked over to her, sizing up her features the same way she'd sized up her clay in class. She walked around her even, as if taking in her whole person. Somehow the assessment heartened her.

"The angels were with you, girl," Lisa Ann said. "Today was a little slow, and now here you are. We're going to have a right fun time. You're ready for a change then?"

"Yes." In so many ways.

"Gavin has a way of looking at people. Touched by the fairies, that one. But so am I. Short would certainly accentuate your beautiful chin and cheekbones. I think you have pretty ears peeking out from behind your current style."

She pushed her hair back to look in the mirror across from her. "*Pretty ears?*"

"Like the elves." Lisa Ann laughed. "But the big question is for you to answer. Shorter would look grand on you, but do you want it? Because I think you've been hiding a little behind your long hair."

Her eyes tracked back to one of the long mirrors. She *had* been hiding. Trying to fit in. Trying not to make waves. Trying to...let everyone else take care of her and her life so she didn't have to worry about screwing up.

But it had still kept happening, and she was sick of it.

She turned and looked the woman in the eye. "I want it."

"Then that's what we'll do," Lisa Ann said. "Put your purse on the table over here and then come with me. We're about to remake you into the woman you are now. Rather like you talked about with the clay the other night."

Megan and she shared a smile at that.

"I have a feeling you haven't had an easy time of things, but I'm thinking those days are behind you."

"God, I hope so." A laugh came out and then tears filled her eyes. "It's not something I ever want to repeat."

"No, I imagine it isn't. Come now. Let's wash it first, and then we'll cut away what needs going."

And so she did, gently washing Megan's hair and then running her hands through the wet locks while studying her in the mirror.

Except Megan thought Lisa Ann was looking deeper than her reflection, at something inside of her ready to emerge. She had that same feeling whenever she was in her Zen place with the clay, as Liam called it. Or riding a horse.

An exultant feeling filled her chest at the first snip of

the scissors. A bubble popped in her heart. It hurt. But she breathed it out.

Lisa Ann started to sing softly, something in Gaelic that made Megan think of angels. Goose bumps broke out over her arms, and then a beautiful calm enveloped her. She watched as decades of her life were cut away with the lightest of touches, almost like a heavy pot trimmed of its excessive weight.

At the end, Lisa Ann ran her hands through Megan's hair again, cupping her skull in an oddly comforting way.

"Yes," the young woman said softly. "There you are."

A tear spilled down Megan's face, but she didn't brush it aside. It felt cleansing. Awe filled her as she stared in the mirror. The woman staring back at her looked wise...and happy. Pretty, even. She could finally see it.

She liked her very much.

"Thank you," she said after Lisa Ann finished styling her hair. Her hand lifted to touch the new line of hair at her nape and chin.

"You're very welcome," Lisa Ann said, resting her hands gently on her shoulders. "Enjoy the new you. I'll see you in class, which I'm loving, by the way. Not only because of the clay but because Keegan O'Malley has finally come out of his shell. The words on his cows come from his soul, and unlike others in the village, I like them. I can't wait to see what he does next."

Megan caught the gleam in her eyes. Did she like Keegan? It sure sounded like it.

She spontaneously hugged the woman after paying her. When she opened the door, she looked down at the hair Lisa Ann was brushing away and felt the weight of all of it. She was so glad to be leaving it behind.

When she stepped onto the street, a patch of sunlight

was waiting for her. It seemed like a sign. She decided to look for some new clothes. Her first stop was the yoga studio where Liam had purchased her *Visualize Sunshine* shirt. They had a couple of shirts she liked in pale blue and pink —*Zen Days* and *Magic Me*—as well as some patterned yoga pants she found, resembling pottery sgraffito. Another sign, she told herself. She wore the *Magic Me* shirt under her windbreaker with her jeans because she was bringing back her magic. People talked about it all the time in Ireland. She was ready for hers.

Back in the bar, she was congratulated for her new look. Everyone offered to buy her a drink, but she looked at the clock. She needed to pick up Ollie, and she didn't want to be late.

She said goodbye to Gavin and Fergal and the other patrons. Eoghan said he'd see her soon, in class likely, and she kissed his cheek, her heart alight, which only made his smile brighten.

As she passed Keegan O'Malley's cattle, she slowed her car, thinking about Lisa Ann and also looking for a message.

She saw the only word she needed. *Date*.

Yes, she wanted one. With Kade. Tonight if he was free.

When she arrived at the schoolyard, Ollie rushed to her. "Mom! You cut your hair! It looks so good."

Jamie strolled over, tucking his hands in the pockets of his brown trousers, much like Carrick did when he sauntered through his fields. "The new hair suits you, Megan."

"Thank you, Jamie."

The man jolted in place, turning green suddenly.

"Are you all right?" Megan asked.

He held up a hand, nodding, his mouth pursed. "Fine. I'm wondering if you wouldn't mind if Ollie came over tonight to help me with..."

She narrowed her eyes. He really didn't look well. She thought he might faint. "With..."

He cleared his throat, tugging on his shirt collar. "With something I'm building for...Carrick and Angie's wedding present!" The man looked visibly relieved.

"Are you sure you're okay, Mr. Fitzgerald?" Ollie asked. "Hey, do you smell oranges? I used to smell them with Aunt Angie."

Jamie gave a nervous laugh. "How about I take Ollie with me right now? I was going to pop by and see Carrick anyway. That way you can show Kade your new haircut."

Kade? How had he guessed that she was hoping to see Kade tonight?

"Kade is going to *love* your new haircut, Mom."

Ollie tugged on her sweater, and she bent over. He touched her hair lightly, his little fingers learning the new texture. Then he patted her on the back of her head, like she sometimes did to him, and they both laughed. Yes, she and her son had come a long way in a few months.

"Okay, let's go see Carrick," Ollie said, turning away. "Bye, Mom. See you later."

"Don't worry about the time," Jamie said, clearing his throat again as Ollie took his hand. "We'll see to his dinner and bedtime. Good luck, Megan."

She still startled when the Irish used that phrase. They used it as a simple goodbye, but her American brain always registered it as *you're gonna need some luck*. Well, maybe she did.

She was about to ask Kade Donovan out on a date.

CHAPTER TWELVE

Megan would be happy about the sunlight.

The berries on the hawthorn trees lining their path glowed like rubies, and the leaves had turned spring green in the bright light—a grand way to start October. Winston paused and gave a shallow bow, as if thanking the weather. Kade had taught him the tricks, as they called them, knowing the pony had poetry in his soul. "We're almost home, boy," he said as he rubbed the pony's neck.

"Pretty lady!" little Fiadh O'Toole called out, pointing straight ahead.

Kade put his hand on Fiadh's underdeveloped leg and smiled at her. Her large blue eyes, slanted upward in the way of many children with Down syndrome, were fixed on Sorcha, who stood in the middle of the mostly dry path. "You can see her, eh, Fiadh?"

"Yes!" She clapped her hands. "Yay, Kade can see them too. I tell my mom and dad sometimes when I see them, but they don't want to believe me. I think they're scared to believe."

"Who comes to see you?" he asked, giving Sorcha a look

as she reached out a slender hand to pet Winston, who neighed.

"My grandma comes to visit me sometimes," Fiadh said, holding the reins like he'd taught her. "She says she's a spirit and that she looks after me. But I see other ones too, and sometimes they're scary. My parents don't like hearing about them. I don't know who they are, Kade."

He'd experienced the same as a boy, but his granny had given him some advice that had helped. He shared it with the little girl. "Tell them to leave your house if you don't want them there, Fiadh. You say it, and they will listen."

Not all of them would listen, but most of the time they would. Better to empower her.

"If you ever need help with a spirit you want gone, Fiadh," Sorcha interjected, "you call Archangel Azrael. He'll take it away for you."

The small girl repeated the name. "Oh, I like him."

Kade wondered if Fiadh had seen the angel before. He'd learned many people with special needs had gifts. "Sorcha, what can I do for you?"

Her white dress waved in the breeze, and her smile was as infectious as the sunlight dancing on the raindrops clinging to the treetops from the earlier shower. "I've done some serious arranging for you and Megan, and I came to tell you to be ready. Jamie is taking Ollie home with him. He turned as green as pea soup when I appeared to him in the schoolyard."

Kade couldn't help but chuckle. Jamie had only started seeing Sorcha recently, after she came back to help Carrick. He'd even fainted once. "You've always been good craic, Sorcha."

She swayed on the path, causing Fiadh to do the same

in the saddle. "Oh, and I prodded a giant of a cow with the word *Date* on it to encourage Megan to ask you out."

"I've been letting her set the pace, Sorcha," Kade said. "You agreed."

"She's ready to take a leap," Sorcha said, looking him up and down. "Someone has a date tonight. Make sure to change out of your farm clothes. You farmers need a guide-book on dating, I swear."

"I'll even run a comb through my hair, Sorcha. Now be off with you. This is Fiadh's pony ride, after all."

"I like the pretty lady." She reached out to Sorcha, who edged closer to them.

The ghost touched her little forehead and then laid a hand on his arm. "*Guh gir'uh d'eeuh uhn tah ort,*" she said.

And then she disappeared.

"What did she say, Kade?"

He patted Winston, marveling over the mystery that was Sorcha. "May God put luck upon you."

She clapped. "I like luck."

A rich breeze rolled over him, the kind that came in from the sea, and all the windchimes he kept in the trees rang like church bells. Fiadh clapped again, crying out in delight. Kade wondered if Sorcha had orchestrated it. "So do I. Come. Let's keep going down our path."

The metaphor wasn't lost on him. When they reached the stables, he spotted Megan speaking with Fiadh's father, who was resting against his red Berlingo. Kade stopped in his tracks.

She'd cut her hair.

The short length accentuated her jawline, making him more aware of her cute pointy chin. The cut made her look taller, and perhaps it was the new way she held herself, but her body looked slender as opposed to thin. God, she was beautiful.

Sorcha's blessing came to mind again. Had she also been speaking it over him? The way his flesh tingled seemed like a confirmation. He felt a smile break out across his face, and Megan looked over at that exact moment.

Her mouth formed the largest, most stunning smile he'd ever witnessed on her. The golds in her eyes seemed to flash like the chestnut and caramel highlights in her short brown hair. "Hello!" she called out.

"It's another pretty lady," Fiadh said eagerly, pointing to Megan.

"She is pretty and then some," Kade said, loud enough for Megan to hear. "As are you, Fiadh."

Megan blushed, which Darragh O'Toole noted with a grin. "You'll be having all the girls with talk like that, Kade Donovan. Sounds like you had a grand time on your ride, and why wouldn't you? The sun finally came out."

"Megan's been visualizing it," Kade said when they reached them, and he helped Fiadh off the pony.

She'd learned to undo the helmet herself, and while it took some time, she managed. "Look! I did it so fast today."

Kade took the helmet and put his arm around the tiny girl as she hugged his leg. "You did at that. Next you'll be jumping fences."

"No, I won't." She ran over to her father, who lifted her into his arms. "Dad, we need to go. Right now. Kade has a date! Bye, Kade. Bye, pretty lady."

He watched as Megan flinched. *Sorcha, sometimes you're too clever for your own good.*

"We'll be off then," Darragh said, shifting his daughter as Kade opened the car door. "See you next week. Megan, it was right fine meeting you. I'm already looking forward to St. Stephen's Day. Good luck."

Fiadh and her father waved as the Berlingo took off, and Kade shifted on his feet. Megan's face was white now. Did she think he had a date with someone else? Oh, Sorcha.

"I hear we're having a date," he said, crossing to touch her arm. "But before I tell you how happy I am about it, I need to share something from my heart. You look beautiful, love. Pretty doesn't do it justice."

Her mouth parted a couple times. "But... How did you know about our date? I'm so confused."

He slowly lifted his hand, making sure she was open to his touch. When she didn't jolt, he smoothed her hair behind her ear, tracing the short lock with his finger. She shivered. A good sign. "A ghost told me and Fiadh. A nice one. One that's helping matchmake us, so to speak. The truth is: I can see ghosts."

Honesty seemed the best way. She would have to know all of him at some point.

"You can see ghosts." She grabbed the lapel of his navy jacket. "And that little girl can too? Excuse me a moment while I take this in. I know you'd never say something that wasn't true. But it's...not something you hear every day. Although we *are* in Ireland, and only today in the butcher shop, people were talking about the Mayo football team being cursed and Summercrest Manor being haunted. No one blinked an eye."

He chuckled as Sorcha appeared suddenly behind Megan and made a face at him before disappearing again. Deciding it best not to confirm what she'd heard in the butcher shop, he said, "I don't imagine the Irish are the only people who believe in the supernatural, but we do talk about it a lot. In my family, you can't go to a funeral without someone mentioning who they've seen from the past. But that's not the point."

She was holding her breath, so he rubbed her back.

"The point is that I was told to dress up for our date." He gestured to his clothes. "I don't even smell the horse anymore."

Her nose wrinkled. "I suppose I still do. Sometimes. I don't seem to mind it as I probably smell the same way. Kade, I... I don't know what to think here. We have a match-making ghost helping us? Do you know who it is?"

So much for diverting her. He thought about it a moment before saying, "The ghost is Carrick's deceased wife, Sorcha."

"You mean the one the arts center is named after?" She put her hands to her face. "I've seen her picture in the entryway. Oh, my! This is crazy. Does Carrick know? I mean, is he aware that she's around? God, I can't believe I'm talking like this."

He nodded. "Yes, Carrick knows. She helped your sister and him get together, after all."

She grabbed his forearms. "You'd better start at the beginning."

He led her over to sit in one of the two chairs at the small table he had outside the tack room. As he took the saddle off Winston, he told her what he knew. By the end, she was even paler.

"But this is incredible." Her fingers lifted to her gorgeous mouth. "She must have loved Carrick a lot."

"She did," he said quietly as he placed Winston in his stall and joined her at the table. "She wanted him to be happy again. He was mired down in grief, you might recall."

"I do," she said softly. "And now us."

"Yes, love, and now us."

She pressed a finger to the space between her eyes, as if trying to take it all in. "Wow, they must think...or Sorcha must think...that we have a really good chance of being happy together."

"I would agree," Kade answered, making her gaze fly to his. "Ghosts typically don't waste their time."

"I see." She looked down at her hands. "Kade, I have a question, and it's really important. Can you see *any* ghost?"

He felt a ripple of something in his midsection, already knowing what she was going to ask, and his heart broke for her. "I can. For me, seeing them is like seeing people."

She clutched the edge of the table. "Can you see Tyson?" Her voice was hoarse.

"No, love," he said softly. "Sorcha told me he's gone on to whatever was next for him. I wish I could tell you what that is, but it's beyond my knowing and Sorcha's as well."

She rubbed the tip of her nose before whispering, "He didn't love us enough...to help us be happy."

He could not bear the pain this thought caused her. "Megan, love, that's not something you can know. I can't tell you why Sorcha is here helping and Tyson isn't. Best let it go, *mo chroí*."

Her hand went to her nape as she exhaled audibly, as if learning her new shape. "You're right. This was a happy day. Eoghan and I did fundraising for the fair, and I got my hair cut, and I came to ask you—"

"About a date." He took her hand now and traced the back of it with his thumb. "I gladly accept. Where would you like to go?"

"Anywhere really." Her brown eyes seemed larger in her face as she laced their fingers together. "Jamie suddenly volunteered to take Ollie with him, so I'm free."

Kade chuckled. "Sorcha's doing, and I thanked her for

it. Come. How about we take a drive up to the Lost Valley of Uggool? There's a nice seafood place on the water that I think you might like."

"The Lost Valley of what?"

"Uggool," he said slowly. "It's past Westport, but well worth the drive. Since Sorcha seems to have arranged someone to mind Ollie."

"That would be great. I should change maybe, right? Oh, I forgot to show you my new shirt."

She turned shy as she unzipped the windbreaker. He smiled when he caught sight of the pale pink cotton with the message *Magic Me*. "Ah, it looks grand on you. The perfect accompaniment for your new look. Me, though, *I* should change." He squeezed her hand before standing up. "Sorcha's orders. Do you want me to pick you up? I won't be long."

He might shave though, to please her. Their first kiss was hovering in the air, and he wanted to make it as memorable as possible.

"No, I'll sit here with Duke while you're gone if that's all right." She lifted the Jack Russell onto her lap. "It's been a big day so far."

Walking toward her, he cupped the back of her neck. "The grandest, and it's not over yet."

When she looked up at him, hope and longing shone in her eyes. He kissed her forehead and went with his instincts.

"Now that you know about a ghost helping us, there's one more thing you should know." He rubbed her nape gently and swore he heard her purr. "I sensed the woman I'd been waiting for was coming two months before you arrived. Megan, that woman is you. I'll go change now."

He started to whistle after caressing her skin one last

time. As he was leaving the shed, he heard her call his name. Turning around, he was struck by the smile on her face as much as how young she looked, curled up in the chair with his dog nestled against her.

"Kade, I'm glad it's me."

"That makes two of us, love."

He left the shed whistling, his hands tucked into his pockets. She was starting to accept what was between them. The signs were as clear as the stormy portent of gray clouds when they came in from the sea.

The pounding of horse hooves broke into his reverie, and when he looked up, an angry black stallion was bearing him down, its eyes wild with fear. His father was racing after it, shouting at the top of his lungs.

Kade set his weight and threw his hands up in the air, trying to halt the stallion.

"Kade!" Megan yelled.

The horse's eyes grew wilder at her cry, and he lowered his head with a snort as he thundered toward Kade.

All was lost.

Moments before the horse would ram him, Sorcha appeared in front of the stallion, making it rear and squeal. That brief break gave Kade the time he needed to throw himself to the side. His father called out his name as he hit the ground hard and rolled twice. The wind the stallion was carrying rushed over him as it raced past, carrying the scent of oranges. He pushed off the damp earth with a hand and looked over his shoulder. Megan was huddled against the shed's doorway, Duke clutched in her arms. Safe.

Thank God.

Then he spotted Sorcha standing across from him, and although her corporeal body didn't need oxygen, there was enough human left in her that she blew out a breath before disappearing. He needed a moment, so he put his hands on his knees and took a few cleansing breaths, his heart pounding in his ears. Megan's footsteps sounded behind him, and then she was on her knees next to him, touching him as Duke barked beside her.

"Kade! Kade! Are you okay?"

"I'm all right," he said, cracking his neck. He'd be a bit bruised, nothing worse.

His father skidded to a halt when he reached them. "Nothing broken?'

"No," he said, gesturing to where the horse had disappeared. "Who was that? For I surely didn't recognize that stallion."

"I'd thought he might be a good choice for Legend," his dad said, scratching behind his ear.

"No, Dad." Kade stood, helping Megan to her feet. "Absolutely not."

Killian Fitzgerald wasn't normally at a loss for words, but he took his time answering, staring in the direction the stallion had gone. "Perhaps not, but he does have fine breeding. Not so much on the manners but that's what training is for. Come on and brush yourself off so we can go after him. We'll be running after him all night, the way he was acting."

Normally Kade would have helped his father chase down a horse. But not tonight. He took Megan's hand. "Can't, Dad. I have plans."

She glanced between them. "But—"

Kade gave her hand a squeeze. "Dad has plenty of people to call, Megan."

"Do I now?" His father lowered his eyes to where their hands were joined. "And this after I gave in and agreed to have your precious St. Stephen's Day fair on my own land so Tom MacKenna couldn't sabotage it?"

He heard Megan's sharp intake of breath. "I already thanked you for that, Dad. We're all grateful."

Megan cleared her throat. "We are, Killian. Thank you for hosting."

His father's mouth didn't soften. "Isn't my own son supposed to be helping me with a wild stallion terrorizing the countryside? You almost got flattened."

Terrorizing was a bit strong. The stallion had bolted for a reason, and his energy would wind down at some point. His father's friends and stable assistants would help with the search. If it had been any other night, Kade would have done the same. "Then you'd best get after him, Dad."

Killian shook his head after a long pause. "Fine, then. Go on your date." His father stalked off, pulling out his cell phone to call for help.

"Ignore him. He's angry the stallion got away from him —and that it's wrong for Legend. Now he's spoiling for a fight. I'm sorry you had to witness that."

"Me too." She put her hand on his chest, looking into his eyes. "Are you sure you're all right?"

He framed her face, seeing the fear staring back at him. "I am. Sorcha helped divert him. Seems she has an angelic side, after all."

"You'll have to thank her for me," she said, lifting her hand to his jaw. "You have dirt on your face."

When she brushed her fingers gently along his jawline, he felt a whisper of arousal roll through him. It wasn't the moment he'd imagined, but the pull to her was as undeniable as an Irish rain.

He lowered his mouth to hers.

She lifted her head to meet him, and the sweetness of it filled him with joy. When their lips touched, they both jolted at the shock of it. There was fire between them. And magic, like her shirt said. And a tenderness the like of which he'd never experienced.

He brought her against his body and cupped her nape, giving her lips another pass. Her breath shuddered out, and her hands gripped his shoulders as she kissed him back. Closing his eyes, he brushed her lips again, changing the angle of his head to enjoy the right side of her mouth and then the left. Her lips were warm and soft, and while his heartbeat had settled some, its pace increased for a whole new reason.

Her.

He'd dreamed of kissing Megan Bennet, and those dreams were finally a reality. As he lifted a hand to caress the exposed line of her neck, she moaned against his lips— the softest of cries, but it reverberated through his bones. She knew what she wanted deep down.

Him.

They were finally where he'd always hoped they would be. He kissed her again with more strength, and she kissed him back, teasing his lower lip. Learning him. He traced the long length of her back, letting her have her way. When she finally raised her head, she was smiling. Grinning actually.

Yes, she was pretty proud of herself. First, a new haircut. And now, their first kiss. His happiness soared to new heights.

"I loved that," she whispered, touching his jaw again. "I didn't know kissing could be that sweet."

He caressed her lower back, making the golds in her eyes fire. "Neither did I."

"Are you sure you don't want to help your father?" She held his gaze. "We can have our date another night."

"No, what's between us is more important." He kissed her softly again, because now he had the right. "Only a stupid man would spend his evening chasing after a wild horse that wasn't his when the woman of his dreams wants to be with him."

"And you're not stupid," she said, the octaves of her voice as sweet as her kiss.

He gestured to the dirt on his shirt. "But now I really do need to change. Would you like to come with me and wait? I don't think the horse will come back, but I'd rather you be inside somewhere just in case. My cottage is down the path."

There was a new awareness in her eyes, one he reveled in. "I'd love that."

"Then come, *mo chuisle*."

She took his hand. "What does that mean?"

"It means the pulse of my heart." He needed to look at her as he said the rest, so he turned toward her, their bodies inches apart. "What it really means is you're the one who makes my heart beat."

Her other hand rose to rest in the center of his chest. "I love that too."

He kissed her again, lingering over her lips. As they started to walk to his cottage, he marveled at how quickly life could change.

When he'd arisen this morning, he hadn't known the events of the day would stray beyond the norm.

When he found his bed tonight, the taste of her lips would still be on him.

Life in all its wonder stole around him as he led her to his home.

CHAPTER THIRTEEN

S he hadn't expected a thatched cottage.

"I love your house," she exclaimed as they reached the end of a path lined with large Monterey pines and ash trees.

The grassy knoll in front of them seemed to be cushioning the white cottage with the red door. Three small latticed windows lined in red graced the front. A small chimney peeked out of the brown thatch, and rose hips and old vines trailed up the concrete front.

He squeezed her hand, which he'd held as they'd walked through the quiet grove of trees. "I'm glad. It belonged to my grandparents, and before my granny died a couple years ago, she invited me to live here after she passed on. It's been good to be on my own. I was living with my parents in the main house before and finding it a little constricting. Come inside."

Duke raced ahead, barking, and then disappeared around the right corner. Kade opened the door—which she noted wasn't locked—and stopped in the doorway. He traced her cheek, a smile lighting up his gorgeous face. She didn't want to let go of his hand, so she just smiled up at him. He lowered his head and kissed her again, slow and achingly sexy.

"Welcome to my home, love. Do you want a cup of tea while I change?"

"I can make it," she said, patting his chest. "Do you want one?"

Another kiss was brushed on her lips before he said, "No, I'm going to shower. Make yourself at home."

He disappeared through the main room, and since she knew Irish cottage floorplans were fairly standard, she made her way to the doorway past the hearth and the single settee. Sure enough, there was a small kitchen. She filled the kettle with water and opened the cupboards looking for tea—she found Lyons—and then chose a simple white mug.

Alone, she touched her lips, savoring their recent kisses. She hugged herself. This feeling coursing through her was unlike anything she'd previously experienced. She felt happy. Excited. Warm. Hopeful.

At the beginning of her relationship with Tyson, she'd been both excited and afraid. It wasn't like that with Kade. She simply wanted to wrap her arms around him and never let go. When the water boiled, she made her tea and went back into the main room, taking a seat on the antique settee. Like the one in her cottage, it wasn't comfortable, but she didn't care. She leaned back against it with the mug on the small table by her side and enjoyed the quiet sounds of the shower running.

Her mind went to Kade again, her mind giving her a tantalizing fantasy of the water running over his naked body. Her belly tightened, and her breasts tingled.

She wanted him.

And she wasn't afraid of that either. What a revelation!

She sipped her tea and let her eyes wander. A trio of photos of him with his family and his ponies graced the bookshelves alongside volumes of Yeats and Swift. She wondered if the books had been chosen by him or his grandparents. The small table in the corner only held a white sugar bowl, suggesting he rarely sat there except to drink tea. She wondered where he usually ate. Perhaps up at the main house? She knew he grabbed lunch there during the day, as he'd made her a ham and cheddar sandwich before. But it was the silver tray holding a cocktail shaker and a collection of liquor as well as a few smaller bottles in the front whose labels she couldn't make out that captivated her curiosity. The Irishmen she'd met usually drank beer or whiskey.

The shower went silent. She had a fantasy of him pulling on his clothes, making her body warm. She shifted on the settee, making it squeak. The sound of his boots coming down the hall reached her, and she looked over to the doorway. When he appeared, happiness and outright arousal rushed through her.

His brown hair was damp and ruffled from a towel. He'd changed into dark jeans and a navy pullover, and he looked good. Really good.

"You look beautiful sitting there," he said, crossing over to her. "Mind if I have a taste of your tea?"

She lifted her mug, and he brushed a caress over her hand before he took the tea from her and brought it to his lips. As he drank, he kept his gaze on her, rendering her breathless.

"Are you ready to go?"

In that moment, she didn't want to go anywhere or do anything but kiss him. Still, she gathered herself and stood up. His smile grew, his eyes crinkling at the corners, and he set the mug on the table and opened his arms to her. She wrapped herself around him, savoring the warm, hard muscles of his chest and the tender way he held her.

"I didn't imagine ever feeling like this again," she whispered. "But honestly, it was never this wonderful with Tyson. Is that terrible of me to say?"

His hand tangled in her short hair, cupping her head. "Honesty is never terrible. I was with Mary Kathleen, my childhood sweetheart, for ten years, and I never felt like this."

She darted back. "Ten years?"

He must have heard the surprise in her voice because he chuckled. "We were fifteen when we started dating. Growing up around here, you know everyone. Mary Kathleen was my first kiss—and I hers. Everyone thought we'd marry, and it would have been good. She's a nice woman. We enjoyed each other. We even had passion for each other some of the time."

Some of the time. "I understand that." When Tyson had come home, she hadn't always wanted him. Ollie was right. Sometimes she'd struggled for what to say to him, and he her. Undressing with him in a bedroom he rarely slept in had filled her with tension, and not the sweet kind. She remembered one homecoming, when he'd taken her quickly, his eyes closed the whole time, and then rolled onto his side away from her while she lay awake, unable to sleep.

Kade rubbed her back soothingly. "In the end, I knew we both had someone else out there. When I broke things off, I told her so. Because she knew I had the gift, she believed me. Four months later, she met Padraig Teskey. Before she married him, she thanked me and said she'd never been happier. They have four children now."

"That's an incredible story." She touched his chest. "How is it you know these things?"

"I simply do," he said, shrugging. "My father isn't much for that answer even though his mother was the same way. He said it drove him mad growing up. Well, shall we go?"

She stroked the fabric of his shirt, imagining the skin under it. "It's tempting to stay here."

He lifted her chin and kissed her. "It is, and yet I think it would be better for us to go. There's no need to rush what's coming. When we're ready, we'll know."

"You don't think I'm ready?"

Her knee-jerk reaction of feeling wrong kicked in before she realized he was smiling at her in the same glorious way he always did. The unrest inside her started to ebb away, like water from the shoreline.

"I think making love with each other is going to be wonderful and more powerful than we both can imagine right now." He caressed her cheek. "Maybe it's because I work with animals, but even in their mating process, there's a courting period where they come to know each other. I'd like that for us."

She realized she did too. She'd only been with three guys—her high school boyfriend, a short relationship in college, and then Tyson. She'd gone to bed with each of them quickly, caught up in the high of liking and being liked and wanting to please them. Perhaps it was time to try another way. "I'd like that too, but I *do* want you."

His brown eyes warmed. "I want you too," he said, leaning down and kissing her neck. "And I really do love this new haircut and look. Megan, you are so beautiful."

She finally felt that way, although it was new and precious—like kissing and touching him. "And I think you're the most wonderful man in the whole world."

169

He laughed. "I wish my father believed that. But let's go. We have a nice drive ahead."

The drive wasn't nice. It was *magnificent*. Brown and purple mountains hugged long planes of green and gold. Cows grazed. Mountain sheep hugged the road, their independence clear from their proud stance. And wrapping around it all was a sky she once would have called gray.

"You're right," she said, holding his hand as he drove. "The skies are pearly."

He lifted her hand for a kiss. "I knew you'd see it when you were ready, *mo chuisle*."

My pulse, she recalled. She was the pulse that beat his heart. But he did the same for her. It gave her the courage to say, "Kade, I'm falling in love with you."

"Good," he said, smiling that beautiful smile of his. "Then we're of the same mind, for I'm head over heels in love with you."

She pressed back into the seat, his words making her want to tap her feet in delight.

When they reached the restaurant, she exited his jeep with her mouth agape. Tucked around the corner of the narrow valley running through mountains covered in pine and stone, a large lake stretched out in shades of mirror and midnight. "It's gorgeous here."

"I've always thought so," he said, taking her hand. "And quiet. When I was a boy, I thought trees absorbed the sound around them. Now I know they do. Especially the ones around here. These are old trees, you see, planted hundreds of years ago. I can't imagine how far-reaching their roots are, but you can feel the wisdom in them. The seafood we're going to eat tonight comes from this lake too, and the magic you feel here is always in the meal."

Some of his comments were startling to her. Until

Ireland, until him, she'd never believed that anything could be magical. But he was right—it *was* quiet, the kind of silence usually found in a church or a library. Yet her heart wasn't only peaceful. She was content in a way she hadn't experienced in a long time. Maybe ever. She touched her shirt. She felt like she was part of the magic now. That was certainly something she'd be writing in her journal tonight.

"Kade, I'm really grateful to be here in Ireland, and I'm really glad to be here with you too."

"Me too, love," he said, kissing her softly and then leading her to the restaurant's bright blue front door. She somehow wasn't surprised that Kade knew their young greeter, a blond teenager, or the charming bartender with the bald head and friendly smile.

"What are you planning on drinking?" he asked after they were seated beside a large window with a view of the lake and mountains. "Tom makes a wonderful Irish Old Fashioned. That's my favorite here. Some Powers Gold whiskey, Bénédictine liquor, and bitters. I think you'd enjoy it."

She remembered the cocktail grouping on the silver tray in his cottage. "How is it you know and like cocktails? Don't most Irish people usually drink whiskey or beer?"

"Do you remember me telling you about my childhood friend who fell off a tractor?" he asked, his face softening. "Ryan is a bartender at his cousin's bar in Dublin. He's a mad scientist with cocktails, I'm proud to say. It's an incredible story of family helping each other. He hasn't only embraced the city and a busier way of life. He's thrived."

"How wonderful," she said, loving the way he smiled as he talked about his friend.

"I tell many of my clients this story," Kade said, his face alight with joy, "so they can imagine something special for themselves. They might not know what it is yet, but hope in the human heart is critical to living. Without it, we wither. I try and go to Dublin every six months to see Ryan, and he's taught me to make a few drinks. He says the ingredients are simple and that's where the magic is. Making them keeps him feeling close to me. He's a wonder to behold, Megan, let me tell you."

She reached her hand out to him. "Kade Donovan—you are quite simply the best man alive."

"You keep saying that, love." He traced the delicate V between her thumb and forefinger, sending a shiver through her. "Do you know what that makes you?"

She shook her head.

"The most wonderful woman in the world."

"I'm not." Then she laughed. "Liam would say I have more journal writing to do."

"He would at that," Kade said softly. "You are to me though, so until you believe, let me tell you why I feel as I do."

Her breath caught as she waited. She found herself leaning forward even.

"Megan, to me you're like the sunrise and the first roses in spring. You're everything good in the world, and I'm so glad you've come to Ireland at last—to be with me."

Swallowing thickly, she tangled her fingers with his. "I am too."

His brown eyes held hers as they drank Irish Old Fashioneds and feasted on a seafood medley of lobster, crab, and cod. She asked him which cocktails he liked to make, and he gave her a few examples, describing the ingredients and promising to make her one anytime she wanted.

She wanted.

Over sticky toffee pudding, which they shared, he asked

her more about her pottery, and she ended up telling him stories about those first years, when she'd had her center and could make piece after piece without thought.

"You're going to have that back and then some, Megan," he said as they left the restaurant and drove home.

Home.

The word had seemed natural. Caisleán did feel like home. And so did the man next to her.

She texted Jamie to check on Ollie and was reassured that she needn't worry—he was staying with Angie and Carrick.

When she put her hand on Kade's thigh, his eyes met hers in the darkness of the car. She knew he was smiling, and as they passed between the pewter-tinged mountains lit by a crescent moon, she knew she wasn't just falling in love with him.

She was in love with him.

He took her back to the farm for her car, and when they arrived beside the shed, he leaned over and kissed her. His mouth started out slow and gentle, but soon his tongue traced the seam of her lips. She opened her mouth to him and fell into a pool of desire. The seat belt was constraining, and she chafed at it holding her in place. Kade nipped her lower lip and edged back.

"We should get you back to your cottage, love," he said, his voice thick with desire and emotion. "I'll follow you home."

"You don't need to." But how she loved that he wanted to.

"A man takes his girl home."

She reveled in the deep timbre of his voice, realizing what he said was true.

She was his.

CHAPTER FOURTEEN

His mother drove into his yard the next morning as he led Legend out of her stall.

Since she rarely came down, Kade knew she'd heard about his date.

"Hi, Mum."

"Hi," she said with a grin after lowering the window of her purple Jeep. "I'm off to work, but your father tells me you had a date last night. With Megan. *Finally*, Shannon said, but you know your mind. Of course, this was after your father came home cursing up a storm chasing down that wild beast that almost ran you down."

"How long did it take him?" Kade asked, pleased he had no guilt over not helping.

"Four hours and then some." Nicola rolled her eyes. "When he curses like that, I remind him that he could sell the whole lot." Her gaze shifted to the horse. "That's Legend, yes? How he could have thought that mad horse would be acceptable to Legend is beyond me. I told him to listen to you, but we know how many times I've said that."

They shared an eye roll. "I still am grateful when you say it, Mum."

"You're welcome."

He walked over to her jeep when she made no move to leave, Legend's soft footfalls accompanying him.

"I wondered if Megan might be for you when you took the boy camping overnight a month or so ago," she said, looking straight at him. "Ollie's a good boy, and she's coming alive again. You'd be the one knowing how to help them thrive. You always have. You seem to be coming alive yourself. Love looks good on you, son."

When she held out her hand, he grabbed it. "I'm glad you came by today."

"I need to leave if I'm going to beat Shannon to the shop." She dropped his hand and blew him a kiss. "She had a date last night too."

He didn't bother to ask with whom. His sister was like Liam that way. She loved to date around. "Wouldn't it be funny if Megan and I ran into Shannon and one of her dates one night?"

"She'd love it. You know her. She's happy for you too, Kade, but I expect she'll tell you that herself soon enough."

His sister did tell him, in fact, coming by after work that day. He'd just finished his last pony ride. Megan had left a couple of hours ago since Angie was hanging out with his aunt. Freshly kissed after a pony ride, she'd told him her hands were itching to mold clay. He'd told her to go to the studio early before she went to fetch Ollie. She had pieces to make for the St. Stephen's Day fair, after all. She'd gone after a few more kisses.

"Your face says it all, brother," Shannon said, lifting the saddle off Winston before he could. "You're in love."

"I am, indeed." He laughed as Winston bowed to her.

175

"You seem to have all the males in the local area wrapped around your finger, my horse included."

"He has good taste." His sister walked over to Legend's stall. "How about a ride? You can tell me all about things. I'd like to ride this girl."

"You think you can handle her?" Kade grabbed a saddle for his sister and set it on Legend when she didn't respond to his teasing.

Shannon took over the task of saddling the horse. "I need fast. Come on, I'll race you."

Legend gave his sister the ride of her life. They thundered across the shore, seals scattering and barking at them. Shannon laughed, her long brown hair flying madly behind her. Kade patted Blaze's side. She couldn't match Legend's speed, but he didn't need her to. He simply took in the sight of a patch of sunlight breaking through the clouds, turning the lichen to a spring green as it danced in the water's shallows. He led Blaze through the water since the horse loved to splash. He thought about Megan and how beautiful she'd looked yesterday, gazing up at him with love in her eyes.

They'd turned a corner, and their roots would only grow stronger.

Shannon was waiting for him when he reached the path they would take back to his yard. "She's wonderful, Kade. I can see why Dad is so tied up to have a foal from her. Did Mom have it right about your deal with Dad?" She parroted back the details of the deal he'd made with his father.

"You have the right of it." He brought Blaze even with Legend as the horses walked past the rows of fresh blackberries hanging thickly from their thorny branches.

"I wish things were different between you two." Her gaze was troubled. "I know you'll find the right horse for

Legend and it will all work out, but you shouldn't have to do it in the first place."

"My relationship with him has always been more complicated," Kade said, "and it's not something you need to feel guilty about." But she still did, and he knew it.

She positioned Legend closer and touched his arm. "The guilt is mine. I've wondered if it would change things if I had an interest in taking over the farm. But I don't think it would. Dad still expects you to want to do it because you're a man. Sometimes he makes me want to scream."

His sister had always been like his horses—in need of her independence. "I hear you're going to be in the St. Stephen's horse race."

She shot him a look like she was angling for him to share his chips with her. "Why do you think I was trying out Legend? I want to ride her for the race, Kade."

He chuckled. "I should have known you were up to something. Legend isn't my horse. You'll have to ask Dad."

Her nose scrunched. "I'll have to think up a way to get him to agree. I can tell you don't think he will."

"We're planning on covering Legend around that time. She should be in season." All they needed now was to find a horse.

"No chance then," Shannon said, making a face. "Any of Dad's horses you could suggest?"

Kade thought about it a moment. "I think you challenge Dad straight on. Tell him you're racing and if you're to have any chance at beating him fair and square, what horse would he give you? His competitiveness will kick in."

"Brilliant!" She grinned at him. "Come on. I'll race you back. The racing looks as good on you as your new girl."

She was off before he could agree. Nudging Blaze, he raced off after his sister. When he arrived in the yard, his heart warmed at the sight. His friends had all come by, as he'd known they would. Brady. Declan. Liam. Jamie. Carrick.

Brady walked over to him, making kissing noises. "At last! You've finally found your woman. How're your lips? Do you need some lip balm? You need to break them in slow, man, or you'll have problems."

"Like you'd know lately, Brady," his twin brother called out. "Your lady love is a sweet woman. As is her boy."

"Ollie is that and more," said Jamie, laughing. "The other day I found him and Chloe Kilmartin in a tree talking about their dreams of the future. It was rather sweet."

Kade thought about Megan's Dream Jar. Like mother, like son, it seemed.

"So he's a romantic like his mother," Liam said, clapping him on the back. "I was glad to hear the news of the date, although I knew it was coming. She's a grand girl, my cousin."

"That she is," he answered, turning his attention to the one friend who had yet to say his piece.

He and Carrick Fitzgerald had always shared a deeper understanding, one where words weren't needed. This time, there was an added piece: Carrick was marrying Megan's sister. His friend put his hands on his hips and rocked on the heels of his navy wellies. "Since we were kids, you always knew the way of things differently than most. I'm glad to see you smiling because that tells me all's right in the world."

"It is," he simply responded.

A powerful scent of oranges wafted through the yard.

Carrick smiled and nodded. "Ah, that pleases my heart. I see the way of it even better now."

Kade hadn't expected Sorcha to communicate with

Carrick again, but she likely knew her efforts on his friend's behalf would please him.

"You see the way of it?" Jamie said, elbowing his brother in the side and looking at Kade. "That's the understatement of the century."

Brady sniffed the air. "Do you smell oranges? Kade, you're not feeding your horses extra vitamin C, are you?"

"Oranges!" Declan shoved Brady gently. "Why would he give horses oranges? You're becoming as daft as Aunt Olive."

Kade grinned as Carrick cleared his throat. Jamie just slapped a hand to his forehead. He'd probably realized what Kade had—if Brady was smelling oranges, Sorcha had plans for him too. He couldn't wait to see what would unfold for his friend, the traveling postal publican.

"I only smell horses and rain in the air," Shannon said, wrinkling her nose.

Liam only shrugged when Brady shot a confused look at him, making Kade curious. His friend was so attuned to certain things—energy and signs and the like—but he'd never mentioned being able to see ghosts like his father and his oldest brother, Wyatt. Time would tell.

Everyone turned at the sound of a car approaching. Kade's heart warmed in his chest, seeing that it was Megan's. His friends all turned to him.

"We'll be leaving you then," Declan said, jerking his thumb in their direction. "New girl always trumps old friends."

"That it does," Brady said, making kissy faces again.

"Off with you," Kade said, shooing them playfully like he would his ponies.

The others grinned and made their way to their cars as Megan pulled to a stop.

Carrick put his hand on his shoulder. "Angie's happy for you both and trying to give you space."

"But she's still the older sister." Kade waved as Ollie shouted his name as he got out of the car. "Tell her I'm happy to have her call if she'd like."

Kade smiled as Megan stepped out of the car too, only to be surrounded by his friends. She touched the ends of her hair, and he imagined they were exclaiming over her new look.

"Don't expect a morning visit," Carrick said, wincing.

He could have been referring to the morning visit Kade and the others had paid him and Angie after they first found their way to each other, but Kade didn't think so. He put a hand on his friend's shoulder and looked him straight in the eye. There was awe mixed with a new love and tenderness he'd never seen there. "Ah... I see the way of it. I couldn't be happier for you two. Congratulations."

"We haven't told anyone yet as it's early," Carrick said, "although I know it will be fine."

Kade sensed that as well. "I do too, if that helps."

"It does." Carrick stopped short as oranges filled the yard again. "More confirmation. I'm happy Sorcha is still around."

"She's got grander plans than we imagined, I expect." Kade chuckled as Declan picked Ollie up and threw him in the air, making the boy cry out with joy.

"She always did." Carrick tipped his head up to the sky, as if lost in thought for a moment. "Well, I'll be off, then. Enjoy your evening."

"Thanks for minding Ollie last night after Jamie dropped him off," Kade said, watching as Shannon bunched up her hair to Megan's length while Brady made slashing motions with his hand as if to dissuade her from cutting it.

"We're happy to mind him anytime," Carrick said. "But you know that."

With that, Carrick strolled over to the parked cars. Ollie ran to him, and Carrick picked the little boy up. How changed he was from when he'd first come to Caisleán. He'd been a tad sad and more than a little rebellious, wanting to break free from the past.

Now, he was flourishing with all the love and attention around him, laughing and playing as boys his age should. Kade took a moment to appreciate the scene. He truly was the luckiest of men to have such friends.

To have such a woman.

When he walked over to the group, he put his hand on Megan's back and rubbed the knot of nerves at the base of her spine, pleased when she settled back against him.

"Her hair is so gorgeous!" Shannon touched it gently again, making Megan blush. "I wish my hair could look like that."

"If you cut your hair like that," Brady said, "it would explode into clown hair after the first rain shower. Better to keep what you have now, as it's completely beautiful."

Liam snorted as Shannon kissed Brady's cheek. "Is it any wonder the women in the village give him jams and jellies and all manner of treats?"

"He makes a living with his mouth," Declan said, "while I make one with my cleaver. Come, friends. Let's go."

"Oh, you don't need to leave," Megan said as Duke raced over to her for some attention of his own.

"Yes, we do," Brady said, steering his brother to the car.

"Enjoy those steaks I dropped off at your house, Megan," Declan called. "Clearly you didn't enjoy them last night."

Cheeky fellow, Kade thought, as he waved goodbye to his friends. The last to go was Carrick, who'd stood aside talking to Ollie. When his friend tousled the boy's head and sent him into the shed, their eyes met again. He nodded, understanding. Ollie knew they were dating too. Oh, how small the village was. He would need to talk to him.

"Megan, love," he said, kissing the top of her head. "Would you mind starting the tea back at my cottage? Duke can keep you company. Ollie and I will join you in a moment."

She put her hand to his chest. "He was quiet when I picked him from Angie's. They went into town for ice cream. Do you think he could have heard something?"

"I do. I'll talk to him. I imagine he'll talk to you too when he's ready."

She picked up Duke, laughing as the dog gave her kisses. "He's happier when I just let him be a little boy. I was too overbearing with him before. All of you have been such a great influence."

"He's been wonderful for us as well," Kade said. "After I speak with him, perhaps I'll bring him by yours to pick up those steaks Declan mentioned? We can make them at my cottage for dinner."

"That would be great," she said with a smile. "I love the idea of having dinner with you again. But with Ollie this time."

"Me too. We'll have a fine dinner. And I'm making cocktails." He kissed her cheek, knowing the boy was watching from the shed. "See you soon."

Megan gave him a trusting look that shot straight to his heart and then set Duke down. The dog barked and trotted alongside her.

Kade strode toward Ollie, who was pretending to make circles in the dust on the shed's floor with his shoe.

"You have something you want to talk to me about, I think." Kade opened his arms as he crouched down. "Come here, Ollie."

The little boy ran over to him and hugged him. "Are you really dating my mom? One of my friends from school told me when Aunt Angie and I went for ice cream."

Kade gently pressed the boy back so he could see him. "That's the way of it. I love your mother very much. As much as I love you. How do you feel about that?"

Ollie's smile started slowly before breaking into an outright grin. "Good. I love you too, Kade, and I'm really glad you love my mom. Liam says we should all be loved."

Such profound words for so little a boy. "He's right," Kade said, cupping the boy's head. "How do you feel about spending more time around here?"

"I love the farm! I love Duke. And I love the horses. Kade, I want to grow up and ride a horse really fast. I even want to jump a fence like I've seen you do. Will you teach me how?"

Kade remembered being that age and wishing for the future. When his friend had gotten hurt, he'd stopped wishing. He'd let life unfold, and it had worked for him. But maybe he needed to start wishing again. Like for the new house he wanted to build for him, Megan, and Ollie. And for seeing that *baby on the way* look he'd noticed in Carrick's eyes in his own mirror.

"I'll teach you anything that's for me to teach." Kade smiled when the boy let out a whoop. "And you have plenty of other new friends to help you learn whatever else your heart desires."

"I know!" Ollie's green eyes sparkled. "I love Ireland.

It's like you always say. It's the best place on earth. Are you going to marry my mom?"

From one thought to the next. A little boy's mind was like a pendulum. "It's early yet, but that's what I'm hoping for—wishing for, in fact."

"Good!" He nodded. "I think it would be okay with my dad."

Kade waited for him to continue.

He put a finger to the side of his mouth, his smile fading. "He was gone all the time. He didn't want to be with us. You do. I like you better. Does that make me bad?"

"No," Kade said, cupping his little arms. "Telling the truth is always good. Deep down you know the way of things. You listen to that, you're golden for life."

"I like how you talk," Ollie said, smiling. "You Irish talk different, but I'm learning. Do you want to know what word I learned today from Aaron Patterson after he told me about you and my mom?"

Kade imagined it was going to be a good one. He'd gone to school with Aaron's father. "Tell me."

"Slobbering. That's when you kiss a girl."

Kade bit the inside of his cheek. He remembered Jamie talking about Ollie and Chloe Kilmartin perched in the trees, sharing their dreams. "Are you thinking about kissing a girl?"

"Maybe." He lifted a shoulder. "Her name is Chloe, and she has the prettiest red hair. The other kids make fun of her sometimes and call her a ginger. They make me so mad I want to punch them, even though I know I could get into trouble."

When Ollie looked down and kicked at the ground, Kade hugged him again, thinking through what to tell the little boy. Many of his special needs clients told him about other people making fun of them for being different. Growing up, he'd witnessed plenty of cruelty to Ryan after his accident, something that had infuriated him. "One of my friends was made fun of for being different. I'll tell you what my mom told me. You can't punch everyone, so it's better to find another way to handle it."

His mother had pointed out how often his dad had punched people growing up, something that hadn't helped him one bit until he joined the local boxing club. That *had* helped him expel some of the anger and frustration he'd felt, but it wouldn't work for everyone.

"Ignoring it will drive those people mad because they're doing it for the attention. But it's okay to tell them to stop. They might not, but at least you'll know you stood up for your friend."

"I want her to know I won't let anyone hurt her," Ollie whispered. "My dad used to tell me that. About taking care of my mom when he was gone."

Kade could feel the boy's complicated feelings toward his father, something he understood all too well. Parents made strong impressions on their children. Still, it was up to each person what their legacy would be. "He was right. It's good for the people you care about to know you'll stand up with them, especially if they're younger or aren't as strong as you. You know, Ollie... You're already turning into a really good man. Even at eight years old."

The boy lit up. "I am?"

Kade smoothed his hair, thin and brown like his mother's. "You are."

"Good, because I want to be like you and Liam and Carrick and Mr. Fitzgerald. Oh, and Mr. O'Dwyer. He's pretty cool too."

"All good company." Kade stood up. "How about we go

and grab those steaks from your house? I'm making dinner for us."

Ollie walked alongside him as they left the shed and headed to his jeep. "Are we having dinner every night now that you and Mom are dating?"

A few rooks called out as they neared their perch, and a magpie landed on a hawthorn tree heavy with red berries. "We'll have to ask your mom about that, but I imagine many nights, yes. There might be a few others where I'll take your mom out to dinner, and you can stay with one of our friends. How does that sound?"

Ollie giggled. "So you and my mom can do the slobbering?"

Kade had to hold back laughter. "Aren't you full of *craic*? Come on. Your mom is waiting."

After their short errand was concluded, Ollie shot out of the jeep with a grin. "I'll race you to the cottage."

Ollie darted off like a slingshot. Kade wasn't one to go full speed, so he jogged after the boy with the butcher bag swinging in his hand. Two swans flew overhead, the sound of their massive wings audible in the quiet around him. He watched the boy run toward his home, a feeling of rightness in his chest.

The scent of oranges enveloped him, and he sent off a blessing to Sorcha for her help. She would know about Carrick and Angie's little secret, of course, and he had no doubt she was delighted. How far they'd all come, and in so short a time.

Megan was waiting for them in the doorway of his cottage with Duke, her short hair shining golden in the soft late afternoon sunlight. She was smiling from ear to ear as Ollie reached her. He wrapped his arms around her leg, saying something that made her face go blank with shock.

Then the boy raced inside with the little dog. Her smile returned, although she was blushing.

"What did he say to you?" Kade asked when he stopped in front of her.

"He said he was glad we're slobbering and that he loves Ireland." Her brow wrinkled. "Kade, what's slobbering?"

He leaned in to her ear. "I'll show you later. Come. I'm about to make you a cocktail. Anything you'd like in particular?"

"Anything?" she asked, taking his free hand when he extended it to her.

"I probably can't make a piña colada, but we Irish don't drink that anyway."

"Make something you think I'll like." There was the hint of a challenge in her eyes.

This time he did kiss her, lightly on the lips. Ollie knew they were together. Now it was time for him to see the affection between them. "I know just the thing."

He led her inside and made her a gin fizz while Ollie chased the dog through the house.

She hummed at the first sip. "I love it. And I love being here with you—with Ollie playing with Duke. Kade, I would love to do this every night."

Ollie had shared that wish easily, but he knew it was difficult for Megan to make such an admission. Taking her hand, he leaned in and kissed her again. "Then we will. How did pottery go today, by the way?"

The golds in her brown eyes shone brightly. "Incredible. I think I've locked into my center."

He wasn't surprised to hear it.

Love was the ultimate center.

CHAPTER FIFTEEN

Donal's answer to their problem was a doorbell.
A doorbell.

"Are you out of your ever-loving mind?" Bets placed her hands on her hips. "No one has a doorbell in this part of Ireland."

He beamed at her. "Exactly! We're to have the finest doorbell anyone around here has ever seen. It has a camera that works twenty-four seven, facial recognition, and automated messages when anyone shows up."

He pulled the user manual out of the box and flipped through the glossy pages. She took the opportunity to look under her gold settee for her car keys. After some serious making out this week, she'd lost both sets. Again.

She was having a horrible time focusing on the myriad details required for the art center's grant application. All she did was fantasize about Donal—so much so she had to carry around bag of ice to cool down. Something had to give.

"This had better work, Donal." The closer it came to

Liam moving out, the more her temperature seemed to rise. She was sure her blood was boiling now.

"It's going to work. Aha! I found the messages. If we're occupied, we can have it say, 'No one can come to the door' or 'you can leave it.' It's brilliant, Bets. We'll be the talk of the village with this new beauty, and we won't have to be rude to any of our friends. Let's go to the pub tonight to tell everyone about it."

That *was* important. She had to give him credit for being considerate. It wasn't like they could tell everyone not to pop by because they planned to have sex on every available surface in her house any time of day. The general consensus was well known—there was no such thing as spontaneous sex, least of all inside one's house. Okay, perhaps the people in Dublin were different, but she couldn't be sure. Also, she didn't have any interest in living there.

So she went along with his plan, and they brought the doorbell to the pub that night. Before long, the men clustered around him, making appreciative grunts, in the corner by the bar.

She'd shared everything with her friends, the Lucky Charms, of course, and they'd shown up to offer their support. Angie and Megan were there too, because Kade had offered to have a boys' dinner with Ollie. Bets was happy for Kade, whom she loved like a son, and Megan, who deserved happiness. They both seemed to be walking on air. She hoped she would be walking on air soon. Her horniness had her feeling very heavy these days, especially in her belly.

She turned her head to see how Donal's plan was progressing. "One might wish men could move past grunting at the newest thing," Bets said, picking up her Guinness.

"But if this works, Bets," Nicola said with a knowing look, "you'll be needing this little book I ordered for you. In case you've forgotten anything."

The other women craned their heads to see Nicola passing a navy gift bag to her under the table. When Bets peeked inside, she sputtered. *The Kama Sutra: A Modern Sensual Exploration* stood out in bold black letters with a cartoon-like picture of two people doing it Indian style.

"You brought this book here?" She immediately lowered her voice when a few of the people at surrounding tables turned around. "To the village pub? Are you insane, girl?"

Nicola only laughed.

Megan fidgeted with the collar of a navy pullover Bets had never seen.

"What book?" Siobhan made a grab for it.

Bets deflected her. "Not here. Jeez! Come to the bathroom. All of you."

Angie sent her a puzzled look, which made her peaked complexion look even sicker. She'd made up a bum excuse about not drinking tonight—a first—saying she had an upset tummy. Her sister had fallen for it and ordered her some peppermint tea.

Bets and her friends had all shared a look, knowing the upset tummy/not drinking routine was code for morning sickness. The worst. Bets had puked every morning for what had felt like forever with her boys. She didn't miss those days.

Of course, no one congratulated Angie and Carrick, who was part of the male grunting committee. They understood it was still early in the pregnancy. But Brigid, who was imagining what it would be like to be a grandma, no doubt, couldn't hide her soft smile. If it was true, she'd be the first in their circle. How fun! Although Bets was glad her boys weren't rushing into anything, she couldn't wait for a grandbaby.

All the better to have Donal install this doorbell so they could get on with wild monkey sex *now*, because she wasn't going to send a message that said *No one can come to the door* if her grandbaby was out there.

When the lot of them had finally squeezed into the bathroom, Brigid plucked the gift bag out of her hands and pulled out the book. Her gasp was almost as funny as Siobhan's squeal. Megan's eyes went wide as saucers.

Angie's grin brightened her complexion. "Now that's a classic. Nicola, I might need a copy for my honeymoon. Just in case Carrick and I miss something. I hope it's okay to say that in front of you, Brigid."

"Of course, dear." Her future mother-in-law patted her arm. "I want you and Carrick to be as happy as you can be in your marriage bed. I think Seamus and I have done pretty well in that area ourselves."

Megan edged back and jumped when she accidentally turned on the hand dryer. "Oh, excuse me!"

That told Bets all she needed to know. Megan wasn't as comfortable about sex as her sister. Their mother was fairly clinical about it, she remembered, being a nurse. Art might have helped Angie. A woman didn't paint nudes without being comfortable in her sexuality. Bets could use a little dose of that kind of confidence at her age. She'd looked at her graying bush in the mirror and wondered if it was possible to dye it to match her hair. But it wasn't exactly something she wanted to ask Lisa Ann at the hair salon about, although she rather thought the edgy young woman would have a response.

Siobhan grabbed the book from Brigid, who had blushed beet red after a few pages, and started flipping through it. "My goodness. It has a checklist. For positions."

"A checklist," Megan squeaked, craning her neck as if trying to see.

"I rather liked that addition myself," Nicola said, leaning back against the vanity. "I know Killian will bluster, but I bought a copy for us too. He's been so on edge lately about his horse, Legend. If I didn't know better, I'd swear he'd never bred a horse before."

"Maybe Legend needs the book," Bets said snarkily.

"Yeah, I definitely want a copy," Angie said, edging closer and making a rather different noise than the men were over technology.

Rather like a hum. Bets spied the picture of the couple doing it with the man behind the woman and found herself making a similar noise. She couldn't wait to try that!

"Are you—" Brigid clamped her mouth shut, thank God. "Never mind."

"Never mind is right," Bets said, sending Angie a wink to cover Brigid's near blunder about the pregnancy. "Now give me that book. I'm taking it to the car right now. It would be just my luck if someone accidentally kicked the bag out from the table."

"I can see everyone staring in shock as it tumbles into the center of the bar," Siobhan said with a cackle. "It might be funny."

Usually Bets was up for a laugh, but not about this. Donal might be embarrassed by such a thing, and that wouldn't do. Since he'd opened up to her about wanting to broaden his horizons, so to speak, she imagined he'd put on his sexy gold-rimmed reading glasses and devour this book overnight. She loved a man who did his research.

"It would explain the doorbell better to the village," Brigid said, elbowing Bets. "It's not like everyone doesn't already know you're forgetting your keys for a reason. You and Donal look ready to combust."

"Combust is right," Siobhan said, fanning herself. "Yesterday Gavin said he thought for sure you were going to burn a hole through the cashmere sweater you were wearing."

Great. The whole village was making jokes about them. She only wished they would pare back their visits or go to more trouble to announce themselves, but they wouldn't. People would think she and Donal would wait until after nine thirty p.m. to draw the drapes in their bedroom and do it. No way. She'd done that. She could tough it out. Donal agreed. But dammit, this doorbell had better work.

"All right, we're leaving this bathroom before one of the men decides to check whether we—or the plumbing—have had an incident."

"I think we should cover for your trip to the car by starting a Lucky Charms special. What's a good dance leading up to Halloween? Angie, you're the new member. What say you?"

"I don't think Bon Jovi has a Halloween-themed song."

"It's 'Wanted, Dead or Alive,'" Megan blurted out.

Bets and Siobhan exchanged a look before Siobhan said, "That's exactly right, dear. Maybe you need to join the Lucky Charms too."

The fact that she'd known the answer was rather funny. When she'd first arrived in Ireland, Megan had been shocked to see the women dance with their colorful boas. She'd worried the village wouldn't respect her sister as a teacher if she joined them. Only the people of Caisleán didn't think any less of a person for enjoying herself. Well, people like Mary Kincaid and Orla MacKenna probably did, she supposed, but she didn't want to think about them. If she did, she'd end up with the tummy ache Angie had made up.

"I'm not Lucky Charms material," Megan said, accidentally triggering the air dryer again when she stepped back, her cheeks red with embarrassment.

"Never say never, dear," Siobhan said, giving her a cheeky wink.

"I think you'd look pretty good with a boa, Megan," Angie said with a warm smile.

She only shook her head in response. Bets imagined Megan was still finding her way. Hell, weren't they all?

Donal met her as she came out the bathroom door. "Are you ready to go? I want to install this tonight."

She eyed the clock hanging over the bar beside the Guinness Toucan sign. "It's almost nine. How long is it going to take? I was going to drop something in your car and then join the Lucky Charms for a dance."

His mouth formed a sexy smile. "It can wait. Watching you dance is more interesting. What's in the gift bag?"

He had his giant hand in there before she could protest, and sure as shooting, he pulled out the book and held it up to see the title in the soft light. He grunted. A very different kind of grunt. "I like this book."

Not missing a beat, he shoved it back into the bag and touched her face. There was heat in his eyes, alongside a tenderness she loved.

"Fancy reading it to me while I install the doorbell tonight?" he asked.

Her mouth parted for a moment in pure wonder. "Donal O'Dwyer, you surprise me sometimes. In the best freaking ways ever."

"Good." He kissed her on the mouth in front of the whole bar. "Now, dance for me. I'll take the book."

She pressed the gift bag into his hand. "Keep it under wraps."

Gavin was putting up a fuss as Siobhan found their music. Brigid efficiently cleared the men sitting at the barstools, and Nicola passed out the boas they kept under the bar for times like these. Since Angie had fallen off the bar while dancing in heels and ended up in the hospital, they only danced on the floor now.

Bets tossed the green boa around her neck as the Bon Jovi classic came on. She let her eyes close and fell into the music, aware of Donal's eyes on her as she swayed to the twang of the guitar. The crowd started to cheer, and she looked up to see Nicola pretending to ride a horse with the barstool as a prop. Saucy.

She found Donal right away, seated at the edge of the room. His green eyes were fiery with heat, and an answering sweat ran down her back. She was so hot, and she wanted a release. With Donal.

When the song ended, she couldn't make a beeline to Donal fast enough. "Girls, I'm outta here."

She made a point of waving to Megan, who'd settled into a chair next to Carrick, and then strode toward Donal. "Let's go home and install that damn doorbell."

He took her hand and led her to his Mercedes. Inside the dark car, she attacked him, fitting her mouth to his, using her tongue to tantalize them both. Panting, she fell back into her seat and put her belt on. "Drive, man."

"I'm driving." He didn't speed though. He never did, saying she was precious cargo and he wouldn't take the risk.

At her house, he carried his tools to the front door and asked her to turn on the front lights. He positioned a portable light on the ground so he could see the area where he was working.

"Book's in the car, Bets." He drilled into the doorframe with easy precision. "Pour us a whiskey and find yourself a chair. Read for us."

Not me. *Us.* She walked to the passenger door, feeling like a young girl again. After arranging everything else, she settled back into the chair she'd dragged out, whiskey in hand, and started to read.

Her cheeks flamed for the first few pages as her imagination went wild. Donal cleared his throat at least four times, telling her his mind was in overdrive too. But then they settled into a rhythm. He drilled—which struck her as funny for a moment, causing her to giggle—and she read. He took a break to cut the power to the circuit he was connecting the doorbell to, but made a speedy return.

After he gave her a sexy wink and gestured for her to continue, she put more feeling into what she was reading. The book wasn't only about positions. It was about intimacy. It was about setting the stage for passion.

Like the man who was installing her doorbell.

"Donal, I love you," she said in the quiet fall night.

He finished screwing in the panel. "And I love you, *mo ghrá*. Now let's try this out. Can you turn the power back on for the switch?"

A solution was finally upon them. She walked over to him and kissed him square on the mouth.

"Betsy O'Hanlon, you'd better be ready for what's next."

She was. So much so her belly tightened in response. Liam, who'd been at the pub, had obviously discerned the reason for the doorbell and told her with a knowing look he'd be spending the weekend elsewhere. God help her if he was sleeping on the floor of Summercrest Manor, because even with some of the rooms cleaned and painted, it sounded like they still had a ways to go. "Tonight then?"

He sat back on his heels, looking so freaking hot she wanted to climb all over him. "Girl, you've lost all your car keys, and me own father pulled me aside a couple days ago to ask if I needed him to go over the basics again. Your own friends are buying you a refresher course in a book, which you just read to me while I installed a doorbell—in Ireland, mind you—while I am fully erect. Have mercy, woman. Once this doorbell is in, I've fulfilled my part." He gave her an intense look, waiting for her to speak, then demanded, "Bets, tell me what you're thinking, girl!"

She opened the top two buttons of her blouse. "I'm going to turn the power on, and then we'll see about giving this book a run for its money."

Because a book couldn't equal the real thing. Ever.

She danced through the house and even managed to keep her good humor when she had to head down into the scary dank basement for the electrical box. Except something popped when she flipped the appropriate switch, and the lights went out. She smelled something electrical burning.

That couldn't be good.

Heavy boots sounded on the floor above, and then a single flashlight beam found her in the darkness. "Jesus, I think we blew your transformer. I'll have to call an electrician tomorrow. We might need to install some new circuits to take the load. I hadn't thought about your old circuits not being able to handle it. Sorry, Bets."

She hadn't known anything about the doorbell's electrical needs, but Bruce had tried to install things before only to discover their electrical box couldn't take it. They were doomed. "It's okay, Donal," she said, although it wasn't.

"My plan hit a snag, but I'm not giving up. I'll be taking the book with me now and leaving you, as I'm dying a painful death wanting you."

She was dying too.

"Maybe this happened for a reason," he called out softly, an odd note in his usually strong voice. "We both deserve some romance for our first time. We'll make sure my plan works and then make arrangements to be together at last. Good night, *mo ghrá*."

She headed up the stairs for ice to cool down her body, although she didn't mind with the warmth permeating her heart now.

CHAPTER SIXTEEN

Megan couldn't make pieces fast enough as the first weeks of October changed the colors of leaves and wild grasses from vibrant green to the earthy colors of burnt umber and rutile, shades she loved for glazing her pots.

Her hands were dry from their constant contact with clay, but she didn't care. Every time she put a new ball of clay on the wheel, she could already see what it wanted to be—a bowl, a pitcher, a platter, a mug, a vase. The Irish countryside outside the windows inspired her, with its rolling hills and multicolored skies hosting swashes and puffs of clouds, sometimes white, sometimes pearly, as Kade would say. She wanted her pottery to reflect the shapes and colors around her, here where her heart had found its home.

Her tools were spread out to aid her. For the leather hard pieces, she'd carve in a design for added depth. A Celtic knot called to her one day while another morning she detailed the gentle sway of the grasses in the fields. For the freshly thrown pots, she'd slowly turn the wheel and dip her tool into the turning clay, initiating the swirls of clouds or a wild rainbow.

The magic of pottery was back. *Her magic.*

It had been gone so long, she sometimes teared up seeing her hands shaping a thing of beauty. She'd made these pieces. Her. The new her. It seemed fitting for her to choose a new signature to fuse into her pottery: a simple but artful letter M. She didn't want any other names to define her. Only Megan.

Her accomplishments rested on the shelves all around her, some drying, while others had been fired in the bisque kiln, ready to be glazed and fired again at a higher temperature to set the piece.

Her three classes were progressing beautifully. She started each with a demo—on the wheel—and then she'd go around helping or encouraging anyone who needed it. In the Tuesday evening class, Hollie had discovered an interest in the clay, while Sarah had dropped out after Liam paid more attention to his pieces than to her. Keegan and Lisa Ann had taken to sitting next to each other in class and leaving together afterward for a drink. Megan had heard through the grapevine that they were dating, and she'd finally pulled Keegan aside. "I really like some of the words you put on your cattle," she told him. He'd blushed and taken a moment before saying, "I've liked learning about pottery from you, and I plan to come back next term."

The praise had made her want to twirl in a circle. She was a good teacher. Even Liam's mastery taking a holiday, as he called it, hadn't diminished her feeling. He was having trouble finding his center sometimes as his impending move grew closer. Transition and growth were pulling at him, he'd told her, but he'd find a new center. She had no worries there.

Eoghan delighted and inspired her by throwing simple pieces like a mug or a bowl and then contorting or pinching their sides so they looked like gnarled trees along the road. He had an uncanny ability for shapes equaled only by his ability to convince the villagers to donate to their fair.

He'd even squeezed out a donation from Mary Kincaid in the produce section of the grocery store, having shamed her into it by asking in front of several other townspeople. That had briefly cheered up Bets, who was bemoaning the failed installation of Donal's doorbell.

Then there was Kade. He could center massive pieces of clay with his large, beautiful hands—hands she loved feeling on her body. His work was a study in simplicity, and he threw his pieces with the same gentleness he used with a horse or one of his clients. Her favorite so far was the cocktail pitchers he'd made for himself and his friend Ryan in Dublin. She'd helped him fashion handles that would fit their hands perfectly, and she couldn't wait to see what glaze he chose after they were run in the bisque kiln.

When Angie stopped by after her painting class, the ever-present smears of paint on her clothes, she grinned despite a sallow completion. Her sister looked tired, but given their détente, she didn't ask why. They'd agreed to let each other live their lives without any more comments or judgments, and it was working for them. So far neither had mentioned her dating Kade, and she was fine with that.

"You look happy, Megan," her sister said, "and your work has never been more beautiful."

Angie's praise meant a lot. Growing up, Megan hadn't always felt as capable as her sister, except when it came to fitting in. She'd always known how to stay in line. Now she felt like she was flying, like she did when she and Kade raced horses on the beach and the Irish wind blew back her hair.

"I can't tell you what it means to have this again," Megan responded.

Her sister touched her heart. "I know. Ireland looks good on you, Megan."

"Yes, it does," she said, smiling as Angie blew her a kiss and left.

A new pattern unfolded. She and Kade and Ollie had dinner together almost every night, either out or at one of their cottages, and she'd show Kade pictures of her daily work on her phone. The habit didn't form because she wanted or needed praise, but because she wanted to share this piece of herself with him. She'd bask in his interest, his engagement, while drinking one of his splendid cocktails, enjoying his hand settled somewhere on her. Her side. Her back. Her thigh.

Ollie was seeing her in a different way. He kept telling her he was *crazy* happy that she was dating Kade because he was the best guy in the whole world. Like Liam and Carrick and Mr. Fitzgerald and so on. His eyes had grown wide the first time he studied pictures of her work, but then he'd made her laugh by pointing to one of the bowls and saying he wanted it for his porridge every morning. Her son loved talking like the Irish.

The tickets for the St. Stephen's Day fair went on sale, and more donations poured in for the arts center. Kade did indeed convince a local band to play for free before the horse race, and Megan arranged for one of the rare food trucks in the area that served fish and chips to be at the fair. Eoghan had told her they needed to come up with a few signup sheets for the donation of baked goods for a bake sale, and so they'd hung them up in Lisa Ann's salon, the Brazen Donkey, and One More Chapter. So far, sixty people had volunteered to contribute something.

Caisleán was behind them in full force.

She had Kade.

And she had her magic back, better than ever before.

All was right in the world in a way it never had been.

When the day came for her to glaze fire her pots, she was a nervous wreck, however. She'd waited until her pots would fill the kiln completely, not wanting to waste electricity.

Barry had always led that effort in her former studio, rendered skillful and fearless by thirty years of experience. Even though she knew kiln disasters weren't common, they did happen. Glaze applied too thickly to a pot could run onto the shelf and sear the pot to it, making it and the shelf unusable. If there was even the smallest trace of wetness in a bisque pot, it could explode in the kiln, breaking other pots. This was Ireland. Dampness was in the air. Everywhere. She feared that the most.

So she tested the kilns and read the safety manual from front to back. She carefully arranged all of her pots on the shelves, feeling extra joy when she placed her first bowl— her soul bowl—and spaced them appropriately to maintain proper clearance and balance the load. Programming the kiln was still a little intimidating, but she punched the buttons on the panel and selected the correct setting. She let out the breath she'd been holding.

Now all she had to do was sit back and let the kiln do its work. Part of her wanted to watch it like she had Ollie when they'd first come home from the hospital after his birth. She remembered hovering over his bassinet, checking to make sure he was breathing. The smallest sound had sent her heart racing.

She didn't want to go crazy over the kiln firing, so she left for Kade's farm.

The sun was out, warming the soft rain still dripping from the trees. She'd seize the moment and bicycle over. These days she didn't have to change into different clothes. Her pottery and farm clothes were mostly the same, although the pottery dust clinging to her had made Winston sneeze once, which had made her laugh.

A gentle breeze blew through her short hair, and she smelled oranges for a moment. The inviting scent made her smile as she rode past hedgerows dotted with blackberries. Ollie couldn't talk enough about how much he loved eating the berries he found along the road. His idols had taught him what to look for, and she'd given up the impulse to have him wash them beforehand. The rain in Ireland was cleansing enough. Something she felt touch her skin just then. A gentle mist fell, the sun making the drops golden. Her face grew wet. The drops grew heavier.

She was upon Keegan O'Malley's cattle. The two cows closest to the fencing said *Grasp. Opportunity.*

As the mist turned into a full-on rain shower and the sun disappeared behind pearly clouds, she embraced the elements. Her pieces were becoming masterpieces in the kiln. This wasn't just a good moment. It was a grand moment, like the Irish would say.

Her clothes clung to her skin as she pedaled down the country lane to Kade's part of the farm. She was drenched by the time she arrived. Kade emerged from the shed and started to laugh.

"Oh, Megan, the rain had its way with you."

She swung off the bike and put the kickstand down, using both her hands to press back her dripping hair. "It was so beautiful earlier."

"That's Ireland for you," he said, extending his hand. "Come on. I have a towel in the tack room. You loaded the kiln then? I can see it on your face. You're lit up like the sun you love so."

Following him into the tack room, she heard her shoes squish. She put her hands on his chest as he started to hand towel the ends of her hair. When he slid the cloth down her neck, she shivered. Their eyes met, and then he was lowering his head to kiss her. Something inside her seemed to burst. It had been straining for freedom for some time. Heat fanned out inside her belly and up to her breasts. She dug her hands into his hair, and the kiss went wild.

She couldn't get enough of his mouth. He must have sensed it because he pulled her hard against him and opened her mouth with his tongue. That was good, because today she didn't want slow and gentle. She wanted him. Wildly. Urgently. Like he was the wind and the rain covering her body. She moaned, a loud, needy cry.

He pulled back, giving her a look that radiated pure heat, those golden brown eyes she loved looking for something. His smile started out slow, but it spread across his face.

"It's time then," he simply said.

A punch of heat blasted her belly again, and her hands slid up to stroke his jaw. "Yes, I think so."

He grinned, tossed the towel aside, and grabbed her hand. They ran out of the shed, mindless of the puddles in the yard. Somehow splashing in them together was fun. She felt young again and alive and so in love that she imagined her heart might fly out of her chest. The sun came out in a blaze of light, the brilliance nearly blinding. But she didn't need to see where she was going. She knew her destination. Home. With Kade.

When they arrived at the cottage, she was breathing

hard. He flicked the door open and slammed it once she'd crossed the threshold.

Taking her face, he looked deeply into her eyes. "I love you. More than I ever imagined loving anyone."

Her heart took flight. With those words and the love radiating in her eyes, it soared like the great gray herons she often sighted along the shore. "I love you too. Kade, you can't know how much. But I want to show you. I need to."

"Then let's make love, *mo chuisle*," he said, caressing her cheek before he lowered his mouth to hers.

She settled against him, savoring the way he pressed one hand to the small of her back while the other tangled in her wet hair. This time she slid her tongue into his mouth, and he shocked her by sucking on it. A tremor rocked her body, and then she was soaking him up, kissing him with complete abandon. He met her passion, moaning low in his throat. She needed skin. His skin. Their skin. She pulled at his shirt, caressing his flesh, and he pressed back and tugged it off.

The pleasure of seeing his bare chest made her mouth water. She laid her hand there, feeling the pounding of his heart. *She* had made that happen, just as he'd set her heart to racing.

She stroked his chest, learning him. God, he was so beautiful. She wanted to tell him so, but the words didn't seem like enough. She wanted to show him, so she pressed a kiss along the lines of one muscle and then another and ran her hand down the center of his body. He hissed as she traced the line of skin along his jeans. Her fingertips felt more sensitive, perhaps because of all the pottery she'd been throwing. She could feel every movement inside him—and an answering rhythm from her own body. Rhythm. Flow. Movement.

Oneness.

She lifted her gaze to find him watching her, his eyes full of heat mixed with love, the perfect fusion she'd been waiting for her entire life. She reached for the soggy hem of her shirt. His hands moved to aid her, and together they unveiled her body. He traced the line of her simple white bra, and the pleasure of his touch was so powerful she let her eyes close. He cupped her breasts, sensing she needed more, and when he reached back and undid her bra, she felt none of the embarrassment from the past. She was ready for him. Ready for him to see her. Feel her. *Touch* her. Like she'd never been touched before.

His hands were gentle, sliding along the sides of her breasts, one of the most pleasurable sensations she'd ever experienced. She hadn't known her sides could be so sensitive, and as he tugged lightly on her hardened nipples, she found herself awash in a new sea of sensation, one she reveled in. She fell into his hands, edging closer, wanting to express the heat building inside her, a heat so strong it could forge anything. A new part of her was coming alive, stirred to wakefulness by their love.

Tugging on her breasts, he took her mouth in the deepest and hottest kiss they'd ever shared. She groaned, the sound shocking to her own ears, but she wanted what was coming. Recognized what was happening in some primal part of her. His mouth was luscious. His touch exquisite. Her entire body flushed with heat, and then she was coming, crying out into his mouth.

She grabbed his shoulders, needing an anchor as the pleasure rocked through her. He continued to caress her breasts, extending her pleasure. When she wound down, her head fell against his chest and his arms slid around to hold her. She came back to herself and raised her head to look at him. "I'm a bit...shocked by that. It's never happened like that before for me."

He traced her face. "The passionate part of you was ready to come alive. Megan, from the moment I saw you, I knew you were holding so much of yourself back. This is life, love. This. *Us*. It's how it's supposed to be."

"I want you to show me more," she whispered. "Kade, I love you so much. Your love has changed everything for me."

"It's changed everything for me too, *mo chuisle*. And yes, together we'll both show each other more."

He held out his hand to her. She took it, and they walked the short distance to his bedroom. The fields were lit with gold outside the window, and the light danced on the ceiling in his small room. He sat on the bed and positioned her between his legs, undoing her pants and sliding them and her underwear down. She toed off her shoes and he lifted her legs onto the bed to peel off one wet sock at a time.

She didn't feel exposed when he held her legs in place and slid his hand along the insides of her thighs to her core. In fact, she felt downright delicious. Heady. The pleasure she'd already had at his hands had made her body more pliant and ready for him. She pressed into his touch and let her head fall back as he parted her with his fingers and caressed her. Heat fanned out in her belly again, but this time she wanted to share it with him.

"I want you bare too," she voiced, the words shocking and yet so right.

He gave her a sweet smile before gently lowering her leg to the floor and standing up. He toed off his shoes, kicking them under the bed. His hands went to his pants, and she covered them with her own, as he had with her. Together they lowered his pants and navy briefs.

His arousal was beautiful and full and thick, and her throat grew tight with emotion as he laid her hand over him and said, "Touch me."

She feathered his length and then stroked him more urgently when he moaned low in his throat. She waited for him to tell her to take her hands away, but he only pressed into her touch, his eyes closed, his jaw tight, and moaned again. She watched in awe as he soaked in every stroke, every caress. Tyson had resisted too much stroking, she suddenly recalled, saying he couldn't hold out. She marveled at Kade, who seemed to embrace every sensation.

His eyes suddenly opened, and the heat in them stoked the fire within her, sending those memories away for good. "Lie back, *mo chuisle*, and let me love you."

She lay back on the bed as he opened a side drawer and took out a condom. She watched as he covered himself, the sight filling her body with glorious tension. She wanted him inside her. *Now.* Without thought, she opened her legs as he settled over her. Hands working together, they guided him inside her. The pressure was intense and sweet, and they both moaned as he slid in to the hilt. Covering her, he raised her hands over her head and tangled their fingers.

He held her gaze one long moment, his love filling her every cell. When he started to move, she lifted to meet him, needing to be with him for every stroke. She'd allowed herself to be taken before, but this time she wanted to be part of the rhythm.

The power of their movements had her straining against him. He anchored his hips, as if sensing she needed more, and increased their pace. Heat started building again, her every muscle straining with it. She raised her knees to take him deeper, and when that wasn't enough, she locked her legs around his waist. He pressed against their hands and lifted onto his knees at an angle. His thrusts rocked her back, making her moan and moan again.

Then she was coming, everything shaking inside her. She cried out as she pulsed around him and felt him groan low and deep in response as he came inside her, pressing her into the bed in the most delicious way possible. Heat suffused her. Pleasure rained through her. He filled her. She floated, as if she had no body, as light as a feather dancing in the wind.

She was aware of the gentle kiss he pressed sweetly against her neck and of his fingers lightly squeezing hers. Part of her didn't want to float down to earth, to end this moment, but the other part of her couldn't wait to see him.

When she opened her eyes, the whole world looked brighter. His eyes weren't simply brown. They were caramel. His thick hair was a rich umber. And his skin, a texture she loved even more than clay, was a sensuous latte.

"Hello, Megan," he simply said, the corner of his mouth tipping up on the right.

She felt an answering smile on her mouth. "Hello, Kade."

"Pleasure, love, and me very own self look good on you, *mo mhuirnín dílis*."

"That's a new phrase," she said, tightening her hands around his, their fingers still joined together above her head.

"I've been saving it for this moment." He kissed her on the mouth, ever so softly. "It means 'my own true love.'"

Her heart rolled over in her chest. "Say it again."

He did. She repeated it to him as well as she could, holding his eyes.

Because he was her own true love too.

CHAPTER SEVENTEEN

K ade marveled at the woman beside him.

She'd fallen asleep after they made love a second time, but not before she called him *mo mhuirnín dílis* in a hesitant but determined voice.

He'd never used the Irish endearment before, and its power had wrapped around his heart. Both in the saying of it and in the hearing of it. He glanced at his bedside clock. With school, most of his clients were coming around four o'clock. There was still time to spare, but she'd need to pick up Ollie soon unless he asked another of their friends to see to the boy. If he did, they could have another hour together. He wanted that. Even if it were only to hold her and soak in her beauty and the feel of her beside him in his bed.

He heard horse's hooves suddenly. The only person who'd come riding this way would be his father. Wincing, he reluctantly rolled out of bed and hastily tugged on his clothes. When he left the cottage and closed the door behind him, his father was dismounting. His breath caught in his throat, seeing the horse. It was a rare gray, almost ghostly, with the lines of a Connemara pony, an Irish draught, and a thoroughbred—a spectacular, rare, and absolutely magical specimen.

This was Legend's match.

"You found him!" He walked down the path as his father charged forward and wrapped him up in a giant hug, lifting him off the ground. He was so startled, he began to laugh.

"If you hadn't mentioned the Connemara, I wouldn't have noticed this one when I went to Galway to look over horses. His name is Sutter's Mill. The owner told me his name had two sources—the fastest meteorite on record and the place where the American gold rush began. Good luck if I ever heard it."

Kade approached the stallion closely, gazing into his dark eyes. They were watchful but calm and held a kindness he knew could be coaxed out. Yes, Sutter's Mill would do nicely for Legend. "Now that's the kind of name you want to give a stallion."

"Exactly!" His dad rubbed the stallion affectionately, his love already evident. "I raced him only hours ago, and son, I can't tell you how he ran. I smelled oranges all around us as we thundered down the path."

Kade smiled as Sorcha appeared beside the horse. Sutter's Mill turned his head and nickered softly.

Thank you, Sorcha, he said in his mind.

She blew him a kiss and disappeared.

His father walked around the horse, running his hands over his sides. "He has the heart of a champion. It's clear as the clouds in the sky. I'm not sure the owner completely understood what he had on his hands, but I knew the moment I saw him. Still, I offered the man a fair price, and he was happy to accept. Kade, I haven't been this excited by a horse in ages. Thank you, son. For encouraging me to look beyond my usual suspects. This horse is going to change things around here. I know it in my heart."

Kade finally extended his hand to the horse, letting the stallion catch his scent. "It makes my own heart happy to see you like this, Dad."

"I was so excited when I got home, I went to find you first thing." His dad laughed as Sutter's Mill bumped him playfully. "Why aren't you down in the yard?"

He didn't want to embarrass Megan. Their business was private. "I had something that needed tending here. I'll be back down in a while, Dad. In the meantime, why don't you introduce Legend and Sutter's Mill to each other in one of the pastures?"

His father put his hands on his hips. "I want you to share the moment with me. Finish what you're doing. I can wait a moment."

He was about to reply when his mother's car appeared on the road. Odd, that. Both men turned, and his father was instantly off, Kade following behind him. His mother lowered the window, her mouth tight. "You both never have your phones on. I swear. Kade, I'm looking for Megan. Her bike was in your shed. Is she here?"

A tremor went through him. "Is something amiss with Ollie?"

"No," she said instantly. "It's the art center. Her kiln set off the sprinklers. Someone called the fire department because they feared a fire. Kade, it's a mess. Angie was looking for her. She wasn't answering her phone."

No, she wouldn't have been. "I know where she is. You two go on, and I'll take her on to the arts center."

His father's brows shot to his hairline. "I see the way of it now, you being at the cottage at this time of day."

He gave him a look. "And that's all you need to say,

Dad. Don't be getting in my business. I love her and she loves me. I want your word that you won't speak of it to anyone."

"What? Am I not a romantic? Son, if you knew the kind of book your mother brought home the other night..."

"Killian, that's enough." His mother poked him in the side. "That's a beautiful horse, by the by, my love."

"Thank you, *mo ghrá*," his dad said, leaning into the car and kissing her on the mouth.

"Listening to your only son looks good on you." She shot Kade a wink. "All right, I'm back to the bookshop. I'll see you both later. Killian, be good."

"Aren't I always?" He headed back to the stallion. "I'll leave you as well. Son, I'm glad you've found your woman. It makes a man's life all the richer. I'll wait for you to return before I introduce this one here to Legend. You deserve to be there. Maybe we'll even share a whiskey."

They hadn't done that in an age. "I'd like that, Dad."

His father swung into the saddle and took the reins, turning the horse and taking off. Kade watched them trot off. Yes, the stallion would do for Legend, and he imagined a whole new generation of horses here at the Donovan Farm. But he wouldn't play a part in that. He knew what he wanted. Once he helped his father with Legend, he would be free to start on his new project. Making a home for him, Megan, and Ollie.

He went inside the cottage. Megan was sitting on the bed, dressed, when he arrived in his bedroom. Her hair wasn't mussed anymore.

"I almost died of embarrassment," she said, her eyes wide. "First your father and then your mother."

Crossing to her, he sat beside her and touched her cheek. He hated for their time together to end like this, but she was needed elsewhere. "Megan, love. We need to go to the arts center. Something's happened. I'll tell you on the way."

He explained in the car, and she fisted her hands in her lap, tension clearly twining around her. When they arrived and went inside, they were met by a sea of water on the floor. The sprinklers had soaked every inch of the building, but it was the sight in the kiln room on the second floor that broke his heart.

Megan cried out and rushed closer. The door to the kiln gaped wide open and her barely fired pots were covered in white powder from a fire extinguisher.

"My pots! They sprayed *my pots*. Oh, no! Everything is ruined!"

"They thought the fire had to be inside the kiln," Angie said, appearing in the doorway. "There was some smoke."

"The kiln is new," Megan said, anguish lacing her voice. "It always smokes a little. I checked the fire alarms."

"The fire alarm didn't go off," Angie said as Carrick stepped into the room behind her, his somber gaze meeting Kade's. "The sprinklers did. The heat from the kiln—"

"Oh, God!" Megan cupped her cheeks, tears filling her eyes. "I screwed up. I didn't realize—Angie, I'm so sorry. Are any of your things destroyed?"

"Oil and water don't mix, remember?" Angie made a show of smiling. "Some of the canvases are soaked through, and some of the acrylic paintings and charcoal sketches took a beating. But nothing is ruined as badly as your work. Megan, I feel terrible. I wasn't here, or I would have insisted they wait for you."

"But you weren't," Carrick said, "and our firefighters didn't know what they were dealing with. They cut the power to your kiln and then opened the door looking for a fire. One told me the pots were all molten red so they sprayed them as a precaution. They'd never seen anything like that before. They're sorry, if that helps."

Kade didn't imagine it would. She'd worked so hard to find her center again and she'd finally locked into it. Her joy over her new art had been a tangible, glorious thing, lighting up her eyes, her face, her smile.

All of that was gone now, much like her pots.

"My soul pot was in there," she moaned, hugging her stomach.

He'd feared that. "You'll make another, love, although I know it's no comfort."

"We've canceled classes for the next couple days," Angie said. "Bets is arranging to have every fan in the greater area brought in to help dry things. She's also arranging a cleanup crew."

Kade started to roll up his sleeves. They would play their own role in the cleanup, like Angie and Carrick already had.

"I'm so stupid." Megan stared without blinking at the destruction. "Why did I think I could do this? Barry always supervised the kiln. I helped, but I—"

"*Megan.*" Kade took her arms. She had a wild look in her eyes, the kind caused by deep and galvanizing pain. This was the sort of hurt that made a person or a horse want to bolt.

He waited to see what she would do. Sometimes he knew it was better to let the person—or animal—bolt. Right now, she couldn't see anything but what was wrong.

"I don't know what to do." She pressed her hand to her mouth, her grief spilling over. "I need to help you clean up, but school's almost over. I have to get Ollie."

"Jamie will mind him," Carrick said, taking Angie's

hand. "We're all going to step outside and take a breath. This looks bad, but it's not the end of the world. We need to remember that."

She nodded, tears leaking down her face. "Right. Not the end of the world. Excuse me a moment. I need to—"

She ran out of the room. Kade rubbed the back of his neck. Only a short while ago, everything had been perfect. They'd made love for the first time, sealing their relationship in a new and beautiful way. Then his father had thanked him for helping him find Legend's match. He'd even hugged him.

And now, here Kade stood, surrounded by Megan's heartbreak and ruined artwork.

Well, there was nothing for it. He would have to help her heal and start over.

CHAPTER EIGHTEEN

M egan had failed.

She'd lost everything again.

The hurt pressed under her ribs as she stared at her crumpled expression in the mirror. She couldn't hold back the pain. She started crying. Her soul pot. All her beautiful creations. Fifty-two of them. She'd been so proud of her work.

All she wanted to do was crawl into bed. Forget everything. The pull was so strong.

Why did you think you could do this, little girl?

Her father's voice.

He'd never believed she could do anything. No one had. Until Kade...

She'd been so happy earlier, happier than she'd ever been, but those feelings had been extinguished like her pots. She couldn't feel anything beyond despair now, and it was overwhelming her like she was drowning in the sea.

She had to fight. Somehow. Or all of the progress she'd made in the past few months would be gone too. She fisted her hands, crying softly. She didn't want to feel like this. She wanted to feel like she did with Kade. Like she did while making her pots. Like she did when Ollie giggled.

She turned on the spout and splashed cold water on her face. Looked into her sorry reflection. *Stop it, Megan. Stop this. Right now.*

"Oh, Megan," she heard Angie say as her sister's arms came around her, pulling her into a hug. "I know it's awful. I can't imagine how I would feel if all my paintings had been destroyed. It would be like someone stabbing me in the heart."

She turned and faced Angie, wiping at her eyes. "It helps a little to hear you say it. I was feeling sorry for myself."

"Of course you were!" Her sister's voice resounded in the bathroom. "You'd created a buttload of pots. Things of beauty. Hours of work down the drain. This sucks. You go ahead and feel bad about it."

She rubbed her tingling nose. "I wasn't just feeling bad. I felt the pull of depression. It...it made me want to get into bed and never try anything again. I even heard Dad's voice in my head."

"Tell it to take a hike," Angie said, cupping her arm. "Forget Dad. Do you want some good news? I checked with Carrick before I came in here, but I thought this was the perfect time to tell you."

"What?"

"We're having a baby," Angie said, her face lighting up.

Surprise breaking through the sadness, Megan looked at her sister's tummy. "You are? Is that why you've looked tired? Oh, I should have guessed. Congratulations! I'm so happy for you and Carrick."

And she could feel a little uptick in her emotions as the

news settled in. Her sister was going to be a mother, and she would be an aunt. Ollie would have a cousin to dote on.

"We are too," Angie said, patting her belly. "I'm pretty sure it happened the night the arts center opened. It's wonderful and a little scary, especially since I've been barfing every morning and wanting to die. I mean, wouldn't you think Mother Nature would have created a symptom that would make you feel happier about having a kid? Like craving chocolate or something? Puking sucks."

"I remember doing that with Ollie, and it's terrible." She'd gone through it alone. Tyson had been off in Iraq or Afghanistan. She couldn't remember. Their mom had told her it was completely normal. But it hadn't felt normal as she'd stared into the white toilet bowl morning after morning, sick as a dog.

"So that's our good news." Angie slid her hand over her midsection and looked down. "It's still early, and you're the first person we've told, although you should know Kade guessed. He's like a vault though, and Carrick knew he'd keep it to himself. Even though the two of you are— Should I say? Or are we still going to keep walking this crazy line where we don't say much to each other?"

"It's been good for us," Megan said, brushing a drop of cold water from her temple. "But maybe it's time we retire it. Mostly."

Angie smiled. "I can do mostly. I'm so happy for you and Kade, and I just love your hair. You look more young and free than ever."

She touched the ends. "I feel young and free, and I love Kade with all my heart. Did you know about Sorcha helping you guys?"

Her sister blinked. "He told you? Carrick told me when we first got together, and I've heard she's helping you too. I smelled oranges in the kiln room when I arrived shortly after the firemen. I think she was hoping one of those eejits talked to spirits. I think she would have told him not to open the kiln."

"I read about some potter saying you should put a padlock on it," Megan admitted, feeling a little stupid again. "At the time, I thought it was overkill."

"I'm the one who managed an arts center, and it didn't even occur to me to change the sprinklers over the kiln to ones with higher temperature gauges."

Probably because Angie had needed to close down the pottery unit at her former employer owing to budgetary restrictions. Much like the problems they were dealing with now in Caisleán.

"We're going to have extra budget expenses to clean the center up," she whispered. "I feel terrible about that."

"Don't worry." Angie rubbed her shoulder. "We have good people behind us. The level of donations you and Eoghan have managed is incredible. My favorite story is about him checkmating Mary Kincaid in the grocery store. How can we not succeed with an evil mastermind like Eoghan O'Dwyer on our side?"

That comment forced a reluctant laugh out of her. "Can you be an evil mastermind at ninety-three?"

"I'd love to find out." Her sister took her hand and put it on her middle. "Meet your niece or nephew. Carrick and I can't wait for Ollie's reaction."

Neither could Megan. "He'll be over the moon. Like I am."

"Come on." Angie wrapped an arm around her shoulder. "Let's start cleaning up. Carrick and Kade are doing a few errands, but they'll be back. With help, I expect. It's not going to be fun or pretty, but we're going to do it together."

Together. Yes, that sounded better.

When they left the bathroom, they found their first volunteer. Brady McGrath was mopping up water in the hallway, humming under his breath.

He looked up and winked. "Hell of a storm in here. I was moving my things into Summercrest with my brother and Liam when I heard you needed a hand."

"That was mighty nice of you, Brady," Angie said, crossing and hugging him. "I know you guys have been working night and day to make that place habitable again."

"I don't feel my back anymore after all the cleaning and the painting we've gotten up to these couple weeks. Whiskey helps, so I brought some elixir of life for us all. Feel free to pour yourself a generous glass. We're going to have this cleaned up in no time."

Megan felt overcome by the gesture, but she managed to say, "Yes, thank you, Brady."

"You're both ours now," he said, blowing them a kiss. "I heard what our firemen did. Megan, is there any hope for your pottery?"

Pain pressed under her ribs again. "I don't think so. When you open a kiln too soon, it causes all sorts of problems. I don't have a clue what happens once it's covered in fire retardant, but I'm sure they're beyond hope."

"Megan Bennet," a craggy male voice shouted.

She and Angie followed the sound to the entry hall. Eoghan O'Dwyer stood in front of at least thirty people armed with mops, buckets, and towels. He came forward, the wrinkles on his face more pronounced than ever.

"Oh, it's worse than a funeral in here." He took her hand and patted it. "But don't you worry none. We'll have this place brighter than it was before this horrible tragedy happened. And if you think I won't be pressing people for more donations, you'd be betting wrong. Girls, it's a tragic day, but money is going to flow as is kindness. Try and remember that."

To her surprise, he hugged her gently. "Thanks, Eoghan."

"Oh, for the love of heaven!" Bets appeared at the front of the crowd with Liam and Declan, each of them carrying an electric fan. "What a mess!"

"That's an understatement," Liam said, resting his fan on the floor and crossing to hug both of them. "You must be so upset."

"It's worse for Megan," Angie said, explaining what the firemen had done to her pots.

"Not that!" He grabbed his head with one hand. "I suppose they were only doing their job, but it's a loss to be sure. Megan! All your beautiful pots for the St. Stephen's fair."

"I'm so sorry this happened," Bets said, setting her fan down with a bang. "I can't imagine how you must feel. But we'll make it right."

"It takes more than something like this to put the people of Caisleán down," Donal said, coming forward with a fan in each hand. "I've got every farmer in the area coming to help. We'll hope it's dry for a few days and let the fans do their work. All right, everyone, let's get started."

Megan found a mop. She wiped up the floor and then grabbed towels to dry the wooden shelves and other surfaces in the main hall. She couldn't face the pottery studio yet.

The progress was slow and painstaking. Her back was hurting when Ollie shouted her name. She turned to see him running toward her, and her heart gave a thump as he wrapped his little arms around her. Looking over, she saw

Jamie behind him, and she mouthed *Thank you*. He simply nodded and went to pick up a mop.

"Mom, this is awful!" Ollie slapped a hand to his forehead like Liam often did. "It's wet everywhere. Did the fire department really come and ruin all your pots?"

She didn't want to throw anyone under the bus. "They were only doing their job."

He hugged her again. "But it's terrible, Mom. You loved those pots! You showed me and Kade everything you made."

"I'll just have to make new pots," she said, her voice catching.

"Megan."

She knew that voice. Her heart expanded in her chest, hearing it. When she turned her head, Kade was smiling softly at her.

"I need to borrow you for a moment," he said, crossing to where her cousin was working not too far away. "Liam, can you mind Ollie for a while?"

Her cousin nodded. "Sure thing. Ollie, do you want a mop or a towel?"

"A mop!" He raced over and took the mop Liam extended to him, immediately starting in on the floor.

Kade walked to her and put his hand on her back, rubbing that special spot he always found. "How are you faring?"

"Better." She made sure to nod.

Gazing at her in that patient way of his, he said, "Come with me."

She didn't know where he wanted to take her. All she knew is she wanted to go.

But when he led her past the volunteers and they exited the building, she gave him a pointed look. "The mess is back there."

"It'll hold." He led her to his jeep and opened the door. "Trust me."

Since she did, she climbed into the passenger seat. The fields didn't seem as bright as they drove to his farm. Even the sight of Keegan O'Malley's cow with its message—*Smile*—couldn't lighten her spirits.

When they reached his yard, Duke's excited yips pierced her heart. When she opened the car door, she picked him up and hugged him to her chest. Tears filled her eyes as he rained dog kisses all over her face.

"When you're ready, come to the shed," Kade said, striding off in that direction.

After crying softly, she got out and followed him. When she reached the shed, she gasped. A pottery wheel sat where he'd once kept a small table and chairs. Her apron, bucket, and tools rested on the chair, and there was a bag of clay on the floor.

"I thought you might work here for a time." His brown eyes were warm and understanding. "I know it's not optimal, but you'll want to find your center again. I thought it might be easier here, with me and those you love around you. Including this new little guy. I've been saving him for the right moment, and I felt like this was it."

He opened the door to the tack room, and a baby Jack Russell terrier tumbled out. He gave a squeak and then found his feet. Kade scooped the little puppy up and walked over to her. She put Duke down and reached for the precious bundle in his arms.

"He's only just arrived and needs training, but he's a dear one," Kade said, stroking his head gently. "You and Ollie have talked about having a dog yourselves, and while I know Duke loves you and you him, he has too many children who'd be sad to see him go to your cottage, as much as

I'd love to give him to you. But this little fella is from Duke, so I thought you'd like him."

"I love him." She raised her head to gaze at him. "Oh, Kade, this is the best present ever. And on the best and worst day ever."

"I know, love," he said, embracing her and the puppy gently. "I thought you might try finding your center. Today. Megan, I can't imagine how hurt you are, but I know you won't let this make you forget how far you've come. If you'd like, your new puppy, Duke, the horses, and me would all like to help."

She glanced over at the pottery wheel. She was *scared* of it. What if today's accident had rocked her center again? But Kade's insight was, as usual, spot on. She had to do what scared her. Face the wheel again and start over. "You're right. I need to do this, and I'm glad you—all of you —are around me."

After nuzzling the puppy one last time, she strode over to the wheel and situated herself. The light was as different as the location. Duke padded over and lay at her feet. Kade pulled a chair from the tack room and sat in front of her, holding the puppy. She grabbed a ball of clay and shaped it into a ball. Without a wedging table, she used the wheel. Then she glanced into her bucket. He'd filled it with water. Of course. That was Kade, always anticipating people's needs. She pressed the ball into the center of the wheel and turned it on, fitting her hands around the disc after wetting them. She immediately felt it wobble.

"Breathe, Megan." His voice was as soft as a whisper. "You know what to do."

She closed her eyes. The scent of hay filled her nose, a comforting smell. She felt Duke stretch at her feet and the puppy gave a sweet sigh. Sweat trailed down her back despite the cool air, but her hands started to come alive. She let go of the tension in her shoulders and cracked her neck. Her back was a little tight, so she wiggled her hips. She hugged the clay, imagining she was hugging herself. It needed patience and love, just like she did.

Today had been hard. But it had also been beautiful. She'd made love with Kade. He'd given her a puppy and an art space in his shed, next to him and the ponies she loved.

Her heart filled with warmth, and a spurt of joy shot through her as the clay centered. Yes, she could still do this. Nothing was going to stop her ever again. Especially not herself.

She opened the clay and started to pull up the sides, wetting her hands as needed. Feeling the sides wanting to lay down, she let them. They were too tired to stand up all the way. They wanted to recline. Like she did. She formed the V-shaped bowl with easy passes, keeping it simple. She didn't have the energy to over-effort anything. When she opened her eyes, she marveled at its beauty.

She'd done it.

Barry's words came to mind. *You find your center. Again and again. That's life. That's the journey.*

Maybe it was being around Kade, but she could feel a piece of her soul settle. Another soul bowl. This one she would make sure would grace her table.

Opening her eyes, she found Kade smiling softly at her, the puppy chewing on a stick he must have found. "Ah, love, I believe all is still right with the world."

She stared at the man she loved. The man she'd made love to.

"Yes, it is."

CHAPTER NINETEEN

The timing of life sometimes annoyed the heck out of Bets.

She'd finally finished the application for the grant after receiving input from Angie and Donal, who both thought she'd aced it. She'd wanted to celebrate some to take her mind off the fact that Liam was spending his last night in their house now that the bulk of his possessions were situated in Summercrest Manor. Her son had suggested the two of them have dinner and a movie at the house for old times' sake, and she'd looked forward to it. Instead, the arts center needed the help of the whole village to clean it up.

"I'd planned a lovely dinner for Liam's last night," she told Donal, putting extra force into her mopping as they cleaned the knitting room. "Dammit! We can't catch a break."

"You sent the grant application in—"

"I meant you and me. The electrician can't get the door-bell to work—"

"I have something else coming," he said, his voice grave. "I know it's been a long haul with the electrician."

"You've already spent a fortune!" she said, leaning against her mop. "Paddy MacFadden keeps trying to upgrade my electric box and the wiring, but that damn doorbell keeps blowing a fuse."

"We're so close, Bets," Donal said. "I know this seems like a trial, *mo ghrá*, but we talked about the kind of sex we want, and by God, we'll have it. Or I'm not Donal O'Dwyer."

She was too tired to argue. Truth be told, she was too dejected. "Maybe we should just plan a trip to Paris. Make love there nonstop. Come back and forget we ever wanted anything different."

He took her by the arms, his green eyes blazing with frustration. "No! I'm not giving you anything less than what we both want. If we can't get the doorbell to work, I'm installing a car sensor. Anyone comes up the drive, we'll be alerted. It's low voltage. It should work. If it doesn't, I'll run an electric cord all the way from my house to yours if I have to."

"Oh, Donal, I love you." She put her head against his chest.

His arms came around her. "Neither of us is going to settle for less than we want or we'd have thrown ourselves at each other weeks ago, when Liam started to make himself scarce. A good boy, that one. You should keep your dinner with him, Bets. There are plenty of people who can clean tonight. Everyone knows he's officially moving out tomorrow. No one would think less of you."

Uncharacteristic tears filled her eyes. She felt pulled in two directions. "This is my center too, and these workshops belong to my cousins and good friend. But yes, it's Liam's last night."

"You'll never get that back, Bets," he said, caressing her

back. "Trust me. I still remember the last night my girls were in my house. It's not the same once they leave. But you know that. With Wyatt and Rhys."

Her tears finally spilled over. Her boys had told her this week they couldn't come home for the holidays. The vineyard was too busy. The news had come as a disappointment since she hadn't seen them in nearly a year. Would she see Liam less? He and his friends would spend more time together, living in the same house, and his dating life was always busy.

"You're right. We should sneak away for our dinner."

He lifted her chin. "You set all this away now. We'll be making love soon, *mo ghrá*. To lift my spirits, I might pack my overnight bag when I get home. How does that strike you?"

She cupped his strong jaw, loving the feel of his five-o'clock shadow. "Make sure it's a big bag. You'll be staying for days, especially in the beginning."

He kissed her soundly on the mouth. "A big bag? Bets O'Hanlon, all I need is a toothbrush and that book Nicola gave you. I plan to fill out the handy little position chart. Just preparing you for how it's going to be."

"I can't wait," she said, pulling him down for another kiss. "And so *you* know how it's going to be, if we can't get either the doorbell or that car sensor to work, I'm calling the quarry and having a lorry deliver an entire load of sand so I can block the entrance but good."

His eyes danced. "Maybe we tell Paddy to eff off and call the quarry tomorrow. I'm tired of waiting too, Bets."

She knew it. "Have I told you how much I appreciate your complete singlemindedness about this whole thing?"

He took her mop. "I always keep my eyes on the prize, and you, my love, are that and so much more. Now, go find

230

your son and have a grand dinner. I'll call on you in the morning."

After kissing him, her heart filled with gratitude, she went off to find Liam. He was in the kiln room with Declan, both of them wearing protective gloves, picking out the ruined pots and placing them in a rubbish bin. The sight made Bets' heart clutch.

"*Liam.*"

He turned, tears in his eyes. "It's such a waste, Mum. Megan worked so hard for every piece."

Declan looked up, a fierce frown on his face. "It shouldn't have happened."

"No, it shouldn't have," she said, coming over and touching Liam's back. "But it's done and she'll make more. Liam, Donal encouraged me to come find you so we can have our dinner at the house tonight. I know it's bad here—"

"There are plenty of people to clean up," Declan said, propping his hands on his waist. "You two go."

Liam's sigh told her how torn he was, but in the end, he tugged off his gloves. "Let's go. Declan, I'll see you tomorrow."

"I'll put the welcome mat out for you at Summercrest Manor."

Liam laughed. "Like you'd buy one."

"See ya, Bets," Declan said. "Best go out the back way or you'll be here another hour."

She waved, realizing he was right. People were upset—herself included—and they'd be wanting to talk while they cleaned up. Sneaking out the back wasn't her way, but so be it. She tried to shake off the heavy feelings as she got into her car and Liam raced off on his motorcycle.

When she passed Keegan O'Malley's cows, she spotted one with *Hope* on her black fur. She hadn't seen that word on one of Keegan's cows before. Had he spray-painted a new cow after he started dating Lisa Ann Walsh? Being with someone gave a person hope, she knew. Donal had brought that and more into her life.

So had Liam.

Tonight they would celebrate their bond, and tomorrow she would face what she hadn't let herself think about. Empty nest syndrome. She'd always thought that phrase overly dramatic—syndrome suggested a condition that needed to be cured with medicine—but there was no denying she would feel the loss of Liam, her baby.

When she arrived, Liam was already in the kitchen, pulling out the ingredients for his favorite dinner: mac and cheese.

"We've had a great run, haven't we?" she said, leaning against the doorway, memorizing this moment.

He flashed her a charming smile, letting her know he'd shaken off the arts center too. "We have, Mum. Come on, let's make dinner and then we'll watch our movie."

"What did you settle on?" she asked.

"*Gladiator*," he said, fingering his gold earring. "I've always wondered what it would have been like to be one."

She rolled her eyes. "Russell Crowe makes it look easy. Better to be the lion in the Colosseum, I think."

He laughed, and she joined in, kicking off what would be the first of many laughs that night. They stuffed themselves with mac and cheese and then changed into their pj's and climbed onto her bed to watch the movie shoulder to shoulder. Growing up, her boys had binged on *Gladiator* more times than she could count. While she'd never had trouble watching Russell Crowe, she still covered her eyes at the more gruesome parts, smiling as Liam laughed at her squeamishness. When the credits started to roll, she laid her head against his shoulder. His arm came around her.

She didn't want their night to end. Once it did, things would never be the same. The word she'd seen earlier flashed in her mind. *Hope*. She reached for it. Yes, a phase of life was ending for them both. But there was always something beginning too. She thought of Donal. He was part of her new beginning. Liam would have new adventures as well.

"I love you, Mum," he said, kissing the top of her head.

"I love you too," she said, hearing the emotion in his voice. "We should have a slumber party like this every now and then."

He squeezed her tightly. "Count on it."

When they said good night, she lay awake in her bed. When he was little, she'd have wandered into his room and watched him sleep. Her boys had looked so cute when they were tucked into their beds. She rolled over and clutched a pillow. She was being nostalgic. It hadn't all been sweet boys in superhero pajamas kissing their mother. There had been war cries and tussles and muddy footprints in the house. Some moments her heart had melted. Other moments she'd wanted to bellow at the constant chaos of three boys.

But she wouldn't change any of it.

She finally closed her eyes and fell asleep.

When she woke, she padded into the kitchen, the aroma of fresh coffee filling her nose. Walking over to pour herself a cup, she discovered an envelope with *Mum* on it beside the coffee maker. Liam's writing. She slit it open, pulled out the plain stationery, and began to read.

Dear Mum,

There is a lot in my heart as I write this, and it would be pages longer if I said everything I feel. So I'll keep it simple. I'm grateful you're my mum and that you're continuing to grow and discover more about yourself and what you want out of life. I've always admired you for being someone who talks straight, wears peacock earrings, and encourages the people she loves to go on adventures. You gave us all wings. Now it's time for you to enjoy your own.

Along those lines, I have a little treasure hunt for you, so get dressed and grab your shoes. And don't read ahead. You know I'll know.

That made her laugh despite her watery vision. She went and got dressed. When she came back downstairs, she picked up the letter again.

Now... You're going to want to walk down the path along the back side of the house and follow the signs. Bring your phone. When you reach the end, open this letter again and go to the next page.

Signs? He had her curiosity piqued. She stepped out, grateful it was dry outside, and the quiet stole around her as she walked in that direction. The first sign was a large purple ribbon tied to a low-hanging oak tree, something she'd done on May Day when the boys were little. There were more ribbons on the trees, every few yards. They led her to the tree house. At the base, there was a hand-painted sign with an arrow pointing up beside the ladder.

Really, Liam?

She hadn't been in their tree house since Bruce had first built it. A *Boys Only* sign hadn't been needed. She'd known her sons wanted it for themselves. She climbed up the ladder and entered. Her breath caught at the sight.

A mattress with fresh, pale yellow sheets covered in rose petals stood on some kind of foot-high frame, a white coverlet folded in the corner. White candles of various sizes were arranged all around the space in glass holders. Her eyes teared up uncharacteristically as she took in the fresh paint smell of the lovely lilac walls.

She opened the letter again, brushing at her eyes, and turned the page.

I thought long and hard about what to give you to say thank you for being my mum. I finally realized you and Donal needed some help, so I created a place for you to go where no one would find you. Call it your secret love lair, if you like.

Mum, the doorbell wasn't going to work, and you really don't want to stop your friends from popping by. Trust me, I understand your dilemma. I feel that way when I'm dating. You only need to be a little creative. When you're ready, climb down the ladder and follow the signs to the right.

She sank onto the bed, fingering the rose petals. *Thank you, Liam.* As she descended the ladder, she felt a thrill of excitement, wondering what he had in store for her next. She followed his hand-painted signs all the way to her newly renovated shed, the one where she'd imagined an arts center flourishing. Since that dream had died, she'd avoided coming out here. But Liam had changed that, and now she was eager to go inside. When she opened the door and stepped into the first floor, she clutched her heart as she walked toward what was tucked in the right corner.

He'd made her another love lair, as he'd called it. Oh, her boy! He'd moved one of the antique rugs and sleigh beds out of the third-story bedroom they never used. (How had he done that without her noticing?) There was a bottle of red wine, two glasses, and a corkscrew on a table next to the bed, along with more white votive candles. A couple of French screens from another room in the house offset the large space, giving the appearance of side walls.

She loved it and could already see a few additions she'd make. There were peacock feathers in a vase in her office she could bring in here. She smiled as she noted the red rose petals on the white down comforter. Her son was such a romantic. She opened the letter again and turned the page.

How do you like your next space? The tree house is great, but not so much on really rainy or cold days. I thought you needed another indoor space, one far away from the house. Now, follow the signs to the right of the shed, Mum. You know what to do when you get there.

She finally wondered if she should be embarrassed. No, she decided. She was incredibly touched that her son had cared enough to do this for her. He hadn't needed to give her anything, but since he had, he couldn't have given her a better gift.

She followed the signs to the next spot and stopped short at the entrance to her secret rose garden, the one Donal had planted for her to ensure her prize roses weren't devoured by any escaped sheep. She looked around the square space. Not seeing anything, she took out the letter and turned to the next page.

This is your last love nest, so to speak. The garden is deeply secluded, and no one goes there but you and Donal. When you're ready, turn the page.

She finally got it. There didn't need to be any bits and bobs of romance. One had only to use their imagination. She could suddenly imagine making love with Donal above her, the sun streaming over them on a warm Irish day, the delicious scent from her roses wrapping around them. She flushed with heat at the image. She'd best keep reading.

Mum, I love you, and thanks for everything so far. I'm only ten minutes away if you'll recall.

Now go call Donal.

This was why he'd told her to bring her phone. Her heart brimming, her body eager, she dialed up the man she wanted. He picked up on the second ring.

"Morning, *mo ghrá*," he said, his deep voice making her belly tight.

"Morning," she said brightly, looking up at the powdery blue sky, feeling young and carefree. "If you could choose between a tree house, a shed, and a rose garden, which would you choose?"

There was a pause. "Did you drink too much last night? What kind of question is that?"

She wanted to smack him. "One you need to answer."

"A tree house without question," he said, "although you're making me wonder where your mind is."

Of course he'd chosen the tree house. "Can you come over? Right now?"

"Are you sure you're all right? Must be tough on you, Liam leaving."

She would miss him, but they were on the same page. Now they both needed to write a new chapter. "Donal, I'm more than fine. But I need to show you the tree house."

Why not be a little mysterious?

"Your tree house? Is this some empty nest thing? Do I need to bring my tools?"

She almost made a dirty joke then and there. "Just bring yourself. I'll see you in five."

Usually it took him ten minutes to get to her, so long as he wasn't out with his sheep. But he'd speed over after what she'd told him. She skipped all the way to the tree house, her belly full of longing and anticipation. After climbing the ladder, she grabbed the matches and started lighting the candles. The room softened, making her heart soar.

Romance.

Who said it was overrated? She thought about pulling her clothes off, but then she had a moment of doubt. What if he didn't want to make love to her yet?

Donal O'Dwyer, you'd better not be stubborn about this stupid doorbell.

She heard his heavy bootsteps on the path six minutes later.

"Bets? Are you really up there, girl?"

"Yes, come on up."

Clenching her hands, she waited for him to climb the ladder. When his body came through the opening—a tight fit—she almost laughed. Yes, it was going to be a tight fit.

"What in the hell is this?" he asked, his towering frame making the space feel better suited to leprechauns and fairies. "You're not planning on sleeping in your boy's old tree house because you're missing him so? Oh, Bets."

She glared at him. "Oh, Donal! Do you not see the rose petals and the candles? This is *our love lair*—one of many—a present from my very romantic son."

His face blanched. "You son made you love lairs?"

She almost laughed. "No, he made *us* love lairs. You should see the one in the shed."

"Jesus," he said, running a large hand through his thick silver hair. "I'm rather embarrassed by this, Bets."

"And the doorbell isn't embarrassing?" she asked. "Even my friends know what we're about. Now we don't have to try so hard to be alone. Liam made us places—well away from the house. He also reminded me of the power of spontaneity and imagination."

Donal's mouth tipped up. "Seems I owe your boy a pint at least."

"At least," she said, clutching the coverlet with a fist. "Unless this doesn't work for you."

He sank to his knees in front of her and cupped her cheek, looking straight into her eyes. "Doesn't work for me? Bets, I feel like a man who's walked a thousand miles through the desert and finally found water."

How lucky was she to have such romantic men around her? "Then make love to me, Donal."

He leaned forward and kissed her, slowly at first, but when he opened her mouth with his tongue, she dove at him. He groaned as she wrapped herself around him like the vine in the very tree supporting them. Then *she* moaned, needing his bare skin. Her hands pulled at the work shirt tucked in his trousers, and from that moment on, they'd kiss and then take a piece of clothing off and kiss again until they were naked and breathless.

All the months of wanting had them gripping each other as they kissed again and again and again. With a moan, he finally pulled away and gently tossed her back onto the bed, his smile downright devilish.

"This isn't going to be slow, *mo ghrá*, but it's going to be so good."

"Yes, it is," she said, panting.

She lay back and opened to him. He cradled her against him as he pressed inside, the tenderness of the gesture weaving with the passion raging within her. Overcome with desire, she pressed her lips together as he slid into her. Carefully. She'd known he was going to be big, but it was tight and hot and absolutely wonderful.

"All right?" he asked hoarsely.

"Oh, yeah," she said, the tension both beautiful and unbearable.

Closing her eyes, she pushed her hips up to meet him, feeling the burn in her belly. He let loose an anguished sound, lowering his forehead to rest on hers, and then he was thrusting inside her. She couldn't get enough of him, nor he her, because he gripped her hips with one of his large hands and pumped into her, groaning deeply in his throat.

"Oh, God," she whimpered.

"Oh, Jesus," he hissed.

She wrapped her legs around his waist, pressing closer, and then she was crying out, pulsing, every cell in her body beating in time with her heart. She heard him call out her name, following her, his body hot and heavy and oh so wonderful.

She let her body sink into the bed, as if she were weightless in the sea. She drifted, loving the feel of their bodies pulsing in time with each other. His face rested against her neck, his breath like the most perfect wind. She felt a kiss pressed to her cheek, and then he was sweetly nuzzling her.

When she opened her eyes, he rose up, his green eyes shining with love and awe.

"Bets, it was more than I could have imagined," he said quietly as the candles flickered around them.

"Me too," she said, touching his face.

"In our haste, I don't believe I managed to tell you how beautiful you are, *mo ghrá*. You take my breath away."

She knew he believed it, but she wouldn't go that far. He, however... "I might have stopped breathing completely for at least a minute when you dropped your pants."

"Breathing might continue to be a problem for me when I see you naked," he said, caressing the line from her belly to her breasts. "But it's my heart I'm more worried about. You have the most incredible impact on it."

He leaned down and kissed her, making her own heart turn a somersault in her chest. When he lifted his head, that new devilish smile was back in full force—a smile she expected would be reserved for this moment.

"I see what you mean," she whispered.

"I'm ready to see the next love lair when you are," he said, waggling his silver brows.

She tugged him down and kissed him.

It could wait.

CHAPTER TWENTY

K ade thought a puppy could change just about any situation, and he was happy to see Pip work his magic on Megan and Ollie, who took to carrying the puppy around everywhere after school. The little boy was more excited about the puppy he'd named, truthfully, than the news that Angie and Carrick were expecting, but that was to be expected. The puppy was a tangible thing, whereas the baby would not arrive for many months.

Kade trained Pip to nestle against Megan's feet as she threw pot after pot to replace those that had been destroyed. He and Carrick built shelves against the wall of the tack room so she could dry her pots there while the arts center dried out. Being Ireland, it took over a week, especially when the rain came in for three straight days.

Long term, he thought it might be nice to have her work around him at the farm. Carrick, he knew, watched Angie paint while he did his work in the fields or the shed. Perhaps he could install a small studio at their new house when the time came.

His additional delight came from the continued

improvement of his relationship with his father. Having listened to Kade about Sutter's Mill, Killian had asked his opinion about Red Zephyr being a good horse for breeding. When Kade responded in the affirmative, his father called the stallion's owner and made an offer, which was accepted. It had felt like another stepping stone in their relationship.

Seeing his father standing beside the pasture where Legend and Sutter's Mill were penned was one of Kade's favorite moments of the day. Kade would walk out with him. Sometimes the sun would be shining on the horses, making their coats bright, and at others, the mist would come, darkening their color. Either way, the pair was beautiful to behold, and they clearly liked each other from the way they carried on, prancing and nuzzling each other. Still, Legend boarded with his lot in the shed, and his father always took the stallion back to stay with the other thoroughbreds, which now included Red Zephyr.

Sutter's Mill wasn't the only one Legend had warmed to—she'd taken to nuzzling both Duke and the new puppy, which warmed his heart. The mare had found a home with them as surely as Megan had.

His clients enjoyed watching Megan throw pottery when they arrived for their pony rides. Some kids were mesmerized by the rotation of the wheel while others peppered her with questions, which she gladly answered.

She was thriving again, and while he knew the loss of her pottery weighed on her, she fought through it. Her bravery inspired him, and when he told her so one night after they'd put Ollie to bed, she'd teared up and wrapped her arms around him before kissing him softly and telling him how much she loved him.

They found times to be together and deepen their intimacy, and the passionate woman he'd known was hiding in the shadows continued to emerge, piece by piece. Together, they both climbed to new heights of pleasure and love, and he had to remind himself to be patient for the right time to ask her to marry him. The other moments he'd hoped for had appeared. This one would as well.

When the arts center reopened, he was excited to return to pottery class, so much so that he brought home some of his own clay and threw a new coffee mug while the sun was coming up. His horses and Duke gave him strange looks in the beginning. It was Megan's spot, after all, but they soon settled back into their rhythm, the ponies grazing on hay and Duke chasing swallows from the shed.

They took Ollie trick-or-treating to their neighbors' houses as a waning crescent moon rose in the night sky. The little boy had delighted everyone by dressing up like a sheep farmer, looking like a miniature of Carrick in work clothes and wellies. After Ollie's bag was full of candy, Kade helped Carrick light a bonfire behind the cottage while Angie and Megan brought out cups of warm apple cider flavored with cinnamon and clove. Ollie chased Pip, whose bark sounded more like a squeak.

When he finally sat down in one of the chairs he and his friend had brought out for the occasion, Kade was surprised —and pleased—by Megan settling onto his knee instead of the nearby chair.

"I like this," she said, snuggling into his side as he wrapped an arm around her waist.

He wondered whether she was contrasting it to past Halloweens, when Tyson hadn't been home. Her face had gone blank with shock when Kade had mentioned wanting to take Ollie from house to house, but she'd shaken it off and rewarded him with a radiant smile. Although she wasn't dwelling in the past, sometimes the differences between past and present were such that she couldn't help taking notice. She'd said as much the other afternoon. And she'd also confessed that she'd never initiated lovemaking with any of her previous partners. He'd only smiled and told her she could initiate anything, anytime, which had made her eyes sparkle. All her blushes were gone, and he was glad for it.

When two people loved each other, there was no room for barriers in the bedroom.

"I like this too," he said, kissing her cheek. "I never much cared for Halloween myself before tonight. I never believed in the reason for it."

Her brow knit in the firelight. "What do you mean?"

Sorcha appeared by the fire and pointed to herself, prompting an eye roll. Angie and Carrick didn't see her, since her time helping them was over, but his heart warmed as he beheld her radiant smile.

"It started because people dressed up like ghosts or witches around the Harvest moon so the spirits wouldn't recognize them as mortals. But I always knew spirits could recognize a person no matter what they wore." *I could wear a clown wig and paint my face white, and you would still know me, Sorcha.*

She laughed. "The person who invented Halloween in Ireland didn't know anything about the supernatural." Then she waved at him and disappeared.

Megan took a sip of cider. "I'm glad I didn't know that was the real reason. It's a little creepy."

He leaned into her ear and whispered, "Do you think it's creepy that Sorcha is helping us?"

She shook her head. "No, not at all. I'm really grateful to her, in fact. Tell her so when you see her again."

He only smiled. He imagined Sorcha had heard.

November blew in with a storm but also a piece of good news. Ryan called to say he was coming home from Dublin to meet Kade's girl. When his dear friend arrived at the farm on a bicycle, Kade waited for him to dismount and take off his helmet, then wrapped him up in a tight hug.

"I still remember how to come here," Ryan said. "My mum was a little worried. I need to text her to tell her I'm fine."

"It's so good to see you," he said as his friend sent the message, scanning Ryan for any changes.

Ryan's muscles were still strong, thanks to the push-ups and sit-ups Kade had suggested he do daily. If you didn't study his face too carefully, you'd see a six-foot-three man with a healthy build. But his eyes were those of a young boy, a boy Kade remembered all too well, running with him and laughing as they chased crows away from the grain bins. Ryan couldn't run after the accident, but he could bike. Fortunately, he had few other physical issues. Most of his problems had been with mental retention and emotional sensitivity, something Kade had done his best to help him with.

Ryan hugged him hard again. "I missed you. Kade, I can't wait to meet Megan and her boy. If you don't watch out, she might leave for Dublin with me. Especially after I make her my new cocktails."

His bright blue eyes were shining, and Kade shook his head at his friend's teasing. "She'll love you, Ryan, but ponies and puppies trump cocktails."

His friend laughed gaily, and Duke rushed out and barked, only to completely change his demeanor when he realized the visitor was a friend. He danced at Ryan's legs until Ryan picked him up, holding him high in the air. "Hi,

Duke! He's still the best dog, Kade. You might be right about ponies and puppies. Where's Winston?"

"He's inside the shed, waiting for you," Kade said, putting an arm around the man's shoulders and ushering him into the shed. "As is Majestic, who can't wait to give you a ride."

"Can we leave now?" Ryan asked, putting Duke down so he could pet Winston. "Who's the big horse?"

He meant Legend, and Kade walked over to her stall. "I'm helping my dad with her."

"If you're helping your dad, you're going to be in trouble," Ryan said, making a face. "He doesn't want you to work with people like me. We scare him."

He sighed. He and Ryan had spoken of such things many times. "He doesn't like thinking life isn't fair or something he can control or shape to his will."

"He wants everyone to be tough like him." Ryan lifted his arm and flexed his muscle. "But it isn't all about physical strength, is it, Kade?"

Kade put his hand on his friend's shoulder. "Are people in Dublin being nice to you?"

He shrugged. "Mostly. But they still look at me like something's wrong. I thought it wouldn't hurt as much the older I got, but it still does."

Kade's throat thickened with emotion. "Of course it does, but it's their loss, isn't it? Are you not the best friend a man could ever have? Don't you make the best cocktails?"

"You're my best friend," Ryan said, his smile full and encompassing. "And I do make the best cocktails."

"When are you going to make them for us?" he asked.

Time was still an issue for his friend's mind, he knew, but he watched with pride as Ryan took his smartphone out of his jacket pocket and opened his calendar. The calendar, which also held his to-do list, aided his mental comprehension. "Today is Thursday," he said, touching the purple dot that indicated the day. "Tomorrow is Friday. I leave Sunday. That means I can do Friday or Saturday."

"How about Friday?" Kade knew Megan's schedule like his own since they spent nearly every evening together in some form.

"Friday is great!"

They went on a pony ride, Kade initiating Ryan's favorite song, "Where the Streets Have No Name." They sang together like Bono and The Edge, and his heart soared. His friend was home, the friend whose tragedy had helped him find his path, and Ryan would soon meet the woman he loved and the boy of his heart.

When Friday night rolled around, Megan fussed with the flowers she'd bought at the store, saying Kade should invite Ryan for dinner. He laughed, saying the Irish didn't invite people over like that. Ryan would pop by for a visit after dinner, and sure enough, his friend arrived by car, driven by his mother.

Kade went out to greet Mrs. Hughes as Ryan waved at him and went around to open the trunk. She declined to come in, but she pressed some euros into his hands. "It's not much, but you give it to your girl for the St. Stephen's Day fair. Everyone wants that arts center to stay open, and we won't let a few mean-spirited people close it down."

Her hardship showed in her face, the wrinkles cutting deep lines. "We'll be keeping it open, don't you worry none. Ryan looks good."

"He does," she said, pressing a hand to her soft white hair. "His cousin in Dublin is an angel, like you."

"You're one yourself. I'll see him home."

"Thank you," she said as Ryan slammed the trunk.

"I have what I need!" He held up the grocery bag. "See you, Mum. Don't worry about me. I'm safe with Kade."

"I know you are," she said, blowing him a kiss and taking off.

Ryan gestured to his clothes. "Do I look okay? I hope she likes me."

"Of course, she and Ollie will love you," Kade said. "And you look like a man from the city. Polished. Respectable."

"Not like you on the farm." He sniffed the air. "The fields still smell like shite."

They both laughed as they went into the cottage. Megan yanked on her sweater set. She hadn't brought one of those out for a while, but apparently she'd wanted to dress up for his friend. He personally wished she'd worn the clothes she felt more comfortable in. She never yanked on her farm and pottery clothes.

"Ollie and Megan, this is one of my best friends ever, Ryan Hughes."

"Hi, I'm Ollie," the little boy said, holding out his puppy. "And this is Pip. Kade said you were in an accident when you were a boy like me. I'm sorry. Did it hurt?"

Ryan set his bag on the table and took the puppy, who nuzzled his jacket. "It did, but it could have been worse. Right, Kade? Now I make cocktails with my cousin in Dublin. Do you want one? I can make it without alcohol."

"Can I, Mom?" Ollie asked, jumping in place.

"That would be very nice." She grabbed Kade's hand, her nerves palpable. "Thank you, Ryan. I'm Megan."

"You're pretty," Ryan said, his grin contagious. "Kade, you found a pretty girl. Good for you. He's waited long enough."

Kade laughed, and Megan's tension had to be dissipating because she joined in. "I waited as long as I needed to," he said.

"Even I've had more girlfriends than Kade." Ryan winked at her. "Would you like to come to Dublin with me?"

Megan blinked. "I live here. I have classes."

Ryan laughed louder, making Pip squeak. "Kade said you'd say no. But I don't blame you. He's the best. Do you want a cocktail too? I brought three choices."

Megan's shoulders finally relaxed. "Three? I can't wait to hear about them. Maybe I should try them all."

"If you do, you might get pissed," Ryan said, handing Pip back to Ollie.

"Pissed means drunk," Ollie informed his mother as the puppy lapped at his face.

Kade bit his lip as Megan sighed. "I won't ask who told you."

"Mom, *everyone* knows what pissed means. We live in a town where everyone goes to the pub. Except us. Ryan, can I help you?"

Ollie edged closer to Ryan, who was looking inside his bag. "Kade, I'm going to make these in the kitchen. Do you have ice?"

"In trays in the freezer," he replied.

"Bad ice, then." Ryan rolled his head dramatically. "We have a whole machine that makes different kinds of ice."

"You're in Caisleán now, Ryan. Not Dublin."

"No Wi-Fi out here either." Ryan winked at Megan. "Means I can't text my girlfriend."

He disappeared into the kitchen, and Ollie followed him with Pip.

"Why are you so nervous?" he asked Megan when they were alone.

She glanced to the open doorway of the kitchen and whispered, "He's important to you. I want him to like me."

This again...

Had the sweater set brought up the old patterns, or was it the other way around? "You should tell Ryan that when he brings out our cocktails."

When Ollie brought out two cocktails, she gave him a look. "One's for me, Mom. It's made with passionfruit juice and something bitter with vanilla."

"Vanilla bitters," Ryan said, carefully setting the glasses on the table. "I make the bitters myself. Megan, I made you all three since you said you wanted to get pissed."

Kade started laughing as she sputtered. "I did not!"

"Yes, you did." He giggled and gave her a lopsided smile. "Don't worry. Kade will drive you home too."

"I'm—"

"Megan, he's teasing," Kade said, glancing at Ollie, who was laughing under his breath.

"Oh, I'm so sorry." She tugged on her sweater set again.

That was all it took. Kade pulled off the hoodie covering his T-shirt and handed it to her. She gave him a puzzled look.

"Take off your sweaters and put this on. You're as uncomfortable as a horse with horseflies."

"Ugh!" Ollie made a gagging sound, making Pip squeal. "I hate those flies. They're even worse than the spiders in our cottage."

Megan's face closed up as she took his hoodie. "Don't I look okay?"

"You look beautiful, as always," Kade said, touching her face softly. "But you don't seem happy to be wearing these clothes."

"She fussed with them the whole way here—like Aunt

Angie used to do when she wore things like that. Why don't girls just wear what they want to? Like boys do."

"Because we're smarter," Ryan said with a laugh. "Teasing! Hurry and change, Megan. Your ice is melting."

Yes, it was, Kade realized, in more ways than one. She'd told him how she used to be chilly and standoffish, wearing her old clothes as a shield, wanting to fit in and not be hurt. She wasn't the same woman now. That ice inside her had indeed melted. Love had done it. "I think it's time to retire the sweater set for good, love. You look really beautiful in your farm clothes."

"I agree!" Ollie said. "Go change, Mom. The ice is melting fast!"

She touched her sweater set with a grimace. "I do like my farm clothes better. If only Baltimore could see me now."

As she was leaving, Ollie tugged on Kade's arm. "Why does she want Baltimore to see her? Sometimes I think she's mad as a March hare. I heard Liam say that about Cousin Bets. Do you know why Cousin Bets was losing her car keys? Nobody will tell me."

According to the buzz in the village, Bets wasn't losing her car keys anymore, and the doorbell was a thing of the past. She and Donal looked radiant and happy, which was good. God knew what the village was saying about him and Megan. Good thing he didn't care.

"Maybe she forgets things like I do," Ryan said, pushing one of the glasses even with the other.

"How's your cocktail?" Kade asked, distracting the boy.

"Good," he said with a slurp. "I need a straw."

Ryan made an affronted noise, making Ollie laugh.

Megan appeared in the doorway in his sweatshirt. She

looked young and sweet again, his favorite. "Do I look okay? It's a little big."

"Of course it's big, Mom." Ollie's voice was filled with drama. "Kade is bigger than you. Come on and drink your cocktails."

She came over to the table. "Which one should I try first?"

Ryan pointed to the first one. "They're in order already. The Maverick martini with passionfruit juice, vodka, and vanilla bitters. The Irish Old Fashioned with a sugar cube, Irish whiskey, bitters, and orange peel."

"I've made her that one," Kade said. "We'll see whose is better."

Ryan snorted. "Mine. Don't interrupt me. The final cocktail is the White Lady with gin, Cointreau, lemon juice, and an egg white. Because the White Lady told me to come visit you, Kade."

His heart started to beat faster in his chest. "What White Lady? Did she have long brown hair and a white dress?"

"Yes," Ryan said with a smile. "She looked like Sorcha Fitzgerald, but I didn't understand how she could be since she's dead."

Megan's face went blank with shock.

"You mean the nice lady Uncle Carrick used to be married to?" Ollie looked from Kade to Ryan, his little brow furrowed. "The one they named the arts center after?"

"That's her," Ryan said, handing Megan her first cocktail, which she looked to be needing. "She was always nice to me. She said coming to visit would make us both happy. I guess she knew I was sad. My girlfriend broke up with me. I lied about texting her."

Kade put his hand on his friend's shoulder. "Why didn't you say anything?"

He shrugged. "I was embarrassed. I thought she liked me."

"I like you," Megan said softly. "I dressed up tonight because I wanted you to like me. I was afraid you might not."

Ryan's mouth gaped. "Not like you? Why wouldn't I? Why wouldn't anyone? You're not different—like me."

She let out a small sigh. "Maybe not, but I feel different. Like I don't fit in. I don't make people laugh like my sister does."

"Aunt Angie's funnier than you, Mom," Ollie said matter-of-factly. "You don't like to joke or play practical jokes. Did you know Aunt Angie put a fake spider in Brady's glovebox because he said he was going to start telling people she wanted more models for her naked paintings? He almost ran off the road when he found it. It was so funny."

Kade bit his lip. "That's not quite the whole story. Brady was going to say she was doing a series of elderly nudes."

"That's the craic," Ryan said, smiling before it faded. "But you don't have to make people laugh for them to like you, Megan. Kade doesn't tell jokes either. He's just kind to people and he listens. Like you. I think that's why you fit. Can I make cocktails at your wedding?"

Kade coughed. "Let me ask her first, man."

Megan put her hand to her mouth, her brown eyes searching for his gaze. "Are you—"

She didn't finish the thought.

"Of course he is, Mom." Ollie let out an aggrieved sound. "He loves you and me. We hang out all the time.

It's what happens next. Kade, where are we going to live?"

"Yeah, Kade, where are you going to live?" Ryan asked. "Your cottage is way too small for more kids."

Megan let out a squeak worthy of Pip. "That's— Oh, my God! I can't believe this. Just...excuse me. I need a minute."

"Your ice is going to melt all the way," Ryan called as she left through the front door of the cottage.

Kade looked at Ryan and Ollie, grinning at him. "Who knew the two of you could be so much trouble together?"

Ollie took Ryan's hand. "I told Ryan—he said to never call him Mr. Hughes—that if he was your good friend, then he'd be mine."

Kade got up and hugged both of them, and they embraced him back. Hard. "I'll go see about Megan."

He grabbed Pip and a cocktail, wondering if he'd need both.

Megan was standing a few steps outside in the cool fall night. The moon was a half shell in a sky filled with curvy clouds. He smelled oranges and looked around for the source.

Sorcha held up her left hand, pointing to her ring finger, then disappeared. He wasn't sure what she meant. Then Megan turned to him, and he knew. Tears were streaming down her cheeks, but her smile was radiant.

"I'm sorry I left like that, but I... Kade, I came out here and all I could think of was being with you and having more kids. Watching them run around the farm like Ollie does. It made me so happy. I've...never imagined feeling as happy as I do with you. It feels like I'm watching the glitter settle in my Dream Jar. I didn't let myself think..."

"That I'd want to marry you?" Kade tucked Pip into the crook of his arm and handed her the cocktail so he could trace the line of her cheek, rubbing away the tears. "Megan, I knew you were the woman I was to marry before you arrived. Then I met you, and I *hoped* you would want to marry me someday. I'd been waiting on you to heal, *mo chuisle*, and to find yourself. Be yourself. That's the woman I love."

"Not the woman in the sweater set."

"No, I love her too." He met her gaze in the moonlight. "She got you to where you are now. With yourself and with me. But you weren't happy being her, love. So putting her on doesn't fit anymore. I like this Megan, the Megan who wants to try three cocktails. The one who moans my name when we make love in the sunlight. The one who cried tears of joy when she thought about us marrying and having a family."

The rightness of the moment stole over him. "I'll be right back, love. Stay here."

He headed back inside, Ryan and Ollie trailing him to his room.

"What are you doing, Kade?" his friend asked.

"If it's okay with Ollie, I was going to ask his mom to marry me." He opened his sock drawer and drew out his grandmother's handkerchief. She'd given him her ring before she died, saying the woman who wore it would be the most fortunate woman in the world.

"Cool!" Ollie took Pip from him and jumped up onto the bed. "Are you going to do the slobbering after?"

Kade rolled his eyes as Ryan pounded him on the shoulder. "Kade's getting married. Oh, I can't wait!"

"Will you stand up with me?" he asked Ryan, putting a hand on his shoulder.

"You know I will," Ryan said. "And Carrick and Liam and all of us will. I'm going to Summercrest Manor tomorrow. Liam said he wanted to learn how to make a good cocktail to impress the ladies. He's full of craic, that one."

Kade smiled, tucking the ring into his palm. "You two stay in here and out of trouble."

He traversed to the front of the house. The cottage's door was slightly open. In his haste, he'd forgotten to close it. Megan stood in the moonlight in his hoodie, touching her short hair. She'd never looked more beautiful to him.

Crossing to her, he looked up as the clouds cleared, moonlight spilling onto the front yard. He took her hand and sank to his knee like he'd always imagined doing. The words were the easiest he'd ever spoken. They were from his heart. "Megan Bennet. I love you with all my soul. Would you do me the honor of becoming my wife and letting me be a husband to you and a father to your boy, whom I also love?"

Tears filled her eyes. "Of course I want to marry you."

He nodded, his own throat thick with emotion. When he held out the ring to her, she pressed her fingers to her lips.

"This was my grandmother's. The stone is small, but it was worn with love for nearly five decades. There's a lot of wisdom in that ring. I thought it might suit you. But if you want another, you have only to say."

"Oh, Kade," she said, taking it carefully and pressing it to her chest. "I love it. I even feel... This is weird. I even feel like her wisdom is wrapping around me."

His skin broke out in goose bumps because he felt it too. Taking the ring, he slid it onto her finger. "Around us, *mo mhuirnín dílis*. You should also know it doesn't only mean my true love. It means my dearly beloved."

She raised her hand to his face and whispered, "*Mo mhuirnín dílis*."

Leaning down, he kissed her softly. Her arms came around him, and the scent of oranges danced in the air with that feeling of wisdom from his grandmother. Then they went inside to celebrate with the boy who was to become his son and the friend who had helped him find his heart. He didn't have to think about which drink he would choose.

He picked up the White Lady and toasted Sorcha.

Then he toasted Ollie and Megan, who held an Irish Old Fashioned, which was only right, and lastly Ryan, who held the Maverick. Because that's what his friend was.

They'd all found themselves through love, and that deserved to be toasted most of all.

CHAPTER TWENTY-ONE

S he was getting married.

     Megan still couldn't believe it.

She rolled over in bed and put her hand on Kade's chest, loving the feel of his skin as much as the sight of his grandmother's ring on her finger. *Her* ring.

They'd dropped Ryan off and left Ollie with Angie and Carrick after sharing the happy news, which had made Angie squeal *"You're getting married!"* so loudly both Carrick and Ollie had plugged their fingers in their ears. Back at the cottage, Megan had asked Kade to see a picture of his grandmother. The request had seemed to please him, and he'd brought down a dusty photobook from the bookshelves around the hearth.

His grandmother's smile hinted at hard times laced with good humor, and her eyes were kind.

Just like Megan's fiancé's.

"I feel like I'm dreaming," she said as he rose up to caress her cheek.

"You wake from dreams." He kissed her ever so softly on the lips. "This isn't a dream. But we might find our clothes. I have a feeling word of our engagement is making the rounds. People will be popping by."

Her body felt like singing crystal, and she didn't want the sensation to end. "For the first time in my life I'm going to say I don't care and stay in bed with you a little longer. I suddenly have great compassion for Bets and Donal and their doorbell fiasco."

His brow rose above sparkling brown eyes. "Well, Megan Bennet... I believe your transformation is complete. I'll just leave a note on the door in case anyone comes, saying we're down at the shore. Either it will keep them occupied or they'll leave. Either way, I imagine it will give us plenty of time for what I think you have in mind. Be right back."

When he returned to bed, lowering down next to her, she slid her bare foot over his calf. The sensation was utterly delicious—and so was his body's answering response. "Kade, how do you feel about *The Kama Sutra*?"

"I'm mostly in favor of it, not knowing the particulars and the like. Why?"

"Your mother gave a book to Bets that I peeked at a month or so ago." She smiled when she realized she wasn't reddening in the cheeks from embarrassment the way she had in the bathroom that night.

Kade laughed out loud. "My father mentioned a book my mother had brought home, and I wondered. They've been having a renewal in their relationship lately, and it's been good to see." His face turned contemplative. "Sometimes I feel hopeful for our relationship, my dad's and mine, but then I remember how we want different things."

She smoothed the brown hair back from his forehead. "If anyone can heal someone's heart, it's you. You do it all the time."

He smiled ruefully. "Isn't it the craic that I can't do it with my own father? But enough of that talk. I believe you had plans for me this morning."

In his bed, she felt bolder than she'd ever imagined possible. "I thought you might like this."

She wrapped her hand around his arousal.

He groaned and pushed into her hand. "I do. What else might you have in mind, I wonder?"

She guided him onto his back and smiled into his grinning face. "How about I show you?"

"I've been waiting for it since I awoke to the sounds of your soft snoring."

"I was *not* snoring!" Her cheeks finally reddened.

"It was adorable," he said, grabbing her waist with both of his large hands. "Especially after you got pissed last night, drinking so many of Ryan's cocktails."

Even though she knew he was teasing, she still picked up a pillow and tossed it at him. "I was celebrating! Plus, they're the best cocktails I've ever had."

"Ouch!" He mimed a stab to the heart. "Ryan does make better cocktails, but thankfully not enough for you to run away with him."

"I'd never leave you," she said, her voice filled with conviction.

He took her left hand and kissed the ring on her finger. "Nor I you. You crossed an ocean to be with me, love. We were meant to be. And I'll love you for as long as I take breath."

She leaned over him and traced his jaw. "And I you. Let me love you now."

After covering him with a condom, she lowered onto him and took him inside her, moving slowly at first, loving his groans and the moment the smile on his face shifted into a pleasant line of tension. That same tension was growing inside her. She picked up the pace, letting her head fall back. One of his hands cupped her breast while the other pressed where they were joined. She cried out, flying back into the clouds, and heard his answering call.

Falling onto his chest, she savored the way his arms gathered her to him, caressing her sweat-slicked back. They lay like that in the quiet of his cottage.

Suddenly a vision started playing through her mind, and the scent of oranges wrapped around her. She could see her, Ollie, and Kade riding ponies on the beach. She could see herself giving birth with Kade supporting her from behind. She could see Ollie running ahead of two twin girls who were chasing him. She could see herself in bed with Kade, whose hair was gray, still watching her with those beautiful, kind brown eyes. The scenes faded, and she shook her head to bring herself back.

"Did you see something, love?"

Her heart started racing. "I think I just had a vision. A few of them."

"I wondered what Sorcha was about when I smelled oranges. Her doing, the visions."

"She can induce visions?" Megan pressed a hand to her forehead. "Kade, we're going to have twins."

He smiled slowly, one of the most beautiful smiles she'd ever seen on him. "I thought as much. Girls. We'll have a grand time with them. Ollie will dote on them rather fierce, I think."

She almost fell off him as she rose up. *"You knew?* How did you know? When did you know? Kade, this is too much!"

"I knew after we made love the first time, and as for how

I knew, I can only say what I always say. I simply did. I can't tell you how."

"Oh, my goodness!" She couldn't sit up anymore, so she flopped onto her back. "I can't believe this. Twins!"

"You looked happy in my visions, so I didn't feel the need to ask if you'd be happy having babies with me, but I'll ask now. Will you?"

She touched her stomach without thought. "Yes. I wanted more with Tyson. But it never happened. Between us, maybe some part of me didn't want it to happen. I didn't like raising Ollie alone."

"Well, neither Ollie nor our twins will be alone." He leaned over her. "We're a family. Now and forever."

Her heart seemed to fill her chest. "I like those words."

"They are grand words, aren't they?" He kissed her again, this time with more haste. "Shall we love each other again and count the number of people fooled by our note?"

She laughed. "Is it terrible of us?"

"No, *mo mhuirnín dílis*. This is our moment to enjoy. One we'll always remember. The mist is coming in from the sea. Come. Let me love you one last time before we let our friends and family shower us with their well wishes."

He did love her well, right up until they heard a car drive up. She stifled her moan as he grew still within her. They heard voices, and then the car drove away. He started to move again, strong and deep inside her, but she was listening now for another arrival.

He pressed in deep, then went still again, grabbing her attention. When she lifted her hips to meet him, he resumed his rhythm until the second car drove up. He stopped again. "This idea doesn't seem to be working as we'd hoped," he said, looming over her. "Do you need me to fill your ears with cotton balls, love?"

When the car drove off, she laughed. "No, but you might pick up the pace. I can't promise what'll happen if another car shows up."

He was chuckling as he began to thrust inside her, but soon they were both moaning and clutching each other. She dug her head into the pillow as she came, and he reared up on his knees and took her deeply, following her over the edge. This time they didn't linger. They were dressing when the third car drove up.

She pulled his hoodie over her head. "I don't know what I was thinking. I can't greet people like this."

He pulled up his pants and zipped them, still mouthwateringly handsome without a shirt. "Why not?"

"I probably look like I've been having sex." She winced as she ran her fingers through her tangled hair. "I'm a mess."

"A gorgeous mess," Kade said, pulling out a navy work shirt from his bureau. "Megan—"

"Kade Donovan! I know you're in there. This is your mother. You have three minutes to present yourself."

Megan's cheeks burned. "Oh, my God!"

"Leave it to Mum." He chuckled as he walked to the door. "I'll hold her off."

She wanted to dive under the covers and hide. But wasn't that shame talking? She didn't want to return to that. She liked being the woman who'd wanted to stay in bed longer making love to her fiancé. "No, I'm going with you."

He smiled as she took his hand. "Brace yourself. I have a feeling it's going to be one hell of a party for the rest of the day."

He was right.

His mother was only the beginning, hugging her not once but three times before Killian showed up and welcomed her to the family. When Shannon arrived and said she'd closed the bookshop and left a note that they were off celebrating St. Kade's engagement, Kade groaned. "The entire village is going to show up."

His dad only patted him on the back and said, "Then we'd best go to the pub so everyone can congratulate you."

And so they did.

Gavin poured them each a whiskey before hugging them both with so much enthusiasm that he lifted them off the floor.

Siobhan arrived with news that everyone in Caisleán had indeed closed their shops for the day so they might come to the pub to celebrate the merry occasion. Declan was one of the first to arrive, alongside Seamus Fitzgerald, who had closed the butcher shop and brought congratulatory steaks.

Megan couldn't believe it, but as she watched the love and affection the people of Caisleán had for Kade, she understood. They knew this was a special moment too, and they wanted to share it with them.

Angie and Carrick arrived with Ollie, who perched on Kade's knee at one of the tables as more people showed up to congratulate them. Liam let out a giant whoop when he arrived, swooping her up off the Brazen Donkey's wooden floor, and Brady kissed her loudly on the cheek before doing the same to Kade.

Pints of creamy-headed stout and drams of whiskey were drunk. Ryan showed up with his mother and father to congratulate them again, and Megan was delighted to see Gavin enlist the Dublin bartender's help in making Irish coffees and any other cocktails the villagers had in mind. She pushed her empty glass of whiskey away and took the first drink Ryan made in the bar, one of the Irish Old Fashioneds she'd enjoyed the night before.

Eoghan, her dear friend, grew so misty-eyed when he congratulated them that he had to pull a wrinkled white handkerchief from his pocket. She teared up too and then hugged the older man gently, feeling Kade's hand warm and strong on her back.

Bets and Donal finally arrived, and Gavin called out a teasing remark about them not picking up their phones. The old Megan might have blushed, but she was happy for them. Her cousin kissed her on both cheeks, saying she was so glad she'd come to Ireland, and Donal embraced her warmly and ordered her another cocktail after finding out what she was drinking.

And then the party really got going.

Gavin put on some Irish music, and Ollie pulled her out of her chair for a dance. From Liam's wink, she knew her cousin had suggested it, so of course she went over and danced with him next. Carrick took the following dance, and then Brady, followed by Declan. Eoghan showed her how to dance a proper Irish jig, and then Kade found her and showed her how downright sexy dancing a jig could be. He was full of surprises, her Kade. The crowd clapped as the patrons belted out songs and danced.

Like the Irish saying, it was a grand time.

They had dinner at the pub, a malty Guinness stew served with piping hot soda bread dotted with Irish butter. The meal was as delicious as the second Irish Old Fashioned in Megan's hand.

Her heart felt like it was tied to a kite, flying high over Caisleán. Kade kept her tucked against his side, his chair pressed against hers all night. Exactly the way she liked it.

Angie and Carrick offered to take Ollie home with them, but she protested. He hadn't been with her last night. Besides, that would be two nights in a row her sister and

Carrick had taken Ollie, and she and Angie had agreed on more balance in their relationship.

Then Liam said he'd love to have a boy's night with Ollie at Summercrest Manor, and the McGrath twins readily agreed. Her son cried out with joy, hugging them all.

She looked at her dear cousin and her smiling boy and said, "All right. Have a great time." She knew people still talked about it being haunted, but she trusted Liam.

Kade leaned in and whispered, "Way to go, love."

She laughed. Before, she'd taken herself so seriously as a mother, but her son had chafed at her rules for him, just as her soul had chafed at the restrictions she'd placed on herself. Their relationship had never been better, and all because she'd lightened up on both of them.

When the time came as it always did for the Lucky Charms to turn on Bon Jovi, she settled back and watched as her sister joined them. They danced to "It's My Life," and for the first time ever, Megan felt the words in her heart.

It *was* her life.

She was going to live it like she wanted to. With Ollie and Kade. In this beautiful community of Caisleán where she'd found herself.

Bets motioned an invitation for her to join them. Her heart warmed. She took a moment to ask herself if she wanted to dance with them in front of the crowd. She didn't. But she *did* want to sing. Louder than she normally would have in the past. Kade's arm came around her, as if he knew she'd made a decision, and she cuddled in closer.

When the evening came to a close, she savored the hugs of her new friends. The old Megan wouldn't have been hugged, least of all liked. She'd been too cold. Too disapproving. Too worried about what everyone would think.

She was so much happier now, and with love in her heart, she waved to her friends as they sent them off in Kade's car with another classic Irish song.

Driving through the village with her fiancé, she already felt like a bride.

The sky was a mix of blacks and grays and a half moon, and the wind traced the land as if lulling it to sleep like a mother might her newborn baby.

She thought of the visons she'd had earlier, of their daughters, and smiled in the darkness.

Her world was complete.

Now she only had to finish the final preparations for St. Stephen's Day, including firing up the kiln again.

This time she realized she had a new reason for wanting to run a successful event.

She wanted to express all the gratitude she felt for her new friends.

CHAPTER TWENTY-TWO

K ade wasn't thrilled about his father wanting to use artificial lighting on Legend.

"I always employ the extra lighting before and after sunset, son." His dad cut his usual stance of hands on hips with a determined thrust of his chin as he stared him down in the shed. "Unless you're telling me that Legend won't take to the lights."

Kade walked over to the mare and looked into her eyes. "No, she'll come into season early like you wish."

Normally a mare needed anywhere from sixty to ninety days of photo stimulation before her first estrous cycle of the season. He wasn't sure Legend was going to need that long. She was happy these days, playing in the fields with Sutter's Mill and exchanging nickers with his ponies. Shannon had taken to racing her—and he did the same when he wasn't racing Red Zephyr, which gave the horse purpose. A horse needed a purpose to be happy, Kade had always thought.

"That's all I need to hear," his father said with a sharp nod. "Maybe with your special magic and the lighting, we'll get twins from Legend."

Kade studied the mare again, and sure enough, he felt the possibility. She would be happy to take care of two foals. Not all mares would be. And in addition to bringing forward the mare's transitional phase as winter ended and spring began, the artificial lighting would encourage the development of multiple anovulatory follicles.

There was a downside though: an unpredictable estrous cycle.

"I'd like to put one of my ponies in the pasture with Legend to alert us when she's ready."

"I've used stud ponies before."

"She and Winston are fast friends. That would be my choice. You'll want to keep training Sutter's Mill, not have him lolling in the field with a mare. Plus, you'll want to decide when to breed her. With the lighting, she might come into season early, Dad."

"I'm good with that plan," his father said, "and I'll be trusting you to keep your pony well tethered."

He snorted. "You keep your stallions away from my side of the farm. You're the one who's had a few break through their stalls at the smell of a mare in heat."

"Not anymore." He glared at him. "I keep the mares well away, and with Legend down this far, none of my stallions are likely to scent her. It's all been brilliant so far. I don't see any reason why that shouldn't continue. I'll bring down the lights and the timers then."

Good fortune was shining on them. But he was going to keep everything buttoned up on his end, per their agreement. He had a lot riding on it.

Once he had his own land, he would be free of his father's hopes and he could live his own life and build his new family a home.

"I'm thinking we'll need to find Legend a new stall. My other ponies won't appreciate the extra hours of light when winter is upon us."

His dad stalked to the stall at the end of the shed and popped the door open. "This one should do. I don't see a problem with you emptying the stall next to her."

Legend loved her pony friends, but Kade knew they would continue to nicker at each other even if she was in the far stall. "Fine, then."

"Fine," his father repeated. His gaze turned speculative. "Son, I'm glad we're working on this. Together. With you getting married soon and having a family, I hope you might consider helping me more with the breeding. For your future. As you can see, there isn't much to it when you have the right partner, and we work well together. It's thanks to you that I found Sutter's Mill. I've already arranged for him to stud twenty horses in the coming season. And I'm working on arrangements for Red Zephyr as well."

Twenty was a lot in terms of stud fees, and they both knew it. "I'm glad for you, Dad. Even unproven, your reputation for knowing your horseflesh is evident."

"Sutter's Mill is going to sire champions." He walked over and stroked Legend's mane. "I've never been more certain. You think on what I said."

He wished his father could be content with their current arrangement. Except he knew better. Perhaps he was like his father. Hadn't he dug his feet into the earth time and time again to pursue what he wanted and make a name for himself? "I can't make that promise, Dad."

His father stroked his jaw. "You might change your mind after you marry. A man's priorities shift when he has his family. Didn't I stop going to all those horse shows and watching my own stallions at the races? I wanted to be home for supper with your mother, you, and your sister. I made sacrifices—ones I don't regret. So might you. Only a stupid man thinks he has all the answers before he's walked a mile in another's shoes."

He could feel a tugging on that invisible chain that his dad liked to pull, the one that filled him with frustration. He took a step back and leaned against the closest stall, not taking the bait. "Dad, all I'm focusing on is enjoying my engagement and the woman I love and the boy who'll be my son. I'll face each day like I do now. With an open heart. It's worked for me so far."

"An open heart." His father let out a sigh. "Talking to you is sometimes like talking to the wind. But I will say again how happy your mother and I are about you finding Megan and the boy. You all suit each other, and I'll be glad to call them family. I'll leave you now."

His father left the shed. Winston let out a gusty neigh, making Kade laugh. Duke appeared from under Winston's stall. "Is that where you were hiding?"

He picked up the dog and rubbed him behind the ears. "How about we go and lend some support to our girl? She'd loading the kiln as we speak."

Last night, she'd been as up and down as the tides during a storm. He'd made dinner as Ollie ran around the small kitchen chasing Pip, who loved it when the boy raced after him. After putting Ollie to bed, they'd sat on the settee, and he'd simply held her, sensing her distraction and disquiet.

In the morning, he'd reminded her everything was going to go fine with the kiln this time. The sprinklers had been changed out for ones set to a higher temperature, and she'd taken the extra precaution of meeting with Caisleán's fire brigade to walk them through the kiln process, pointing out the difference between a perfectly working kiln and one actually on fire. Lastly, he'd helped her put a padlock on the kiln.

When he arrived in the pottery room at the arts center, he was pleased to see Angie siting on a stool beside the loading shelves, keeping Megan company. She looked peaked from the morning sickness, God love her, especially against the deep hues of her burgundy jacket. He slid an arm around her and hugged her.

"You two seem to be managing all right."

Megan looked over her shoulder, a glazed pot in hand, and smiled, although he could see the tension in the cut of her shoulders.

Angie uttered a little moan and dug a cracker out of her bag. "Do horses have morning sickness?"

"No," Kade said, feeling terrible for the Yank. "I rather think the phrase 'healthy as a horse' referred to a pregnant mare."

"I want to be a horse." Angie crunched on her cracker. "Did you know I can't get near any sheep now that I'm pregnant?"

"Of course. Cows too."

Megan turned around, pot in hand. "Whyever not?"

"There's something about an infection the animals might have—when they're pregnant and birthing themselves." Angie shivered. "Carrick is even having his mother wash his work clothes just to be safe."

Though Kade knew of the precaution, he wanted to reassure Angie. "While the incidents are rare, it's wise to be cautious."

"I had no idea," Megan said. "Should I tell Ollie not to play with the sheep?"

"Carrick already talked to him," Angie said. "He's getting all kinds of education at the farm. Megan, I hope you won't mind that Carrick told him what the ram was up to with the ewes. Ollie was watching from the fence line. He kept it clinical."

Kade bit his lip as Megan grimaced.

"Are you laughing at us city girls, Kade Donovan?" Megan asked.

"Never." He went over and put an arm around her. "But you're living around farms. Breeding is a way of life. It's nature."

"I have to say I was shocked the first—and second time—that I saw a cow's penis," Angie said, making Kade laugh. "It looks like a really long carrot."

"Does it really?" Megan's voice held a shocked note as he released her so she could resume her work.

"There's even a Gaelic word for a man's that implies it's a carrot," Kade said, watching as they both blinked at him. "*Bliúcán.*"

"*Bliúcán.*" Angie laughed as she gave a theatrical wince. "Tonight I'm going to tell Carrick that I want to see his *bliúcán.*"

"I would pay good money to see his face, but I'll bet he'll show it to you all the same," Kade said, winking at his future sister-in-law.

"You two are terrible." Megan picked up another pot and set it carefully inside the kiln.

"But your shoulders aren't inching up to your ears anymore, so I'd say this talk is helping." He waggled his brows, feeling impish. "Want to learn other naughty Gaelic words?"

"I do!" Angie said, looking less peaked already.

Megan chuckled as she continued to load the kiln, and since Kade would do anything to make her laugh, he taught the two Yanks naughty words in Gaelic. He couldn't wait to hear what Carrick had to say. His friend would laugh like crazy to hear what "St. Kade" had gotten up to.

He regaled the women with classical poetic phrases like "*tá breac ar mo dhuán,*" which meant "I've got a trout on my hook," and "*an seinnfeá port ar mo dhiúdalín,*" which meant "will you play a tune on my flute?"

Seeing the two sisters laughing easily with each other warmed his heart. They'd had their struggles, but here they were laughing over naughty Gaelic phrases while Angie sat in support for her sister.

When he smelled oranges, he grinned. Sorcha, being a poet, had loved Gaelic. He wondered if she'd inspired some of the more colorful phrases he was sharing. They weren't his usual, as Megan knew, but maybe he'd try using them more—if only because they made her laugh.

He was changing too, he realized. Like Megan, he'd lightened up some. It felt good.

Later that month, Kade had something else to be thankful for. Bets, Megan, and Angie arranged an American Thanksgiving celebration for the family. Liam basted the early turkey Donal had secured from a local farmer, wearing a girly apron that his older brother, Wyatt, had given him one Christmas as a joke. It surprised no one when Bets and Angie kept ruffling the pink lace, except Donal did it too.

Before the meal, Bets invited everyone to take a moment of silence to count their blessings, and this year, Kade's cup was overflowing. He squeezed Megan's hand under the table, already looking forward to their Thanksgiving next year. They'd be married by then, as they'd already agreed to have a small ceremony after Angie and Carrick since Megan's parents would still be in town. She'd made the suggestion with a pinched face, so he'd asked if she'd prefer to wait—or elope.

The new Megan wasn't quite ready for eloping, she told him, although she could see the wisdom in it. Since both of them wanted to live together and start their lives together sooner rather than later, he'd agreed, saying he'd handle the details like the officiant and the wedding supper as she was preoccupied with the final preparations for the St. Stephen's Day fair.

He would start building their home in the new year, but until it was ready, their family would reside in his cottage. He couldn't wait to see what touches Megan would bring to his very basic living space. His granny would be pleased, looking down from heaven.

December rolled in with more pearly skies, colder weather, and rain. The wind had its way with the remaining leaves on the ash, hawthorn, and oak trees. Their bare branches rose up like bones, giving the land a mournful feel. The days grew shorter, and he both awoke and went to sleep in darkness. But he didn't mind. Angie and Carrick had offered to have Ollie stay with them two nights a week, which meant Kade had at least two mornings of waking up next to Megan, and they found other moments alone in the early afternoon hours. But her scent was always with him.

Legend basked in the artificial lights in her new stall, as if she were one of the girls in town lying on Lacken Strand Beach hoping for more color. His father proclaimed he'd never seen a mare so ready for covering, and Kade had to agree. Before long, Legend would be an expectant mother like Angie.

Soon Megan would be one too.

The holiday season blew in like an Irish storm, soft and gentle one moment and tough and bracing the next. Megan loaded kilns for herself and the class and suggested people bring in holiday treats for their last class, which fell mid-December. He had to tell her the Irish didn't really prepare the kinds of cookies and holiday baked goods she and Angie had been making since the beginning of the month. So she'd pivoted and told people to bring in their favorite drink. That had worked. The Irish knew how to drink, after all.

No one actually made anything new that last night. Lisa Ann and Keegan sat holding hands, their affection clear, and everyone collected their fired pots. Kade was pleased with his takeaways. He'd made bowls for his mother and sister, a mug that would fit his father's large hand, a cocktail stirrer for Ryan (as well as one for himself), and candlesticks for his cottage as he loved seeing Megan in candlelight, whether at his table or in his bed.

The week leading up to Christmas found him and many in their community setting up for the fair. He and his friends hauled in tables and chairs and constructed booths where baked goods and Megan's pottery would be sold. She had nearly a hundred pieces, all stunning to the eye, and he had a good feeling she was going to sell all of it. Siobhan had also knitted up a storm, producing a variety of hats, gloves, and even a few blankets.

He walked the horse racecourse with his father, Eoghan, and Donal, and they all agreed the course was wet but not unsafe. Cormac O'Sullivan's betting book was packed full, with Kade's father as the favorite to win.

The joy of the season had never been more palpable.

That is, until he met Megan's father for the first time with the rest of the family.

When Colonel Dan Newcastle strode into Bets O'Hanlon's parlor after arriving from the Dublin airport, he approached Megan, looked her up and down, and said, "You're still too skinny, and that haircut and those clothes only make it worse."

And Kade, who'd always been a man of peace, had the shocking urge to punch Dan Newcastle right in the face.

CHAPTER TWENTY-THREE

Her father wasn't any different.

But Megan had changed, and she stared back at him instead of looking away. He still had the thick neck of a man who lifted weights daily and did the calisthenics he'd learned in the military. No emotion had shown in his flat eyes, the size and shape of hers, as he delivered his jab, although there was a charming smile on his face that suggested he'd done her a favor. Because, after all, he knew better. He had the medals of distinction to prove it.

She'd once believed that.

She didn't anymore.

But Kade's hand came to rest on the center of her back, a silent reassurance, and she decided to ignore her father's insult. "Did you have a pleasant drive?"

"I can't say I like driving on the left-hand side of the road, but I mastered it. All it takes is focus. Ollie, you remember that when your time comes. Are you doing the calisthenics I taught you to make you strong?"

Tyson had joined her father in supporting that lunacy, she remembered. Ollie had only just turned six, and his face

AVA MILES

had gone white when his father and grandfather had dropped into push-ups and gone through a series of exercises in front of him, showing him what he "needed" to do to be strong. He hadn't felt accepted by either of them. Neither had she.

"Ollie's helping Carrick and Kade out at their farms," she said, putting a protective hand on his shoulder.

"I can do the fencing and chase down sheep," he said, lifting his chin proudly.

"He's an incredible helper," Kade said at last. "I'm Kade Donovan. Megan's fiancé."

Her father looked him straight in the eye. "You're the pony guy, right?"

Megan's throat burned with anger. How dare he say that to Kade. "He's—"

"I own a pony therapy farm, and I help championship horses heal when no one else can help them," Kade said, his mouth tipping up on the side. "Welcome to Ireland."

Again, his father took Kade's measure. "Thank you. My wife has been wanting to come back for a long time. I imagine the girls will want to go off and do girl stuff, especially since Angie is in the family way before the wedding. Not that I'm surprised by that. I did my best to take the hellion out of that one. Maybe we can have a beer at the pub."

Megan dug her fingers into her palms at the insult to Angie. In the past, she'd gone along with him calling Angie things like that in the hope of gaining his approval. She'd even started to believe it was better for her sister to fight her so-called artistic tendencies. How could she have been so blind?

"I imagine there's plenty of time for a beer," Kade said. "Megan, am I remembering correctly that you and Ollie

280

needed to check on a few things for the St. Stephen's fair?"

Megan looked over to where her mother stood, talking to Bets and Donal in front of the fireplace. Angie and Carrick had offered to help Liam with the tea and coffee in the kitchen. She envied them, but she would take Kade's tactical retreat and run with it.

"Kade is right. We have some pressing items to attend to for the fair. We'll see you later."

"Fine. Be good to get a run in before it's too dark." Raising his voice to be heard over the chatter, he said, "Patty, Megan and Ollie are taking off, and I know you'll be chatting with Bets until I drag you off to bed. I'm going for a run. Bets, if you'd show me where we'll be bunking..."

Bets pasted a smile on her face, but Donal put a hand on her arm. "I'll show you, Dan. We can haul the bags up together."

The two men left the room. Megan relaxed immediately. Her mother came over, her short silver hair frizzed as much from the plane ride as the humidity in the air.

"You're leaving already?"

"We have some last-minute matters that need attending for the fair," she said, telling herself not to feel guilty. She loved her mom. They just weren't close.

"I understand," her mom said, smiling at Ollie. "You have a full plate, what with the fair, Angie's wedding, and your own. But I'm here now. I can help."

She'd heard these words all her life. The old Megan would have ceded to her, presuming her mother could do it better. Heck, her mother could run circles around her. But not this time.

"You and Angie can talk about what she'd like help with for her wedding." That was her sister's prerogative. "As for me, I'm good with the fair, and we're fine on the wedding front. You just enjoy yourself."

Her mother's unpainted mouth parted. "Oh, I see. Well, if you change your mind... Ollie, why don't you stay here with Grandma while your mother does her errands?"

He clutched Megan's leg, which squeezed her heart. "He can't, Mom. Ollie is vital to our efforts. Aren't you? He's helping with the pony rides."

He raised his head and gave her the most beautiful smile she'd ever seen. "Yes, I am. Come on, Mom. Let's go. We have important things to do."

She kissed the top of his head. "I'll just go and say goodbye to Angie and Carrick. And Liam." Her cousin had come over to see her parents, but he'd almost immediately retreated to the kitchen.

"I'll join you," Kade said. "Ollie, can you check on Pip in the jeep?

Her son raced off after giving Kade a big grin.

"The drinks are taking an awful long time, probably because Angie feels so ill," her mother said. "My God, her color is downright sallow from morning sickness. I'll have to do something about that."

Megan hoped her mom could, being a nurse. She patted Kade's arm as she walked away. When she reached the kitchen, Angie had her hand to her head while Carrick stood beside her, tapping his boots hard into Bets' ancient wooden floors. Liam was banging around in the kitchen.

"It won't have to be murder, Yank," Carrick said. "Any of our friends would agree to serve as witness and say I killed your dad in self-defense."

"You can count me in," Liam said, slamming the cupboard door.

Megan bit her lip. She didn't know what her father had

said to Angie's face, but the comment he'd made earlier had been bad enough.

"He actually used the phrase 'knocked up.' Why did I agree to have them come to our wedding?"

"Because you like your mother," Carrick said, "and it's not like you can only invite one of them."

Kade firmly closed the kitchen door behind her. "I might serve as a witness too, Carrick. He's the first man I've ever wanted to punch."

"A flaw in St. Kade," Liam said, arranging the cups on a tray. "I'm glad I'm not staying here. Poor Mum, although I expect Donal will be at her side whenever Dan is around. Patty's not too bad. She's a busy one though, isn't she?"

"She wants to help with your wedding, Angie," Megan said.

Angie blew out a breath. "I might let her. Liam's right. She needs to keep busy. It's Dad I'm worried about. What are we going to do with him?"

"He's going on a run now," Megan said.

Kade put his hand to her back again. "He mentioned drinking beer at the pub. Let him go down there. There's plenty of men who will talk to him. They'll either be insulted or they won't. What did your mother see in him, I wonder?"

"He was a high-ranking soldier with a lot of charisma," Angie said. "You should have seen him back in the day. Straight out of *An Officer and A Gentleman*."

"I like that movie," Liam said, "but it's really fucked up."

"Word," Angie said. "Mom deals with sick people all the time, so she likes a strong man who knows his own mind. Plus, he doesn't talk to her like that. He respects her work as a nurse. He gets almost emotional talking about all of the nurses who saved the men who were injured under his command. He's an asshole but not a psychopath."

"That's a hell of a distinction, Yank," Carrick said, putting a hand on her shoulder, "and it doesn't make me want to punch him any less."

"Me either," Kade said.

"Same here," Liam agreed. "I'm going to have to release all this pent-up anger somehow. Anyone up for a holiday meditation at Summercrest Manor?"

They all groaned.

"What are we going to do?" Angie asked, tipping her head up to the sky.

A loose plan suddenly formed in Megan's mind. "Keep Mom busy. Encourage Dad to go to the pub. And don't talk to them alone. Ollie doesn't want to be around them either."

"Who can blame him?" Liam pushed the tray aside. "We'll look out for him, cousin. Not to worry."

"We will," Carrick repeated, and she heard the vow in his voice.

That made her tear up. "Thank you. We'll keep him busy with the fair. After that, we'll figure things out."

"I have plenty of fencing that needs tending," Carrick said with a grin. "Kade, aren't your ponies hungrier around the holidays? I could have sworn you give them some extra hay to see them through these long, cold Irish nights."

Angie laughed. "We sound like we're planning for the Battle of the Bulge."

Megan had never liked talking military. Tyson had done it all the time and driven her nuts. "Do you know what? I just realized another good thing about moving to Ireland."

"We're far away from Mom and Dad?" Angie laid a hand over her belly. "It's sad, really. Part of me still wishes it could be different."

"Wishing is one thing," Kade said softly, "and it's not a bad thing. But when it doesn't present itself, you need to make other arrangements."

They shared a look. "So let's make them," Megan said.

No one was going to ruin her first holiday with Kade, the St. Stephen's fair, or her and Angie's weddings. For the first time in her life, Megan Bennet was going to rebel against her parents.

God, it felt good.

CHAPTER TWENTY-FOUR

Bets was going to kill Dan.

"I'd forgotten how much I disliked him," she said to Donal as they snuck out of the main house toward the shed, or their love lair #2 as Donal liked to call it. "The way he talked about Megan and Angie made me see red."

"He's a difficult man. You'll get no argument from me there."

"Patty is the same as ever, but I feel different." *Set in her ways* was the phrase that came to mind for her cousin.

"How so, *mo ghrá?*" he asked as they entered the shed and he hit the lights.

She loved that he was already pulling off his boots. "I looked at her buzzing around to clean up in the kitchen after I told her to leave it, not taking a moment to connect with who and what was around her. Liam's been a good influence on me that way. I used to be crazy busy like that when I was a bartender."

"You're nonstop when you work in a pub." Donal tore off his jacket and then went to undo the buttons of his shirt.

Bets decided to sit down and enjoy the view, enjoyment

being her new *modus operandi* about life. Since they'd dived into this part of their relationship, she couldn't get enough of him. "I was nonstop, and then I had three boys."

He tugged on his pants playfully. "And now you have me."

She did, thank God. "But you aren't busy like that, even with your sheep and the doorbell incident. You look around and take in your surroundings. You sit and read with me or hold my hand. You listen. You don't make me tired." All the oxygen seemed to be sucked up from the room when Dan and Patty were in it. Mostly Dan.

"Are you too vexed to make love?" he asked softly.

She cocked a brow. "Now, why would you think that?"

"I'm used to such things ruining the mood," he said, scrubbing his jaw.

"Come here," she said, patting the comforter.

He strode toward her, his broad chest making her mouth water. He was crazy if he thought she'd let Dan ruin her evening.

"Don't sit down yet," she said when he reached her.

His green eyes fired as she reached out and grabbed the waistband of his pants, angling him toward her.

"Let me show you just how much I'm in the mood."

When he was spent—and then later when she was—she crawled onto his body. He was so large, she could lie comfortably on him like he was her own heated mattress. When they slept together, and they were doing so more and more, she slept on him.

"You might need to bring over a few more things than your toothbrush," she said, tracing the muscles in his arms. "I love watching you leave in the same clothes you had on, but you might shock my cousin."

He laughed. "I doubt that. I suspect I could be bleeding

from an artery, and she wouldn't blink. She's fierce. Like her husband. I can see why they suit."

She rose up. "Couples are weird sometimes."

"Do you think we're weird?" he asked, caressing her cheek.

"Sometimes," she said, kissing him lightly on the mouth. "We've known each other for decades, but now we're wild for each other. Except...I guess I never really knew you at all."

"Nor I you," he said softly. "But I'm glad to know you as I do now. I love you, Bets."

She hugged him, settling more into the rightness of the feeling. "I love you too. How would you like to go to Paris after the new year? Heck, maybe we should be cliché and go for Valentine's Day."

He rolled her onto her back, looming over her. "Took you long enough to ask."

She blew a raspberry in response.

"Do you know why you weren't sure about coming away with me before?"

She traced the middle of his chest, feeling his heartbeat against her fingers. "You're going to tell me, huh?"

"You wanted to know we'd be good together first." He made a triumphant sound. "Admit it. And now that you—and I—know the full of it, you're starting to imagine what's next."

She almost cracked "A baby?" but it wasn't funny, even if it was impossible. "Living together?" she asked, knowing he meant marriage.

He kissed her hard on the mouth. "If you want. Maybe it's my age, but I know a ring won't make me love you any less or treat you any different. I'm trusting the same is true for you."

He was right. It wouldn't change. But she still wasn't sure about marriage. "Something screwy happens to people when they get married."

"Please, for the love of God, don't say that to the Yanks," he said with a sigh. "You have something else on your mind. What is it?"

She startled. How had he—

"I wasn't going to say until after the weddings. There's nothing we can do about it anyway."

"You'll tell me since it's been weighing on you for a week now." He tapped her nose, his green eyes steady. "You can always unburden yourself to me, *mo ghrá*. I thought you knew that."

"I do." She leaned over and punched the pillow. "We didn't get the grant funding. They somehow heard about our 'fire' and the resulting damage. They even read the report. We don't seem to know what we're doing yet, the letter said. Maybe next year, when we can show we've addressed some of our issues and have more experience running the arts center. It pissed me off."

Donal sat up and pulled her into his arms. "The only way they could have heard was if they contacted the county council. This sounds like Tom MacKenna's doing."

She thought so too. "I still feel like I'm to blame. Maybe I didn't write a compelling enough application."

"Angie read your responses, as did I," he said, taking her by the shoulders. "It was a right fine application."

"But we don't have the money, Donal." She started to bite her fingernail and thought better of it since she had a fresh manicure. "We're going to have to do more fundraising."

"So we have another fundraiser," he said, pulling her onto his lap. "I'll sell my sheep if I have to—"

"We talked about this. You—or Carrick—aren't selling your sheep. Dammit! None of us can start funding the center like that. It needs to be independent."

"Still..." He tipped her chin up. "It's as I told you when I first came to call. I'm retiring soon. I'll be selling sheep and land, likely to Carrick, since I like him and he's starting to feel like family."

Her throat grew tight. *Family*. What a powerful word.

"I want to be with you, *mo ghrá*. Always. But we'll leave that for now."

She put her head to his shoulder. His girls were coming for the holiday, and they'd agreed he would spend it with them and Eoghan. He had his family, and she had hers, only things would feel strange this year without Wyatt and Rhys. She was grateful for her cousins and Carrick and Kade— along with Liam, of course—but there was still Patty and Dan to contend with.

"You're sad, and you're thinking too much," he said, laying her back and cradling her against his body. "The holidays can do that to a person. I'll be missing you at Christmas dinner, Bets."

Her eyes grew wet. She felt so emotional with him sometimes. Her heart could feel like a bunch of birthday balloons in one minute and raw meat in the next. *Love*. New love. She'd forgotten the highs and lows of it.

"Will you make love to me again?" she whispered.

He turned them onto their sides and pulled her leg over his hip. "Always."

His kisses were tender and sweet and so filled with love, she had to clench her eyes shut so tears wouldn't leak. This wasn't how sex was supposed to be...or at least she didn't remember it being like this.

Except this was what she needed, and he knew it. He

always knew. The unhurried kisses turned into a slow rhythm as he finally entered her. Her body seemed to stretch in response, infused with a love it needed and craved —a love she always found in his arms.

When he turned off the light, he pulled her onto his body. "Go to sleep now."

She cuddled into him, comforted by his touch as much as his warmth. Her mind started to replay what he'd said to her. He had a way with words, her Donal, and she loved remembering them. Yes, they needed to go away to Paris and explore what was next for them. She also needed to brainstorm some more ideas to solve the arts center's problems. Tom MacKenna, Orla, and Mary weren't finished. They'd shown they wanted to go another round by sabotaging the grant application. She had to find a way to stop their machinations completely.

His hand settled on the back of her head as if to calm her racing thoughts. She remembered her desire to enjoy the moment and told her mind to shut it.

She could think up a plan after the holidays.

CHAPTER TWENTY-FIVE

Megan surveyed her art stand in the corner of the main Donovan shed.

Pride shot through her as she glanced over the varying pieces—everything from mugs to vases and bowls. She hugged herself. She'd done this! Her. She dug out her phone to take a picture, and there was a text from Bets.

Your mother is on her way.

Her happiness deflated even though she was grateful for Bets' heads-up. She'd managed to mostly stay away from her parents, what with the final preparations for the St. Stephen's Day fair the day after tomorrow. Ollie was with Kade and the other men, checking out the racecourse one last time. Tonight they would have a traditional Irish dinner for Christmas Eve.

"Megan! I thought I'd grab some exercise so I walked over here. Are these all yours?"

Her mother. She turned, bracing herself. Her mom walked into the shed with her brisk power walk, her intelligent eyes assessing everything in sight. "Yes."

"They're beautiful." She came forward and picked up a

cobalt blue mug. "I'm glad you're creating again. You seem happier than I've ever seen you. Even with Tyson. I hope you don't mind my saying so."

Her mother had never said a word about Tyson other than to say how much he was like her father, who'd adored him. "Ireland has been good to Ollie and me."

"So I see." She picked up a vase this time. "Kade especially. He reminds me of a male nurse I used to work with. He knows how to heal people."

She could feel defensiveness rising inside her. "Are you saying I needed healing?"

"Yes." Those direct hazel eyes turned on her. "It wasn't in my power. Or Angie's."

"Certainly Dad was no help," she blurted out.

Her mother set a hand on her thin waist. "You and Angie have a tough time with your father, but you're no better at seeing him for who he is than he is at seeing you two. He's a natural leader. There isn't a single thing that could faze that man. Trust me. We've both shared our horror stories—mine at the hospital and his in battle. He knows how to help men reach full potential. That's all he's been trying to do with you girls."

Megan felt tongue-tied and wrong again, looking for approval that would never come. She cleared her throat. Today she was going to speak up. Even if her mother got mad at her. "I didn't want to be molded, Mom. I wanted to be loved."

Her mom fingered the simple gold necklace she always wore at her throat. "You need both. You're a parent. Kids don't come with instruction manuals. You need to help them figure out who they are. Push them to become the best versions of themselves."

Something popped inside her. "Then you failed. Both

of you." The words seemed to burn in her mouth. "Because until I came to Ireland, I had no idea who I was. I'd always tried to be what Dad wanted. A sweet and quiet little girl who didn't make waves. Angie resisted his model for us, and he punished her for it. I didn't want to be punished, so I played it safe. And you let me."

Her mother's mouth tightened. "While I tried to soften some of your father's harder edges, I didn't disagree with his methods usually. He pushed you to discover who you were. That you didn't until now isn't his fault. It's yours."

Her chest tightened at her mother's version of tough medicine. The adult she was knew there were slivers of truth to it, but the child she'd been wanted to throw something.

"But we're getting off track." Her mom smiled then, as if the shot was over and it was time to dispense the lollipop. "You've found yourself. You've gotten back into pottery and teaching, which you loved, and you're going to marry a good man who will take care of you and Ollie. I'm proud of you. Your father is too, even though he doesn't say it."

Megan didn't believe that. Her father didn't respect Kade or his work. It wasn't macho enough for him. As for her mother, the gulf between them felt as wide as ever, except she didn't want to bridge it like she had with Angie. While she and her sister had been through some rocky bumps, they'd communicated honestly about it. Both of them had also changed, which had helped them forge a new bond. But she could tell that experience wouldn't be replicated with her mother—and certainly not with her father.

"Mom, I need to finish up here." She picked up one of her pieces—a green pitcher—and clutched it to her stomach. "I'll see you back at Bets' for dinner."

"I can help," her mother said, scanning the shed. "I miss keeping busy. Put me to work."

No. Her inner voice practically shouted the word. "It would take more time to explain. I'm good here."

Her mother's nod was crisp. "Fine, then. I'll head back to the house."

Watching her mother walk away, her pace brisk as always, came as a relief. Megan clenched her eyes shut, feeling raw from old hurts, old patterns. She promised herself to continue being a better mother to Ollie. To forget all the pushing and molding that clearly hadn't worked on her. She wasn't going to pass her feelings of inadequacy and hurt down to Ollie or her future children with Kade. Her mind showed her the girls, and then she jumped and let out a scream when something touched her shoulder.

Her eyes flew open. A beautiful woman with long brown hair stood before her in a white dress. The smell of oranges touched her nose, and every hair on her body stood on end. "Oh, my God! You're Sorcha. I can *see* you."

Her smile was soft and slightly crooked. "I asked for a boon, for us to meet. This seemed like a good time. Your parents' visit has stirred up deep wells of emotion inside you. You need to keep your eyes on the prize, as you Yanks say. Don't let the past pull you under again, Megan. If you feel yourself falter, reach for Kade. You couldn't be in better hands."

She disappeared. Megan's legs gave out, and she sank to the floor. She'd just seen Carrick's dead wife, a thought that made her belly tremble. There had been wisdom as much as a warning in Sorcha's advice.

Hurrying from the shed, she called Kade.

"Hiya," he answered after a few rings. "Are you finished with the display? We're wrapping up on this end. If you can, I'd love for you to meet me at my shed. I have some-thing to show you and Ollie. He's high on the Christmas candy Eoghan had in his pocket as we walked the track."

It occurred to her it might be better to tell him about Sorcha's visit in person. "I'll be there soon."

"Are you all right? Your voice sounds funny."

"I'll tell you when I see you."

And she did tell him after he sent Ollie to check on Legend in her small pasture beside the shed.

"Well, that's quite a boon, isn't it?" He had his arm around her already, but the other one lifted to touch her cheek. "She must have wanted very much to tell you those things."

Leaning against his chest, she savored the feeling of his arms around her. "I'd just had a fight of sorts with my mother."

"It's been brewing," he said, rubbing her back. "You and Angie both have things that seem to be bursting out of you. Carrick made a similar observation. If it makes you feel any better, he and I have things brewing inside, seeing the way they treat you."

She felt tears burn her eyes. "I realized I don't *like* them. Not even my mother. I used to be able to ask her to do anything, and I should probably be more grateful that she was always willing to help. But she never asked me how I felt or sat down and listened to me."

"She knows how to do busy love," Kade said softly as the ponies nickered in their stalls. "That's what I call it. The kind where someone only does things for others. Some people don't know how to do any other kind of love."

"You do," she said, pressing back to look into his face. "You give the kind of love I've wanted my whole life. The kind that nurtures and supports and loves and heals. The kind where I never feel wrong or less. For that, I am beyond grateful."

He leaned down and kissed her, and some of the tightness in her chest eased. When he inched away, she cupped his jaw, needing more.

"Ugh! Are you two slobbering?"

Kade gave her a wink before turning to look at Ollie. Her little boy had a bold grimace on his face, but underneath, she could see the smile in his eyes as he bit into a candy cane. "We are. It's something people in love do."

"I know!" He rolled his eyes dramatically, crunching on the candy a bit more before he spoke again. "Aunt Angie and Uncle Carrick do it all the time too when they think I'm not around. Kade, what's my present?"

She blinked at the rapid change of subject. "Your present? I thought we were doing presents tomorrow morning?"

Kade grinned. "These presents would be a little tough to bring into the house. Come with me."

Ollie jumped and let out a whoop. "Presents! You said presents."

They walked through the yard to the pasture where he usually held his healing hospital, the sun's rays powering through clouds of white and baby blue, the only kind she'd ever seen in Ireland. The last horse he'd been helping had left the previous week after overcoming his depression over a leg injury. There were two horses she didn't recognize, both close to the fence line. One was a black pony about four feet high with white socks. The other was a full-size horse in the most beautiful shade of russet.

Kade walked to the gate and turned to face them as the big horse nuzzled his back. "Merry Christmas, you two. I thought it was time you had your own horses."

Megan's mouth dropped.

"He's mine?" Ollie asked after an audible gasp.

"He sure is," Kade said, stroking the mane of the pony, who gave a sweet whinny. "His name is Socks."

"Oh, Kade!" Ollie raced toward him and wrapped his arms around the man. "Thank you! Thank you! Thank you!"

Tears filled Megan's eyes, and this time she let them spill, her throat thick for a different reason. "Kade, it's the most beautiful present I've ever been given."

His brown eyes were shining. "I'm glad she pleases you. Her name is Breezy. Another sign she's right for you. I decided a horse might suit you best as I feel you have a rising urge to ride like the wind."

Every time they rode on the beach, she wanted to urge her mount into a gallop and race the current in the sea. "You know me."

"I do at that," he said, making her heart burst with joy.

She and the rest of her party got through Christmas Eve dinner. The turkey Bets had basted was the best she'd ever tasted, which helped. Kade said he and Carrick had something planned for the evening, so the two couples—and, of course, Ollie—excused themselves shortly after dinner, inviting Liam to come with them.

Megan felt a little bad about leaving Bets alone with her parents, but that guilt ended when Liam rubbed her arm and confessed that his mother had called in the troops. Those troops being the Lucky Charms. They were arriving with holiday-themed drinks and so much Bon Jovi that Dan —and perhaps Patty—would inevitably head to bed early.

Megan and Kade and the others had a few drinks at Jamie's small cottage, joined by the McGrath twins. They followed a similar pattern on Christmas Day. Kade joined her and Ollie to see what Santa had brought him. Afterward, they met Angie and Carrick at Bets' house for a late Christmas brunch and to open gifts. The tension with her parents was noticeable, but they got through it. The Lucky Charms and their husbands arrived to take over and help Bets so she and the others could go off to Angie and Carrick's for more holiday cheer.

When they finally returned to her cottage, Kade carried a sleeping Ollie into his room, giving Megan an opportunity to retrieve the gift she'd wanted him to open while they were alone together.

When they nestled together on her small settee, she handed it to him.

He kissed her even before seeing it, which touched her deeply. After laying the bright red wrapping paper he'd torn apart aside, he opened the box. She saw his throat move and was equally affected.

"It seems we had a similar theme for our gifts," she whispered.

Lifting out the sculpture of the white horse she'd made, he ran his hands over the curves she'd lovingly made from clay. "My God, Megan. It's beautiful. The most beautiful thing I've ever seen."

"It's not only because you love horses." She put her hand on his arm, and their eyes met. "It's because you've been my white knight, my champion in all things. My love."

A smile shot across his face. "You saved the best for last. Being your *mhuirnín dílis* is all I want to be, and Megan, you make that easier than you'll ever know. Although one day soon, I hope you know the full truth of it."

She wanted to know the truth of it all the way to her soul. Sorcha's warning came to mind and she shivered. As she cupped his jaw and pulled him down for a kiss, she felt a powerful stirring in her heart.

Kade would say there was something in the wind.

She felt it.

Only she didn't yet know what it was.

CHAPTER TWENTY-SIX

The day of the race dawned glorious and beautiful, with a sunny sky and no wind to speak of.

Of course, Kade had known people would come out for the St. Stephen's Day fair even if the day was miserable. The Irish didn't let weather deter them. But as he closed his eyes and soaked in the warmth of the winter sun, he had to smile. Good fortune was all around them, potent and undeniable.

Still, he was on the lookout for the source of Sorcha's warning to Megan. She hadn't steered them wrong yet.

He was in the shed preparing the ponies for the pony rides when Megan and Ollie arrived.

"Hi, Kade! Carrick says this is the best day we could've hoped to have for a horse race. I can't wait for it to start."

Winston nickered as Ollie ran toward him and hugged his neck. "Hi, boy! Have you met my new pony, Socks?"

Socks gave an answering neigh upon hearing his name. "He's going to make a lot of children happy today, Ollie. It was nice of you to suggest he give pony rides with the rest of our crew."

Ollie grinned, rubbing Socks' mane. "He'll be a good pony for kids to ride, but I get to go first."

Kade and Megan shared a smile. Then he walked over and kissed her lightly on the mouth. "I have another present of sorts for you."

Her face lit up. "You've already given me so much, Kade. I can't imagine anything more."

As far as he was concerned, he could never give her too much. "You can always say no if you'd like, Megan, but I thought you might want to race Breezy today. If you do, I'll race at your side. We wouldn't be racing to win. Only to have fun. It's your call."

She sputtered and pressed her hands to her face. "Really?"

"You've got to, Mom." Ollie threw his hands up and turned in a circle. "It's going to be awesome. I wish I could."

"You'll be big soon enough," Kade said, tousling his head. "What say you, love?"

"Oh my God! I'd love it. Kade, it's...going to be so great."

He smiled, aware she didn't know that he'd never raced before. Growing up, he'd avoided competing in horse jumping and racing, refusing to cede to his father's wishes. The goal of those contests was winning, beating others, something that had never mattered to him. But racing with her, for no reason but to give them both joy, the same way they did on the beach? Yes, he would do that today and any day. "Yes, it's going to be grand."

"Is Brady really going to ride his donkey?" Ollie asked, giggling.

Kade chuckled himself as he thought of his friend. "He is. Technically Spark isn't a horse. But everyone loves Brady, so they're making an exception."

"Mom, that's why Mr. McGrath called his pub the

Brazen Donkey. They've always had donkeys. Did you know?"

"I did. Brady is good craic."

Kade sent her a wink. "He is. Shall we saddle up our ponies? Carrick, Jamie, and Liam will be here soon to help."

He was grateful that his friends had offered their time. There would be a line of children wishing for rides, and each pony needed a handler.

"I wish I could help," Megan said, rubbing Winston behind the ears, "but I have to sell my pottery. Listen to that. *Sell my pottery*. I thought that was going to be the big event today, but I'm going to be in my first horse race too."

"You're killing it, Mom," Ollie said, holding out his fist.

She eyed it with confusion. "What's that? Oh, a fist bump."

Her fist glanced off Ollie's, making him groan. "That was so weak, Mom. You need to practice."

"I never thought of myself as a fist bumper." She held it out again. "One more try?"

Their fists connected this time, and Megan let out a sound of delight. "All right, I'm ready to kill it."

The words didn't sound right coming from her, but he liked the sentiment very much. "Let's saddle up the rest of the ponies and tell Legend not to miss them too badly."

He'd thought about leaving one of the ponies with her for company, but they needed all his stock. Breezy was new to the shed, since he'd kept both her and Socks in one of his father's sheds to maintain the surprise. They could become acquainted. He walked over to Legend's stall and opened it. He was keeping her inside today, given all the stallions about, so he was going to leave the lights on. He heard one of his ponies stomp its hoof and turned his head. Winston blew loudly and stomped again. Kade studied the pony. He was showing mating signs.

Well, he'd thought Legend would be in season early, hadn't he? He would tell his father. They would put her and Sutter's Mill together tomorrow in the pasture and let nature take its course.

He was smiling as he played with the light timers. His goals were so tangible his fingertips tingled. When Legend was pregnant, he'd have his land. He and Megan could begin planning their new home. It would be a fine wedding present.

"You enjoy your new friend," he told Legend, rubbing her neck as he closed the stall. "We'll see you later."

His friends arrived as he finished saddling Eve. He'd elected to bring some of his larger ponies in addition to the smaller ones, knowing they could safely give some of the older children a ride.

"Morning," Carrick called as he walked into the shed with Angie, who looked peaked and was carrying a large gift bag.

Ollie ran over and greeted his aunt and soon-to-be uncle. "Who's the present for?"

"It's for your mom," Angie said, making a valiant effort to smile over her probable nausea. "I didn't want to give it to her yesterday when we were opening presents in front of everyone."

Kade didn't have to wonder why. The celebration had been strained, especially when Megan opened a lilac sweater set from her parents. Of course, they hadn't known about her changes, but the gulf between them had been noticeably uncomfortable.

"It's been a morning of presents," Megan said, taking the bag when Ollie brought it over to her.

When she pulled out the painting inside, her gasp filled the entire shed. A few of the ponies nickered in response.

Tears filled Megan's eyes, and he watched as rare tears welled in her sister's eyes too.

"I thought you might like to see how you look to me right now," Angie said softly. "I hope you like it."

Kade stepped up behind Megan as Ollie ducked in to see. "Wow, Mom," Ollie said with awe. "You look really pretty."

And she did, Kade thought, staring at the portrait. Angie had certainly captured the new air around Megan, from the way her short hair seemed to dance in the wind to the extra light in her brown eyes. Still, it was the full smile on her beautiful lips that touched his heart the most. She hadn't arrived in Ireland smiling, and she'd told him she'd never smiled as much as she had since meeting him. "She's captured your joy, love."

She brought the portrait to her chest as if to hug it into her heart. "It's beautiful, Angie. Thank you."

"You're welcome. Now, if you'll show me to the toilet, I'll just take care of things."

Carrick took her arm, wincing. "It's this way, but if you need to retch, don't wait. It's only a farm."

Ollie made a disgusted face. "Being pregnant is the worst. Why do women have to get so sick?"

"One of the great mysteries of life," Kade said, ruffling his hair. "I think I hear Liam, Declan, and Jamie's voices."

Ollie raced out of the shed, leaving them alone, and Kade pulled Megan to him, knowing she was awash with emotion. Eve nickered her support.

"It's one of the best presents ever. Kade, do I really look like this?"

Tilting up her face, he smiled. "You do and more."

"Then I've accomplished what I set out to do." She

brushed away her tears. "I've become someone I'm proud of."

He kissed her softly. "Good for you, love. Come on. Let's head to the fair. It's going to be a grand day."

When they arrived in the main shed, Eve in tow, Eoghan met them at the door wearing a formal wedding jacket from decades ago, paired with a bright red bow tie.

"Megan, me girl!" he said, hugging her enthusiastically. "You've customers already. A few of the villagers came early, wanting to look over the wares. Your pottery is a hit. Not that I thought any differently. Go on, now. You have a queue already."

She pressed her hand to her forehead. "A queue? Really? Oh, this is wonderful."

She was so discombobulated that she wandered off without saying goodbye.

"Did you happen to put out the word that you'd be letting people in a little before ten?" Kade asked the older man.

He made a scoffing sound. "I might have, and then again, I might not have. I'll never say this side of me own grave. Now, go on with you. We don't allow ponies inside the main shed."

He was chuckling as he took one last glance inside. Bets was walking around with his mother and Siobhan, making final arrangements with the other stalls. The baked goods made his mouth water. He'd have to send Ollie back to buy some fairy cakes and perhaps some of the scones he spotted on the front table. Later, he would browse the cake table, if there were any left. Today might be a day to end with cake.

After all, he and Megan were going to join the race.

Ollie brought Kade updates and treats while he and his friends gave pony rides. "Mom's pottery was selling like crazy," Ollie said, stuffing a fairy cake with white icing in his mouth. After the initial rush of kids, Carrick told Kade to take a break and go see how his woman was faring. He would do the same with Angie once Kade returned.

The shed was buzzing with people when he returned. Eoghan was chatting with Cormac O'Sullivan, keeper of the bets, who lit up when he spotted him.

"I heard you and your girl were entering the race." His bushy gray eyebrows rose to his thin hairline. "Are you planning on trying to win or is this only a recreational ride with your lady?"

Everyone knew he could ride—maybe even win if he had a mind to. "I only want to ride with my fiancée."

"The people of Caisleán are going to be disappointed yet again." Cormac made a clucking sound. "Maybe someday St. Kade will race for good. Any bet on whether it will be your father or your sister to cross the finish line first?"

He felt his mouth curve. "No bet, Cormac. I'll see you later at the race."

"Your bet could send people over the edge," Cormac called after him.

Kade imagined it could. But right now, he'd say the race was too close to call. After all, he'd been watching his sister practice. Although she'd be riding a horse other than Legend today, he had no doubt she'd be fast.

When he finally wandered over to Megan's booth after being intercepted by several people he knew, he couldn't help but smile at the sight. Half her stock was gone.

"Kade! It's been crazy here. People love my work. I've sold much more than I thought I would."

"And it's only noon," he said, tapping his wristwatch.

"I even found out who made my favorite Irish pitcher,"

she said, putting her hands to her cheeks. "I thought I'd set it out with a note asking if anyone knew the artist. A woman from Inniscrone said it was done by her cousin who has since passed. Her name was Niamh, and she was trained by a potter in Dublin. Isn't that lovely?"

"It's so lovely, and you know what else is?" He set his hands on the front table between her mugs and bowls and leaned in to kiss her, wanting to share in her joy.

She looked around for a moment and then laughed. "I don't know why I'm embarrassed. We're engaged."

Her mouth pressed into his again, and he heard a cough behind him. He turned, doing his best not to frown at the sight of her father. His bearing was so rigid Kade wondered if he ever relaxed it. In the past few days, he'd done his best to keep an open mind about Megan's father, only to find there was nothing much about the man that he liked.

"Megan, your mother said your pots are selling well. Pick out a big mug for me, and I'll buy it."

Some of the light in her eyes dimmed. "Okay. Sure."

"Kade, while she's doing that, there's something I'd like to speak to you about." Dan started to walk away, making it apparent their talk wasn't to be in front of Megan, and Kade pushed back a spurt of frustration.

"I'll see you at the shed a half hour before the race. Have fun, love. This is a grand moment for you."

She nodded, her eyes brimming with good humor again. "Have fun with the kids."

He nodded and strode over to her father, who'd left the tent. "You wanted to speak with me?"

Dan's mouth twisted. "My wife just told me it was your idea to have Megan enter the horse race. I don't think that's wise, do you?"

Obviously he did, but he strove for patience. "I'll be

with her every step of the way if that's what you're worried about."

"Worried?" He scoffed. "Son, I don't worry. I solve problems. I mitigate risk. My daughter isn't a good enough rider to enter a horse race. She certainly has no chance of winning one. You putting ideas into her head is only going to lead to someone getting hurt."

Kade met his hard gaze straight on. "I grew up here, and I've been to country races my whole life. Each one features riders of all levels. We're not entering to win. We're entering because it's going to be fun."

Dan put his hands on his hips. "Fun? Son, a horse race is a serious proposition. We have the Pimlico Race Course in Baltimore, and it's all about winning. Fooling my daughter into believing she's a good rider only does her a disservice. Worse, it will embarrass her."

Kade bit the inside of his cheek before saying, "I'm a good judge of horses and riders. Ask anyone. Megan is more than able to race. She certainly won't be embarrassed. You have my word on that."

He strode off, anger bubbling up inside him like stew in a pot. Not even the lively music from the band whose performance he'd helped arrange could lighten his mood. With effort, he calmed himself down as he walked back to the pony riding area.

"Kade!"

He turned his head to look for Ryan. His friend held a fairy cake in one hand and what smelled to be hot apple cider in a paper cup in the other. "Hi, Ryan! Are you having fun?"

"Yes." His blue eyes were alight with happiness. "I bought a mug from Megan that I'm going to use for a new cocktail. I heard you were going to race today. Kade, I hope you win."

He put a hand to his friend's shoulder. "You know I don't race for that."

Ryan rolled his eyes. "But you could. If you can, why don't you? Are you afraid to beat your dad? Kade, you can't keep letting him think he's stronger than you just because you don't want to hurt his feelings. You're a man too. Just like him. Pretending is like lying."

Studying his friend, he realized what he was saying. Part of him hadn't wanted his father to see him as an equal because he feared his dad would push him harder to take over the farm. Maybe Ryan was right. "I promised Megan I'd stay with her."

Ryan took his arm and led him over to the station for the pony rides. "Carrick!"

Kade nudged his friend. "You're meddling."

"I'm being a friend," he said enthusiastically as Carrick led Eve over with the little Hodnett boy beaming in her saddle.

"Hi, Ryan!" Carrick smiled broadly. "Did you check out my fiancée's paintings?"

"I bought one of your field and the sheep, but what I really wanted was a nude." Ryan laughed gustily. "She said she didn't bring them."

"You've taken to some wild ways in Dublin, my friend. What do you need?"

"Kade needs to race to win today, so we need you to enter the race and take care of Megan."

The silent understanding that had always existed between Kade and Carrick kicked in, and his friend nodded after a moment. "It's done. Ryan, if you'd enter my name and put a bet down for me with Cormac—on Kade, of course—I'd be grateful."

Kade groaned as Carrick handed Ryan a wad of euros. "No, not this!"

"Yes, this!" Carrick started to lead the pony back in a circle. "It's about time. Ryan, you did grand!"

"I did! I did! See you, Kade."

His friend stuffed the last of his fairy cake in his mouth and started to run off, waving bills in the air.

"What was that all about?" Declan asked, coming up beside him.

When he told him, his friend laughed out loud. "It's official. I believe St. Kade has been laid to rest. At last! I'm off to find Cormac for a bet."

He stared after his friend, only for Liam to approach the fencing leading Winston with a little girl Kade didn't recognize. "Was Carrick telling the truth? Are you finally racing like you're meant to?"

Kade nodded. He was going to hear about it until the time of the race if this was any indication.

"You've finally found the last piece of yourself, away from your father," Liam said, his gold earring winking as cheekily as his smile. "You and Megan have been on a grand journey. I can't wait to see what's next."

Neither could he, he realized, as he entered the ring and began to give rides again. Ryan had seen a part of him he'd buried.

His father wasn't so pleased when he found him shortly afterward. "You're racing, and people are betting that you're going to win."

Shannon hurried over, a grin on her face. "I have to hear this."

He shot her a look. "Yes, I'm racing. I haven't made any bets."

"And you shouldn't," his father said. "You'll only lose money."

His mouth started to curve, and his grin was unstoppable. "We'll see about that, Dad."

Shannon rubbed her hands together. "I can't wait for this race to start. What happens if I beat you both?"

He winked. "You'll have bragging rights, and your older brother will buy you a pint."

Their father only grumbled. "Your mother won't be pleased by any of this."

"Yes, she will. See you at the track, Kade. Dad." Shannon waved and rushed off.

His father only stared him down for a few more moments before nodding and strolling away.

He suffered through more conversation, congratulations, and meddling by Cormac. By the time they closed the pony rides, he was awash in as much irritation as excitement. When he finally found Megan, she was cleaning her mostly clear tables. Only a few pieces remained. "A good day then," he said.

She lifted her face. "You're racing to win, I hear. Did my dad insult you?"

No, he insulted you, he almost said. "'Twas Ryan who helped me see my way to it. Carrick will be riding with you. I hope that's all right. I realize I promised you—"

"I want you to race," she said, taking his hand. "And I very much want you to win. For you. If I weren't racing, I'd be waiting at the finish line for you."

He kissed her full on the mouth. "I'll be waiting for you, and that's the way of it, love. Thank you for understating."

"We understand each other," she said, squeezing his

hand. "That's why we work. Come on. Let's go saddle our horses."

"I need to go for Carrick's and my own horse," Kade said. "I'll meet you at the shed."

As he walked to his father's part of the farm, he briefly considered having Carrick ride Legend. They needed a horse who wouldn't mind being held back, if necessary, who wouldn't mind racing neck and neck with Megan's mare. Legend would ride well, he knew, and she loved Megan, so she'd stay close, but she was in heat. It was a risk he couldn't take.

He strode into his father's stables, eyeing the stallions. He selected one of the more peaceable ones—a chestnut stallion named Sunset's Brew—to ensure the animal would hold back when they needed him to.

As for the stallion he would race, there was no question. He and Red Zephyr would do grand together.

"I thought I'd find you here," his mother said, coming inside the shed.

"Hi, Mom," he said, leading the stallion out of its stall. "When was the last time you were here?"

Her mouth twitched with mischief. "You likely wouldn't want to know the particulars, but your father didn't mind me interrupting his work, I can surely tell you."

He chuckled. "You're right. Best keep that to yourself."

"I'm glad you're finally racing, is all," his mother said, wandering over to one of the stallions and petting his mane. "What you're doing today will have a profound impact on your father, but don't let that stop you. It's needed, and it's time. For you both."

His throat thickened. "It couldn't have been easy to let us fight it out all these years."

"No, but it wasn't my fight," she said, crossing and

touching his arm. "I can't tell you both how to be men. I can only love you."

He leaned down and kissed her cheek. "And you taught me how to love others."

She tugged on his chin playfully before saying, "You did that yourself. Your sister is still learning, like your father. But they know how to race and fight and win. You do it your way today, and you'll come out just fine."

When he and Megan finally reached the course with the horses, Carrick was waiting alongside Angie.

"I suppose I should have told Carrick to run this by you," Kade said.

Angie only shook her head. "It was a good idea. But I do like the idea of him not going as fast as I expect you will. I even put twenty euros on you, so don't lose my money."

Red Zephyr nudged him as they all laughed.

Then it was time for the race. Ollie hugged all of them, and so did Kade's mother. He only nodded to his father, who was riding Sutter's Mill, and Shannon, who'd finagled a ride on Hunter's Bounty. After helping Megan into her saddle, he pulled her head down and kissed her softly.

"See you at the finish line, love."

She shook her hair out before pulling on her helmet, looking as free as he'd ever seen her.

He walked up to Red Zephyr and looked into the stallion's eyes. They were calm and focused, but Kade knew the stallion was taking in the other horses around him. He'd been bred and trained to run. After caressing his neck, Kade swung into the saddle.

"Good luck, Kade," he heard Brady shout. "I'll be rooting for you from the back."

Kade turned to wave at his friend on his trusty donkey,

then nudged Red Zephyr to the starting line with the other horses.

Eoghan stood on a mounting block and raised a white handkerchief in the air. Kade set his weight in the saddle, prepared to spring forward when the man brought down the handkerchief.

The moment came, and the stallion shot forward. In ten seconds, the leaders were established. As his stallion thundered straight down the course on his family's land, Kade glanced at them from the corner of his eyes. Shannon. Their father. Donal, holding his own on a stallion he'd borrowed from a friend in Sligo. The last contestant surprised him. Keegan O'Malley was to the left of Shannon, slightly ahead of her.

They raced past the ash and hawthorn trees lining the path and then climbed slightly as they passed his father's pastures. Kade urged Red Zephyr then, knowing they were coming to the first right turn that would take them on the path down to the shoreline. They could use it as an opportunity to surge ahead of the others if they played it right.

His father knew his mind because he spotted him coming up along his side, close but not in a way that skirted the rules. Killian Donovan had won many a horse race by being aggressive, so Kade hadn't expected anything less. Only his father didn't know what he knew. Red Zephyr hated to be crowded.

The stallion lurched forward, his hoofs solid and powerful as they tore up the dry earth under them. As they neared the turn, Kade kept his eyes straight ahead, not bothering to watch what his father did. He wasn't racing his father.

He was racing for himself.

Red Zephyr's neck continued to rise and fall as they

galloped onto the shore, not missing a beat. Seagulls screamed overhead, and a heron took flight in front of him.

Kade could feel someone behind him, but he knew not to look back. His father had always told him, from his very first pony rides, that you look where you want to go and the horse will go with you. Kade wanted to go to the finish line, and as they hugged the last of the shoreline, angling left toward the final neck of the race, he told Red Zephyr where to go. The stallion didn't disappoint, eating up the dark earth below them.

Shannon surged ahead of him, making him smile. She'd never been patient and was running Hunter's Bounty straight out. *Too soon, sis.* The stallion would tire. His father appeared next to him, probably confident in his chances. Sutter's Mill was younger, his training equal to his pristine form. But while Red Zephyr was older and coming off an injury, Kade knew his heart. The stallion understood this was his first race in over a year, and he would make it count when the time was right.

Kade watched as his father came even with Shannon, only a length ahead of him. Donal appeared to the right of Shannon, a half-length behind. Kade sensed someone behind them, but he didn't look back.

No, he prepared for the final stretch.

They raced past the fairy fort between his father's pastures and then declined gradually into the straight path leading to the finish line. Kade heard the crowd start to cheer as they caught sight of them. He shook the reins and gave a guttural sound to Red Zephyr to ask the horse to go faster. The stallion lurched forward, passing first Shannon, whose mount was tiring, and then Donal, and lastly his father.

They tore the white ribbon as Red Zephyr crossed the

finish line, and Kade felt a part of his heart tear open as the cheering deafened his ears. He'd raced and given it everything he had, as had Red Zephyr. He brought the stallion out of a gallop and finally into a trot, letting one of his hands drop from the reins to stroke the sweaty stallion. When he finally came to a stop, he sat back in the saddle and lifted a fist to the sky, giving in to the urge to cry out his victory as the scent of oranges enveloped him.

His father appeared beside him and punched the air, his frustration evident. "Third! That Keegan O'Malley beat me out of second, after your own self." Then he grinned. "Congratulations, by the way. You raced well."

"Thank you," he said in surprise.

"Then again, I always knew you would. You should listen to your dad more." With a cheeky wink, his father turned his horse around and headed to the edge of the crowd.

"I wonder if your father liked having the last word with you," he said to Red Zephyr, who let out a hearty sigh.

Kade turned his stallion back. He would be at the finish line for Megan, exactly as he'd told her.

He didn't have to wait long, he was pleased to see. Carrick was right beside her, as promised, and while they weren't galloping full out, they were close. When she crossed the finish line, he dismounted from Red Zephyr and handed him off to Shannon, who'd come over to congratulate him.

When Megan brought Breezy to a halt beside Carrick, he held out his arms to her. "Did you win?" she asked with bright eyes.

"I did at that," he said, laughing as she launched herself at him, congratulating him.

"It was wonderful!" She peppered his face with kisses. "I loved it! She rides like a dream. I want to do it again."

"Then so you shall," he said, hugging her to him. "And so shall I."

Carrick dismounted and came over, grabbing them both in a huge hug. "I've always been proud to call you my friend, but never more than today. You've finally found yourself."

"You sound like Liam," he said, laughing.

"Liam knows everything," Megan said, kissing Carrick on the cheek. "Thanks for having my back out there."

"You didn't need it," Carrick said. His friend gave him a look, and Kade knew he spoke the truth. Not that he was surprised. He'd known she had wind in her veins.

"You're the man of the hour," Carrick said, clapping him on the back. "Everyone is going to want to buy you a pint."

They would indeed. "I look forward to it."

And so it went. The entire village congratulated him time and time again at the Brazen Donkey. When he actually took a moment to sit, Megan sat on one side of him, grinning from ear to ear, and Ollie on the other, laughing at the attention from his dear friends.

The Lucky Charms pulled off a lively dance number to "I'll Be There For You," which Gavin followed up with "The Ballad of the Irish Horse" by the Chieftains. Everyone sang along, his friends' voices mingling for song after song.

A man couldn't have passed a better day or night, and when Bets announced that the fair had brought in over three thousand euros for the Sorcha Fitzgerald Arts Center, he raised his glass with everyone and let out a cheer and kissed Megan right on the mouth. Later he would tell her he was also donating his five hundred euros in prize money.

All told, they had raised a proper sum for the arts center. They likely would have to raise more, but all was well tonight. Megan had sold most of her pottery. He'd raced his first race and won with a horse he'd healed. Tomorrow he and his father would cover Legend.

His dreams would finally come true.

CHAPTER TWENTY-SEVEN

St. Stephen's Day had been one of the best days of Megan's life. She'd sold most of her pottery, and she'd raced in a bona fide horse race. The center had money for operating expenses for the next term, Kade's dear donation included, and while they'd need to have another event, Megan was actually looking forward to it.

Like she was racing Breezy again.

Her skin tingled as she remembered the wind racing over her body as they rode down the shoreline. She eyed the clock. It was after seven, but she was wide awake. Kade's head was nestled into his pillow. She'd stayed over last night because Liam had offered to take Ollie home. Usually Kade was an early riser, but perhaps he was more tired than usual after his big day. He'd snored softly for the first time, which had made her smile in the dark.

Maybe she could get a ride in before he rose. The sun would be rising by the time she reached the shed and fed and watered the horses before saddling Breezy. How fun would that be! She slid out of bed and dressed quietly. He didn't stir. After grabbing a granola bar, she tugged her new riding boots on—courtesy of Liam, who'd given them to her for Christmas.

When she left the cottage, she took a moment to pause. Mist was all around her, and the skies were the color she would have previously called gloomy gray. But now all she could see was pearly magic. She exhaled slowly, enjoying seeing her breath in the air. The world looked so different than it had months before, and she took a moment to feel grateful for that.

Finished, she nearly skipped to Kade's red shed. Duke and Pip greeted her as she reached the yard, and she bent down and picked them up, giggling at the double doggie kisses. The horses had their heads out of the stalls already when she entered the shed. A few neighed, including Breezy, while Winston gave a high-pitched call, stomping his foot.

"Who needs attention?" she asked, putting both dogs down and crossing to open his stall and rub his neck.

He nodded his head vigorously in three beats and then let out another high-pitched call. Legend gave an answering nicker.

"Were you missing each other yesterday?"

He stomped again and started to walk toward the stall's open door.

"Hey! Come back here."

When she tried to get in front of him, he blew out his nose and ignored her.

She rolled her eyes. "What are you doing? I know Kade lets you hang outside of your stall, so we'll forget that you ignored me."

When Winston walked over to Legend's stall, she wasn't surprised. The mare lowered her head to reach the smaller pony, and they nickered softly, their affection as obvious as always.

She put on her gloves and pulled some hay from the bale to give to the horses, greeting all of them. Breezy leaned into her hand the moment she raised it, delighting her. "We did great yesterday. You ready to go again? I think we're both meant for speed."

Winston gave another high-pitched neigh, which Legend answered. The mare started to pee—something Megan had gotten used to from being around the animals so much, and Winston gave another high-pitched sound. Legend answered, this time knocking against the mare's stall.

"You must have missed each other something terrible yesterday," she said as Winston stomped his foot again.

He looked over his shoulder at her, his big eyes almost beseeching. Legend knocked the stall again with a hoof.

"Fine, I'll open the stall door so you can hang out together, but you'd better not ignore me. I'm only doing this because I believe in friendship."

It was rather sweet that two animals so different in size had befriended each other.

"Kade told me last night it's a big day today, Legend. You and Sutter's Mill are going to get together and make a baby. It looks like you're in an affectionate mood."

She edged around Winston and popped the door open. Legend rose up a little on her front hoofs as if delighted and let out another neigh, which Winston answered. Then the mare turned around and lowered herself to the ground.

"Figures," Megan said, laughing as Winston walked into the stall proudly. "All you two like to do is sit in the pasture and eat grass."

Legend's tail flicked back and forth and then the small

pony got close to her backside, nuzzling her. Then she realized his penis was out like he was going to pee. Only he climbed on top of Legend and he—

"Oh my God!" He was— "Oh my God! Winston, stop that! No, no, no, no!"

She rushed into the stall and tried to push Winston off. He wouldn't budge.

"Oh God!" She hadn't known this could happen. Legend was seventeen hands, and Winston about four feet. He was a pony. She was a thoroughbred.

Megan's cheeks flamed. She needed help, and she needed it fast. The cottage was too far. She'd find Killian up the way. Running out of the shed, she was trailed by the barking dogs.

"Killian!" she yelled as she reached his part of the yard.

He rushed out. "Megan! What's wrong?"

She stopped, breathing hard. "Winston is mating with Legend. I can't stop it."

"Oh, Jesus!" the older man called out, racing toward and then past her.

Running after him, she arrived in the shed only to hear him swearing.

"You stupid pony!" He pushed Winston from the stall and herded him into his own, slamming the door.

"Why did you let them out?" Killian's angry face had her cringing. "You know Legend is ready to be covered."

"What's the matter?" Kade asked, bursting into the shed, panting from the effort. "I heard some commotion."

"I'd say you did." Killian lifted his fists to the heavens. "Your girl has messed up but good. She let Winston and Legend out, and Winston covered the mare."

Kade's face went blank with shock.

Megan's chest hurt. "I didn't know that could happen. He's so—and she's so."

Suddenly Kade put his hand to his mouth, quiet laughter trickling out.

"What are you laughing about?" Killian strode over to him and gave him a slight nudge in the chest. "This is a fucking disaster, son, and you know it."

"It's a little funny," Kade said, clearing his throat. "Megan, it's not your fault."

Killian made a rude noise. "Not her fault? Of course it's her fault. She let a male horse into the stall of a mare in heat. What did she think was going to happen?"

Kade put a hand on his father's shoulder. "Dad, Legend wouldn't have taken Winston if she hadn't wanted him."

"But she was supposed to take Sutter's Mill!" Killian walked over and kicked the stall. "I promised Joris Christiansen that foal for a fine price, and *you* promised to deliver. Dammit, Kade! Don't you remember our deal? Do you want to break your own father's heart?"

Megan watched the color drain from Kade's face, her heart pounding in distress as the full impact hit her.

"I don't want to do this," Killian said, wiping his eyes furiously, "but we made a deal and a man honors it. You've lost your place here and the land where you were wanting to build a house for your family."

"No!" Megan cried out.

"Megan, be quiet," Kade said softly. "Dad, you're right. I gave my word."

"Kade, no!" She rushed over to him, putting her hand on his chest, but he only patted her back in response.

Killian pinched the bridge of his nose, his head lowered, a picture of agony. "This will break your mother's heart right in two and your sister's as well. Maybe Legend won't be pregnant. We can keep her locked up and scan her in a few weeks. Maybe—"

"She'll be pregnant, Dad," Kade said, his eyes locked on his father's.

"I won't ask how you know," Killian said, running his hand through his gray hair. "You know."

"I do, but it gives me no pleasure."

Megan clutched his shirt, hearing the grief in his voice. "Please, this is my fault. Don't blame him. Isn't there something I can do?"

Both men responded, "No," in unison.

"You can take your horses and everything in the shed," Killian said, wiping his nose.

"I'll pay you for the foal, Dad, when I can."

Killian shook his head. "You won't be able to afford it. Let this madness end here. I'll go now."

He strode out of the shed, leaving them alone in the quiet. Megan put her hand on Kade's chest. "Kade, please! I didn't know this could happen. I'm so sorry."

He took her hand and kissed it. "Of course you didn't. Why would you think a small pony could mate with a giant? It's rare, but it happens and sometimes produces grand breeds. Mating never goes as we expect. Even I didn't expect it would happen, which means I wasn't meant to. Don't trouble yourself."

"Are you serious?" Tears burned her eyes. "I just cost you this place and our new home. Kade, this is your family's land as much as your place of business."

"I'll find another one," Kade said, looking around. "But I won't lie. This hurts. Oh, my mum. Shannon."

She felt tears spill down her face. "You can't accept this, Kade. I can't accept this. This is all my fault!"

"Megan, love," he said, hugging her to him. "It's done.

I'd best start thinking about finding a new place and figuring out how to pay for it. I'm afraid we'll have to stay at your cottage at Bets' for a time after we get married."

How could he still want to marry her? She'd screwed up everything. She needed to talk to one of his friends. Carrick! He would know how to fix this.

"Kade, I need to go." She hugged herself as she backed away. "I'll see you later."

She rushed out of the shed and ran all the way to his cottage, tears burning her face. When she entered to grab her purse, she stared at his beautiful parlor. He'd inherited the cottage from his grandmother, and he was going to lose it because of her. She couldn't allow that. Running to her car, she got in and drove to Angie's house, but they weren't home.

Panicked, her mind raced for someone else she could talk to. Donal! He was as tough as Killian if not tougher. She steered her car toward Bets', knowing he usually took his morning coffee there. It wasn't until she arrived that she remembered her parents were staying there too.

Please let them not be around. Please let them not be around.

When Bets opened it, her face fell immediately. "What happened?"

Megan looked over her shoulder, her desperation sharp. "I need to speak with Donal."

"I'm right here," the large man said, striding into the hall. "What's the matter, Megan?"

The whole story tumbled from her lips. Bets took Donal's hand, their faces grave. She was aware of her parents coming and standing at the top of the stairs, and her father's curse resounded in her ears as she finished her recounting.

"I won't tell you any tales," Donal said, putting a comforting hand on her arm. "Both Killian and Kade are men of honor. If they made a deal, they'll plan to uphold it. I can talk to them both for you, of course."

He didn't sound optimistic. "But it's all my fault! Kade shouldn't lose everything because of me."

"Megan, it's not your fault," Bets said in a decisive voice. "I've lived in Caisleán for thirty years, and I wouldn't have imagined a pony mating with a mare like Legend. Stop blaming yourself. Let's focus on a solution. Kade can move into your cottage after the wedding, and he can use one of our sheds for his pony riding. That has to continue."

She thought of all the children, all the people who counted on him. "Oh, Bets!"

The woman pulled her into a hug. "None of that now. You just keep telling yourself that it's not your fault."

"That's crap!" she heard her father bark out.

"What did you say?" Donal asked, lifting his head.

Her father's boots seemed to pound in her head as he descended the stairs.

"Dan, don't," her mother called.

"Patty, stay out of this." Her father strode over to her. "You've mollycoddled the girl enough. I told that boy yesterday that he wasn't doing you any favors making you think that you knew anything about horses, Megan. You don't. That much is more than clear."

"Now wait just a minute—"

"Bets, you stay out of this too." Her dad took her shoulders. "It's time for some tough talk, young lady. This is your fault, and if you don't take responsibility for it, you'll never amount to anything except the weak girl you've always been, always leaning on people to tell you what to do or to do it for you."

She had to force herself to meet his eyes. "I'm not like that anymore."

"Aren't you?" he all but sneered.

"You stop talking to Megan like that," Bets said again, her voice raised.

"I won't tell you again. This is between me and my daughter. Donal, you'd better take Bets out of the room."

"No, we won't be leaving Megan," Donal said harshly. "Unless she comes with us. And you'd best mind yourself in this home."

"I'm only talking to Megan." He stared her down with flat eyes. "Isn't that right?"

Megan's mouth started to tremble, and all she wanted to do was run away and hide, but her father's hands kept her in place as much as the truth of his words. This *was* her fault. All she ever did was ruin things. Fail at them.

"Tyson couldn't make a woman out of you," her dad said, his mouth hard. "Certainly Kade can't, not if he's puffing you up with bullshit about you knowing things you don't. That's as stupid as it is dangerous. Megan, you march back there and tell Killian it's your fault and that you'll find a way to make it up to him. How much did this *snafu* cost? Donal?"

The older man shook his head. "It wouldn't be right for me to say."

"In my country, a man answers when he's asked."

Donal stepped forward. "Then you'd best stop flogging your daughter for an accident and calling her names."

"Yes, stop calling me names!" Megan all but shouted as she wrested his hands from her.

"I'll call it how I see it," he only said, reaching for her again.

Donal stepped in front of her, his chin out.

"Stop this!" Bets grabbed Donal's arm, and he reluctantly took a step back. "Megan, don't listen to your father. You're doing great here, and you and Kade are lucky to have each other."

"You're as crazy as ever, Bets," Megan's father said, "thinking a man is lucky to have a woman who made him lose everything."

Megan started to shake. She *had* made Kade lose everything. She was the worst thing that had ever happened to him.

Kade didn't deserve to be with someone like her.

CHAPTER TWENTY-EIGHT

K ade had trouble shaking off the altercation in the shed.

He sat on Megan's stool in front of her pottery wheel and tried to sort out his feelings so he could make a plan.

Carrick's jeep pulled to a halt in front of his shed, and the man came leaping out. "Jesus Christ, man, I'm sorry!"

His friend had him wrapped up in a giant hug before he could blink. He pounded him back in return, blinking back tears. "It's rather funny when you think about it. Until it isn't. How did you hear?"

"My mum called me after your mum called her, crying. I hustled over here. Angie went looking for Megan. She must be hurting something fierce."

"She is." All the color had leached out of her face, and she'd looked much like she had when she'd first come to Ireland. He'd tried to call her after she left, but she wasn't answering her phone, and he hoped giving her some space would help.

Carrick set a heavy hand on his shoulder and looked him straight in the eye. "We'll find a way to set it all straight.

You'll come and take over one of my sheds for your business. We can make a path for your rides through my fields. I don't have the shoreline, but there are some nice vistas. As for a new home for you and Megan, if this had happened in August, I could have given you the house I'd built."

Kade's throat thickened. "But then we wouldn't have an arts center."

"Come on!" Carrick said, giving him a shake. "We'll call our friends and get you moved. You don't want to keep running into your father after this."

"No, I don't suppose so," he heard his father say.

He looked over, feeling answering tears the moment he saw them in his father's eyes. Kade could count on one hand the number of times he'd seen his father so emotional, and it usually involved tragedy. He looked like he'd aged twenty years. Kade wondered if he looked like that too. Megan certainly had. All her hard-won joy and vitality had left her.

They stared at each other for a moment before his dad cleared his throat. "You and I understand the need to keep our word even if we don't always see eye to eye. I love you, son, and this hurt isn't going to follow us all our days if I have anything to say about it. It would be a favor to me if you'd help me put a stop to that. And to the hurt your mother and sister are feeling. Will you hear me out?"

Carrick clapped him on the back. "I'll leave you two."

Kade waited until his friend had left the shed. "Dad, you don't have to do this because of me. Carrick was just offering me a place on his land. I'll figure out the rest, so I will."

"It's good friends that you have," his dad said, stepping closer. "I know they've wanted to take a punch at me for not being more understanding, but it doesn't mean I don't love you. Kade, it's not only for your mother and Shannon that

I'm coming to you. I can't live knowing you're not here on Donovan land, the land you love as much as I do."

Kade braced himself for the deal. He expected his dad wasn't going to make it easy on him.

"What do you propose?"

His dad took out an envelope and threw it on the table at the end of the shed. "A bit of mail for you. I say we settle this like the old-timers did. With a horse race. If you win, you've everything back. No strings. No rules about what you do with it."

He had to rub the tightness in his throat. "What happens if you win?"

"I'll think of something," his dad said, inclining his head. "Suit you?"

His mind spun. "Sure."

So they saddled up the horses they'd ridden yesterday with Carrick looking on with watchful eyes, and they raced the same track, neck and neck until the finish.

Sutter's Mill edged out Red Zephyr in the final moment, and his father let out a giant cry.

Kade felt his heart break again. He'd lost, and he didn't know what it meant. He steered the horse to his father and waited for him to say the words Kade dreaded most.

You'll work for me and the farm now. My way.

He'd have to say no. The hurt would be double this time.

His father's face was flushed as he dismounted and approached Red Zephyr. Kade eyed him suspiciously as he checked the stallion's front hoof.

"We might need to race again," his father announced, standing up. "Your horse isn't shoed properly."

His horse was shoed just fine, and they both knew it. His father had supervised it, in fact.

"Does tomorrow suit?" his father asked.

Kade laid the reins in his lap, trying to understand the meaning behind those words. "And if I lose tomorrow, what will you want?"

"To race again..." His father's mouth tipped up on one side. "Until you win."

He bit the inside of his cheek as emotion flooded him. He finally understood. His father only wanted him back. Nothing more.

"I love you, Dad," he said softly.

His father's earlier tears returned, but he smiled through them. "I love you too, son. You might take a look at that piece of mail I brought down for you when you get back to the shed. I'll see you later."

With that, he remounted and took off. Kade sat there for a moment, letting everything sink in. When he finally turned his horse toward Carrick at the finish line, he took in his friend's somber expression. He looked like they'd be attending a wake tonight given his loss in the race.

Only he told his friend there would be no wake. In fact, there was much cause for rejoicing.

When they went back to the shed, Kade felt the urging to read that piece of mail his father had mentioned. There was no address on the thick envelope. He pulled the papers out, his heart pounding in his chest as the scent of oranges wrapped around him.

"You old codger," Kade said with affection.

"What is it?" Carrick asked.

Kade held out the papers, not surprised his friend couldn't smell the oranges.

Carrick swore softly. "But this is the deed for the land he promised you, and it's dated yesterday."

"Before today's race," Kade said, shaking his head.

Carrick blew out his breath. "He could have said something and saved us all this worry."

No, he couldn't have, Kade realized. "We're both too proud for that."

"This is where our womenfolk would say we men are eejits sometimes," Carrick said.

Sorcha appeared in front of Kade. "*Most* times."

Then she disappeared.

"I need to find Megan," Kade said, taking back the papers.

Carrick checked his phone. "Angie tried to call, but I had my phone on silent for the race. She texted to say Megan is in a bad way. Their father said some awful things apparently, so bad that Bets took Patty aside and told her they need to stay elsewhere."

His heart sank. If there was one person who had the power to bring back the old Megan, it was her father. That woman would think she was a failure and he was better off without her. But Kade anchored himself in positivity. If he could finally find peace inside himself about his own father, she could do the same. He only hoped she would fight bringing that old Megan back.

He didn't want to lose her over this.

CHAPTER TWENTY-NINE

S he'd run.

The moment Bets and her father had gotten into it. The last thing she heard before she left was Bets telling Patty they needed to find someplace else to stay.

Everything was in shambles.

Liam still had Ollie, thank God. She needed some time. If she could just lie down for a while to help calm her pounding head...

The cottage was quiet when she entered it, and she headed to her room. Tears started to fall again, and she flung herself onto the bed, sobbing. She'd ruined Kade's life. All because she was stupid. So stupid.

She buried her head in the down comforter, agony needling down to her bones.

How could he love her after this?

She knew how. He really was St. Kade. Wouldn't a normal person be mad at her? Perhaps, but he'd accept her with open arms, which meant she'd need to be the one. That she'd need to...

A chill hit her, and she pulled the comforter on top of

her, curling into a fetal position. She lay there as depression stole over her. She could feel it covering her, stealing any hope she had that she had changed. That she'd made a new life for herself and found a man who could love her for her.

Her Dream Jar, sitting on the table by her bed, looked empty of all its magic.

She sat up, trying to fight back. If she kept lying down, she knew what was next. She wouldn't have the energy to rise. Depression leached everything good. She didn't want to succumb to it again.

Her mouth started to tremble, and she pressed a hand over it. Her whole body hurt. Was she really going to break things off with Kade?

Sorcha appeared at her bedside. She startled. "My God!"

"No, only Sorcha," the woman in white said with a soft smile. "As for Kade being better off without you, doesn't he strike you as a man who knows what he wants?"

Megan shivered for a different reason. "You read minds?"

"When needed." Sorcha clasped her hands together in her lap. "You didn't answer my question, Megan."

She sniffed, wiping her nose. "He does. He always does."

"Then you know he loves you and wants to be with you," she said with a firm nod. "You're here and not with him because you don't yet know your own mind. Are you the girl your father scolded today? Or are you the woman you were yesterday? The one who sold some of the most beautiful pottery this county has ever seen and raced with wild abandon in her first horse race. The woman who planned to marry Kade Donovan and live out her days here in Ireland with her family."

Megan balled the comforter in her fist. "I want to be that woman."

Sorcha reached out her hand as if to touch Megan's face, but it was only a whisper of wind as it neared her cheek. "You *are* that woman."

"But I felt like that girl again."

"I imagine you did, hearing such cruelty from someone who's supposed to love you."

"I don't know how to let go of that girl," Megan said softly.

Sorcha smiled. "It's simple. Say goodbye to her. I'll leave you to decide. Only know this is the last time we'll see each other. So this is me saying goodbye to you, Megan."

"Goodbye, Sorcha," she said as the woman gave her a final smile and vanished before her eyes.

Decide. Liam had told her something similar when she'd first arrived. He'd talked about moving forward. He'd talked about changing. And she had, hadn't she?

She opened her dresser drawer and pulled out her journal. Then she read. Her transformation into the woman she'd been yesterday colored the pages she leafed through. When she finished, she pressed the journal to her heart and let it fill with new light.

Then she stood up and walked over to the mirror. She touched the short hair that she loved and looked into her big brown eyes, the ones that sparkled now. The tears and white complexion she knew. They were from the old Megan.

Pretty. Girl. Smile.

The phrase formed by Keegan O'Malley's cattle came to mind.

She found the strength to smile. "Goodbye, little girl."

Then she blew her a kiss and wished her a grand send-off. Picking up her Dream Jar, she shook it for all she was worth, watching the colors sparkle and dance.

After putting it down, she stepped into her bathroom and washed her face. She needed to find Kade.

She heard a knock as she was changing into her *Visualize Sunshine* T-shirt. As she made her way to the front door, she prayed it wasn't her mother. But if it was, she would handle it. Her. The woman.

She planned to tell her mother she could come to the wedding, but not her father. Not after what he'd said about her and Kade. People were supposed to stand up with you at a wedding, as the Irish would say, not bring you down. She wasn't going to let her father do that to her or her family ever again.

She took a breath as she reached for the door handle. Opening it, she felt her throat catch. "Kade."

His brown eyes were filled with love, and his beautiful smile was back on his face. "If you're wearing that shirt, then I'm hopeful I won't need to say what I'd planned."

She felt joyful tears fill her eyes as the scent of oranges touched her nose. *Ah, Sorcha.* "No, you won't have to convince me that you're not better off without me. Or persuade me to see the best in myself. I have to do those things on my own."

"And you have." He held out a hand to her. "It looks good on you, love."

She took his hand, but it wasn't enough. She rushed into his arms, and they came around her in a gentle and yet powerful embrace. "I love you, Kade. So much. I can't wait to marry you and be your partner. In every way. But it does hurt me something awful to think about what you lost."

He pressed back and cupped her face. "The loss was

ours, love, but thankfully it's no more. Let me tell you what's transpired since you left my shed."

She hadn't imagined crying again as they sat beside each other on her settee, but tears trailed down her cheeks when he told her what his father had done. He wiped away his own tears. "So not all is lost."

She remembered Sorcha's words. "We're back to how everything was yesterday."

His brow rose at that. "That's one way of looking at it."

Linking her hands around his neck, she said, "That's how I want to look at it."

He studied her before nodding. "I see the wisdom of it. Any other wisdom you feel like sharing?"

"Only that I plan to love you and our family as the woman I am." She smiled. "Let me tell you how much that woman really loves you. In fact, I'd like to show you. Right now."

"I'd like nothing better," he said, rising and locking the door. "We'll hope and pray no one comes knocking and looking around. Although after everything, we might be granted some space for a while."

She took his hand and led him to the bedroom. "But this is Ireland so who knows who might pop by."

Oddly, she mostly liked that. In her other life, she'd never had good friends pop by to see her. She'd never been close enough to anyone for that.

"We'll hope any callers will see my jeep and leave us in peace just this once," he said as he shut the bedroom door and proceeded to love her.

She loved him back, letting the woman inside her surround him.

When she lay in his arms later, she lifted up on an elbow. "How do you thank a ghost?"

Kade caressed her arm, his brow knitting. "I don't know. I've never thought of spirits wanting thanks. Are you thinking of Sorcha?"

"I am," she said, touching his face. "She came to see me earlier. She helped."

"She helped me as well," Kade said, "but the last words she gave me were about men being eejits. I wonder if that will be her parting salvo."

"I wonder." Sorcha would call the men that, Megan thought with a chuckle. "I think we'd have been friends."

"I suspect so," Kade said, pulling her on top of him. "We're lucky she was here to help us."

"We were." Megan grinned. "Me especially. Wait! I just got it. I know how to thank Sorcha."

She could already see the tall fluted vase she'd make. She'd sgraffito a drawing of the woman. The wind would make her white dress dance, and somehow she would capture her etherealness along with her compassion and strength. They would put it in the entry hall of the arts center to welcome all who came.

"I can't wait to see it," Kade said, giving her a sexy wink after she told him. "But I'm even more eager to see who she'll be helping next, as I suspect she has plans to stay around for a while."

"If only we could tell Cormac O'Sullivan about all of this. His book would be filled to the brim with bets."

Kade laughed. "Look at you, talking like an Irish woman."

She liked the sound of that as much as she did hearing the cars finally pull up outside her cottage. Their friends. Their *family*.

Coming to Ireland had been the best decision of her life. It had brought her here. To Kade. It had given her a place to teach and practice her art again. And to find herself as a woman.

"Perhaps we can make that official after we marry," Megan said.

He pursed his lips. "I expect we can at that if only to make sure you stay here for the rest of your days, *mo mhuirnín dílis*."

"Where else would I want to be?" She rose to dress and looked out the window, her hear lifting at the blend of clouds and sky.

After all, there was nothing like living beneath pearly Irish skies.

EPILOGUE

Two weddings in two days. That was what Brady McGrath called more than a measure of good luck.

The feeling of it hung in the air, so much so that the candles at Kade and Megan's celebration danced with it. Bets' parlor was lit up in grand style with all the candles he'd delivered only days before. Laughter bubbled like hearty Irish stew, and the whiskey flowed—poured by his own hand from behind his bar station. His father let him pour at weddings, something he never did at the Brazen Donkey. The pub was Gavin McGrath's until he was ready to sit on one of the ancient barstools and let the next generation pour for him. Brady couldn't wait for that day. He loved being a postman, but his favorite part of the job was sitting around with people and telling tales—all the better if he could do it with a whiskey.

Eoghan O'Dwyer also loved telling tales, and he certainly had a lot of them, being ninety-three and counting. But he was going to be telling tales to a doctor if he didn't mind the candles around him, the most dangerous being the flickering, wax-dripping candelabra on the table behind him. Eoghan grew excitable at celebrations, waving his arms about. Caching on fire would negate some of the good luck, Brady imagined, and they couldn't have that.

"You'd have thought Kade would have told sweet Megan about the last wedding with too many candles," his brother Declan said, coming up to his bar station and extending his empty glass.

He poured his twin a generous portion. "We managed to put out poor Sinead's dress before it hurt her or torched the extensions she'd gotten. Thank God she'd padded her bum with those new gel bottoms some women favor."

His brother shook his head. "I don't understand why women can't like what they have—I do, being a connoisseur of all parts—"

"Is that supposed to be a bad butcher joke? Breast, thighs, and legs?"

"You know it, but don't interrupt me. I also can't understand why you know so much about such things."

"It's my job to scan packages, brother," he said, sipping his own drink. "You should see what some people order. I don't rightly know if they realize the customs description is on the front for anyone to see."

Declan leaned his elbow on the bar. "Tell me something interesting you've delivered lately."

"No, it's confidential." He gave his brother a shove. "Give me some room. I'm trying to keep an eye on Eoghan."

"He'll be fine," Declan said, glancing over his hulking shoulder with a grin. "That man defies age and is as canny as they come. I hear Donal is planning on selling his sheep and land to Carrick. I told Carrick he's lucky to be buying them from the son and not the father. Eoghan would drive a harder bargain."

"Times were tougher back then." Brady grabbed a rag

and polished his station like his father had taught him, aware his father was keeping an eye on him because he was the McGrath, after all. A bar was never supposed to have spilled whiskey. Bad luck, his father would say. The wood remembered the loss of it, and good whiskey wasn't to be lost. Not in his pub.

"Carrick and Angie's wedding was grand, wasn't it? But they didn't have candles, thank God."

No, Carrick and Angie's celebration had been filled with color at the local estate turned hotel. "In my experience, usually a couple chooses two or three shades to set the theme."

His brother raised a brow. "What?"

"Look at Megan and Kade's setup." He waved his arm. "Sea tones. Blues and creams with a splash of green. Kade said they wanted to have the land around them."

"That explains the platters and clear vases holding seashells and sea glass," Declan said. "I had no idea what to make of them. I hoped they weren't party favors."

Brady laughed. "I bet Kade would let you take a shell home if you really want it."

His brother didn't laugh in response.

"It suits them. Just like the rainbow buffet of colors at Carrick and Angie's do suited them. Everything they selected was colorful—flowers, tablecloths, china, and lights. I rather liked it."

Declan stood to his full height, but he was still the shorter twin by two inches, something that had always delighted six-foot-five Brady. "Did you just talk about rainbows and tablecloths and china?"

These were the moments he enjoyed. He took pleasure in getting a rise out of his brother. Still, he said for cover, "Why not? I delivered it all!"

"Right, but you still scared me." His brother shuddered. "If you start bringing in tablecloths and china and the like to Summercrest Manor in... What did you call it? A rainbow buffet of colors? I'm going to put you out of your misery while you sleep."

"You wouldn't." He extended his whiskey to toast. "You love me too much."

"I'd live," his brother responded, clinking their glasses together.

"Although I think a magenta tablecloth *would* look incredible on a table in the dungeon. Isn't that where you're planning on taking your dates?"

"You—"

"Are you two keeping an eye out for Eoghan?" Kade interrupted as he stepped up to the bar.

Brady laughed as his brother shot him another look, but he turned to Kade and dutifully nodded. "I'll pull him back if he gets too close. Don't worry. No accidents like Sinead on my watch."

"Or at your wedding," Declan responded.

"I know I can trust in you both," Kade said, putting a hand on his shoulder. "Declan, can you man the bar for a while? Brady and I have business outside."

He turned to face his friend. "We do?"

Kade only gave him a mysterious smile. "Come outside with me for a moment."

"You're leaving your bride—the love of your life, whom you just exchanged vows with—to step outside with me?"

"Did you remember he owes you money from when we were kids?" Declan asked.

"You know I never bet," Kade said with a laugh. "Besides, Megan's mother has retired from the party and I feel better about taking a break for a moment. Let's go. Oh, and leave your glass. Wouldn't want you to drop it or anything."

Why would he do that? He shared a puzzled look with his brother before following his friend out to Bets' sleeping rose garden, which oddly smelled of oranges, just like he'd smelled at Kade's a while back. Could his friend have a new cologne? Usually he would have teased him, but this was his wedding day. "You're not going to hit me, are you?" he asked, mostly joking.

"I've never hit anything in my life, as you know," Kade said, inhaling the cool night air. "Ah, it was a grand day, and I'm soon to be off with my beautiful bride. But you and I have business apparently before we go, according to some-one. Are you ready for your surprise?"

He pointed to himself. "*Me?* This is your wedding, man. We're obliged to give *you* gifts."

Kade rubbed his clean-shaven jaw, more dressed up than Brady had ever seen him before, in a fancy formal suit with an ascot tie. "I don't know that I'd call her a gift per se, but she has been very sweet and helpful of late."

A woman in a white dress materialized next to Kade. Brady would indeed have dropped his drink if he'd brought it out—he practically jumped out of his bones. "Jesus! Is that—"

"Sorcha?" Her smile was full of the same mischief she'd had in spades while alive. "Hello, Brady."

"Saints preserve us!" He crossed himself. "Oh, I don't know— I don't want…"

"Stop your mumbling," Sorcha ordered, crossing her arms. "If you weren't ready to see me, you wouldn't. It's your time, man."

He clutched his chest. "Am I going to die then? Tell me it will be quick and painless."

Kade slapped him on the back. "You're not going to die. You're going to find your woman. Your love."

His mouth dried up. "My love? Oh, Jesus, she's not a spirit, is she? We Irish have too many tragic tales. I can't take that kind of love."

Sorcha's laugh rolled out in the night. "A spirit? Oh, Brady, you and your imagination. No, she's flesh and blood, I assure you. And you're going to need some help coming together. I'm your help."

His eyes widened as her dress rippled, and he heard himself utter a little cry some might mistake for a whimper. There wasn't a trace of wind out. What the hell? "I'm going to faint or be sick. I'm not sure which."

"You're not." Kade pounded him gently on the back. "Take a breath. Sorcha's gotten Carrick and me married. Her track record is rock solid. Plus, she's a friend."

"She's dead!" He winced when Sorcha cocked a brow. "No offense or anything. But I don't usually see spirits. This shouldn't be happening to me."

"You'll only see me for a brief time, Brady, so brace yourself for what's ahead."

Brace himself? She was out of her mind. Or her body? Maybe it came to the same thing.

Sorcha turned to Kade. "You'll leave me alone with Brady as we come to terms. This will be the last you'll see me, my friend. I wish you and Megan well. You know you can call me if you ever need help, but honestly you won't. Your path with each other is lined with gold, as they say."

Brady watched as the two shared a smile. The whiskey he'd been drinking roiled in his stomach.

Oh, Jesus, this was too much.

Kade put his hand to his heart and bowed like he'd

taught Winston to do. "Thank you, Sorcha. *Guh gir'uh d'eeuh uhn tah ort.*"

His mind spun. *May God put luck upon you?* Could you say that to a ghost?

"You remembered my words to you." She blew Kade a kiss. "I'll take them to heart. Thank you, Kade."

With another smile, the man turned and left him alone —alone!—with Sorcha. She faced him, hands on her hips, all business. "Brady McGrath, I've known you since you were a boy with knobby knees. Don't think you can out talk me as we work together."

The scent of oranges wove around him, and he gasped. "Your hair! The oranges are from you. But how—"

"Brady, didn't I just warn about the talking? You'll stay on point. I might be dead, but I don't have time to waste with all your chattering."

"*Chattering.*" He shot her a look. "But I have questions! You can't tell me you didn't expect that."

"Didn't I say I knew you? Only, you must keep your questions pertinent. Otherwise, you'll be asking me everything that pops into that busy mind of yours."

He gestured to her with another cry. "You're dead, but I can see you. And there's wind blowing your dress even though the night is still. Have mercy, Sorcha. A man's entitled to have questions."

"No, he's not." She narrowed her eyes at him. "You get five. About your woman. I reserve the right not to respond."

"What is this? Only five questions. That's hardly—"
"*Brady!*"

Could she blast him with fire or something? He'd watched ghost movies. Best not to find out. "Fine, what's her name?"

"A good start," she said. "Ellie."

"Ellie." It rolled around on his tongue like custard as he thought about his next question. "What does she do?"

"Hmm... I thought for sure you'd ask if she was pretty."

He snorted. "If she's mine, of course she's pretty. Don't be obvious, Sorcha."

This time she chuckled. "Fair point. She's a stained glass artist."

The picture clicked, and he glanced back at the well-lit house. "And she'll be a new resident at the center named after yourself. I see the way of it. Is she a Yank?"

"She is," Sorcha said with a smile.

"I like Yanks," he said, tapping his mouth. He only had two questions left. He had to make them count.

"I told you I don't have all day."

Day, night, what did it matter to a ghost? But he couldn't ask that. Didn't want to waste his questions. "Don't be rushing me. All right, I have it. Does she like stories?"

"Because you're always telling tales?" Sorcha's long brown hair blew in an otherworldly breeze, something that made his formerly knobby knees knock. "She creates them in her own way. You're a good match like that, although you tell them differently."

He would have to muse over that detail later, when he returned to Summercrest Manor and found more whiskey. Jesus, if there were ever a night for it.

"Last question, Brady. Make it good."

He thought of all the heroes in the Irish myths. Love might have elevated their spirits to heights untold, but it had also usually led to their downfall. Since he'd been a boy reading those myths—everything from Grainne and Diarmuid to Clíodhna and Ciabhan—it had bothered him. They were legendary characters, and he but a simple man. How was he to overcome what they couldn't? The answer to that riddle had plagued him.

Suddenly it appeared to him, as if written on water.

"Does she have a grand laugh?" he asked, his heart pressing against his chest as if it were leaning forward to hear the answer.

Sorcha's mouth tipped up at the right before she said, "You lovely man. Is it any wonder I like you so? Yes, Brady, she has a grand laugh. Full and rich like Guinness, yet fiery and smooth like whiskey."

He sighed, his heart nestling into his warm chest. "Then I'll be happy to have her and love her all my days. When do we start?"

"That's the sixth question." She gave him a cheeky wink. "Oh, this is going to be fun."

She disappeared before he could persuade her for one more answer.

"Well, hell—" He took a moment to compose himself before strolling back inside, whistling an old Irish love tune he hoped Sorcha might carry on the wind to his beloved.

Every time you leave a kind review, a rainbow appears in the sky.

Leave a review for Beneath Pearly Irish Skies and get ready for a splash of color!

Surround yourself in light and love with Brady and Ellie in Through Crimson Irish Light, the next Unexpected Prince Charming novel!

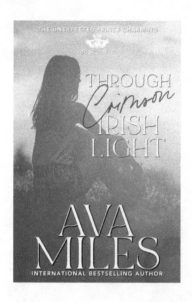

A romantic classic about an artist journeying to Ireland to stand on her own, only to discover support and romance in the most surprising of men.

"One word for Ava Miles is WOW."

Get Through Crimson Irish Light!

Available wherever books are sold.

ABOUT THE AUTHOR

Millions of readers have discovered International Bestselling Author Ava Miles and her powerful fiction and nonfiction books about love, happiness, and transformation. Her novels have received praise and accolades from *USA Today*, *Publisher's Weekly*, and *Women's World Magazine* in addition to being chosen as Best Books of the Year and Top Editor's picks. However, Ava's strongest praise comes directly from her readers, who call her books unforgettable and life changing.

If you'd like to connect with Ava or hear more about her upcoming books, check out the links below:

https://avamiles.com/
https://avamiles.com/newsletter/

facebook.com/AuthorAvaMiles

twitter.com/authoravamiles

instagram.com/avamiles

bookbub.com/authors/ava-miles

pinterest.com/authoravamiles

DON'T FORGET...
SIGN UP FOR AVA'S NEWSLETTER.

More great books? Check.
Fun facts? Check.
Recipes? Check.
General frivolity? DOUBLE CHECK.

https://avamiles.com/newsletter/

CPSIA information can be obtained
at www.ICGtesting.com
Printed in the USA
BVHW040455180522
637272BV00024B/78